One Life
A Thousand Souls

FOR DIANE

ONE LIFE
A THOUSAND SOULS

Jim O'Sullivan

© Jim O'Sullivan 2025
second impression 2025

ISBN 978-1-0684583-9-2

Published by Rymour Books
45 Needless Road
Perth
PH20LE

A CIP record for this book is
available from the British Library
BIC Classification FF

cover and book design by Ian Spring

The right of Jim O'Sullivan to be identified as the author of this work has been asserted in accordance with sections 77 and 78 of the Copyright Designs and Patents Act 1988.

All rights reserved. No part of this publication may be reproduced, stored in a retrieval system, or transmitted at any time or by any means, electronic, mechanical, photocopying, recording or otherwise without the prior permission of the copyright holder or holders. This book is sold subject to the condition that it shall not by way of trade or otherwise be circulated without the publisher's prior consent in any form of binding or cover other than that in which it is published.

ACKNOWLEDGEMENTS

Thanks to my Mum and Dad and siblings, Joan, Noreen, Mike, Mary and John, for their love down the years.

Thanks to Stuart and Morag Campbell and Lee and Stephanie Healey for their endless encouragement. I am indebted to Ian Spring at Rymour Books for championing One Life—A Thousand Souls.

Thanks also to; Chris Banks, Billy and Rosie Baynes, Mary and Michael Brogan, Peter Brockwell, Mark Devereux, Kevin and Sally Boyle, Rob Brien, Lu Matchett, Jo Cornish, Steve Costello, Maria Costello, Russell Gardner, Bill and Debbie Harding, Tim and Deborah Harrison, Simon and Lynda Hackwell, John and Julie Henderson, Sarah and Jared Head, Paul Holland, Lee Howells, Rob and Julia Hughes, Emily Justice, Stephen Lee-Foster, Mark and Ruth Leveson, Katie and James Lord, Denny and Aggie Lucey, Eileen and Terry Madigan, Pete and Sarah McCormack, Lesley McKeown, Stuart Marrington, Barbara Mautterer, Graham Mautterer, Keith Mautterer, Rosie Mautterer, Sheena Mautterer, David and Rebecca Mollison, Peter and Caroline Mollison, Rebecca Newman, Dave Cleaves, Rob Newman, Emily Rushton, Kerry and Nick Newman-Hill, Ryan O'Sullivan, Nick Pearson, Stewart and Heidi Reid, Julie Slinn, Eddie Smith, Steve Smith, Gavin Smyth, Deris Out, Jamie Victory, Mark and Philippa Walsh, John Wilgoss, Paddy and Meritta Wiggall, Dale Watkins, Iain Watson and Zoe Woodward.

Emma Bovill remains a perpetual source of brilliance and Rebekah Harrison's wonderful artwork inspired the novel's design.

Doctor Matt Campbell provided invaluable medical insights whilst Mary Gardner and Holly Brockwell happily shared their embroidery and sewing knowledge.

Cheltenham Synagogue patiently set the author straight on medieval Jewish burial customs and several collared residents of Lavagna and Genoa patently answered many (often ridiculous) questions.

Staff from The British Library and Gloucestershire Libraries (Charlton Kings in particular) proved a great help in sourcing texts. Archivists from The Imperial War Museum and The International Committee of the Red Cross helped to shed light on the plight of Italian prisoners of war on the Russian Front.

Thanks also to Cheltenham Town and Steve Cotterill.

Any errors or inaccuracies are solely the responsibility of the author. Finally thank you, Diane, my very own angel, for your editorial advice and unstinting belief in my madcap notion that one day I'd see my work in print.

Jim O'Sullivan, 2025

PART ONE

PART ONE

CHAPTER ONE
Lavagna, Italy, July 1189

Guzco Domar crouched beside the long abandoned boat's decaying spars, waiting for the collected souls in his possession to fall silent. Their unease surprised him, as he'd thought the collections had gone well. True, the ailing Ostler had pleaded for his life but the Weaver had accepted her fate with stoicism, whispering, "Please, make it quick."

Guzco had obliged.

Distracted by the winning crew's raucous celebrations, he glanced out to sea. A broiling knuckle of sea mist rolled inland, enveloping two fishermen struggling to land their catch. "Plant the feet, bend the knees, take hold then haul for all you are worth," Guzco muttered, hoping the fog would help with the next collection.

Adjusting the string of terracotta pots, each the size of a child's fist, slung across his chest, he trudged along the black sands towards the winning boat. The rowers back breaking efforts had rekindled centuries-old memories of his own rowing victories; victories that had earned him a measure of fame, the attention of women, and, more than once, from men of ungodly persuasion. Life back then had been hard, with food and hope in thin supply but what he would give to return to those days, to be with Luisa, and the cherished uncertainties of a fisherman's life.

"My friend!" one of the crew shouted, startling Guzco. "A drink to toast Lavagna's victory!" He raised a gourd to his lips, took a draught, and then collapsed in a gurning, slovenly heap, much to his squat, powerful crewmates' amusement. Licking his brine stung lips, Guzco forced a smile but hurried on, threading a path through a smattering of near comatose revellers who had spent the searing afternoon spurring their village's boats onto victory before rounding on each other with garbled insults and flailing fists.

The rowers' racket thinned as he neared the bay's fog-bound southern headland. Shunning the drover's track, he chose a steeper but more direct route towards the summit. He soon regretted his decision, as the higher he climbed, the colder it grew with the thickening mist making each timid step treacherous. Worse yet, the calico binding wound around his chest left Guzco breathless, sometimes giddy, further agitating the collected souls stowed in the pots.

As the slow, fearful ascent ground on, a baby's sobs mingled with a woman's softly sung lullaby. To Guzco's relief, both fell silent as the path levelled out. A mist-shrouded wagon loomed ahead. A giant of a man, twice Guzco's height and breadth, stood beside the wagon soothing two braying mules in between muttering to a heavyset woman, busy stirring a cauldron hung over a fire. A mongrel, hoping to cadge a morsel, sensed Guzco's presence and growled, only to fall silent at the woman's waspish command.

To the right of the fire, sat a low slung tent, from which emerged a handsome young man.

"How is she?" the woman shouted over the mules' din.

"Tired," answered the young man.

"And little Marta?"

"Beautiful, Rosa. Just like her mother."

Ladling broth from the pot into a bowl, Rosa said, "Take this to Isabella, Giacomo. Make sure she eats."

Flickering candles threw a wan, yellow light across Isabella's flushed, exhausted face as she coddled her grizzling, hour-old daughter. Something felt off, wrong, dreadful. She looked at Marta, then at Guzco, her eyes wide with fear. Whispering manically, she implored, "Saint Michael, Benedict, Martin of Tours, Nicholas of Myra, Virgin Mother, please, I beg you, intercede on my child's behalf."

Giacomo entered the tent carrying the broth.

"He's here," Isabella said, unable to tear her eyes from Guzco.

"Who?" Giacomo asked, uncertain what she meant.

She pointed her trembling hand at Guzco. "Death. There, right beside you, cowering like Judas himself."

Giacomo turned to his right and brushed Guzco's shoulder. Guzco flinched. The pots rattled. The souls howled. But none the wiser, Giacomo forced a smile, knelt beside his wife, and said, "There's just the three of us here, my love." Raising a spoonful of broth to her lips, he added, "Eat something. You'll feel better for it."

Isabella pushed the spoon away and again called on the saints to intercede. Giacomo stroked her cheek, uneasy with the stranger who now lay before him, babbling about demons, saints, and the Virgin Mother. He'd heard tales of women driven mad by childbirth, but seeing *his* Isabella so reduced, shook him to the core. True, her dance could calm the wildest seas or set the forests alight, but now, to see her teetering on the edge of sanity, well, he had no words.

"He's come for Marta," she said. "You have to stop him, Giacomo."

At a loss, Giacomo replied, "I'll fetch Rosa."

Isabella gripped his hand. "Stay."

"I'll only be a moment. Rosa will know what to do."

Guzco took Giacomo's place beside Isabella. She instinctively drew Marta closer and asked, "Why my daughter?"

Guzco shook his head. "Not your daughter, Isabella. You."

"Me?" Her voice quavered. "But why?"

"I don't know."

"Spare me. For my daughter's sake."

"It's not in my gift."

"I don't want to die."

"Forgive me." He leaned closer. Isabella, heart racing, mouth dry, again called on the saints and the Virgin Mother. Her voice cracked as she repeated her babbled pleas. Guzco allowed himself a moments doubt, but obedience drove him on. Isabella's tears brushed his cheek, and as with the Ostler and the Weaver the day before, her final thoughts overwhelmed him.

The agony of Marta's birth—the joy of holding my first born—Giacomo's wit—the dance—the taste of honey—the summer's warmth—hiccups—the sow's grunts—Mama, Papa, Claudia—the first winter snows—life—death—the dance - tired - want to rest —the Angel in my midst—beautiful Marta—beautiful Mar...

She died.

Struggling to steady himself, Guzco untied one of the pots, and cackhandedly swept Isabella's fledgling soul into it. After reattaching the jar, he brushed away the few stray hairs matted to Isabella's forehead. Marta's tiny right hand stretched out and grasped his left forefinger. Life's beginning voiding life's end. In thrall to the child, for the first time in centuries, Guzco sensed he belonged. Age old instinct bated him to pick Marta up, to shelter her. From the likes of him. For all time. But not now. He had his orders.

Gently prising Marta's fingers apart, he hurried outside but in his haste, tripped on a sagging guy rope. Again the pots rattled. Again the souls protested.

"What was that?" Giacomo asked, stooping to enter the tent.

"Hearing things now," Rosa replied, with a shake of the head.

Moments later, Giacomo's caterwauling sobs rented the air.

"What is it? What's happened?" shouted the giant, blind to Guzco slipping past him. Rosa stepped outside with Marta in her arms. She had no words.

This time following the drover's track, Guzco listened out for chasing footsteps but only heard the bellowing mules and the mongrel's occasional bark. The descent was swift, uneventful with the souls calm and the fog now an ally.

He reached the shore, the brume now so thick he could only hear the rowers' celebrations and the fishermen's grunting efforts to haul their small vessel ashore. *What I would give for one day of their lives.*

Stepping onto the Via Julia Augusta, an ancient Roman road grooved by centuries of use, he raised his salt streaked hood, and set off for the mountain village of Badur, hoping Maria Bascuali's collection would prove less taxing.

Again the souls mithered. Again Guzco pleaded for silence.

It would be a long three days.

CHAPTER TWO
East of Genoa, Italy, July 1189

Struggling to shake off his guilt over Isabella, Guzco headed east for a day and night toiling in the broiling, pine scented, summer heat. Some passing travellers hurled stones and issued caustic threats to ward off this leering, bedraggled hermit before them.

Exhausted, unable to take another step, he sat against a crumbling wall, removed his thin soled sandals and winced at the state of his raw, blistered feet. Maria Bascuali's village seemed further away than ever.

If he followed the rules.

Nobody would know. Better to arrive fresh, with my wits about me. The coast clear, he disrobed and carefully unwound the calico binding.

At first the wings hung limp, almost forlorn, matching Guzco's mood. But for once the scorching breeze came to his aid. Relief-tinged euphoria replaced guilt as the wings extended to their glorious, majestic breadth, a head and shoulder above Guzco. He flexed the wings. Branches swayed, birds took to the wing, and dust swirled as the down draft lifted Guzco an inch, maybe two, above the baked earth. He rarely, if ever, felt worthy of the wings, thinking his brother Jose the more deserving, but now, their numinous majesty signalled that, despite his shortcomings, Guzco Domar, *really* was an Angel.

From the east, a larger spiralling dust cloud accompanied by a low craven rumble, cut short his reverie. Furling the wings, he ducked behind the wall as a caravan of ox-drawn wagons and ten dozen horses appeared through the clagging dust. From the lead wagon, a man draped in fine silks, bellowed orders to dirt-encrusted wranglers struggling to control their horses, skittish in the Angel's presence.

Keeping out of sight until the caravan had all but disappeared from sight, and now heeding Azekiel's instructions, Guzco rebound his wings and resumed his pain-wracked trek. An hour on, with night falling, the rich scent of roast mutton carried in the air. Campfires lit up an abandoned farmhouse set back from the road. Ravenous, Guzco crept towards the camp, taking in the corralled horses and drawn up wagons.

"You're welcome to shelter with us." The man spoke in a rich, foreign brogue and was dressed head to toe in fine silks. He popped an orange slice into his mouth, spat out the pips and continued, "As much wine and mutton as you please, a fire to ward off the mosquitos, and, if you can bear it, my company."

Without waiting for an answer, he walked on. A man and woman stepped from the shadows and followed.

The lure of food, rest and companionship tugged at Guzco, as did Azekiel's warning. *But what harm could be done? I'm an Angel and, besides, rest and a good feed will make the trek to Badur all the easier.*

"Wait!" he shouted.

Dropping the orange, Massandar beckoned Guzco to him.

Settling by a fire, Massandar said, "You strike me as someone of substance. A holy man perhaps?"

"Pilgrim," Guzco replied.

"Then can I ask in return for my hospitality, you pray for my soul when you reach your destination."

"Of course."

"Your accent; Andalus?"

"Further west, where the sea meets the ocean."

"I know the place! Passed through it many years ago. Traded a dozen slaves for a brace of fine Kuhaylan stallions." Massandar's bland features softened as he smiled at the memory. "I think we shall have a most enjoyable evening, Pilgrim."

With wine-numbed thoughts, Guzco wallowed in the easy kerfuffle of the everyday chores taking place around the campsite. He wolfed down his food listening to Massandar recall at great length his First Crusade heroics before recounting Jerusalem's capture by the Moors. "Couldn't believe my fortune when the Kings of England and France decided once again to take up the Cross. Horses by the hundred at six *English* shillings a piece! The Saladin tithe is a blessing." He tempered his avarice with a penitent's look. "But there's no greater honour than to welcome a guest, who like me is on a pilgrimage. But mine involves a profit and yours a prophet!" His laughter prompted the man and woman, now standing behind him, to follow suit.

Suddenly, Massandar's mood darkened. "You are brave to travel alone, these roads invite the attention of rogues and robbers."

"I'm under God's protection."

"No doubt. But many of these knaves once took the Cross yet now prey on the helpless. You display a fortitude I cannot begin to countenance. And I have journeyed to the darkest parts of a man's mind to secure my treasures. Feel free to travel under my protection for as long as you wish."

Guzco nodded his appreciation, thanking his good fortune for coming across such a generous host.

"To safe travels," Massandar said, raising his beaker.

"To safe travels," Guzco answered.

Massandar belched while beckoning the frail, olive skinned man standing behind him to come closer. "Spinoza! A song for our guest."

While Spinoza sang a doleful madrigal in his obscure language, Massandar nudged Guzco then whispered, "Spinoza's been mine since Acre. Traded him for three Arab bred Palfreys with an Armenian who had caught him stealing from his orchards. Good worker. Arshadne on the other hand," he gestured to the po faced woman behind him and shook his head. "Lazy. Had her for too many years. What horrors she has witnessed I will never know. Quieter than the mute of Decapolis that one."

After Spinoza finished singing, Massandar asked, "More wine, Pilgrim?"

"I'm full thank you."

"Then how about a game of dice, Master Domar? The perfect way to bring such a pleasant evening to a close." For a bleary moment Guzco wondered how Massandar knew his name, but intoxication smothered any concerns. He recalled exciting if hazy memories when playing dice.

"Why not!" he said.

"Splendid! One denarius per game?"

"My circumstances do not allow me to wager such sums."

"My apologies. Thoughtless of me to place you in such a difficult position. Allow me to forward you a few denarii. It would be no hardship. Trust me."

Guzco spotted Spinoza, once more behind Massandar, gently shaking his head, but he ignored the warning and said, "If you are happy to do so, I accept. But on one condition."

"And what is that?"

"I pay you back in full."

"A wonderful gesture. Bold too." Massandar offered his hand. It was clammy but its grip powerful, surprising for such a spare-framed man. "Well, Master Domar, shall we begin?"

Half a dozen curious drovers looked on as Spinoza smoothed a patch of dirt two or three steps from the fire. Arshadne handed Guzco a plain wooden beaker holding two ivory dice. He tipped the dice into his hand, studied them then returned them to the beaker.

"Eight or more," Massandar said.

"Ten!" Guzco shouted as the dice rolled to a halt. Massandar handed over a coin. "Next throw, nine or more."

Eleven showed. The surprised spectators to a man, avoided catching their master's eye. Handing over another denarius, Massandar then said, with a hint of sourness, "Seven or less."

The dice showed six.

"Ten or more."

Again Guzco celebrated.

"Three more wins and you'll be able to afford one of my brood mares," Massandar mused.

"Maybe two at this rate," Guzco answered, excited at the prospect of arriving in Badur on horseback, even if he hadn't a clue how to ride a horse. *How hard can it be? I'm an Angel after all.*

"Eight with two fours. For two denarii."

Guzco clenched both fists. Two fours showed. Thoughts of Isabella receded.

As Spinoza smoothed the earth, Massandar dropped both coins into Guzco's hand and said, "I see I have picked a worthy opponent."

"It's mostly luck," Guzco answered, convinced his skill was the decisive factor.

"And your bravery in taking the bet! But now, please allow me the chance to regain some of my losses." Shaking the beaker, he asked, "What score, Master Domar?"

"Eight or more."

Massandar rolled ten. Guzco returned a denarius. For the next three throws Massandar made the required score with the relieved drovers applauding his efforts. With his winnings dwindling, a long dormant compulsion snared Guzco, prompting him to claw back his losses. Until he handed over his last coin.

"One last game?" Massandar asked.

"I've no money left to wager."

"Those pots." Massandar half-heartedly pointed at Guzco's chest. "What's inside?"

Guzco knew he shouldn't wager the collected souls, but lust for victory trumped caution. His luck would turn. "Spices; tarragon, lavender, pepper, saffron; salt too," he answered matter-of-factly.

"Shall we play for them? And if you win, my cook will provide you with mutton and wine for your journey into the mountains."

"Very well," Guzco answered, surprised Massandar knew his plans.

"You may have the honour of throwing."

As he wagered and lost each pot, Guzco's urge to gamble thinned. "Can I at least have a chance to win them back?" he asked.

Biting into a slice of mutton, Massandar chewed his food slowly, swallowed, then wiped his chin on his sleeve. He smiled, revealing slivers of meat between his teeth and carefully stacked the pots, all the while studying Guzco. "There is something I'll happily wager against these." Swotting away a moth, he said, "These souls for your wings, Angel."

Guzco affected a look of surprise, hoping the souls would not react.

"Do not take me for a fool, Domar. Do you think I'd choose to pass the time with a simpleton such as you? Besides, what else have you to wager? Those rags you wear? Do you see the fine silks that adorn me?" He stroked the pots. "Your wings for these poor fretful souls pleading with you to save them." He smiled, "Yes, I hear them. No doubt the mighty Lord Azekiel does too."

Darker memories of the dice resurfaced in Guzco. Centuries earlier, they had cost him everything. *How did I fall for this stranger's flattery?* He was snared. Lose the souls or forfeit his wings?

He *knew* he would win. It was ordained. More than that, he had to win. "Very well," he said, "What score?"

"Eight or less." Massandar smiled, his easy flattery returning. "But let me salute you, Master Domar. For an Angel to gamble would be unusual, but to gamble his wings on the roll of dice is highly unusual. Some may call it reckless, but *I* consider it bold."

The drovers, some eager, others appalled, crowded Guzco as he dropped

the dice into the beaker. He shook it eight times and once more for luck. The dice rolled.

The first dice showed five. The second dice showed four.

"Seize him," Massandar said.

As he was dragged towards the farmhouse, Guzco realised he was in the presence of evil.

CHAPTER THREE
East of Genoa, The Abandoned Farmhouse, July 1189

Arshadne and Spinoza pressed Guzco face down into the scullery's earth floor. He tried to resist but a series of sharp blows to his head and back stymied him. With Massandar's instructions increasingly frenzied, the slaves tore away his cloak and tunic and then unravelled the calico binding. The pair took hold of a wing each, both beguiled by the beauty fanning out in their dirt-stained hands. There followed the soft, elegant whisper of metal on leather as a blade was withdrawn from its sheath.

"Azekiel," Guzco whispered.

"No one is coming," Massandar answered, stuffing the sheath into Guzco's mouth. "All's fair. You staked your wings. And lost. Debts must be honoured. But as an act of mercy, I shall use Caballero, my sharpest blade." Holding the knife in front of Guzco, he continued, "Beauty isn't he. Sharp as sin. Cleaved a few in his time."

Placing his left foot between Guzco's shoulder blades, Massandar clasped the base of the right wing. Spinoza and Arshadne tightened their grip. The blade pricked the Angel's skin and bore into the right shoulder. The pain was sudden, sharp, unbearable. Guzco writhed. Arshadne struck him.

The knife sliced, tore and scraped at flesh, tendon and bone. Massandar worked deftly, cutting, sometimes sawing with long, steady movements all the while instructing the slaves to keep Guzco still.

Feeling the wing separate from the joint, Guzco bit down on the sheath and begged Azekiel, his Mother, even Jose to come to his aid. As the final cut severed the wing, he lost consciousness.

Massandar wiped his sweat-shined forehead on his sleeve and studied the intricate, gossamer-thin plumage in his bloodied grip. A near narcotic ecstasy coursed through him. No matter how many Angel wings he'd sheared, he still savoured this pure, perfect moment. "Blessed," he muttered, handing the cleaved wing to Arshadne.

Spinoza threw a pail of water over Guzco, jolting him back to consciousness. "More to be done, Master Domar," said Massandar, now placing his right foot between Guzco's shoulders. "Wouldn't want you to miss it."

Caballero's tip pierced Guzco's left shoulder. "Always considered butchery to be an art," Massandar whispered, as the blade slowly moved deeper into Guzco's flesh and exposed the joint.

Broken and pain-wracked, Guzco tried to dredge up Luisa's smile, and with it oblivion. Stupefied, his jaw slackened and the sheath flopped like a lolling tongue from his mouth. Half alive, half dead, neither Angel nor human. Alone. Thoughts barrelled and blended into a fug of pain-seared confusion. *Why has Azekiel allowed this? Is this where it ends?*

The wing came away. Two gaping wounds on Guzco's back announced the extent of Caballero's carving.

"Such beauty," said Massandar, stroking the wing and again enjoying his fleeting arousal before handing the wing to Arshadne.

Wiping the knife on Guzco's back, Massandar retrieved the sheath from the Angel's slackened jaw and rehoused Caballero. Arshadne was ordered to stow the wings while Spinoza was told to bind Guzco's wounds using the dead brigand's shirt. Bloodied boot prints marked Massandar's path from the farmhouse to his pergola. With no one looking, Spinoza gathered up the pots.vPicking her way through a slew of jittery horses, Arshadne had forgotten how much Angel wings weighed and her arms burned by the time she climbed into Massandar's wagon. She pulled back a tarpaulin to reveal a wooden chest inlaid with ivory and ornate carvings of mythical creatures. Taking the key looped on a leather string from around her neck, she unlocked the chest and raised the lid. Beneath a silk cloth nestled three more pairs of Angels' wings, one pair hers. Reciting a prayer for protection, she stowed the wings, locked the chest and replaced the tarpaulin. She left the wagon and returned to Massandar.

Guzco's leathery skin confused Spinoza who'd always believed an Angel's skin to be pale, soft, unfettered by the toils of the mortal world. After washing the wounds with tepid water, he doused them with the powder he'd taken from the dead Saracen doctor in Acre. Using a bone needle threaded with goat gut, he stitched the lesions and then applied a poultice of lavender, myrrh, lard and pepper. Lastly, he dressed the wounds using Guzco's bindings and not the brigand's shirt he wore beneath his tunic in defiance of his captor.

"I'm with you, Angel," he whispered.

"Why?" Guzco asked.

"Because he can."

Massandar, now a touch wine-flushed, returned. He spat on Guzco then said, "I trust Caballero was not too brutal, Master Domar. Man, beast or even Seraphim, all flesh tears. I would wager that even Ottobano Scriba would be keen to include this tale in the Genoa Commune's annals. Now *that* would be a lasting tribute, one even the Mighty Lord Azekiel would approve of."

CHAPTER FOUR
East of Genoa, The Abandoned Farmhouse, July 1189

It would take another day for Massandar's train of the damned and their chattels to reach Genoa, the staging post for launching the Crusade the following spring. Rising before dawn, the drovers had fed the horses, loaded the wagons and then harnessed the oxen to them. With the day's heat already oppressive, the commotion surrounding the caravan disturbed the visions tormenting Guzco, still lying on the scullery floor. Without thinking, he flexed his shoulders. The searing pain reminded him of his folly to the dice.

Spinoza snuck in, untied the dressings and drenched the wounds with the stolen powder.

"Your souls are safe, Angel," he whispered, while expertly rebinding the wounds with fresh strips of cloth.

"Where? Guzco asked.

Spinoza pointed at a cracked, earthenware pitcher lying skew whiff beneath the shuttered window. "In there. Food and flints too. Remember me." He threw the window open and climbed out, snagging the hem of his shirt on a nail.

Massandar's tunic sleeve brushed Guzco's face. "Such a shame we cannot spend more time together. Genoa offers opportunities through the fevered exhortations of the pious or the baser demands of warmongers. Rest assured, although Caballero has left his mark, I'm sure you will still assist deserving souls. But stay away from the dice. But if you must play, make sure they are not loaded against you."

He stood at the window, the toe of his boot catching the jar. "This heat," he muttered. "Unbearable". The fragment of linen snared on a rusty nail head caught his eye.

Minutes later, the air rang with whistles and shouts followed by scuffling hooves and squealing wheels. An old brindled mare tied to the final wagon reared up only to be hauled down by her wrangler. The wagon's pasty-faced driver pointed to the farmhouse and said to the boy beside him, "Say what you will, but that Massandar's a smart fella. Smarter than God."

Guzco clung to the caravan's heaving racket until it fell silent, leaving him alone in the sultry morning heat. The fresh dressing did not lessen his agony, every movement tortured. Light flooded through the open window, settling on dust-coated jars and pitchers standing on a stone plinth opposite a long dead hearth. Cobwebs, some holding the desiccated remains of captured insects, flexed in nooks. Words were scrawled above the hearth in a language Guzco didn't understand, not that he could read. Fired tiles, some chipped, framed the doorway, a sign that a wealthy family had once lived here. But the only item he cared about lay in the shadows.

Shivering with fever, he upended the pitcher and, just as Spinoza had promised, the pots, flints and food spilled onto the floor. He gingerly slung the pots across his aching shoulders and forced himself to eat and drink.

Night fell and in the stifling darkness with blood-bloated mosquitoes circling overhead, Jose asked, "Why me, Guzco?"

Memories as painful as the wounds resurfaced through Guzco's shock.

Jose's course followed the whales into the Atlantic's deeper waters, madness in Guzco's eyes, terrified of what lay beyond the horizon and the languid, arcing leviathans leading him there.

"Don't fret, Guzco," Jose said. "The whales will hand us our fortunes. Soon we won't have to slog against the currents or risk our necks for paltry catches. Rome, Byzantium, even lands further east beckon!"

"I have enough. Besides, I've Luisa to think of now."

Jose's intelligent, if world weary features soured hearing his sister in law's name. "And I'm your brother; raised you; looked out for you. Never forget that."

Guzco held his tongue. He'd learned from a young age the safety silence offered, even if many thought him an imbecile because of it. Before Luisa, he vented his frustrations at being seen as Jose's simpleton brother through the dice. But he was a poor player, racking up large debts with no means of repaying them. Luisa had changed him, made him a better man who no longer saw life as a game of chance.

Keen to change the subject, he said, "I blame that merchant," recalling the slippery trader dressed in shabby silks who had passed through the village a month before offering to buy horses in return for bushels of eared wheat.

"Didn't he speak the truth about the Moors' cruelties?"

"Maybe."

"So why should he lie about the lands in the east, where the women are beautiful, the wine rich and three-headed dragons roam."

"A ruse to make you part with your money for that rag."

"Dragon hunter's cloth," Jose snapped. "Cost me half a dozen bacalao. A bargain! Ever since, we've had calm waters and good catches."

The revelation startled Guzco. His misfortune had not been a chance event. Massandar had stalked him for centuries.

"Azekiel," he whispered.

Clenching his fists, Azekiel sighed. "When will the collectors learn? I teach them to be wary of all offers of companionship. Why won't they listen?"

Death, short, stocky and sarcastic replied, "Many collectors have been tricked by Massandar, wiser ones than Domar."

Life, floundering on her optimism interrupted, "But Guzco has fortitude, loyalty, strength of purpose, the very virtues that made you select him ahead of his brother."

"Perhaps the kilns are his natural level," Azekiel replied. "I erred in allowing him out. I need to make an example of Domar. His actions are worthy of death but instead I shall banish him."

"A fair assessment," Death muttered. "Harsh on Domar but given Massandar's successes, the obvious choice. It appears you are mellowing, Azekiel. Not so long ago you would have taken the sulphur-tipped lash to his back."

"Scourging would be appropriate," Azekiel replied, gripping the teak handle of his bull whip and hankering for the simplicity of earlier times.

"I do not agree," Life said.

"I would not expect any different," Death replied.

"Abandoning Guzco will embolden Massandar. He was our brother once and as such I still hope he can be reconciled."

Death stifled a laugh. "Massandar is nourished by his accommodation with evil. We have lost too many to him. If we show Domar clemency it will not offer a cautionary tale to others."

Azekiel weighed up Death and Life's judgements. "Domar will be cast out. All collectors must learn from his mistakes. We will purge all vices from them." He levelled the whip at Death then said, "That will be your responsibility."

"And the souls in Guzco's possession?" Life asked.

"A price worth paying."

Returning to her chamber, Life summoned her steward, Philomandra.

As usual Life was taken aback by grace and earnestness that marked Philomandra out from her other stewards. "I have an errand for you Philomandra. The protection of Master Guzco Domar."

"The hopeless mariner?"

"The very same."

CHAPTER FIVE
Lavagna, August 1928

Eyes shut tight, Greta Perazzolo prayed to the Virgin for the strength to survive the forthcoming ordeal. She hadn't wanted to come to the old woman's funeral, but it was her turn to accompany mother, and neither her sister Oona nor brother Alesandro were willing to swap places with her. Not even for a week's pocket money.

Opening her eyes, she took in Santa Stefano's ornate, marble basted splendour as the congregation's echoing voices swelled then faded in response to Father Biavati's bidding. Sure she was being watched and thinking a vision as glorious as Saint Bernadette's was in the offing, Greta glanced across the aisle to see the oddball Luca Meazza poking his tongue out at her. Startled by such blasphemy, she juddered, earning a terse instruction from her mother to keep still. She did as she was told but from the tail of her eye, she again spotted Luca sticking his tongue out. This time, *he* received a hissed scolding from his mother.

"Mama," Greta, ever the goody two shoes, whispered, "Luca Meazza has poked his tongue out at me. Twice."

"Ignore him," came the curt reply.

"But isn't it a sin to poke your tongue out in church?"

"Of course. Now be quiet." Baffled by the answer, Greta peered around the Blackshirt officer to watch Biavati, gabbling softly in Latin, sprinkle holy water over the coffin. After that, he swung the bronze thurible over the casket releasing choking clouds of incense that caught on the back of Greta's throat.

The pallbearers, spick and span in black morning suits, bore the coffin from the church with the solemn mourners, some dabbing their eyes with crisp, white handkerchiefs, filing in behind. Watching Mama adjust her black headscarf then drop her rosary beads into a purse, Greta tried to quell her growing dread by daydreaming about her impending first communion. Her beautiful white dress bought, taken in and up, her new sandals still pinching, despite Mama's best efforts to stretch them. As she mithered over this forthcoming blistered catastrophe, Greta had an epiphany. To receive her first communion, *she* would be poking her tongue out at Biavati's beaky face as he said, "Corpus Christi." How could she avoid such a sin? But

Mama's grim face told her this wasn't the time to raise the matter.

Outside in the afternoon's rising swelter, a fugue of nerves and tight-throated fear gripped Greta upon sight of the high walled cemetery. Behind the wall stood scores of weathered sculptures of Angels in various states of repose, creating a macabre, petrified forest of penitence, suffering and remembrance. Peppered amongst the Angels were solemn, life-size effigies of once well-to-do Lavagnans, all staring out towards the Mediterranean, a stone's throw away.

She always found visiting her family's mausoleum to be harrowing. But ever since Alesandro had told her the ghosts of dead children skipped among the sculptures, the cemetery had put the fear of God into her. According to Alesandro, the only way to avoid being haunted by the dead children was to hold your breath upon entering the cemetery and avoid staring into the stone Angels' eyes.

Clasping her mother's hand and taking a deep breath, Greta stared straight ahead as they followed the funeral party into the cemetery. Eyes cast to the ground, she avoided the stone Angel's glare but sometimes caught sight of a brass-collared picture of a dead man or woman, their headstones shrouded in long dead flowers, brittle to the touch.

She grew lightheaded as Biavati droned on and on beside the old woman's freshly dug grave. Many thought the priest destined for greater things, a future bishop, cardinal. Even Pope. "Be good to have another Genovese as Pope," Greta's father once told her. "This fella could be our man." Greta didn't understand why having a Genovese Pope should matter. Surely what was important was that the Pope was a good man and could speak to Jesus. Besides, if Biavati got the job, he'd be away south to Rome and all the finery that went with it. But she decided on balance that it would be good if Lavagna's priest became Pope. For starters Papa would be happy, and it would be nice to say she received her first communion from the Pope.

Thinking these holy, giddy thoughts, she rested her eyes on the statue of a long dead Lavagnan woman, who wobbled then grew hazy. Slumping against her mother, the last thing Greta remembered was two ghost children peeking from behind the statue. *The children ran off but a scowling Angel dropped from its plinth to scold her for breathing in its presence. A young boy's voice echoed nearby.*

Waking with a start, Greta found herself lying on a stone bench. In the shade. A damp cloth rested on her forehead. Again she heard the young boy's voice. "Where am I?" she asked, panicking in this blurred, uneven world of shifting faces and voices.

"In the Portico. You had a little too much sun and fainted," her worried mother replied. Sitting up, Greta straightened her spectacles. The world became clearer, less fearful. Biavati, still wearing his cassock and surplice, arrived with a glass of water. Mama held the glass to Greta's lips and with one sip, her mood brightened, delighted the future Pope had brought her water. Even if damnation awaited for breathing among the Angels, she could count on the Pope to do her bidding.

Hearing the echoing voices once more, she panicked and gripped her mother's hand. "Don't let them take me, Mama."

"Who?"

"Stop shouting, Luca!" Luca's flustered mother ordered. He stepped out from behind one of the Portico's stone columns. As his put upon mother apologised to all and sundry for her son's behaviour, Luca again stuck his tongue out and crossed his eyes for good effect. Greta didn't have the strength to complain but after the Blackshirt enquired after her, she noticed Luca's furrowed scowl and his mother's eagerness to be away.

CHAPTER SIX
East of Genoa, The Abandoned Farmhouse, July 1189

The thought of reaching Badur only to incur Azekiel's wrath terrified Guzco as much as Massandar returning. Desperate to get away and avoid another charlatan exploiting his flaws, he gathered his paltry provisions, hauled himself up and staggered to the window. Despite the heat, the fresher air was welcome.

With slow, fitful steps he reached the farmhouse's back door. Relishing the sun's warmth, he studied the olive grove stretching before him. Further on, chestnut and beech trees covered the lower slopes of a mountain, its higher pastures, a checkerboard of small, roughly rectangular plots of land studded with knuckles of rock and wind-carved shrubs. The mountains promised seclusion and, with luck, safety. After all, his ancestors used to climb to higher ground when Berber pirates threatened the village. If it was good enough for them, it was good enough for him.

A walk that should have taken a few minutes, took the best part of an hour until beset by pain, he leaned against an aged olive tree powerless to stem the memories any longer.

"How did they know to follow the whales?" Jose seethed watching boats laden with fish and riding low in the water head for home. Guzco busied himself repairing the nets, afraid to tell Jose that he had revealed their secret in order to settle a gambling debt.

"Now those bastards profit from my efforts," Jose spat. The sail slackened. "You'll have to row, Guzco."

Happy to pit his strength against the sea, after all, he'd won the year's races, Guzco let out the oars and began to row. A whale and her calf drew alongside. "Ever seen such a thing, Guzco? It's an omen, a king's ransom is in the offing!" Jose shouted, excitement coating his spray-flecked face. Moments later Guzco cowered as the cow raised her giant, jagged fluke and dived, leaving the calf under the brothers' protection.

Tacking starboard, Jose shouted, "The whales are breeching!" Rictus-grinned guillemots, hundreds of them, dived into the foaming water to gorge on the sardines. Reaching the shoal, Jose hurled the net overboard and shouted, "Remember. Plant the feet, bend the knees, then haul for all you are worth!"

Three heaving catches were landed, leaving them knee deep in fish. "Enough for one day," Jose said.

Thanking Poseidon that his voyage across the horizon was nearing its end, Guzco put out the oars and began to row. The boat shuddered and yawed as the cow breeched the water and arrowed skywards. "Pull, Guzco!" screamed Jose with the cow toppling towards them. Guzco hauled as if the Devil himself were after them.

"Pull, Guzco!"

The landing cow splintered the surf and a flume of water erupted over the boat. Opening his eyes, Guzco saw Jose gripping the tiller for all he was worth. "They want me to follow," he said in unfamiliar, near stupefied tones.

"Have you gone mad?" Guzco replied, setting down the oars. Jose's drenched features screwed into a look of contempt. "All my life I've carried you. Without me you would have been little more than a beggar, sold off to the Berbers. I know it was you who told them to follow the whales. But you lacked the balls to tell me. My idiot brother, who offered up my future just to please his fucking wife."

"I love her."

"She's turned you against me."

"She's made me a better man and carries my child."

"You sure it's yours?"

Guzco's punch floored Jose. Egged on by a rich, foreign voice, whispering, "Finish him, Guzco, free yourself," he carried on the assault only stopping when the boat tilted upwards on a surging wave. Certain they had reached the tumbling edge of the world, Guzco clung to an oar as the boat plummeted towards the water, turfing him and Jose overboard.

Numbed by the cold, Guzco continued his befuddled ascent through the woods, grateful to escape the harrying memories. A shadow flitted among the trees. At first he tried to wish the shadow away but as it came closer, he picked up a fallen branch, tapped it against the nearest tree and shouted, "Show yourself."

Philomandra stayed hidden.

Hounded by the unknown, Guzco stumbled on, the search for safety now a trial of endurance. He tripped over exposed roots, clung to branches and thrutched between fallen trees, all the while trying to crowd out the pain and fear lurking inside him, until to his relief, he faced the mountain's bare slopes. Exhausted, he leaned against the final bough and disturbed a carpet of dead leaves, releasing the sweet odour of decay. With the dawn sun tinting the sky with flecks of orange, he followed a track up the mountain's western slope, often stopping to rest and check if the wraith still followed. Certain it wasn't, he calmed and felt safer with each step despite thinking himself a fisherman in the mountains.

CHAPTER SEVEN
The Ligurian Alps, Italy, October 1189

For weeks, Guzco scrabbled deeper into the mountains, deciding his route on whims and fanciful notions. The scree lined slopes offered a barren, lifeless world, the thin air hampering breathing and leaving the starlit nights bitterly cold. Except for the odd flower or mushroom, he found nothing to eat, making him rue not being more sparing with Spinoza's rations. Even so, he skirted isolated hamlets, farms and mills pressing on to the next valley and then the next one.

One day as a thick fog cut visibility to an arm's length, he sat and waited for the mist to clear. Off to his left, bleating goats clattered and scraped over bare rock. Growing cold, he gathered stones around him and cursed his immortality and his creaking, frozen bones in equal measure. Safety had come at the cost of exhaustion and loneliness. The last spiteful moments with Jose returned.

His fingernails scraped along the hull but the boat squirmed away. "No, please no," he pleaded making one last desperate effort to clamber aboard. Again the boat slinked away. Exhausted, he sank, spinning in the eddy, before clawing his way back to the surface, eyes brine stung, gagging for breath, unable to fathom what was happening.

Jose lay face down, motionless save for the swell, which slowly carried him further away. The dragon hunter's cloth lay in his wake. Hoping it possessed the magical powers Jose swore by, Guzco grasped the cloth and prayed to Poseidon.

He sank into the crushing darkness, his final thoughts accompanied by the whales' exquisite chorus.

The joy of the sea—the pride in my strength—Luisa—she saved me from myself—the whale's giant, jagged fluke—a red sky—the Saharan dust clouds—rasping nets—aching wrists—the love of the dice—Mother's songs—the sea's scent and its endless motion—the child I'll never know.

Jose asked, "Why me, Guzco?" He had no answer.
"Work to be done, Master Domar," Lord Azekiel said. "Work to be done."
Even for a man who has murdered his brother?

He only ever craved the simple life: a full belly, a woman to love, children to raise and more luck with the dice. Stability. That's the word, like a good boat in a storm. If only he'd been brave enough to reject Jose's greed, he would have had all those things and died a happy man.

Hoping it wasn't too late, he shouted, "Offer me a new choice Azekiel; death or Angel. Like a snake shedding its skin, I now know what I'd choose. Who wants to live in this fog-bound world, half alive, half dead?"

Punching through the stones, he hollered, "Answer me, Azekiel!" Only his echo replied, yet he continued to shout, slicing his throat hoarse with the effort. The rage that possessed him to kill Jose, burst through the fissures in his mind allowing lungful's of frustration, shame and misery to erupt. Tasting the sea in his tears, he beat the rocks, oblivious to shredding his knuckles all the while bawling, "Why me? Why me?"

The only response was the piercing cry of a hawk, plummeting out of the sky towards a huge boulder, set on the crest of a pitted ridge. The hawk pulled out of its dive and wheeled over Guzco before flying off. Curious as to what the bird had spotted, Guzco headed for the boulder. He found nothing remarkable, although the nearby fast flowing stream was welcome. After drinking the cool, redemptive water, he stripped then lay in the river. The water soothed his wounds but soon proved too cold to withstand. He climbed out, dried off and sat beneath the overhang on the rock's leeward side that offered some protection from the sun and buffeting winds. Drawing his knees to his chest, he again asked, "Why me?"

"Guzco." A woman whispered in a sensuous, soothing voice.

"Who's there?"

Philomandra didn't answer.

"Show yourself."

Philomandra stayed hidden.

He grabbed a rock and scrambled up the boulder. Mountains extended in every direction, their jagged, pleated, snow tipped summits forming an impenetrable barrier. The only living things were a one-eyed lizard, no bigger than a field mouse, feeding on a column of ants, some lugging fragments of moss, across the stone's weathered surface. Guzco smarted from the stings as some ants crawled over his feet to avoid the lizard, who, after eating his fill, scrabbled down the boulder and fell from view.

Curious, Guzco probed the rock's base and discovered a small opening, hidden beneath layers of moss and lichen. Peeling the gauze away, his heart leapt. A hole, wide and deep enough for him to shelter in lay inside.

The lizard carried as much threat as possible but couldn't thwart the Angel entering his home. Drawing the lichen back across the opening, Guzco lay in the cool, mottled darkness, relieved to be free from Azekiel's glower and Jose and Isabella's harrying.

Days passed. An agreeable routine of bathing followed by resting beneath the overhang took hold, allowing Guzco's wounds to slowly heal and his shame to thin. Despite foraging far and wide, he found little to eat except grass and the occasional treat of a flower. He tried to feast on the ants but their stings and bitter taste, soon put paid to that idea.

Most mornings, a piebald Rove goat arrived to drink from the stream. Each time Guzco tried to catch the goat, the dead-eyed buck trotted away, bleating with derision and leaving his would be hunter to ponder how such a feeble-minded beast could outwit him.

On the odd occasion while bathing, Guzco released himself to the current and floated downstream for a second or two, before grasping the riverbank or the riverbed. Each time he allowed himself to be carried a little further. Reckless he knew, but liberating, a test of his loyalties.

Badur is where his best, perhaps only hope of salvation lay and allowing himself to drift, perhaps as far as the ocean, however appealing, had to stop. To stem temptation, he took off the pots and left them on the bank before bathing. Even if the urge to release himself to the current for good proved impossible to resist, the souls were too precious to leave behind.

He'd heard of holy men, from earlier times, living in the mountains, fasting and praying in order to seek enlightenment. He'd always left thinking and praying to others, and given the mess he'd made of things, quite right too. Up here, life was quiet, safe too but perpetual hunger and the approaching winter weighed heavily. He'd grown idle. Soft. Weak. Skin once thick with muscle started to sag, and his ribs protruded. His strength had always been his greatest, maybe only, asset. It was time to resume his long delayed journey to Badur.

Lying in the stream on the morning of his departure, the goat gave him its usual dismissive look upon arrival before drinking.

Won't miss you.

The buck raised its head, bleated softly then scuttled away. None the wiser, Guzco climbed out, pleased with himself for still refusing the river's siren offer to carry him away from his troubles. But while dressing, he looked along the ridge and discovered the source of the goat's unease.

He counted ten men in total, all on horseback, slowly trudging up the valley towards him. Long swords, battle-axes, shields and cross bows were slung around their shoulders or hung from their saddles. Thinking it wise to hide, Guzco slid into the hole.

The lizard sat on his chest, twitching, as the riders dismounted and stamped their feet to leech the stiffness from their legs. The lichen shrouded them from Guzco, adding to the sense of menace.

"We'll eat here, water the horses and then press on," one said.

"When do you think we'll reach Badur, Captain Fachetti?" another asked. Mention of the village stirred Guzco's interest.

"If we ride through the night, tomorrow morning or afternoon."

"And after the village?"

"Genoa and then onto The Holy Land."

His companion said. "Nothing here, save for that hawk above us and these ants underfoot."

"Godforsaken place," another said.

"What's that you're rinsing out, Sanchez?" asked Fachetti.

"Just some jars, Captain. Figure I'll find a use for them." Sanchez's bland words sucked the breath from Guzco. Fresh pain arched through his shoulders. He'd forgotten the pots. He'd given up the Ostler, Weaver and Isabella's souls. Massandar's laughter rang in his ears.

Seconds later, he flinched as the pots smashed against the boulder. "Stupid fucker," shouted Fachetti, "I don't want a man beside me more interested in collecting trinkets and baubles than having my back."

"Sorry, Captain, I just thought,"

"Fuck thinking, Sanchez. No more. No less. Start acting like a soldier and not a whore's fica."

"Azekiel," Guzco muttered.

"Hear that?" Sanchez said.

Guzco froze.

"Hear what?" Fachetti answered.

"A voice."

"By God's teeth these mountains are driving you mad, man. Even the rocks mock you. Let's rest up, eat, then head on away from this God forsaken shithole."

Farts, belches, and bawdy jokes showed the squadron to be comfortable in each other's company. One or two urinated against the boulder, their steaming yellow piss dripping onto Guzco, while the canny lizard found a more sheltered spot.

Within the hour, the soldiers were gone but wary of them doubling back, Guzco only risked leaving his hiding place an hour, maybe two later. With the lizard feasting on squashed ants, he picked up fragments of the shattered pots, wound the discarded twine around his wrist, and wondered how the Ostler's, Weaver's and Isabella's souls would fare flowing down the mountain. To be washed away, like dirt from a shoe was a thought to trouble the mind of the highest king or lowest fisherman. Atonement now rested in Badur with Maria Bascuali. There was no time to waste.

He dropped the fragments into the stream, gathered up the scraps of bread, cheese and cured pork discarded by the soldiers, and set off. After an hour, the track split in two. One route wound down into a valley, skirting a small lake with the bluest water imaginable. In places patches of bruised snow sat in shade and in the valley beyond the lake, lush meadows of wild barley spread towards a dense forest of beech and larch. A place to shelter. To call home.

The second route shadowed the ridge before dropping towards another valley, its forests dissected by streams. Fresh horse pellets marked this route. Guzco chose this path.

Please be alive Maria, I need your soul.

CHAPTER EIGHT
Lavagna, December 1930

Unlike Oona and Alesandro, Greta preferred wintertime. With few if any day trippers arriving from Genoa, life in Lavagna grew quieter, less obtrusive. Donning her wellington boots, favourite overcoat, the one with the shiny buttons, and the bright red bobble hat Mama had bought her for Christmas, she loved to scour the shoreline for shells and driftwood, whilst listening to the grey sea's ever-changing song.

This Saturday afternoon, out beachcombing, she spotted Luca, also shod in wellingtons and wrapped in a sturdy winter coat far too big for him, skimming stones from the breakwater. Ever since the Meazzas had arrived in Lavagna from Genoa, "under a cloud" as Mama said, although what type of cloud Greta wasn't sure, Luca seemed more shadow than real. Apart from the rumpus at the old woman's funeral, he rarely spoke, marking him out as an imbecile with no friends. Not that he seemed to care. At school, he suffered taunts and cuffings from fishermen's sons who found the brainy, pinched-faced Genovese newcomer easy prey. Why they bullied Luca, Greta had no idea. In a few years most of these boys would put to sea with fathers, uncles and cousins, and like Christopher Columbus, sail beyond the horizon. No doubt Luca would follow his father into boring old medicine.

In two minds over approaching him, she heeded Mama's advice that it costs nothing to be nice so asked, "What are you doing?"

"What does it look like?" he shot back, his cowlick dancing in the breeze.

"Skimming stones?"

"Then that's what I'm doing."

Stung by his rudeness and now understanding why he hadn't any friends, she watched Luca hurl another stone. "Fancy a go?" he asked as an onshore gust threatened to lift his willowy frame into the air.

Greta picked up a flat, smooth pebble, ideal for skimming. She planted her feet and leaned into the wind. Although she knew perfectly well how to skim stones, often beating Alesandro, she let Luca explain the technique involved before demonstrating his prowess by achieving a fourer. His cockiness evaporated when she threw a sixer, citing beginner's luck.

"Want to hear an echo?" he asked after chucking one final stone for a paltry twoer. Unsure but intrigued, Greta replied, "Very well."

"Come on then." He skipped along the breakwater's rocks then ran along the harbour, passing trawlers landing their catch. Struggling to keep up, Greta shouted, "Wait for me!"

They reached the level crossing the moment a Pisa-bound train rumbled past. Luca disappeared into a cloud of steam, reappearing moments later smiling. "Was I invisible?"

"For a second," she replied, wiping her steamed up glasses on the sleeve of her coat.

"Good. Keep up."

They crossed the tracks and bolted up a narrow alleyway towards Santa Stefano. Fearing the cemetery, Greta waited near the Portico watching Luca climb one of the glowering marble lions guarding the church's grand steps. He offered to haul her up onto the lion but she refused.

"In that case, this way!" Luca leapt from the lion and ran into the Portico. He darted among the columns shouting, his echo triggering Greta's memories of fainting at the funeral. But this time Greta stepped inside the Portico and shouted her name, revelling in the booming echo.

"Mussolini is an idiot! A fucking idiot!" Luca bawled.

His outburst shocked Greta. The teachers at school went to great lengths to stress Mussolini's genius in turning Italy from a backwater into the greatest nation on earth where everybody had work and food and led happy, fulfilling lives. Where Luca got his notions from, she'd no idea. Also, she'd never heard the word "fucking" before and would have to ask twelve-year-old Alesandro what it meant.

"Mussolini is a fucking idiot!" Luca repeated.

The kerfuffle caught the attention of the crabby cemetery caretaker, locking up for the night. "Who's there?" he asked, "Come out! Show yourself!" Luca giggled, grabbed Greta's hand and hid behind a column.

"What'll we do now?" she whispered aware that saying nasty things about Mussolini was frowned upon by grown-ups.

"Trust me."

"I've no choice."

"In that case, run!"

Not sure what Luca's plan amounted to, Greta followed, swerving to avoid an old man labouring uphill on his boneshaker then leaping over a

slathering terrier eyeing up strings of tripe in a butcher's window. As always when running, she wore a determined look but was taken aback by the rich thrumming sound her wellingtons' soles made on the stone pavement.

Reaching their apartment block in Piazza Bella Liberta, and laughing through heaving breaths, Greta struggled to remember when she'd had so much fun. "Enjoy that?" Luca asked, leaning against the wall, red-faced and sucking in the air. Still struggling for breath, Greta nodded and said, "Did you see the caretaker's face?"

Luca's perfect mimicry of the caretaker's sourpuss features made her laugh so hard she almost wet herself. "I've an idea," she said. "After school tomorrow, we'll climb the southern headland and shout from there. Our echo is bound to reach Genoa."

"You're on," Luca replied.

Two cars pulled up across the road. Blackshirts piled out and crossed the road towards them. Greta recognised the Blackshirt from the funeral and wondered if the miserable cemetery caretaker had told him about Luca's bad language.

"Not again," Luca muttered.

"We're sorry," Greta said to the Blackshirt, "We didn't mean to be naughty."

Ignoring her, the Blackshirt barked, "Apartment five, sixth floor." Luca's home. The Blackshirts left the stale odour of cigarettes and hair oil in their wake.

"With me," Greta whispered, taking Luca's hand. At first, he pulled away but soon tightened his grip. Stopping outside her front door, they watched the Blackshirts barge past Luca's mother and storm inside the apartment, ignoring her protests. Luca now gripped Greta's hand so tight, it hurt.

"Inside, the pair of you," said Greta's mother.

Once inside, Greta pressed her ear to the door and heard muffled shouts before heavy footsteps barrelled downstairs, amidst which a man protested his innocence.

From the living room window overlooking the Piazza, they watched the Blackshirts bundle Luca's father into the first sedan then drive off. Luca's mother ran alongside as far as the Town Hall.

Luca's usually mischievous eyes brimmed with tears. "See you tomorrow?" he asked Greta with an air of quiet desperation. Rubbing her sore hand, she nodded but wasn't sure.

Returning to the living room, she found Mama rummaging in the large mahogany cabinet where the bone china crockery for Easter and Christmas was kept. Shifting plates, cups and saucers, she fished out a bottle of brandy, took a nip then said, "Lay the table, Greta."

It was Saturday, so her turn.

CHAPTER NINE
The Ligurian Alps, Italy, November 1189

Guzco made good progress, even finding time to hatch a new plan of action once he'd found Maria Bascuali. The Crusader armies needed ships to reach the Holy Land. Ships needed sailors. He was a sailor. Of sorts. But a voyage to the Holy Land would be risky. Best be cautious. Find work on a merchant ship travelling west to France, Iberia, maybe even as far as home. Thinking of home brought a spring to his step. The incline became shallower making progress easier despite the thick, heavy heat clinging to the valley. He reached a meadow ablaze with tumbling colour and strumming with the sound of insects. Life. Beyond the field lay dense woodland bisected by a river.

Stopping to drink, he spotted a stone bothy, dilapidated but empty. Perfect for holing up for the night. The roof was constructed from weather-beaten timbers, some all but rotted through. A rough opening, hacked out from one beam, allowed smoke to escape.

The door sat heavy on its hinges and scraped over bare earth.

After gathering kindling and wood for a fire, he ate the last of the scraps and drank sour tasting water from an aged, creased leather gourd hanging from a peg. Despite its bitter taste, the water slaked his thirst and he set about refining his plan for going home.

At first the scratching was barely audible. Probably mice searching for food. The scraping grew louder, more persistent, accompanied by a dull, guttural growl. Peeking through the gap between the door and its jamb, the wolf's bulk surprised Guzco, its scarred snout adding to its threat. He slid the flimsy lock into its cradle and leant against the door, his breaths short and shallow. The wolf's probing continued for ten, maybe fifteen minutes, before it trotted off. Relieved, Guzco reached for the gourd to slake his renewed thirst.

The bolt splintered and the door buckled as the wolf tried to force its way inside. Terrified, Guzco flayed the gourd, striking the wolf's snout and forcing it to retreat. Out of breath, thoughts a blur, he heaved the shattered door closed and leant against it, expecting the next assault.

Instead, the wolf jumped onto the roof and padded across the creaking timbers. Guzco stood anxious, near powerless. He could make a run for it but the wolf would be on him in no time. Better to stay put, keep the fire high and door closed. The timbers around the smoke hole started to splinter as Scarface, ignoring the smoke, chewed and clawed at the rotten beams.

Night fell, the bothy's fire Guzco's sole comfort as the beam gradually disintegrated under the wolf's patient assault. Hours passed, the wolf's efforts remorseless, oblivious to Guzco's shouts and jabs with flaming branches. It began to howl, in triumph or frustration Guzco couldn't tell. He lowered the branch to rest his shoulders. It was enough. The wolf forced his head through the gap but his shoulders and chest were too broad to breach the opening. Guzco thrust the branch into its face. Yelping, Scarface retreated, leaving the scent of singed fur in its wake.

Time and again, the wolf tried to fight his way into the bothy and time and again Guzco repelled him until, at sunrise, Scarface lay down on the timbers to rest. Time was on his side.

The cool dawn gave way to a stifling, oppressive heat. Desperate to slake his thirst, Guzco drained the gourd's dregs and then pressed his face against the shattered door, to draw in cooler air. His heart sank, his clever plan evaporated.

Two more wolves, fangs bared, ears flattened, angry eyes focussed on the bothy, stood before him. He braced himself against the door, last burning branch in hand, eyes closed. Waiting. Expecting.

Whatever way they come, plant the feet, then fight!

The two newcomers leapt onto the roof, the timbers flexing under their weight. Snarls filled the air. A fight broke out, giving Guzco a chance. He flung the door open and ran full pelt towards the river. Within seconds, Scarface had him pinned to the ground only for the two other wolves to set about Scarface. Guzco's would be hunter bolted with the other two in close pursuit.

"Are you alright?"

The man was tall, broad-shouldered and wore a sheepskin-lined jerkin, its right sleeve empty. His face, weathered by a life in the mountains, sported a deep scar over his right eye and wore a haunted, weary expression. He jabbed his staff into Guzco's face. The Angel leaned away but the staff followed him. Two bleating piebald Rove goats appeared, the bells around their necks clanging.

"Are you with the soldiers?"

Guzco raised his hands in supplication.

"Be still."

The other two wolves returned and sat beside their master. One growled whilst the other, larger, more powerful, eyed Guzco in silence.

"Away, Drago," the shepherd ordered. The larger dog obeyed and moments later he guided a herd of Rove goats towards the bothy, some edgy after picking up the wolf's and Angel's scent. Again, the staff twisted into Guzco's cheek. "Are you with the soldiers?"

Guzco pointed to the staff. The shepherd lifted the pressure. Guzco stood, spat out a mouthful of blood then said, "I'm a priest, from Carcassonne, on pilgrimage to Rome. I was robbed. The robbers stole everything. I've been wandering the mountains trying to find the village of Badur. Bascuali."

"Bascuali the farrier?"

"The very same. His wife is my cousin, on my mother's side. I planned to rest there before resuming my pilgrimage. After the robbery, I thought it wiser taking to the higher ground but lost my way. Then the wolf found me."

"He's a bastard that one. Cunning too. Never gives up. Comes off the mountain early to lie in wait for the herds moving to the lower ground for winter." The shepherd shook his head. "First those brigands, and now wolves. By Christ's Cross I fear for the valley." He spat and ground his staff into the earth. "Hope does not carry much weight around the mountains anymore."

"I'm not a man of the mountains."

"Plainly. If you were, you would have known the wolf was trailing you." He propped his staff against his shoulder and wiped his mouth, weighing Guzco up. "Badur is half a day's walk from here. Bascuali is a good man, returned last winter from the Holy Land. A fine farrier too, shod the King's horses in Jerusalem." He spat then continued, "It takes courage to set off into the unknown. Even though you think you have failed you have succeeded by staying alive."

Guzco couldn't recall the last time he had received praise, even if he was

undeserving of it. The shepherd retrieved a portion of cheese from his satchel and offered it. "It's not much but take it. Please."

The cheese was smooth, creamy with an exquisite salty taste. Next, the shepherd offered his water gourd. After taking a long, deep draught, Guzco smacked his lips then said, "Thank you for your kindness."

"Many are in need at the moment."

"Do you live in the valley?"

He shook his head. "Three days to the east. In Cresson. The mountains are my home. I take solace in them. Especially after the Crusade."

"You took the Cross?"

"Yes. My brother also. It's how I lost the arm. Outside Aleppo. The Saracen lost his life. Never got paid, nor granted the land promised. Made it back alive though. A redemption of sorts."

"And your brother?"

"Seven years and still no word of him or any of the men from these parts. Nine of us headed to Jerusalem to fight the Infidel. Now the valley is prey to men like those who robbed you. Did you hear any names?"

"Their leader was called Fachetti". The shepherd frowned. "Do you know him?"

"Of him. A mercenary who took the Cross but only for land and privileges. When he didn't receive them, he came back to take what he thinks he is owed either in coin or in blood. You were lucky, Fachetti holds all people in contempt. Priests above all." He drove his staff into the ground to emphasise his point then said, "Follow the river west, towards Badur."

"And the wolf?"

"You'll have to take your chances. But Drago and Vladko have seen him off, at least for now. Stick to the path. Don't dawdle. He'll be stalking you, doesn't give up, that fella. But you'll be safe in Badur. Did you see the scars on his snout?"

Guzco nodded.

"Bascuali's handiwork from a few years back. Took a scythe to him to protect a smooth-talking merchant, horse trader I think, and his serfs. Ever since, the wolf skirts Badur."

CHAPTER TEN
The Badur Valley, France, November 1189

The Badur valley was more modest than the arrowing ranges and peaks Guzco had blindly wandered for months. The muggy air hung heavy, studded with the scent of pine and beech, while the thick forest canopy offered shade and protection from the mountain winds. But moving deeper into the forest, the atmosphere grew still, dark, chocked with secrets. He grew cautious, easily startled by shrieking birds or the sudden, darting movements in the undergrowth. Fearful of running into the soldiers, he was tempted to turn tail. But heeding the shepherd's advice about the wolf, he hurried on, desperate to reach Badur.

Sediment built up along the river's bends had slowed the current allowing dragonflies and midges to skirt the surface and fish to rest in the stiller waters abutting the bank. On the next bend, a series of large flat rocks formed a narrow bridge. Across the bridge, the track meandered through another forest.

He crossed the bridge still alert to Scarface and entered the forest, hoping for signs of life. There were none. The silence grew oppressive, out of place. Uneasy, Guzco broke into a trot. A village came into view beyond a shallow ford.

Roosting birds scattered as Scarface broke from the shadows. Guzco waded into the freezing calf-deep water, hoping the shepherd was right. He stumbled, landing face down and swallowed a mouthful of freezing water. On the riverbed lay a child's wooden doll dressed in a ragged woollen smock. Shouting for help, Guzco struggled to his feet and scrambled onto the riverbank, lined with tunics, dresses and britches. A young dog, little more than a pup, held its ground, barking in defiance at Scarface now looking on from the far bank. He raised his snout, turned tail and retreated into the forest.

Gasping for breath, Guzco hoped his tale of woe-begotten misfortune would survive scrutiny, even if the irony of a lying Angel wasn't lost on him. He got to his feet and for the first time noticed that most of the buildings were razed, including a still smouldering church. Upturned furniture, smashed pots, wrecked spinning wheels and torn clothes littered the ground while chickens scratched and pecked at the soil.

He entered a forge, warmed by still glowing coals, and stepped around a swing plough awaiting repair. He ducked to avoid a dozen or more fleeing crows, the musky draught of their wings confusing and threatening. One crow, bolder than the others, pecked at the left eye of the dead man hanging from a creaking rope looped over a beam.

Bascuali? Guzco dry heaved.

In its jaws, the sopping wet pup clasped the toy doll Guzco had spotted in the river. The pup dropped the doll then yapped furiously, forcing the bold crow to fly off and perch on the charred beams of another hovel.

Guzco entered the farrier's home, shouting, "Respite for a stranger!" Nobody answered. A lukewarm pot of stew hung over a dying fire. Beside the fire, lay a doll and hawk both carved from single pieces of wood. Jars of chestnut flour, dried barley and pine nuts sat on a ledge to the left of the fire while a bowl of fresh eggs lay on a table beside a worn green woollen dress with a threaded darning needle pinned to it. His spirits lifted. Looks like he'd missed the seamstress by a few minutes and she'd be back soon. Even so, it seemed wrong to wander unnoticed among the lives of strangers.

Outside the church, acrid smoke stung his eyes and throat. Two six foot long iron staves, secured by boulders, damp to the touch, were jammed against the church's heavy wooden door. Sure someone was watching, Guzco scoured the trees behind the church and shouted, "I'm a pilgrim bound for Rome. I offer no harm." Nobody stepped forward.

Ignoring the pain in his shoulders, Guzco rolled the stones clear then worked the staves free. Pulling the door open, the stifling air, fused with the smell of roast pork, reminded him of once celebrated Saints' days.

Before him lay a grotesque, woebegone sculpture of charred human remains, entwined in agonised shapes and lit by shafts of light pouring through the partially collapsed roof.

Unable to understand such reckless hate, and wolf or no wolf, Guzco thought it better to take his chances in the mountains. But if Maria Bascuali lay among the corpses, there might still be a chance of redemption. Steadying himself, he untangled the limp, blackened bodies. A woman clasped a crucifix, whilst a child's sullied hand protruded from beneath her. A seared joist rested on a prone man's shoulders whilst a woman and two children lay beneath him. Beside them lay an old man and woman together in a final, loving embrace. At the bottom of the pile he came across a soldier clad in chain mail. Sanchez groaned.

"I am with you," Guzco said, reaching for him.

"Fuck you," Sanchez replied, with his final breath.

To his left, beneath the remains of two women, a dry, cracked voice asked for help. Hoping he'd found Maria Bascuali, Guzco rolled the two corpses aside. The young woman was naked and bore terrible burns across her face, torso and arms. Her lidless, blood red eyes scoured Guzco.

"They were Crusaders heading to the Holy Land," she whispered. "Bascuali saw them so sent his son and daughter to hide in the woods. After the soldiers hanged him, they came for us."

"Maria Bascuali?"

She shook her head then doubled up after a coughing fit but refused Guzco's offer to fetch her water from the river.

"Why?" she asked.

"Because they can."

Her breaths weak, her ruined fingers tracing imaginary shapes, time and again she refused the offer of water until she beckoned Guzco to her and whispered, "I'm ready, Angel."

Her final thoughts overwhelmed his.

The choking smoke – the young soldier on the roof – the one I thought handsome – he falls - our fear gives way to hatred – we set about him – but he is unrepentant, goading us, 'Is that all you have? Do your worst upon me. Cleanse me with your hate." - Maman, Papa, Sandro – I will be with you soon – Life! Life! – to swim in the river – the starlings dance – the dance - winter's first snows – the summer breeze upon my naked skin – Life! Life! - An Angel?

As he kissed the women's cheek, Guzco reached for the string of pots before remembering. He looked about him hoping to find something, anything to use to store her soul. *This is a church. There must be something.* Nothing. Until he remembered. It wasn't perfect but would have to do.

He emptied the first jar he came across in Bascuali's hut and hurried back to the church. The girl lay still, her eyes dulled, her soul lost.

CHAPTER ELEVEN
Badur, November 1189

Sitting on one of the dislodged rocks, Guzco followed the course of a track winding over the valley's western ridge. Instinct told him to run. He'd only avoided the soldiers through luck and poor judgement. Besides, there was enough food to steal to allow him to see out the winter somewhere safe. Far away. The shores of the blue lake sprang to mind but with night falling and Scarface lurking, the odds of reaching the lake unscathed seemed poor.

He barricaded himself inside Bascuali's hut with the pup. Revived by the stew and a raw egg, he plotted his route from Badur; what provisions to take, tools too. Satisfied he'd thought of everything, he coddled the pup and stared into the fire, trying to crowd out his guilt, certain that if he'd reached Badur on time to claim Maria Bascuali's soul, the villagers wouldn't have perished.

"Help them, Guzco," *She* asked.

But the soldiers, the wolf. Everything about this place reeks of danger.

"Be true to yourself."

In that case, I'll run.

"You're better than that. Be true to yourself, to Luisa and your daughter."

The following morning, equally girded and ashamed by her words, Guzco cut Bascuali down then searched the forge. He found a sack, scythe, spade and also a dozen iron staves planted inside the now dead coals. A lump hammer, its handle smoothed through years of use, lay propped against an anvil. He pictured Bascuali, face blackened with grime, setting the hammer down and stepping outside to watch Fachetti and his men arrive.

Using the scythe, he set about cropping a patch of thick, knotted grass behind the church after which he drove a spade into the cleared earth. Within the hour, he had carved out a grave large enough to lay a grown man to rest. Shoulders burning, he stripped to the waist, stepped two paces left and dug another grave, finding solace in the back-breaking work, that reminded him of his toils at sea. Then his strength had fed into the ocean. Now it fed into the rich black earth. He worked long into the night, until exhausted and hands raw, he counted enough graves to bury the villagers.

With Scarface nowhere to be seen, he washed in the river's icy waters, wondering if the stream he had almost surrendered to in the high valley was a tributary. Either way, he was pleased that his efforts had silenced *Her*.

The next morning, wearing a clean tunic scavenged from the clothes scattered along the riverbank, he returned to the church. Fending off gorging flies, he covered his mouth with a strip of cloth and using the sack, hauled each corpse towards their grave. While interring them, he daren't look at the corpse's face, considering it wrong to look upon such sorrow but paused to honour their suffering. The two boys and three girls burials were the hardest to accept. Of the five women he buried, he wondered which one was Maria Bascuali.

Even after stripping him, Guzco struggled to haul Sanchez's muscular remains towards the furthest grave all the while cursing himself for not thinking to bury the soldier first. But he did not grieve or pause to remember Sanchez's suffering. Others could do that. If they cared to.

Returning to the forge, he thrashed the chainmail to peel the feeding crows from Bascuali. Removing the noose he lifted the farrier's remains onto the sack.

I should have been here for you, your wife and your children. Forgive me.

The burials complete, he fashioned eighteen rough wooden crucifixes. One for each villager but not Sanchez.

He sat on the riverbank, eyeing up Scarface, looking on from the far bank. Watching. Waiting.

The whining pup, its tail wagging ten to the dozen, growled at the wolf and then slobbered over Guzco. "I suppose you'll be after a name. How about Poseidon?" The pup yapped. "That's settled then." Scarface slipped away.

Returning to the hut, Guzco warmed up the stew and ate two more raw eggs. He considered boiling the rest of the eggs but decided to postpone such pleasure for another day. A boy and girl, both barefoot and dressed in rags, stood by the door. Stick thin, skin tinged yellow, they shivered, with the cold or fear, Guzco couldn't decide. The girl, the younger of the two, leaned against the boy, who said, "The soldiers, they killed everyone. With swords and axes. Fire too. Our Papa told us to hide in the woods and stay there until they left. Have you seen him?"

"No. What is his name?"

"Matteo Bascuali."

Startled, Guzco asked, "And your mother?"

"She died a month ago. Poisoned by a thorn."

"Come inside and eat." The girl stepped forward but the boy barred her path. Guzco picked the doll and hawk up from their resting places and set them on the table.

"Ilia!" Smiling, the girl entered. The boy, cautious, fearful, followed, his eyes fixed on Guzco. The children shared a stool. The girl hugged the doll, while the boy allowed the hawk to swoop and soar.

Guzco set bowls of stew before them each and then headed to the river to draw water. Returning, he watched the children enter the church. The doll and hawk lay beside the bowls, the food untouched.

He found no trace of the children in the church. No surprise. After what they must have witnessed, it would take time to gain their trust. But he couldn't abandon them. To desert them to the approaching winter and Scarface was wrong, the act of a coward. He left the food and toys on the altar and returned to the hut in a sharpening frost.

The following morning, snow reached halfway up the door jamb. The trees creaked under the weight of snow while out of sight, a woodpecker struck a bold rhythm against a bough. The mountains crowding the valley were no longer barren rock but jagged, white monoliths. As Poseidon walked alongside him, yapping at the scurrying chickens, Guzco knew he was trapped. But if he couldn't leave then no one could enter. With luck he'd be forgotten in no time at all. Redemption began and finished here.

After all, Azekiel had ordered him to come to Badur. So this is where Azekiel would find him.

CHAPTER TWELVE
Lavagna, March 1931

"Where's Ustica?" Greta asked.

"A small island north of Sicily. Looked it up in the atlas," Luca announced confidently, whilst whittling the bleached length of driftwood into a whale.

"How long will your father stay there for?"

"Hard to say. Mama says it won't take them long to realise they've made a mistake and let him come home."

"Will he return home on a boat?"

"Guess so."

"That's exciting. For my fourteenth birthday, my uncle has promised to take me to Corsica aboard his trawler."

"That's a long way. Have you got your sea legs?"

"The only legs I've got are the ones I'm standing on," she answered, thinking what a daft thing to say.

Snapping his penknife shut, Luca said, "Sea legs aren't different sets of legs, it just means that you won't get seasick."

"I'll be fine. The sea runs in our family. Uncle Antonio crews the Lavagna boat in the regatta and swears Zoagli and Chiavari both cheat by paying outsiders to crew their boat."

"Why don't they stop them?"

"Mussolini has friends in Zoagli, and nobody dare upset Chiavari's merchants. According to Papa anyway."

Puffing out his chest, Luca said, "In that case, I'll take them on. One day I'll row for Lavagna."

"Never seen you in a boat."

"You wait and see. Can't be difficult, rowing. And when I win, I'll carry on rowing to Ustica." Startled, he then said. "Hear that?"

"What?"

"A woman's voice, coming from the sea."

"What did she say?"

"Hope."

Greta arched her eyebrow, a mannerism she'd learned from her mother. "Hope of what?"

"Dunno."

"It's just the wind playing tricks."

"It *was* a woman's voice. I swear," Luca answered, upset with her for not believing him. "There it is again."

"Oh yes, I hear her now," Greta lied.

After Luca's father's arrest, she'd tried her best to avoid him. In school, classmates sniggered behind his back. The bullies thumped him and some called him a communist. Keen not to tar herself with Luca, Greta had avoided taking up Luca's ideas for more adventures and refused his offer to help her with the mathematics homework.

One day, after hiding behind the living room sofa when Luca knocked for her, Mama insisted Greta invite Luca for tea the following week as he seemed lonely. Something we should all fear. Mama was right. Greta grew to enjoy Luca's eccentric company. Better still her maths scores improved. Although quiet and studious for the most part, Luca's anarchic streak made him exciting and different to Alesandro and his pals who delighted in teasing and embarrassing her with rude words while puffing on illicit cigarettes.

Now first thing every Saturday, she looked forward to hearing Luca's forceful rap on the front door, signalling the beginning of another day's adventure. Today the plan was finally to walk to the southern headland, climb the tallest tree, look beyond the horizon and shout so loudly, people in Genoa, forty or so kilometres away, would hear them.

Buffeted by a strengthening breeze, the two friends clambered up the steep, narrow path towards the headland's summit. "Can we stop?" Greta pleaded, desperate to draw breath and give her aching thighs a rest.

"But we're almost there," Luca replied, staring up at the summit.

"This is where the Angel rested." She hoped her lie wouldn't catch up with her. "We're standing on sacred ground."

"What Angel?"

"The Angel of Lavagna. This is where he walked ashore hundreds of years ago."

"Thought Angels flew everywhere."

"Not this one. He was an Angel of the sea." Luca frowned. "He fought the Devil who was on his way to Genoa to do terrible things."

"Did he win?"

"Yes but lost his wings."

"What happened to them?"

"They're buried somewhere in the mountains. Then the Angel wandered off and ended up in some village in France."

"Why didn't he stay in Italy? Italy's much better than France. More Catholics for starters."

"Dunno."

"Is he still there?"

"Where?"

"In this French village."

"Guess so. Years ago, Lavagna used to send fish to this village to thank for the Angel for fighting the Devil."

"Wouldn't they have gone off?"

Greta was stumped. She'd never thought to ask Papa this question. "That's not the point."

"What is the point then?"

"That Lavagna continued to honour the Angel."

"When did they stop?"

"Stop what?"

"Sending fish to this village?"

"Dunno."

"I see. Anyway, I'm going to climb the tree."

Luca soon proved himself to be as good at climbing trees as he was at shouting. Within minutes, he sat on a branch halfway up an ancient beech tree staring out over the choppy sea. To her surprise, Greta climbed up easily enough, and joined Luca in this shady hiding spot, both of them relieved to feel the wind easing. After sharing a tomato sandwich, Luca finished carving the whale then held it up for her to see.

"What do you think?" he asked.

"Very good. What sort of whale is it?"

"A big one."

Stumped once more, Greta decided to risk it. "What did your father do wrong?"

Stabbing the branch with his knife, Luca withdrew into his awkward, snarky shell.

"Sorry," Greta said. "You don't have to tell me."

"He wrote things about Mussolini."

"What things?"

"That he was a bad man and that Italians should stand up to him."

She was surprised and a touch fearful anyone could think so badly of Il Duce. "But Mussolini is a hero."

"Papa doesn't think so. He said it was his duty to speak out. That's why they came for him. It happened before and it's why we moved to Lavagna."

A breeze caused the branch to pitch, forcing Greta to grab Luca. For a slither of a moment, something beyond friendship passed between them.

"Why did Mussolini arrest him?" she asked.

"Because he can."

"Why should he fear a doctor?"

"Mama says it's because Papa spoke the truth, and whatever I hear people say about him I should always believe that. All I want is Papa to come home."

"Perhaps the Angel can help."

"How?"

"If he saw off the Devil, he'll be a match for anyone. We'll find his village in the atlas then head there. Can't be that far. Let's set off on Sunday. After mass. You bring tomato sandwiches and I'll bring a flask of milk. Bring an extra jumper. It gets cold in the mountains at night." Handing her the whale carving, he said, "This is for you."

Again something beyond friendship passed between them. "Thank you," Greta said, pleased as punch, "It's beautiful."

Despite the carving, her enthusiasm for heading into the mountains waned on the walk home. What if the Angel didn't want to be found? How would they recognise him? Would he try to smite them? She'd feel safer if Papa or, better still, Il Duce came with them. But after Luca's father insulted Il Duce, that was unlikely, while Papa liked Sundays to himself. Besides, she'd heard wolves still roamed the mountains. Hawks and eagles too.

To her relief she realised she *couldn't* go. Her grandparents were coming for dinner on Sunday. And it was her turn to lay the table.

Luca wasn't disappointed when Greta told him she'd changed her mind about heading into the mountains to search for this Angel of hers. Chances are that the Angel, if he ever existed, had long gone and besides, it all sounded too far-fetched to be true. With Sunday afternoon now free he would head to the Lavagna rowing club and learn how to become a champion rower.

CHAPTER THIRTEEN
Badur, December 1189

The snow fell for days.

The wretched crows roosting on the church roof, scattered when Poseidon burst from the hut to harry them each morning while Guzco cleared a fresh path to the river to collect water.

There was still no sign of the children, whose toys and food lay on the altar still untouched and, truth be told, as the temperature dropped, Guzco's enthusiasm for finding them waned.

In this cold, silent world, the dawn chorus grew thin and spare. Desperate for noise, Guzco hollered his name and rejoiced upon hearing his echo. One morning the echo answered with, "Priest!"

The shepherd stood on the far bank with a goat slung around his shoulders. Catching sight of Drago and Vladko, sporting thick winter coats, Poseidon snuck behind Guzco. Fording the river, the shepherd said, "I've come to honour the promise I made to Bascuali last spring."

He nodded towards the goat.

"Bascuali is dead," Guzco answered. "The soldiers, they killed everyone."

"Even Lampedusa the charcoal burner? A relation through marriage but family all the same. Where are they?"

"I buried them behind the church."

Tying the goat to the anvil, the shepherd hurried to the graves. The roughly hewn crosses were barely visible amidst the drifts. He stood in silence, his weathered features a mixture of anger and shock. "At least they received a Christian burial. Thank you for that. Most would run from such slaughter."

He entered the snow covered church and prayed before the altar. Contrition complete, he stood, picked up the wooden hawk then said, "Bascuali carved this for his son. The doll for his daughter."

"They're still alive but stay away from me."

"Be patient. Don't drive them into the mountains. They can be treacherous this time of year with the risk of avalanches and starving wolves." He made another sign of the cross then returned the hawk to the altar. "Bascuali told me about a dispute he had with Fachetti in the Holy Land. Unpaid bills for shoeing horses or some such. Bascuali took his case to the courts in

Jerusalem. Even though they found for him, his priest advised him to leave as Fachetti was known for bearing grudges."

"But to kill women, children over an unpaid bill?"

"To men like Fachetti, honour outranks life. Trivial slights have to be settled quickly. That is why Bascuali came home, thinking Fachetti would never return to settle a score. Seems he was wrong."

Returning to the forge, the shepherd patted the goat's head and drew out a long-bladed knife. Holding the blade against the goat's throat, he said, "She was to help Bascuali see the winter out. She's yours now."

Flinching at the sight of a knife, Guzco said, "Please, let her live."

"But you'll need her meat and fur."

"Her milk will be nourishment enough."

Puzzled, the shepherd sheathed the knife and returned to the hut to warm himself. They sat in silence, for how long Guzco couldn't say, but he considered the shepherd's silence to be a sign of trust and not enmity. He'd grown weary of men who talked too much.

"Come to Cresson. You'll be safe with us," the shepherd finally said.

"I cannot abandon the children."

"Bring them with you. Reach the bothy and head east for two days." He spat into the fire. "There's talk of an Angel in the mountains. An Angel skinned by the Devil. Have you seen him?"

How do they know I am here? "If I did, I'd have some choice words for him."

The shepherd broke into a smile. "Not much of a life up here truth be told. But these mountains offer sanctuary." The smile left him. "Even so, when you find the children, bring them to Cresson."

Chores, ablutions, foraging and less than enthusiastic searches for the children attuned Guzco to the pace of mountain life. He obsessed over keeping the fire lit and his feet warm, wrapping them in rags and wearing Bascuali's old clogs. When raging storms forced him inside, sometimes for days on end, he took to rambling conversations with the goat over the size of the day's catch, or with Poseidon wondering how young Marta fared. In turn, the goat and Poseidon struck up an unlikely friendship, foraging together during the day and nestling beside each other in front of the fire at night.

The days grew colder. Mist clung to the frost-stung woods and bitter eastern winds cut man or beast in half. Guzco's conversations with the goat and Poseidon dried up and his search for the children dwindled to standing outside the forge to shout promises of warmth and food.

The food ran out and the goat ran dry, forcing Guzco to survive on a meagre, rancid soup of boiled bark and thin tufts of grass plucked from the riverbank. The soup brought on boiling stomach pains and fevered images of a woman of tumultuous beauty beckoning him to her. "Such a day as this," she'd whisper over and over in soft, near soporific tones. "A day for hope."

The day his fever broke, Guzco awoke beneath a heavy woollen blanket with a roaring fire in the hearth. A pot of mutton stew hung over the fire.

Woozy after standing, he found cheese, fresh bread, boiled eggs and water laid out on the table. Grapes too. He petted Poseidon, guarding the door, and said, "Good to see you." The goat bleated, "You too."

Wrapped in the blanket, he shuffled outside, his breaths framed in the freezing air. Roosting crows took to the wing and chickens bolted as Poseidon, released from guard duties, sprang towards them. Bascuali's son and daughter stood outside the church. Guzco waved to them. The girl waved back. He wrapped the blanket tight around himself and laboured through the drifts towards the church. For once the children didn't bolt, allowing him to hope that they were beginning to accept him. And with their trust gained, he would take them to Cresson.

Exhausted from his efforts, he paused to regain his breath. The fever had taken its toll. He was about to speak when the boy pointed towards the river and said, "They've come back."

He ordered his sister into the church.

Looking over his shoulder, Guzco's heart sank. He hurried after the children.

CHAPTER FOURTEEN
Badur, February 1190

A horse-drawn wagon and eight horsemen drew up outside the forge. The men dismounted and stamped the cold and stiffness from their bones. A shirtless man bound to the wagon, slumped to his knees. Guzco recognised Spinoza, Massandar's slave.

One rider, tall, broad with a loping stride, ducked and went inside the hut. Seconds later he came out, examining Sanchez's chainmail. Drawing swords and knives, his comrades turned from weary travellers into alert, vigilant warriors, scouring the village and trees beyond. Yapping, Poseidon bounded through the snow towards them only to veer into the trees under a volley of stones and coarse threats.

A wiry, lithe individual with keen eyes and a thick blond beard, removed his helmet then said, "Marlinka, with me."

"Coming, Captain Fachetti," Marlinka answered, handing the chainmail on.

Fachetti and Marlinka tracked Guzco's footprints towards the church. Guzco studied the church's unsullied snow covered floor. It had to stay that way.

Beside the door, sat a stack of beams and joists Guzco had salvaged for firewood. There was a small gap between the stack and the smoke scarred wall. He crawled inside barely seconds before the church door opened a fraction more. Fachetti and Marlinka, swords drawn, approached the altar, the fresh snow compacting under their boots.

"Only footprints in here are ours," Marlinka said. "Expected bodies too."

"Not our concern."

"But Sanchez."

"The fool shouldn't have climbed onto the roof. He was always destined for an unmarked pit. What's that you've found?"

"Children's toys."

"What was that?" Fachetti sounded nervy, on edge. Guzco heart leapt into his mouth.

"What, Captain?"

"Thought I saw a young girl behind the altar. Small little thing, stick thin, dressed in rags. Barely alive."

"Sorry, Captain, didn't see anything. Something's not right though. Sanchez's armour, the warm stew, the grapes, the child, the goat, these toys. Perhaps the slave was right about this Angel hiding out in the mountains."

"You take seriously the word of a man who sold his soul for a shirt? We'll stay the night then tomorrow I'll head to Genoa to demand payment from Massandar. You make for Cresson and find the shepherd. We're long enough chasing down debts."

"Heard there's a thousand ships moored in Genoa. Stretch so far, a man could walk across them and reach Jerusalem."

"Just think about finding the shepherd."

"Yes, Captain, but keep your wits about you around Massandar. He fawns and flatters but underneath he's an evil bastard."

"I know. But remember, he's a *rich*, evil bastard. Now, let's find that goat you heard in the woods. Probably a runt on its last but a bellyful of meat will calm you."

They left.

Cowering behind the door, Guzco watched the soldiers scavenge for food. The crosses marking the villagers graves were uprooted and used as kindling for a fire upon which half a dozen chickens were cooked. But the goat remained at large.

Returning to his hiding spot, he wrapped the blanket tight, and fought the gnawing cold, made all the worse when night fell. Outside, the soldiers laughed and joked, a fire crackled and the sumptuous smell of roast chicken left him famished. All he had to eat were the white breaths forced from his chattering teeth. He hoped the children were safe. The shepherd's offer sounded more enticing than ever.

At daybreak, frozen to the marrow, he watched Fachetti draw lines in the snow with the tip of his knife and issue instructions to half the squadron. Another soldier traipsed from the woods, pulling up his britches. Another, sucking on a chicken bone, kept an eye on Spinoza as he watered the horses. Marlinka busied himself examining Sanchez's mail and weaponry. Thinking the coast clear, Spinoza picked up the now discarded bone and sucked the last dregs of goodness from it.

"Who said you could eat?" Marlinka shouted. Spinoza lowered his gaze. Marlinka flayed him with the chainmail. Spinoza crumpled. The beating was savage, relentless and only stopped when Marlinka grew bored. Heaving for breath, he spat on Spinoza before throwing the chainmail inside the wagon.

Fachetti examined Spinoza with the tip of his boot. Shaking his head, he picked out a coiled length of rope from the wagon then said, "Didn't think he'd reach Genoa. You've made sure of that." Handing Marlinka the rope, he continued, "Don't need another mouth to feed. Finish him. After that, burn everything left standing. Should have done it the first time. Purge yourself of this godforsaken place."

Marlinka, still flushed from his efforts, watched his comrades ford the river and enter the forest. When the last rider fell from view, he dragged Spinoza into the forge.

Strung up from a thick joist, Spinoza thrashed wildly, his flushed, spittle-flecked face a mixture of fear and incredulity. Marlinka tested the rope's tension and then carefully wound a length of cloth around one of the iron staves. Distracted by Spinoza's rasps, he didn't hear Guzco step into the forge and pick up the lump hammer resting against the anvil. He brought the hammer down twice on Marlinka's crown. The soldier fell, unconscious.

Grabbing a rusted scythe, Guzco set about severing the rope. But more than once, his clumsy, hacking efforts, embedded the blade in the beam and it took him all his strength to pull it free. Slowly, hack by clumsy hack the rope frayed under Guzco's assault, and as Spinoza dropped to the floor, Guzco blacked out. He woke to feel a knife rasp against his throat.

"Fucker," spat the blood streaked Marlinka leaning over him.

Odd to think I'll die here in this remote mountain village and not at sea. And at the hand of a soldier whilst saving a slave.

Marlinka dropped to his knees. The knife slipped from his grasp. Spinoza struck him again with the hammer. Marlinka toppled over. Spinoza, his neck framed by the noose, whispered, "You remembered me."

The slight, swarthy man who had risked his rope burned neck three times for Guzco, collapsed.

Guzco helped Spinoza into the hut then laid the blanket over him. As he set about building up the fire, he spotted the blackened remains of the doll and hawk in the hearth. Both were still warm to the touch. The doll's head and right arm were missing as was the hawk's left wing.

Remembering Fachetti's orders, he stripped Marlinka, his clothes were too fine to destroy, then dragged the corpse to the nearest hut. It was soon ablaze with the bitter breeze, spiralling a swirling black plume into the sunlit morning. With luck, Fachetti would assume Marlinka had struck out for Cresson leaving the shepherd safe.

He unsaddled Marlinka's stallion, a jet black, heavy set colt, probably traded from Massandar. With no fodder, the horse's chances of survival lay in the valley. "Sorry," Guzco whispered, leading the restless, sweating charger across the ford. Reaching the far bank, he removed the bridle, reins and copper browband. The horse bolted as Guzco cut it loose. Scarface sprang from cover to give chase.

While Spinoza, guarded by Poseidon and the goat, lay unconscious, Guzco tried his cack-handed best to whittle a new doll and hawk for the children. He soon discovered he lacked the dexterity or patience after comparing his carved efforts against Bascuali's fire damaged originals. Odd, given how he used to love mending the nets. Perhaps something to do with the sea instead. He set to work on carving a whale from a piece of beech. While he shaped the whale's fluke, Spinoza stirred. Guzco set the carving on the table and raised a beaker of water to Spinoza's lips. The slave drank only to endure a blood flecked coughing fit. After the fit subsided, he said. "If only I'd done Massandar's bidding and bound your wounds with the brigand's shirt." Lost to exhaustion, he passed out again. A jaundiced pallor spread over him and in rare moments of lucidity, he hummed the tune Massandar had ordered him to sing.

"Angel?" Spinoza muttered, confused and fearful.

"Rest. There's plenty of time to talk. Up here, time is all we have."

"I've endured time long enough." He passed out again.

The following night as Guzco finessed the carved whale's head, Poseidon began to whine and paw at the slave's hand. Spinoza petted Poseidon and scoured the room for Guzco. When their eyes met, Spinoza swallowed and sighed. "I'm ready, Angel."

Guzco set down the carving, laid his cheek against Spinoza's and allowed the slave's final thoughts to overwhelm him.

Larissa and Maladron forgive my follies—I hope you are safe now—safe from Massandar's depravity—of warm feet—sunshine and the still, cold waters of the lake—of shade on a hot summer's day—I hope for a God—that my sorrow and pain are no more; neither sighing, but life everlasting—the cockerel's lazy crow—my poems to be sung in years to come—the Angel—calm—so tired.

Guzco decided to take no chances. Losing the girl's soul had taught him a lesson. He placed his mouth over Spinoza and inhaled. When he withdrew, shock followed horror. His own corpse lay before him.

Tracing the unfamiliar contours of his face with a scribe's elegant but unsteady fingers, his rugged features, borne with pride and no little arrogance, were now smoother, the skin softer, the nose longer. He hurried to the forge and stared into the water barrel beside the coals. Spinoza stared back.

"No!" he shouted, punching the water, distorting his new reflection. Clawing at his face, he shouted, "I am Guzco Domar, a fisherman, nothing more, nothing less. I never asked for this life. Lord Azekiel, I know I have angered you but please, let me be. I have endured crippling sickness, seen off brigands and wolves and met every test you have set me. And what is my reward? The theft of the one thing sacred to me. My very existence."

Guzco hauled his remains towards the freshly dug grave. Possessing only Spinoza's sparse strength, excavating the frozen soil had taken hours of tortuous, backbreaking toil. He gained no pleasure from his labours.

There are no words.

He stepped into the knee deep grave and dragged his corpse towards himself.

There are no words.

Frozen clods of earth slowly covered his remains.

There are no words.

He placed a roughly shaped crucifix at the head of the grave and threaded the whale carving onto the cross-piece.

There are no words.

CHAPTER FIFTEEN
Lavanga, August 1938

"And finally," said Father Biavati, much to Greta's relief, "We pray for Lavagna's victory in today's regatta."

The Lavagna crew dressed in Sunday best, and wringing the life from their caps, assembled for the ritual blessing.

"We've no chance this year," whispered her father. "Zoagli have brought in a national champion, from Bari of all places. And Rapallo are paying two Olympic silver medallists to row for them. How can that be right?"

Ignoring Papa's complaints, Greta watched Biavati spray the crew with Holy Water, dousing Luca most of all. She should have heeded his bold pronouncement all those years ago. Luca had proved to be a dedicated, if average rower. Always prepared to toil in heavy seas or under a burning sun while building his strength with press ups, squats and climbing trees. These years of back-breaking toil had earned him a place in the Lavagna boat. As coxswain.

At first, he seemed disappointed at not being selected as an oarsman but soon brightened after learning that the coxswain's job involved both piloting the eight crew goiter boat and then shinning up the ten-metre on-shore masthead to claim the race winner's pennant. If his crewmates could stay within touching distance, Olympic rowers or not, Luca was confident his climbing prowess would deliver a rare victory and glory for Lavagna.

Following the blessing, the crew lined up on the church steps to have their picture taken by a fussy photographer. Giving up on the photographer's endless efforts, the town's drummers beat out a percussive challenge to all comers as they led the crew and most of Lavagna's population, towards the harbour. Chants went up, and much to Greta's surprise, her prim mother also joined in, with gusto. The other crews were already assembled and their tanned, muscular torsos, to a man twice the size of the Lavagna lads, further dented Greta's hopes of victory.

"Giants," complained her father. "What chance do we have against them?"

"Have faith, Papa," Greta answered, more in hope than judgment. Reaching the harbour wall, she spotted her mother's aunt, the Widow Rigazzi, sheltering under a parasol. A rare sight as the Widow rarely left her apartment on account of her numerous conditions. As usual, Greta shrank from her great-aunt, recalling the tellings-off meted out to her by the Widow for her slouching, dawdling, choice of dress and for wearing glasses.

Dressed in a starched, high-necked, full length dress that would have graced the turn of the century, the Widow summoned Greta and Oona in her reedy, gasping voice. "Either of you two betrothed yet?" she asked. A mischievous smile took hold of Oona. "Greta is, Aunt."

The Widow's wrinkled, sour features lit up with intrigue. "Really? Who to?"

"Luca Meazza." Greta flushed and thumped Oona on the arm. Too late.

"The Genoa boy? Father a communist? Why wasn't I informed of this betrothal?" The Widow asked Greta's mother.

"What betrothal, Aunt?" Mama answered, looking confused. Oona sidled away whilst Greta wanted the ground to swallow her up.

"Your daughter," the Widow jabbed at Greta with her parasol, "Is engaged to Luca Meazza." With passers-by earwigging, Mama replied, "I think you are mistaken, Aunt. Greta will be going to university next year. To study biology. She and Luca are just friends."

"Then why did this one," the Widow jabbed her parasol towards the returning Oona, "Tell me something different?" Now it was Oona's turn to squirm.

"I've no idea, Aunt. You know how excitable the girls get." Casting her great-nieces a withering look, the Widow shook her head then took the arm of her companion and limped away. Greta and Oona, both keen to avoid a telling-off, hurried to the beach to find a good spot to watch the race.

"What were you thinking?" Greta asked.

"Oh, come on, everybody knows you two are sweet on each other."

"No we're not," replied Greta, immediately disappointed with her insipid reply. She and Luca had never kissed and the times she hoped they would, he became tongue-tied and retreated into his shell. Besides she wasn't sure if she felt *like that* about him. They revelled in each other's company, he still helped with her mathematics but she saw him more as a brother. Besides, with university beckoning, now was not the time to be thinking about boyfriends or marriage.

For once she was pleased to see Alesandro and his pals, dressed in the black Balilla uniform of the Fascist Youth, strutting across the black sands like sweaty, spotty peacocks. Several times Papa had torn Alesandro off a strip over his associates, but he had refused to change his ways and it saddened Greta to watch her older brother change from an amiable fool to an angry idiot wrapped up in fascism's arid certainties. She despised Mussolini for his hateful popinjay speeches and the reckless quests for glory that Alesandro found irresistible. Unlike Luca, whose hatred of Mussolini grew deeper yet bolder after his father's jailing.

He fought the Balilla inside and outside school where, to Greta's shame, Alesandro had become Luca's chief baiter. She longed for the day when Italy could breathe again.

"See your streak of piss boyfriend made the Lavagna crew," Alesandro said, pointing to the Lavagna boat as it rowed out to the starting buoy. He called one of his comrades over, this one older than the others, toting a sidearm, his uniform a better cut. He carried an air of confidence that matched his handsome, playful features.

"Massimo, meet my sisters, Greta and Oona." Massimo Ferrari gave a fascist salute then smiled, revealing even, white teeth. "An honour to meet you. But apologies, I must run, my father is expecting me." He returned to the group but not before turning back to look at Greta.

"His dad's a bigwig in the Genovese OVRA," Alesandro bragged. "Made a name for himself flushing out the Reds. And when the new laws are enacted he's going to go after the Jews."

"Mussolini just wants to crawl up Hitler's backside," Greta muttered.

"That's sedition!" replied Alesandro, red faced with anger. But any argument was postponed as a maroon rocket soared skywards.

To cheers, the crews drew on their oars and powered their sleek goiter boats through the choppy waters towards the first buoy. "Come on Lavagna! Come on Luca!" Greta shouted, as much to annoy Alesandro as to show her loyalty to Luca and her home town.

"Rapallo takes the lead!" said an old man standing on a rickety deck chair watching the race through a tarnished brass telescope. "Lavagna already falling behind."

It soon became clear to all those watching, that Lavagna was no match for the other crews. "Biavati's blessing isn't doing them much good," Oona whispered.

"Rapallo leads by eight lengths rounding the second buoy, Lavagna out of contention." The old man sounded a touch disappointed.

"Papa will be fuming. We'll never hear the end of this."

"Rapallo now by twelve lengths, with Zoagli matching their pace."

"Two Olympic rowers in their team. Never fair."

"Rapallo first to shore!" The Rapallo coxswain leapt from his boat and dashed towards the masthead, with Lavagna yet to round the final buoy. Grasping the pennant, the Rapallo coxswain fell to earth and raised his arms aloft in triumph.

"Rapallo wins!" hollered the old man, to the delight of several Balilla, busy launching their tasselled hats into the air. Several minutes later, the Lavagna boat reached the shore and its shattered crew slumped over their oars. Even so Greta couldn't have been prouder of Luca. For this moment he'd given everything, to the point of foolhardiness.

But he lived with passion and was the reason she loved him. "Fuck Mussolini," she whispered.

Running a hand through his cowlick, Luca consoled his exhausted crewmates and looked towards the horizon. Ustica, and Papa, remained as far off as ever.

CHAPTER SIXTEEN
Badur, August 1207

Since Spinoza's death, Guzco's first act each morning was to stare into the water barrel hoping to see his old features. A desperate, scowling version of Spinoza, hair longer and beard thicker, stared back. Only the scarred shoulders reminded Guzco of his former self, the disfigurement bringing on bouts of powerless rage that could often last for days.

He sought solace in nature and tramped the valley. No longer fearful of Scarface, presumed long dead, he discovered the best spots to fish and where to harvest berries, chestnuts and pine nuts. The goat led him to copses where edible mushrooms grew alongside green leafed plants that once boiled up, made a nutritious stew. As nature uncoiled his tightly wound sense of betrayal, the valley taught him that life, death and the points connecting them lay in abundance; cycles within cycles, seemingly haphazard but governed by the seasons. As the years passed, he learned that life in the valley was all he needed it to be.

With Spinoza's slender fingers, he became a proficient woodcarver, marking routes around the forest with carvings of fish, whales and boats to honour his former life. The ghostly Bascuali children still shrank from him. The doll and hawk still lay untouched on the altar.

Life remained hard, with the winter snows lowering a lid of silence over the valley. Guzco once used silence to shield himself from mockery, but in those frigid months, often barricaded inside for days at a time, he yearned for sounds beyond the hiss of burning wood, a scraping spoon or the goat's sarcastic bleat. When able to venture outside, he feasted on ghostly cracks and groans hidden among the trees, the thunderous, grinding roar of far off avalanches and even his own frost baked breath. He clung to each sound like flotsam from a shipwreck, replaying them when the cold forced him inside. Some days he spotted travellers tramping along the valley's western slopes. He hoped they were bound for Badur. But none came.

Poseidon and the Doe endured rambling monologues about crossing the horizon, the art of rowing and what tactics he'd employ in the summer's rowing races across the bay. Other times he serenaded his ageing, less than interested companions with his mother's lullabies. When Poseidon died, Guzco buried him beside the Doe, beneath the tree the two old friends had liked dozing under during warm, still, summer days. Their deaths allowed the silence to become permanent, knotting and narrowing Guzco's thoughts until words and noise became distant, twisted creatures to be feared.

Silence instead then. Better off in silence. Silence will protect me. Better off on my own up here, where no one can disappoint.

And the further he travelled from words, the more scabrous and uneven became his memories until he could no longer recall the colour of Luisa's hair, the smell of the sea or the sound of whale song. Only slithers of memories such as Isabella's fear or Jose's greed-filled final moments bound him to his past.

When the thawing snows heralded the arrival of spring and a thickening of life, he craved silence like an adulterer craves their lover, raging at the thundering melt water or the startling dawn chorus. Above all, he reserved a deep contempt for the millions of starlings who descended upon the valley in the summer. Their regal murmuration seemed designed to mock Guzco for losing his wings and he turned his back from such a glorious, shapeless display.

In this mute languor, nature and its creeping reclamation of the village, passed him by. The saplings that once sprouted around the ruined buildings now towered over them allowing a riot of colour and scent from the thick carpet of foxgloves, lupins and bluebells to grow in the shade, drawing in the hectic thrum of insects.

His only wish was for the winter to drive life underground and conceal the valley from the world as he waited for the tantalising but never realised hope of Azekiel appearing.

Why speak when there is nothing worth speaking of.

Badur became a fable, somewhere to be feared, only mentioned in neighbouring valleys when all other conversation had petered out or, *"The Angel Skinned by the Devil"*, was used to strike fear into the hearts of wayward children.

Then on a late summer's afternoon so hot the heat shaved the sky, while fishing in his favourite spot up river, Guzco heard the clink of hammer striking metal. Keeping to the riverbank, he reached the ford. Two wagons stood outside the steam-shrouded forge, the source of the sharp, rhythmical hammering. One wagon, with a wheel missing, rested on a pile of stones drawn from the river. Beside the other wagon a heavyset woman stirred a pot warming over a fire whilst issuing instructions in a no-nonsense fashion to two men, one young, the other middle-aged, over where to pitch a tent. Two mongrels sat nearby hoping to cadge a morsel.

Bemused to see people, Guzco hunkered down. The fear of God entered him when he saw a sweat-soaked giant, roll a wheel from the forge. With the giant bearing the wagon's weight, the two men fixed the wheel to the axle. All three congratulated each other for a job well done and then began to disagree over where to pitch the tent.

Stepping closer to get a better look at this ragtag bunch, Guzco stumbled and dropped the three brown trout he'd caught. The mongrels stirred. A slim shadow slid over him.

"Are those fish for sale?" She looked about eighteen with sharp, attractive features set on the edge of a smile. "My name is Marta. Do you live here?"

Her name drew out Isabella's memory. Unable to think of what to say, Guzco gathered up the fish and nodded. Marta squatted beside him, set down the pail she was carrying and said, "Sorry if I scared you." Her voice was warm but unnerving. "Lonely old place though."

She gasped, as overhead a gathering murmuration performed its intricate choreography. "Papa!" she shouted, pointing towards the starlings. The older man looked skywards.

"Beautiful," Marta whispered, "Yet threatening." Guzco couldn't see what all the fuss was about.

"Would you like to join us? We have food and drink to share." Without waiting, she picked up her pail and returned to the village. Guzco stayed put, watching the giant stack shields, swords and lastly a trident against the newly affixed wheel. With Marta and the other woman looking on, the giant then lowered a wooden chest to the floor, from which both women retrieved a selection of garish, if tatty, costumes, and dented, dulled armour.

Several times Marta looked towards Guzco. Each time he ducked from view, until sensing little threat, he plucked up the courage to approach the strangers. Marta and the older man, tall, with a shock of greying curly hair, and an open inquisitive face, walked out to meet him. "I see you have had a good day fishing," he said, pointing to Guzco's catch. "Can't beat the taste of fried fish."

"Keep your distance, Marta," said the giant. "He could be a leper." The smile leaving her, Marta took a step back then asked, "Are you?" Guzco shook his head and began to fret. *Words will be needed.*

"That is good news," said the man. His features edged towards old age but his bright eyes and disarming smile calmed Guzco. "Lupo is by nature cautious, a surprise given his size."

"Better safe than sorry," Lupo muttered.

"Forgive us," said the man. "One of our wagons needed repairing and I remembered Bascuali. We're heading to Pinerolo for the late summer festival. Spare pickings in France but I'm hopeful those wily Savoians will look upon us more charitably. I hope we haven't alarmed you."

Unsure how to answer, Guzco shook his head. "Devil's got his tongue, Giacomo," said Lupo, sizing Guzco up.

"Giacomo?" Guzco uttered his first word in years.

Marta and Giacomo? The coincidence is too great.

"Yes." Giacomo looked surprised. "Have we met?"

To avoid answering, Guzco held up his catch. "Fish. Yours. If you want."

"Most kind!" Giacomo answered.

"I'm a priest," Guzco blurted, unsure where the words had come from or what his next ones would be. "Arrived here on a pilgrimage to Rome. The villagers. Slain by soldiers. I buried them. Then stayed. I do not know why. I wish I could answer that question. If I could, I would know where I'm going. There was a shepherd. Tall. One arm. Two dogs. Big dogs. Very big dogs. I haven't seen him. You are the first people I have seen. In years."

"That much is obvious," Giacomo said. "These days, Badur only crosses people's lips if they talk of the Angel."

"Do not mock our host, Papa," protested Marta. "He attends those poor murdered people and in return the valley shelters him. And a beautiful spot it is too."

Guzco melted in her smile and asked, "What do you sell?"

"Awe and wonder," Giacomo replied, throwing in a deep, theatrical bow for good measure. "We are Players bringing succour to the hardy, good-natured people of these lands. Songs, recitals, fortunes told, which will remain a matter for your purse and conscience. Biblical performances too! David and Goliath a speciality given Lupo, whilst my Solomon is known from Genoa to Marseille and all points in between. But if a kick up the arse brings you mirth, we are happy to satisfy your wish. We'll play the courts of kings, the courtyards of merchants, even the doorways of hovels, any place where a penny or two can be earned. Alberto's strumming can move you to tears whilst Lupo's displays of strength have, on occasion, caused women with a persuasion for the larger man to swoon." Lupo reddened. Alberto and Marta sniggered.

"And what about me?" shouted the older woman.

"Rosa! How could I forget you?" Giacomo extended his arm to Rosa. "Signore, meet Rosa, seamstress, cook, painter, mother to us all. She treads the boards with a poet's wit and illusionist's sleight of hand." Picking the trident up, his face darkened. "Bascuali forged this a lifetime ago; it added great depth to my Poseidon. I'm sad to hear of his death. He was a good man." The smile returning, he continued, "We are an unusual family, bound by love and dependence but please share what we have." He turned to the giant. "Lay the boards Lupo. We cannot pay our host for his hospitality but we can endeavour to entertain with our words, tunes and, if needs must, the Fool's humour."

"What is your skill?" Guzco asked, turning to Marta.

"I dance."

CHAPTER SEVENTEEN
Badur, August 1207

The stew, a watery gruel of gristle, the odd near rotten vegetable and sparse grains of rye, was only edible by adding enormous quantities of salt and pepper. And Guzco's fried trout fillets. At first Giacomo took exception to Guzco refusing his offer of wine, but soon forgot, as his drink-fuelled tales grew more fanciful and lurid. Lupo, grumpy and solitary, sat opposite, his eyes fixed on Marta, whilst Alberto and Rosa endlessly ribbed each other.

After eating, Giacomo recited a poem of inordinate length about the Crusades, fermenting glazed looks on everyone's faces. "Enjoy that?" he asked Guzco after finishing. Before Guzco could answer, he said, "Now, Priest, prepare to be amazed!"

Even to Guzco's untrained eye, each act was pitiful. On the odd occasion Giacomo remembered his lines, the wine rendered them unintelligible, whilst the only mystery surrounding Rosa's illusions was how she had the nerve to perform them. David and Goliath, played by Alberto and Lupo, carried menace, until Alberto's slingshot crowned a roosting crow. Lupo's strongman act was short lived after he strained his back lifting a boulder then staggered away as if he'd soiled himself. "Amazing strength, Lupo," Giacomo slurred. "Wrestled a mountain lion once."

"Who won?" Guzco asked, understanding why the troupe had fallen on hard times.

He wanted the night to end, for them to be on their way and allow him to wallow in his hard earned silence.

Alberto strummed a spare, haunting tune on a lyre. Lupo stuck up a steady, simple beat on a small drum. Beside them Marta swayed, the sparse sound giving her movements a lupine, sensual quality. Her steps, simple yet impossible, seeped into Guzco's bones and carried him back to the sea. Something old and hidden stirred inside him, something that ached with the fear of being forgotten. From beneath the tumbling waves, he walked ashore at Lavagna, where Luisa, holding a baby whispered, "Your daughter, Guzco. Her name is Bia."

A daughter.

Luisa and Bia melted, replaced by Marta's spinning, arcing form, which aroused the long-lost spectres of hope and optimism in Guzco. When

Marta's piercing green eyes settled on him, *She* whispered, "There's always hope, Guzco. Protect her when she comes. Life."

Lupo's drum fell silent as the lyre's final notes faded. Her face masked by her jet-black locks, Marta remained still, her voluptuous rapture now receding with each breath. But in that tranquil, sparse moment Guzco remained under her spell, as did the Bascuali children looking on from the church.

"Such beauty," Guzco whispered.

"When Marta dances," Giacomo said, looking rueful, "She carries my poor wife's soul. Eighteen years I've lived without my beloved Isabella, God be with her. Marta didn't utter her first word until she was three. Took her first steps at four. To my shame, I thought her an imbecile, that growing up without her mother had damaged her."

"What changed?"

"Long story."

"Time is the one thing I have plenty of."

"We were in Nice for Easter, ten, maybe eleven years ago. I was about to enact my soliloquy, the one that just held you in raptures, when Marta strides onstage and without any prompting, performed the exact same steps my Isabella once danced. How she knew them baffles me to this day, but within moments those watching, even the mouthy drunks, were in thrall to my eight-year-old daughter. In that moment people saw themselves for what they were. Some fearful, some indifferent but most crying tears of joy. When she stopped no one stirred. Signore, Marta lights a path for those who have lost their way. Just as her mother once did."

"Why isn't she dancing before kings?"

Giacomo sighed. "Two years ago, again in Nice. Frankish priests, whose stock had risen since the failure of the Crusade to prise Jerusalem from Saladin's grip, denounced Marta, calling her a whore, an incarnation of Satan." He shook his head then waved his hands as if pleading. "Why do they fear women so? A woman dances and men of scripture decide that she is blasphemous. What right do they have? But these men without reason are listened to, so we now have to eke out a living in the high country, free from the zealots' prying eyes. To stop Marta dancing would be a much greater sin in my eyes."

"Beauty should never be hidden."

"I'm glad you agree. To live up here, amongst the dead, must be exacting. Rosa thinks you have endured great loss but haven't let it harden your heart."

If that were true.

"Besides, who comes to Badur these days? You have no one to tell, apart from the Angel."

"I've met him," Guzco blurted.

"When?" Giacomo's features curled into one of opportunity. Possible profit.

"In the village of Lavagna, outside Genoa." *Shut up you fool!*

"I know the place. Tight-fisted locals, slow to praise."

"For three days and nights he fought the Devil there. Cost him his wings, but he saved the village."

"Such nobility."

"He came ashore to search for his brother, thought long lost at sea."

"His brother?"

Warming to his lies, Guzco nodded. "He'd been a fisherman, a simple life lived fair and true. One day far out to sea, closer to the end of the world than the beginning, he and his brother were fishing when a giant whale rose from the deep and capsized their boat."

"By God's teeth, I've never heard such a tale."

"The Angel was plucked from the water whilst his brother was allowed to perish."

"A wrenching loss." Giacomo shook his head with feigned disbelief. "And now this brave Angel still searches for his brother."

"Something like that," Guzco answered, unsure how Giacomo had come to this conclusion. Giacomo's eyes lit up at the opportunity offering itself. "Then he appeared in the valley a year or twenty ago, carrying a flaming sword. Having searched the seas without any luck, he began to scour the earth." He smiled. "Such a sacrifice, such a story. Worth a coin or two in the recitals." Leaning forward, his wine-soured breath whispered, "If the zealots hear them, you'll be burned for blasphemy or branded a mad man. Probably both. These are dangerous times. But don't fret, I'll carry your secret to the grave."

Relieved that his loose talk would cause no more trouble, Guzco refilled Giacomo's beaker. Marta, still flushed from her dance, approached them with Lupo beside her. Butterflies filled Guzco's stomach.

"Did you enjoy the dance?" she asked.

"Beautiful." Guzco wished he had the words to give full voice to his feelings.

"Too much wine again, Papa?" she joked, as Lupo helped the unsteady Giacomo to his feet.

"Must be," Giacomo replied, with a sly nod to Guzco.

While the players slept, Guzco stared into the fire imagining Marta dancing, this time to the tune of one of his mother's lullabies. A stout, middle-aged man, possessing the stride of a saint but the air of a charlatan, stepped through the fire. Neither the actors or the dogs stirred. Guzco recognised the Ostler, the first soul he had collected. Behind him walked the second, the wary, careworn Weaver, glancing from side to side, her shawl drawn tight. She looked at Guzco and said, "Do you know the agonies we have suffered, Angel, cast into half-life and half-death? Yet here you sit with poor Isabella's husband and daughter. Have you no shame?"

"Soldiers fed you to the river. I couldn't stop them."

"We should curse you, but the fight left us long ago. Please, just tell us when our torment will end."

"I don't know."

"Don't know!" shouted the Ostler, his jowls wobbling with indignation. The hubbub set the mongrels on edge.

"Don't forget us," pleaded the Weaver. "Death was meant to liberate. Yet we are still trapped."

"Trust me."

"I'd rather take my chances with Massandar. Or your brother."

The following morning, Giacomo, a touch green around the gills from last night's overindulgence, shook Guzco's hand then said, "We promise to return this time next year."

"I look forward to it," Guzco replied, eager to see Marta dance again.

"As to the other matter we touched upon, I vow to remain as silent as

Tacita herself."

Without a clue as to what Giacomo was talking about, Guzco approached Marta. Still tongue-tied, he handed her a carving of a hawk. "Thank you for lifting my spirits last night."

Brushing the hawk's intricate, refined plumage, Marta's eyes settled on him. He blushed. She smiled. "I was wrong," she said, "This is a lovely spot. I *would* like to live here one day."

Rosa laughed. "By all that's holy, I think the thin mountain air has turned you Marta. There's nothing up here but wind and trees, daresay wolves too."

"Saw the wolf off," Guzco boasted, to his, and everyone's surprise.

"There's something else," Marta said, annoyed at Rosa's flippancy. "I felt it last night as I danced."

"What's that then my girl?"

"Hope."

"No offence, Priest, but I imagine hope is spare up here."

"Once," answered Guzco. Alberto held out his hand and helped Marta aboard the second wagon. They shared a gentle, private word, without taking their eyes off each other.

"A word, Priest." Rosa beckoned Guzco to her. "Marta is as headstrong as her mother, God be with her. That passion is what makes her such a wonderful dancer. For your own sake don't dwell on her. She means no harm, but she's not of this world. Hundreds have fallen under her spell. Besides, she is betrothed to Alberto." She looked at Alberto and then again at Guzco. "Not an hour after burying poor Isabella we found him. Barely a week old and wrapped in a blanket on the side of the Julia Augusta. We'd only stopped to let a Genoa-bound caravan of horses pass. Never forgotten the smarmy look the man in the lead wagon wore, as if we were his oldest and dearest friends. Marta and Alberto were destined for each other. Fate can be a strange mistress. Please, do not get your hopes up."

As Lupo led the first wagon across the ford with the mongrels following, Giacomo shouted, "Next year Priest! You have my word."

Crushed by Rosa's revelation, Guzco raised an arm in salute.

Best to forget them. Return to silence and safety.

Marta's dance flickered across his mind's eye and he allowed a morsel of hope into his once bitter heart. Hope for what he couldn't say, but he clung to the thought more tightly than a sinner clings to the relic of a saint.

Marta had bewitched him.

CHAPTER EIGHTEEN
Badur, November 1943

With the echo of the firing squad thinning, the SS officer stood over Henri Velous, levelled his pistol and fired. Once into Henri's chest and once into his head.

"Get away from the window," whispered Irene Fontaine's husband, Pierre as the departing German truck's headlights briefly lit up the café. Unable to tear her eyes from Henri, Irene ignored the instruction. Clasping her stomach, she wondered how, or if, she would ever tell the child growing inside her that the Nazis had murdered their father.

She'd only told Henri she was pregnant yesterday.

"Pregnant?" he had answered, looking baffled.

"Doctor Chamonix confirmed it this morning."

"Are you sure I'm the father?"

Stung and vulnerable, Irene snapped, "Of course. Pierre and I haven't been intimate for months."

Henri's handsome, bold features creased into a smile and with impish certainty he blurted, "I'd planned to dodge the Work Obligation by going into hiding, maybe joining the Resistance but not now." He wiped his mouth while wracking his brains. He smiled. "I've a friend in Nice who can help." His smile broadened as he took Irene's hand. "We'll elope. To Nice, Marseille, Paris, Christ, even Genoa. Wherever you wish, Irene. We'll start a new life together, the three of us.

"What will we live on?"

"I can turn my hand to anything and you can pick up seamstress work. All that matters is that we're together." She knew the idea to be fanciful, frail at best what with the War and everything. But he seemed *so* certain, she allowed herself to share his reckless nineteen-year old's optimism, the very thing that had drawn her twenty-five year old self to him in the first place. That and his beautiful face.

"But what about Pierre?"

Waving away her concerns, Henri said, "He's old before his time and you're always complaining about his penny-pinching."

"But he doesn't deserve such cruelty."

"Yet you cheated on him and would happily let him raise my child as if it were his. How will he react knowing he is not the father?" Irene knew he was right, having counted on Pierre's infatuation with her to mask what she and Henri were up to. The baby changed all that.

Sensing her vulnerability, Henri took her hand and whispered, "I love you, Irene, and swear, I'll do whatever it takes to give you and our child the best life."

Hours earlier, Irene had stood on the cusp of a new, daring life. But beneath a blemished dawn sky, that bold promise now lay lifeless beside Badur's bullet scarred war memorial, a silent witness to the men who had left the valley hollowed out and in mourning ever since.

Shirt and trousers thrown over his pyjamas, Pierre left the café and ran towards Henri now surrounded by a group of villagers. Irene stifled the tears watching her husband go to the aid of the man she loved. *'I'll tell our child all about you Henri. About our dreams and hopes. They'll love you as much as I do.'*

Returning to the café, Pierre poured himself three fingers worth of cognac, four star, none of the cheap stuff he served the regulars. He lit a cigarette, took a deep drag and said, "An SS guard was killed in the mountains. They executed Henri out of revenge. He was unlucky. It could have been any of us." He drained his cognac. "And to think he was here this evening, drinking a beer and talking about a new life. 'Freedom beckons, Pierre,' he told me. "Poor bastard."

Irene knew different. Henri had come to the café to tell her that his friend had found work for him in Nice. He would send for her after finding a place for them both to live. Excited yet fearful for the future, she had watched him head for home and probably take the short cut through the woods. The Germans must have arrested him there. Coming to the café, to her, had cost him his life.

After refilling his glass, Pierre said, "You look pale. Fancy a nip? A drop will calm you."

Nauseated by the cognac's smell, she shook her head.

"Forgive me, I'd forgotten how close you two were." Her heart skipped a beat. What was he hinting at? Did he know about the affair? He'd never mentioned anything. Besides she and Henri had always been careful, arriving and leaving the woods separately and from opposite directions. Her skin pricked with lust and loss recalling the first time they had made love there.

His taste and touch engulfed her.

"Fucking Germans," Pierre said while stubbing out his cigarette. "Well, better get to bed. Turn out the lights when you come up."

Irene stepped outside, lit a cigarette and looked towards Henri. She wanted to scream but couldn't take the chance. Not now. Not with the baby to think about.

Doctor Chamonix knelt beside Henri checking for a pulse. He turned to look at her and they held each other's gaze, until like an errant schoolgirl caught red handed, Irene flicked her cigarette away and went inside. She turned off the lights and climbed the stairs, with tears streaming down her face.

CHAPTER NINETEEN
Badur, August 1211

Grateful to be rid of the rowdy but devout pilgrims drawn to Badur by the troupe's burgeoning fame, Guzco drew in the wildflowers' rich, giddying scent and tilted his head towards the sunrise. Today he hoped Marta's dance would once more lead him to Luisa and Bia and, for a few minutes at least, allow him to live the life fate had denied him.

Holding the freshly carved whale, to go with the doll, hawk and boat he had given Marta in the past three years, he gave full reign to his hopeless infatuation.

This is the year, the year she'll stay. The starlings are a sign, as was the early thaw.

Buoyed by these favourable omens, he turned for home, aware that before Marta danced; Rosa's stew, Lupo's glare and Giacomo's rambling monologue still had to be endured. But from childhood stories, he knew a hero's suffering allowed victory to taste all the sweeter.

Makes me that Odysseus fella then. Or someone like him.

Besides, things always took a turn for the better when Lupo, wearing that shoddy whale's head, wrought terror upon Alberto and Marta's cowed fishermen or Giacomo, if sober, severed Alberto's wooden wings or Rosa's malicious Fachetti laid waste to Badur.

Guzco's tales, brought to life by Giacomo's words, granted the troupe a fame their once thin repertoire scarcely deserved. Now wherever they played, *"The Angel Skinned by the Devil"* enthralled and terrorised all watchers in equal measure. So much so that Giacomo's new velvet purse bulged with coin allowing new wagons, larger tents and more fanciful, elaborate costumes to be bought. Giacomo even treated himself to a garish yellow cap topped out with ostrich feathers to bring "added majesty" to his madrigal of extraordinary length about the Crusade.

Nearing the bothy, Guzco's optimism over the unfolding day was dampened by the sight of a twisted, naked woman, pleading with a masked man tearing the woollen mantle and hood from another woman's corpse. Beneath the mantle she wore a silk tunic. The robber stripped the tunic to reveal the woman's bruised skin. Her face, neck and arms were covered in pustules and sores, her fingers little more than stumps. The smell of rotting flesh clung to her.

A second robber whose saturnine features spoke of a weary intelligence little used, examined a silver bracelet. His thin beard half covered still vivid scars, whilst notches on both ears signalled punishment for thievery. A dulled, dented breastplate hung from his torso whilst the sole of his scavenged right boot had split from its leather upper. "Mean you no harm," he said, waving the bracelet at Guzco. "Best if you pass on." Pointing at the women he sniffed then said, "Lepers."

Clutching the dead woman's clothes, and blind to her nakedness, the other robber lowered his mask to reveal a weak chin and scarred features. He also wore a breastplate and helmet, both far too big for him. Tipping the helmet back, he rested his spare hand on the empty scabbard slung around his waist then said to Guzco, "Rich pickings to be had off her sort."

"What sort is that?"

"Jews. Even their lepers are loaded. Just have to know where to look, before putting them out of their misery. Nobody need know. Doubt they'd care if they did."

"I would," Guzco answered, watching the leper struggle to drape her tattered mantle over the corpse. Although revolted by her broken, decaying form, Guzco was moved by her efforts to offer her companion a measure of dignity, at the expense of her own. He took off his tunic and offered it to the leper. At first she shrank back, her face a mixture of awe, fear and loss.

"Please," Guzco said. The leper cloaked herself.

"You a Jew lover?" the first robber asked Guzco. "You know they killed Christ. Reckon we're doing the Lord's work ridding the world of them. After all, a man must eat and this dead one don't need her finery anymore." He held up both women's tunics. "See these? Silk. Wash the sweat and poison from them and they'll fetch enough to feed us for the month."

Slipping the bracelet over his thin wrist, the second thief said, "We'll leave them to you then, friend. Help them or yourself, it's of no concern to us."

The robbers left, taking the lepers' clothes, even the fetid mantles and hoods with them. What use they would be, Guzco couldn't fathom. Probably out of spite. Their rattling, oversized armour gave them an awkward, misshapen gait.

"Why would they do such a thing?" she asked.

"Because they can," he replied, setting his water gourd before her.

Using her knuckles to grip the flask, she drank and then hacked up a tar of bloodied phlegm. Guzco recoiled. Breathing in a leper's air, invited their pestilence. After the fit subsided, she looked at him through her pained, half-closed eyes and asked, "What is your name?"

"Guzco Domar."

"An Iberian. Al-garve? Must be a fisherman by trade."

He nodded.

"Long way from home. Even though I've nothing, do you still plan to rob me?"

"No."

"Tell me, are you leaving or arriving, Guzco Domar?"

"Wish I knew. What about you?"

"Of Spanish blood but Genovese by birth. Family of merchants. Provided alms for the poor, medicines for the sick and food for the starving. Our ancestors even raised tithes to fund the Crusades. For all the good it did us." Another coughing fit ensued. Guzco stepped further back, thinking it wise to head on. "Forgive me, leprosy pays no heed to polite conversation. Where was I?"

"Crusades."

"Was I? Long time ago, not that you would know given all this talk about Saladin."

"Leprosy?"

"Yes, of course, my apologies." Shaking her head, she pointed at the corpse then shook her head. "My daughter, Miriam." Her voice wavered. "We were banished to a colony outside Genoa's walls. There we stayed, praying, wishing, hoping. News of the Angel of Badur reached us. When summer began, or maybe spring ended, I cannot remember, we set out to find this Angel. Proved a long journey, short on kindness, long on hate, but we're used to being mankind's scapegoat. Our malady fuelled that hatred." After another coughing fit subsided, she continued, "We arrived here last night." She baulked at the still vivid memory. "Within the hour poor Miriam lay dead. She was a kind, decent girl. Never wished harm to anyone. I can't believe God intended this to be her fate." Clasping her daughter's right hand, she asked, "Help me bury my daughter, Guzco Domar."

Her request stung. Times were hard enough without risking your neck for a leper. Besides, he didn't want to miss Marta's dance and the chance to see Luisa and Bia. Somebody else would come along, someone with time to spare. A deeper truth emerged.

They came here to find me, hoping I could cure them. Misplaced hopes I know but I can't let her down. Not now. Luisa will understand if I'm a little late.

He found a patch of bare earth, its topsoil loosened by foraging boars. Overhead, shards of sunlight pierced the trees, spearing the earth as the shrill birdsong, no longer wary of the robbers, thinned. Guzco scraped at the soil, alive with the scents of decay and life. All the while, the leper stood over her daughter, half singing, half chanting a mournful air.

Stripped to the waist, Guzco snapped a fallen beech branch in half, and dug in long steady draws, his efforts once more rekindling his days at sea, even if he only possessed Spinoza's wiry physique. An hour later, wrists aching and hands blistered, he set the splintered branch down. Still fearful of sharing the leper's air, he covered his mouth and nose with a rag and hauled Miriam into her shallow grave.

"Baruch dayan HaEmet," whispered her mother, watching Guzco scrape the displaced soil over her daughter's remains. As he tamped the earth down, the leper continued to chant in her strange tongue but fell silent to watch Guzco climb into the nearest tree and stash his whale carving among its branches.

"Why did you do that?" she asked, after he had climbed down.

"To remind me to pay my respects next time I pass this way."

"Mitzvah goreret mitzvah, Guzco Domar."

"Sorry?"

"Years ago, in Salamanca, there lived a humble candlemaker. His hands were rough with wax and soot, but he had a good heart. Every Friday before sunset, he'd set aside his tools, wash his hands, and take one silver coin from his paltry earnings to give to the poor, so they too might have light for the Shabbat. One day, a footsore traveller arrived in the city. His clothes were torn, his eyes hollow. Most people shunned him but the candlemaker gave him bread and water. A week later, the traveller returned, this time clean, well-dressed. Turns out he was a merchant whose caravan was attacked on the road. He gave three gold coins to the synagogue to help the city's poor. His kindness sparked other kindnesses. The butcher forgave a poor widow her debt. The baker gave out free loaves. The scribe taught orphans without pay. The weaver clothed the new born, again for free. The candlemaker's kindness, lit in secret, became a flame across the city. So, Guzco Domar, just as one spark can light a thousand candles, one act of kindness awakens a thousand others. One good turn begets another. And on it goes."

"I look forward to it. Where will you go now?"

"Here, with Miriam, for the Shivah and after that, well, I'll leave that up to the Lord."

"There's a place close by. It sheltered me once. It can protect you."

"From what? Robbers? Death?" She shook her head, "Thank you but no. I'll stay with my daughter."

The trees flexed in the strengthening wind. It grew dark, ominous, the morning's sunshine a memory. Lightning shredded the sky, and claps of thunder shook the earth. A second peal of thunder announced the arrival of stinging hailstones, slicing the canopy.

"Please, let me take you to shelter," Guzco shouted.

She waved away his offer. Setting his gourd and food down at a safe distance, Guzco then said, "I'll come back tomorrow."

"Don't forget me, Guzco Domar."

Despite the pouring rain, Marta's dance carried Guzco to Lavagna's shore where Luisa and Bia waited to greet him. *"Will you be staying Daddy?"*

"Maybe next year my love."

"I'll count the days."

He kissed them both, delighting in their company but distraught at the years lost. Alberto's final note came as a relief, as truth be told, the leper's faith in his far-fetched fables, troubled Guzco. His efforts to impress Marta had led to a young woman's death.

Giacomo straightened his bedraggled ostrich feather then said, "Still thinking about the leper?" Guzco nodded. "You should have been more careful, Guzco. Common knowledge you can breathe in their pox."

Wiping his rain soaked face, Guzco replied, "It's not that."

"What is it then?"

"The lepers were heading here. To find the Angel."

"A good thing," replied Giacomo, admiring his dapper new hat.

"But if the Angel brought them, he also brought the robbers here."

"And these other good people around us."

"Maybe he never meant that. Maybe he just wants to be left in peace."

"Has he told you as much?"

"No."

Giacomo waved his arm across the scores of sodden pilgrims bedding down for the night. "See all this, Guzco? Thanks to your stories, for the first time in years I have money, status, enough to eat. Best of all though, Marta can dance without fear. Tonight, two of those zealots who once condemned her, looked on spellbound. Think Guzco, if those bastards can take heart from her steps, that *must* be a good thing."

"But what if the stories aren't true?"

Giacomo raised an eyebrow. "Are they?"

"In part. Maybe."

"Who else knows?"

"Just me. And now you."

"Keep it that way. People need to believe, to cling to dreams. The Angel offers that."

"But robbing the dead and dying?"

"The price we pay for our own freedoms. Besides, I think the lepers' tale will be a welcome addition to the acts. Tugs at the heart, and purse strings."

"It's too heavy a price, Giacomo. This morning my heart leapt at the thought of watching Marta dance only for it to break watching the robbers set about those poor women."

"Nothing in life is perfect, Guzco. Tomorrow we'll leave and the silent, simple life you crave will return. But for now, don't deny others the chance to find peace and support their families."

The revelation further dismayed Guzco. His fables, or lies, had turned Giacomo from an open-hearted dreamer into a grasping knave, revelling in his newfound wealth and fame. Marta and Alberto approached. Still flushed from her dance, Marta seemed nervous, out of sorts. Guzco fished in his satchel for the whale carving before remembering where he'd left it. "I've another carving for you, Marta. A whale. Fluke and everything."

She smiled. His heart melted. "Thank you, Guzco. I treasure your gifts but there's something I have to tell you."

What did the leper say? One good turn deserves another. Some good has come from

today after all. She's going to stay!

Marta looked at Giacomo and then at Alberto before turning to him. "I'm pregnant, Guzco."

"Can you believe it?" Giacomo beamed, "I'll soon have a grandson!"

A whale's fluke reared over Guzco. Disbelief and confusion flared through him. *Pregnant? She promised to be with me. Luisa and Bia depend on her. Doesn't she understand? How can she be so selfish?*

In the chaos of surging emotions, he forced a smile and heard himself say, "I'm pleased. For you both." Desperate to be gone, he opened his satchel, sighed and shook his head. "I've left the carving in the woods. I'll just head on and fetch it."

"Won't you stay to celebrate with us?"

"I won't be long. I want the carving to mark the day."

Holding aloft the dress, stolen from the troupe's burgeoning collection, he waded across the storm swollen river. Nearing the far bank, he slipped and sank. The torrent carried him downstream.

Carry me away. To peace.

But between Marta and the leper, he knew he had no choice. He breached the surface to part swim, part fight his way to the far bank. He scrambled onto dry land and lay on his back, chest heaving, mind racing.

True, Alberto is a good man, accomplished plucker, handsome too. If you went for thin, greasy types. But how can he compare with me, an Angel? Especially as I've sacrificed so much for so little.

He got to his feet, slung the wringing wet dress across his shoulder and headed into the woods. With every step, his frustration grew, tipping into anger before landing on fury. Picking up a fallen branch, he flailed a tree to vent his rage. His obsession with Marta had collided with his lies and like a confluence of rivers, the two nostrums tainted each other.

Why did I ever think she would move here to be with me? The doll, hawk, boat and whale carvings were expressions of love. Marta sees them as tokens, trinkets at best.

He ran on, until so tired, he feared his blood would turn to stone, he found the leper curled into a ball, beside her daughter's grave but still chanting in that strange tongue of hers. He handed her the dress. She thanked him, her

voice now thin, barely audible. A fresh second grave lay ready.

Guzco climbed the tree in search of the carving. It was nowhere to be seen. He shinned down and rummaged around the tree's base, brushing aside sodden carpets of leaves and twigs. Still nothing. Growing desperate, he clawed at Miriam's grave until his efforts exposed Miriam's ashen, disfigured features.

"What are you doing?" the leper asked.

The thing I once vowed to protect, I now defile? But I must find the carving. Why, I don't know. But I must.

He rummaged around and beneath Miriam's deformed corpse, even ripping her shroud away, his delusions unabated.

The slap stung. The leper fell, exhausted yet raging. Shaken from his hopeless obsession, Guzco finally summoned the courage to look at her.

"Why claw at my daughter like a rabid dog?" she rasped.

"I've a chance of happiness. A slim chance, probably misplaced, but one that will allow me to be with my wife and daughter. If I told you my tale, I'm not sure you would believe me. And besides it would be a long tale, badly told."

"Perhaps the Angel could help you."

"Doubt it."

"Ask him."

"Ask him what?"

"Why he ran through the storm lashed forest to search for a worthless carving, a token at best, yet still has the wit to attend to a dying leper."

"How did you know?"

"A fisherman in the mountains buries a leper without a moment's thought. Unlikely at best. Then he has the grace to clothe another leper, despite undertaking a fool's errand. Better still you haven't judged me, stoned me, called me the Christ killer or driven me away. You helped me." She paused, allowing her words to sink in. "Have you met God?"

"No. Not very impressive I know."

"But a comfort knowing you are fallible." A rasping, bloody coughing fit consumed her. Once the fit passed, they sat together in silence, easy in each other's company. "An odd combination," the leper finally said, "A Jew and an Angel. Both fleeing their old lives for different reasons, both stumbling towards death."

"Some truth in that," Guzco agreed. He offered her the water gourd but she refused. Violent bursts of sheet lightning lit her waning, intelligent features. She shrank inside her thoughts, reconciling herself with what was about to unfold.

"Thank you for coming back."

"Least I could do." He pointed to the freshly dug grave. "Your work?"

"Exhausting. Left me in awe of gravediggers." Tears rolled down her cheeks. "Baruch dayan HaEmet."

"Baruch dayan HaEmet," Guzco replied, struck by her beauty and courage.

"I'm ready, Angel."

Guzco kissed her scabrous cheek and allowed her final thoughts to overwhelm him.

What awaits me?—Jacob, Miriam, Abraham, Isaac—may our souls find rest in the Garden of Eden, beneath the Tree of Life, among the holy and the pure, in a world filled with light, and may they merit resurrection at the time of the righteous—Mother—Father—no fear—Life! Life!—I tried my best—warm ocean breezes—the thrum of the market—of laughter and music—the kindness in Jacob's eyes—my children's first words—No fear now—the Angel—found him.

Ragged and pain wracked, Guzco raised his withered hands to his face and traced a gnarled finger over his putrid bottom lip and closed right eye. Every movement however slight, offered only agony. The thin, pendulous breasts felt awkward but what sat between his poxed legs, the greatest shock. *A woman?* He wondered if this was Azekiel's final humiliation, but accepted it, knowing the leper was at peace.

Rolling Spinoza's corpse into the fresh pit, he spotted the whale carving's fluke dangling from a lower branch. Hours before he'd hoped it would win Marta's heart. But now in this new shattered, broken body, she would run from him. Good. Dreams are foolish. Better to accept fate and make for the boulder.

Slowly, painfully he drew the earth over Spinoza. The grave was too shallow. Probably offer foraging animals a feast. But Spinoza's soul was safe.

At daybreak, he crawled the short distance to the river, stripped and struggled to take in his deformities. The water washed over him. Sinking beneath the surface, he found safety from his delusions. For once the current didn't tempt him.

He climbed from the river and struggled to dress. A stone flew past, skipping four times on the water before sinking. A second stone struck him on the side of the head, drawing blood.

"Fuck off," Lupo boomed.

Alberto and Marta sat beside him in the lead wagon. Giacomo and Rosa looked on from the second wagon. Lupo took aim with another stone but Marta shouted, "Enough Lupo! The poor woman means us no harm."

"Leper, Marta. Can't take the chance."

Marta climbed down from the wagon then lowered the tailgate. All the while, Lupo and Alberto kept a beady eye on Guzco. Marta returned with a loaf of bread and to Guzco's regret, a flagon of Rosa's stew. She set them down on the river bank and backed away, struggling to hide her revulsion. Lost for words, Guzco wiped a smear of blood from his face.

"Mute as well as a leper. Bad," Lupo said, climbing down from his seat.

"Sorry," Guzco blurted. "Don't get much sympathy. Horde it when I do." He held up the whale carving. "Odd, don't you think, a whale carving so far from the sea." He offered it to Marta. "Take it. I met the man who wanted you to have it."

"Guzco?"

"The very same."

"When did you see him?"

"Last night. He sat with me as the storm raged. Gave me this dress too. Mine was little more than a rag."

"One of ours," Rosa said with a hint of sourness.

Guzco nodded. "This morning he headed into the mountains. But before he left, he told me a beautiful, kind woman, whose very presence lifts the soul, would pass by. And when she did, I was to hand her the carving and wish her, and the child she carries, a happy life." He stroked the whale's fluke. "Lot of love went into this, I'd say." He tossed the carving towards Marta.

"Leave it Marta," Lupo growled, "It's unclean."

"Please," Guzco insisted, "It was made with love."

"How do you know the carving is meant for me?" Marta asked.

"Not many beautiful women in these parts. Nor kind ones."

She picked the carving up. "It's beautiful," she whispered, holding it up to the grey morning sky. "If you see, Guzco, tell him I'll always dance for him."

CHAPTER TWENTY
Principe Railway Station, Genoa, November 1942

"I still don't know why you weren't allowed to finish your medical studies, Luca." Mama fanned herself with a copy of La Stampa as she and Luca waited on Principe Station's concourse for the Milan train. She was dressed in Sunday best, Luca in one of his father's old suits. "And why Mussolini thinks supporting Hitler in Russia is a good idea is beyond me."

"All part of Il Duce's master plan Mama," Luca replied, his hopes of seeing Greta, thinning with every passing second. Around them other conscripts, some in uniform but most wearing threadbare suits and scuffed shoes, said their goodbyes to tearful sweethearts, wives, children and parents. By habit, Luca weighed them all up, diagnosing future ailments from skin tone, gait and excitable natures.

"First they steal your father from me, and now you. We should have gone to America when we had the chance."

"Why didn't we?"

"Your father, God be with him, didn't want to give Mussolini the satisfaction. He could be pig-headed, unaware of the dangers around him." She fanned herself with more vigour.

"Brave though."

"The bravest man I knew. As if that's any compensation."

The comings and goings covered the awkward silence that now fell between them. Words waiting to be spoken. Luca pondered the irony of the son of a communist traitor now conscripted to fight the communists. Papa had died two years ago, less than a month after returning home. His stooped frame and haunted expression sharply at odds with the tall, languid man, quick to laughter, who'd been arrested the day Luca and Greta had shouted down Mussolini in the Portico. Mama's strength and grace had shielded him during those dark times.

He thought back to the elaborate, far-fetched plots he had dreamed up to break Papa out of prison. Each plan involved Greta in some shape or form even though she couldn't swim or handle a knife and had proved herself a poor sailor, as witnessed by that short-lived voyage with her uncle on her fourteenth birthday. Even so, it never occurred to him to undertake such an escapade *without* Greta by his side.

He could still recall details of the day he was pulled out of an anatomy class to be told Papa had died. The lovestruck graffiti scratched onto the lecture hall's desk, the seven people he shared the carriage with on the train back to Lavagna. Three of them smokers, while the man sitting beside him performed several decades of the rosary. The headline on La Stampa's front page bragging about the North Africa campaign. Rushing to the Piazza. Passing Greta's mother on the stairs. Mama burying her head in his chest. Swearing vengeance on Mussolini and his bastard cronies.

Her heartache when a week later, Father Biavati denied her a burial plot in Santa Stefano. Unlike Greta's brother Alesandro, killed outside Tripoli in forty-one and now feted as a hero. The plans to raise *his* statue were in full swing.

"Platform four," Mama said, fighting back the tears. She picked a piece of lint from Luca's lapel and tried to straighten his cowlick. For once he didn't pull away and fought the urge to return to being four years old, hoping she'd hold him then squeeze the life from him.

"I've packed extra socks and a jumper," she said. "The Russian winter is freezing. Did for Napoleon."

Overwhelmed by the moment, they clung to each other. "I'll write as soon as I'm in barracks," he whispered.

"Keep your head down my beautiful boy, my life." They pulled away, tears running down their faces. He checked his watch, a twenty-first birthday gift from Greta. *"She promised."*

Walking along the steam shrouded platform in search of an empty carriage, a woman shouted his name. Probably Mama, with food for the journey or worse still, some underpants she'd forgot to pack. Greta, red-faced, glasses fogged, squeezed past a couple locked in a clinch and stood in front of him.

"Cutting it fine," he said, his usually serious face for once breaking into a smile.

"The tram broke down, I had to run." In truth she wasn't going to come, the thought of Luca leaving was too painful to bear and she didn't want to cry in front of him. But at the last moment, she *had* to see him.

A passing Alpini infantryman muttered, "Tell the girl you love her. That's what she wants to hear and it's what you want to say." The Alpini was right, Luca longed to tell Greta his feelings but up 'til now he had always found an excuse to hide them: they were too young, too much ahead of them; Papa's then Alesandro's deaths. Even now, with Russia looming, he was torn between telling her or sparing her the burden of knowing.

"When you come home," she said, "We'll look for the Angel in the mountains. Even head to that French village."

"What's its name again?"

"Badur."

He nodded, took a deep breath then said, "I love you Greta. I hope you don't mind." Her muted reaction confirmed he should have kept quiet. Oblivious to the scuttling latecomers and whistle-happy porters, she threw her arms around his neck and said, "I love you too Luca. Come home to me."

"Trust me."

CHAPTER TWENTY-ONE
Badur, August 1349

A braying donkey, chivvied along by its drover, hauled a cart up the valley. Another man, stooped and malnourished, leaned into the wagon to help propel it over the rough, slushy terrain. The cart drew up where the track split, one for the blue lake, the other towards the boulder. An argument broke out between the men, the driver keen to press on, his companion less so. After a minute's wrangling, the driver dragged a bundle wrapped in a blue sheet from the wagon and set it on the ground. The sheet caught Guzco's eye.

The leper's ragged clothes had long since worn away, exposing his emaciated, deformed body to the pitiless mountain climate. The sight of the discarded cloak, something to prize, filled him with a desperate hope.

Even so, he thought it wise to slip beneath the boulder. Just to be sure. Hiding had become second nature to him, a strategy honed over lifetimes of waiting and watching. Let the men pass on and then investigate. That had stood him in good stead up to now.

For centuries he had eked out a naked, silent, pain-wracked existence, never straying far from the boulder, with the occasional wandering goat his only company. He had done the right thing to take the leper's soul, but his kindness had brought him little comfort. Why he had never strayed he couldn't say. Safety, perhaps. Or maybe no zealots to berate him, no one to consider his disfigurements divine punishment. There's nothing mystical about pain.

In the early days, he pined for the sea's endless motion, its brine tang, and his long-lost strength. Later, Marta's dance, the leper's chants, his mother's lullabies, and the infant Marta's grip had offered a vestigial happiness that swaddled him in memory. But one thought trumped these warm, comforting memories.

Why won't Azekiel rescue me?

A diet of rage and bitterness at this injustice had sustained him above all else.

The hangdog duo approached the boulder with the men still arguing as they drew near.

"But the priest said to drown her in the lake," said one.

"It's too far. Take us all day to get back," replied the other. "She'll perish up here if she hasn't already. Besides, serves her right, she's a witch after all."

"Says who?"

"The priest. He made it clear we're doing God's work. She brought the pestilence. Harlot deserves everything coming to her."

"Still don't seem right to me."

"What you think don't matter. Let's eat then head home. Wolves been busy this year. Want to get off the mountain before nightfall."

Sensing Guzco, the donkey grew skittish, earning itself a whipping from the driver.

They ate in silence except for the occasional snort and belch.

Minutes later, the creaking cart moved off, the driver and his companion resuming their argument. Guzco waited, listening, until the sound of their voices faded. When he was sure they had gone, he crawled from his hiding place. The wagon had almost reached the treeline, its wheels sliding over the slushy ground. Guzco scuttled forward, snatching up the discarded crusts and cheese rinds. But it was the bundle that claimed his full attention.

Drawing closer, he froze. A shock of roughly shorn hair jutted from beneath the blue sheet. His hands trembled as he drew the cloth back.

The woman, no more than twenty, struggled for breath. Bruises covered her face, welts scarred her feet. A swaddled child, barely a few hours old, suckled from her right breast. "Help me. Please. My daughter," she asked, blind to Guzco's disfigurements.

"But don't you see me?" answered Guzco, noticing the bloodstains on her shredded rag of a dress. Offering him the child, she said, "No matter. Please. Take her to the nuns at Sacre Coeur."

"Never heard of the place."

"It's half a day east of Badur."

The child fixed her drowsy, milky eyes on Guzco.

Can't you see little one, I'm no use to you. I'm cast out, a pain-wracked leper to boot, with no food or shelter to offer.

Sensing his anxiety, the woman's bloodied hand brushed Guzco's face. Her touch drew tears to his eyes. *It's been so long.* He picked the child up. Her tiny, perfect right hand gripped his gnarled, left forefinger.

"She said you would help me," the woman said.

"Who?"

She lacked the strength to answer. Guzco leaned forward and kissed her cheek. Her final thoughts overwhelmed his own.

My beautiful child—I did not wish this for you—they called me a harridan—for fending off the priest—why did you have to perish Marco?—I had no chance without you—but you my beautiful child—I give you my life—grow to be wise and happy—relish the mountain air—take the birdsong into your heart—dance the dancer's steps—no fear now—only life—The Angel.

Guzco took on her appearance, and finally, thankfully set the leper's sufferings aside, at a cost of unknown cruelty and the exhaustion of childbirth. The baby sighed and yawned. Overwhelmed with love, Guzco suckled her. After feeding, she threw up over him. Wiping the milky vomit from his face, Guzco set the infant down on her mother's cloak, put on the bloodied dress then buried the leper's remains beneath a small cairn of rock and scree, all the while chanting, as best he could, the leper's prayer.

Now a woman with a child to look after, brawn would only carry him so far. He drew on the leper's intelligence, intuition and instinct for survival.

Hampered by the lingering exhaustion, the journey down the valley proved slow and stuttering. Even the lower slope's scent and riot of colours failed to lift his spirits and a glorious murmuration, for so long missed, went unnoticed. He reached the bothy and suckled the child, these new maternal instincts, at odds with his fisherman's stoicism. As he half sang, half whispered a long forgotten lullaby, the child gazed up at him.

What life awaits you? No mother or family to rear you. If I could, I would raise you in the mountains but that is no life. But to part from you will bring me such sorrow.

Voices spilled from the dark. A man and woman tramped towards the bothy. Snatches of their conversation carried on the breeze, "Landed in Genoa…Came from the Holy Land…the Angel will protect us… Badur's a blind spot in God's ire." The voices thinned, leaving Guzco to wonder what awaited him in Badur, unsure if his legend still carried weight.

The next morning, a short distance from the bothy, he came across a man lying face down, arms outstretched towards Badur. Festering black boils ringed the man's neck. Robbers had picked him clean. Guzco panicked. It's one thing to hide in the high valley, away from judgment or wrath. But to see the dead left to rot?

Leave her here. Somebody would pick her up, somebody who knows how to care for a child. Back to the mountains. Away from all this.

The child grizzled. She gave him no choice.

Badur then. I'll leave you there. Somebody will take you in.

A stone bridge, blockaded by a jerry-built stockade of logs and rocks drawn from the river, straddled the ford. Pallid, grubby men, their bravery girded with wine, stood guard. Thick, choking smoke drifted across the bridge from the village adding to the fearful air. A column of nervous, desperate people, some herding goats, waited to gain entry. Yet only those with money were allowed to pass. Taking payment from an elderly, wealthy couple, one of the guards spotted Guzco and waved him forward. As the couple hurried across the bridge, the man telling his wife to not look back, the guard weighed Guzco up.

"Got any money?" he asked.

"The child. I found her in the mountains. Her mother. She was dead."

"Not what I asked."

"Just these rags I stand in."

"You carrying the plague?"

"Plague?"

"On Christ's Cross, where you been hiding? You one of them hermits?" The guard took a long draught of wine then wiped his mouth on his filthy sleeve. "From the east. A malady so strong no man or beast survives it. Badur is safe though. The Angel sees to that. Today we celebrate him with poems, song and dance. All shit but it serves a purpose. Grub too. Tastes horrible, like slurping sin. Fills the belly though."

"Won't the Angel want you to protect the child?" Guzco answered.

"Doubt it." He smiled, revealing a handful of twisted, near rotten teeth. His mood shifted from indifference to one sensing opportunity. "If I let you pass, what'll you do for me?" He nodded towards the opposite riverbank. "We'll find a quiet spot over there and, afterwards, Badur is open to you. And your bastard."

"But what will the Angel think?"

"What he don't know won't harm him." He pushed Guzco aside to allow a wagon to draw up. Guzco glanced at the driver, a crabby-looking giant of a man twice his size and breadth. Costumes, weapons, ropes, canvas sheets

and a giant whale's head, its paint faded, were piled inside the wagon.

"Didn't think you'd make it this year," the guard said.

"Very nearly didn't. The roads are clogged with people fleeing the cities."

"Wouldn't have bothered coming."

"Tradition says we should."

With the blockade lifted to allow the wagon to pass, people rushed the bridge but the guards barred their path. Another wagon crossed, the driver and passenger bearing striking resemblances to Alberto and Marta. Unable to help himself, Guzco shouted, "Marta! Alberto!"

"How do you know our names?" asked the woman, as the driver struggled to calm the edgy horses.

With the guard distracted, Guzco took his chance and returned to the forest, angry for his moment's weakness but proud Giacomo's ancestors still came to pay their respects to Guzco Domar once a fisherman now a broken, abused woman carrying a child through disease-riddled lands.

He moved upstream to find another crossing point. Within the hour, he stood in the woods overlooking Badur. People were gathered outside the church, beside a freshly dug pit filled with corpses. Fires burned from each corner, spewing out the noxious, black smoke drifting over the bridge. Two gravediggers leant on their shovels, the two men Guzco had seen on the mountain yesterday. Despite the troupe's arrival and the awful stew warming in a large cauldron, the air lay riven with grief and fear, far removed from the noisy gaiety that had once annoyed him.

A priest dressed in plain brown robes, face hidden beneath a leather mask sporting a hooked bill, stepped from the church and into the smoky mire. He made the sign of the cross over the bodies and thundered, "This is God's wrath descending upon you for wantonness and licentiousness, punishing you for your sins and abhorrent lives. Repent now or face the same agonised end as these sinners before you." The gravediggers began to cover the dead as the priest roared, "Hell awaits unless you abandon sin and carry out God's will. Look to the Angel for survival. Only he can protect you."

No I can't.

The wind shifted, the smoke choking the priest and mourners. Taking his chance, Guzco, eyes smoke stung, entered the church. Clutching the baby in his left arm, his right hand groped for the altar. The child began to mither.

Offering her a knuckle to suckle on, he whispered, "Hush now, I can't take you with me." Outside, the priest grew ever more manic. Guzco's brushed the altar's plinth with his spare hand and disturbed carvings of a doll and a hawk.

"Have you seen our father?" asked a young girl. Bascuali's children stepped through the smog. Neither had aged and both wore the same clothes and wan expressions. Before Guzco could answer, they receded into the murk. The baby grew restless and began to cry, leaving Guzco no option.

With the mourners and priest retreating to the river to avoid the choking smoke, he slipped into the forest and travelled east, hoping to find the convent of Sacre Coeur.

For an hour he crouched behind a thicket, watching the nuns scythe and then winnow harvested wheat with flails and sieves. The scene was tranquil, serene, a lifetime away from the frenetic corruption that had engulfed Badur.

The half-built convent was clad in wooden scaffold with stonemasons hauling and shaping fresh lifts of stone. An iron crucifix, the height of a man, rested against the convent's gate beside a statue of the Virgin slowly emerging from a block of sandstone.

"Close enough," a nun ordered, as Guzco approached. She shielded her eyes with her left hand and looked over his shoulder. The other nuns, dressed in rough woollen dresses and shod in clogs, looked on, red faced and glistening with sweat. Some took the chance to straighten aching backs and sip water from the plain wooden bottles hanging from their belts.

"What do you want?" she asked.

"I found this child in the mountains. She needs food, shelter. Someone to raise her."

"Why bring her to us?"

"Her mother asked me to."

"Where is she now?"

"Dead."

"Was she with sin?"

"Not as far as I know."

"Are you?"

"Yes, but repentant."

"Do you carry the malady?"

"No. At least I think not."

"We should help her," said a novice with bright, attentive eyes.

"Back to work, Sister!" barked the older nun. As the novice returned to work, her elder said, "Set the child on the ground then step back."

Guzco kissed the child on the forehead. Her eyes opened. "I'm sorry," he whispered, "I've no choice. Know your mother loved you." He kissed her again, set her down and stepped away, each pace a stab to his heart.

"Far enough," said the nun. She stepped towards the mewling child and picked her up. "She'll be safe with us."

"Thank you," Guzco answered, relieved but heartbroken.

"Have you eaten? We have food. Clean clothes too." Guzco brought a hand to his cropped hair then straightened his filthy dress. "Thank you but no. I must go."

"Where to?"

"The mountains. A day or so west."

Offering Guzco her water bottle and satchel, the nun's features softened a touch. "Food and water for your journey. The Angel would demand nothing less of me."

"You're right. She would."

"She?"

"Yes. She."

"Does the child have a name?"

"Her mother called her Isabelle."

Cowed by the loss of the child and Badur to disease, Guzco returned to the woods, unsure if he could survive this broken, feral world shorn of his strength. Different notions came to the fore. Nurturing, guile and a sense of making do, not giving up or abandoning hope. Attitudes that would see off this plague and the hopelessness it wrought.

Grateful for his new, female instincts donated by the leper and Isabelle's mother, he skirted Badur and made tracks for the mountains, only stopping at Spinoza's and Miriam's graves to pay his respects.

PART TWO

PART TWO

CHAPTER TWENTY-TWO
The Badur Valley, November 1943

Out of breath, legs aching, Guzco knelt and drank from the stream. The water was cold, redemptive. Overhead a hawk's shrill cry pierced the silence. He rested beneath the overhang and examined the muscular fingers inherited from Louis Foucault, the widower farmer whose soul he had collected in late forty-two.

Louis' reclusive, eccentric manner meant most villagers went out of their way to avoid him thus making Louis, for once, a perfect fit for an errant Angel. It mattered little to them the horrors Louis had experienced in Verdun in the first war that left the farmer grateful to Guzco for releasing him from his demons. Many lads from the valley had given their lives for France, while those, like Louis, who had made it home, left a part of themselves on those killing fields.

Startled by the crack of rifle shot, Guzco looked below. A man broke from the treeline and ran towards him. Minutes later, German infantrymen cleared the trees and gave chase. Shots rang out. The man fell.

The Germans had arrived a few days before, scouring the valley for Italian Jews fleeing to Switzerland. Their plight reminded Guzco of the Plague years when people, full of misplaced hope, sought sanctuary in Badur and in him.

Yesterday, as his farm and outbuildings were searched, he caught sight of the tangle of partially covered bodies piled aboard a German truck. When the lorry lurched into motion, a child's earth-caked hand and a woman's shoeless, stockinged foot jostled and bounced over the lowered tailgate. The soldiers and the bastard Vichy Milice sat on either side of the bodies, smoking and sharing a joke the corpses piled between them little more than cargo.

More gunfire. The man got to his feet, cradled his right arm and ran on. As he drew nearer, Guzco recognised the tall, slim figure of the blood soaked Doctor Chamonix, his distinguished, aloof air overrun with exhaustion. He'd been shot in the shoulder and stomach. Two German motorbikes cleared the woods and accelerated up the slope in pursuit overtaking the slow moving infantrymen.

Chamonix reached the boulder. Chest heaving, he leaned against it, smearing the surface with his blood. The motorcycles angry, straining growl grew louder.

"Doctor Chamonix?" Guzco said.

"Help me, Louis, please."

Without answering, Guzco shepherded the doctor beneath the boulder then climbed in after him. He drew the lichen gauze over the opening with seconds to spare. The bike riders barked at each other then rode on, leaving behind a cloud of exhaust fumes and displaced scree.

The sweltering foot soldiers arrived and to a man rushed to the stream to drink except for the officer who flexed the gauze covering with the tip of his boot. He removed his cap, wiped his forehead then issued orders in a calm, matter-of-fact voice.

Fachetti?

Guzco nudged Chamonix and raised a forefinger to his lips. The bikes returned. More orders were barked. The bikes roared away, as to where, Guzco couldn't figure. But a relief, nonetheless.

"You said you knew these mountains," snapped the officer.

"I do, Captain." Guzco recognised the voice of his neighbour, Jean Velous.

"Well, where the fuck is he?"

"I thought we'd have him once he broke cover."

"Velous, you are being paid to find Jews, not help them escape."

"He's not far. I can sense him."

"For your sake, you better be right."

The Captain gave the order to move out. Guzco waited, gesturing again to the stricken doctor to keep quiet. When the engine noise thinned, he climbed out, relieved to see the soldiers had fanned out and were heading off in the direction of the blue lake.

A rifle's bolt action slid. Guzco spun around and knocked the rifle from the soldier's grasp. The German regrouped to land a series of heavy blows to Guzco's face and stomach. He fell. The soldier was on him. Flecks of spit pushed through his gritted, tobacco-stained teeth as he gripped Guzco's throat. Dazed, slipping from consciousness, Guzco flailed at the soldier.

The German fell. Chamonix struck him again and again with the rifle butt, until exhausted, he dropped to his knees and let the rifle spill from his hands. Gagging for breath, Guzco steadied himself. No time. He dragged the unconscious soldier to the stream then held his head underwater. The shock of cold aroused the German. He grasped the bank, leaving an imprint of his hands in the wet earth. Guzco pressed harder, thoughts a mixture of feral rage and revenge but above all survival. Air bubbles breached the stream's surface as the soldier fought for life, his garbled words lost in the current, until he lay still, face down in the water.

"I need to tell you something, Louis," Chamonix said, refusing Guzco's offer of water. Struggling to breathe, he clasped Guzco's wrist then whispered, "There's seven Jews hiding in the forest, where the river bends toward Badur."

"I know it. Good spot for fishing."

Chamonix examined his wounds and blood spattered hands. He looked heartbroken, weary, aware of his fate. Shock kicked in, mingling with the bitter cold and he began to shake. Guzco placed the dead German's filthy field tunic around Chamonix's shoulders then helped the wincing doctor to lay down. Silence enveloped them in the buffeting wind.

"Didn't expect to die up here," Chamonix, now ashen-faced and blue lipped, whispered.

Overhead, the hawk let out a wistful cry.

"He's after Choughs," Chamonix muttered. "They breed up here. The chicks will fledge in a few weeks and then head south to Africa for the winter. Africa. Always wanted to visit. To see an elephant. One day maybe."

"Rest, Doctor, I need to get you off the mountain."

"It's too late, Louis…I know it. Just, promise me. Find them. Before Velous does. Help them."

"I will," Guzco answered, keen to get away in case the Germans doubled back in search of their comrade.

"I'm ready, Angel."

Guzco leaned forward and kissed the Doctor's cheek. Chamonix's final thoughts overwhelmed him.

Is this how it ends? Here? On a mountain with a stranger?—The pain—I wish I'd known more—seen more—fucked more—Hugo my love my love—I'll be with you soon—shame will not follow us—the pain must end soon—Mother—I could do with a cigarette—The Angel—it's so cold.

Guzco took on Chamonix's soul and haughty patrician's appearance but to his relief, not the bloody wounds. With no time for ceremony, he lay Louis' corpse beside the dead German, hoping to confuse a returning search party.

Anticipating the fizz of bullets around his ears, he never felt more grateful to reach the forest. A motorbike's throaty growl grew louder. Shouts in German went up. Guzco ran further into the forest and then climbed a large beech, shorn of its leaves for the winter but home to a heavily weathered whale carving. Why he'd placed the carving in the beech, he couldn't remember. He brushed the fluke and it disintegrated.

A machine gun opened up, sending squalls of roosting birds skywards. Bullets shattered branches and split the earth around the tree's base. Light from the bike's headlamp streamed through the trees and grew brighter as the rider edged further into the forest. He loosed another volley, this time off to the left.

The headlight arced one hundred and eighty degrees, illuminating a woman to Guzco's right. The machine gun spat but she had vanished.

Torches bobbed and weaved like rabid insects as the soldiers scoured the woods, with the officer bellowing orders. Guzco lay flat against the naked branch as German boots tramped the earth and kicked up mulched leaves below him. More orders were barked, rifles slung, and they headed further into the woods, with Velous offering directions.

An hour, maybe two, passed. With no sign of the Germans returning, Guzco made for the river. The bodies in the truck foretold his future if he helped the Jews. He could be at Chamonix's house within the hour. Nobody would know. The Jews could look after themselves.

Only ever meant to collect the dead, not determine the fates of the living.

He reached the bend in the river, where, to his disappointment, a woman whispered, "Doctor?" She looked about thirty, painfully thin, wearing oversize, tatty labourers clothes, her hair tumbling from beneath a man's beret. A toddler squirmed in her arms.

"Thought you'd abandoned us." Cautious whispers broke out around them. People stepped from the shadows, the sense of hunted terror among them palpable.

"Gather up your belongings," Guzco said, "We've a long walk ahead of us."

"To the border?" Guzco studied her hope-filled face. Unable to leave the valley, he couldn't lead them into Switzerland while their bedraggled state left him doubting their ability to endure a trek through the mountains. "It's too dangerous. The Germans are everywhere. I know a place. A place of sanctuary."

"Couldn't we hide in the forest?"

"They'd find you in no time."

"Then where are you taking us?" she asked, with a hint of mistrust.

"To a nearby convent. Sister Francine is a good woman. I'm sure she'll take you in."

"Sure? Is that all you can offer?"

"The Germans may not think to look there."

It wasn't the most convincing of arguments. Furthermore, he didn't know if Sister Francine would risk Sacre Coeur for these poor wretches but it was the only place he could think of that might offer them sanctuary.

"It seems we have no choice but to trust you."

"Believe me, if I knew any other way to help you I would take it. Follow me. Single file. Total silence." As they set off, an elderly man whispered, "Mitzvah goreret mitzvah."

"Waited long enough," Guzco muttered to no-one in particular whilst wondering how many more good turns he was expected to complete.

The dawn chorus was in full, rich voice by the time Guzco reached the outskirts of Badur after a three-hour trek from Sacre Coeur. Sister Francine had taken the refugees in without hesitation, after which she sent Guzco on his way in her usual no-nonsense fashion.

He squatted behind a wall to avoid a German patrol. Judging by the rancour in the soldiers' voices, news of their dead comrade had reached them. After the troops moved on, he made for the bridge but found sentries, their cigarette tips glowing in the murk, posted at either end. He crossed upriver but struggled with the current and thick layers of sediment on the riverbed. Reaching the bank, he lay flat, wary of more patrols. The coast clear, he ran along a back alley, huddling in a doorway when a dog began to bark. Despite the sun rising over the church, the sign for the village to stir, shutters and doors remained closed. A muted, suffocating atmosphere closed in around him.

Nearing the square, he spotted a man lying in front of the war memorial. Moving closer, he recognised Jean Velous' son, Henri. He had been shot in the head and chest. Without thinking and driven on by duty and habit, Guzco kissed Henri's cheek. He collected a slither of the young man's soul while Henri's final thoughts were wrapped around Irene Fontaine, the sometime flighty wife of Pierre, the café owner.

I've made a mistake.

Fearing the worst, Guzco ran his hands over his nose, chin and forehead.

Still Chamonix. What was I thinking?

Relieved, he turned towards the café and met Irene's gaze. She tossed away her cigarette and went inside. Moments later, the café lay in darkness.

Behind the closed shutters and doors of the homes and shops, Guzco sensed he was being watched. Panicking, he hurried to Chamonix's home and surgery, a short walk along a lane running behind the church. Entering the house, he locked the door, throwing the bolt for good measure. The hall clock showed five-fifty.

He changed out of his bloodied clothes into a grey pair of flannel trousers and a crisp, white shirt. The bed looked inviting. Warm. Safe.

What I wouldn't give for a good night's sleep.

The front door's handle rattled. "Doctor!" The woman's hushed, but insistent voice startled him. He looked out from the bedroom window to see a slight, middle-aged woman pushing against the door whilst glancing over her shoulder.

"Doctor, please!" Guzco stayed put, unsure what to do. If Jean Velous was a collaborator, perhaps other villagers were too. They were everywhere. Couldn't trust anyone by all accounts. But it wouldn't do to not answer the door. Only raise more questions.

He looked outside. Apart from the woman, the lane appeared deserted. He bundled the soiled clothes into a fine mahogany veneer wardrobe and went downstairs but let his hand hover over the door handle.

"Doctor! It's me, Lydia!"

He opened the door and the frumpish Lydia barged past him, her pungent odour something of a surprise. Without stopping to speak, or take off her overcoat, she hurried into the kitchen. Familiar where the coffee,

utensils and crockery were kept, she loaded the cafetiere with water and the ground acorns that passed for coffee these days and set it to boil.

"Have you heard?" she muttered. "A soldier was killed in the mountains. In revenge they shot poor Henri Velous." She made a sign of the cross. "It could have been one of my boys, even you, Doctor. Watching your blessed birds could have cost you your life."

She sighed theatrically before lighting a cigarette. Despite her pained expression, Guzco sensed Lydia was revelling in the tumult. "His poor parents must leave Henri untouched for twenty-four hours. Why do the Jews bring their problems to us?"

She poured herself a coffee. Guzco did the same.

"Thought you didn't drink coffee, Doctor."

"Must be the shock of everything."

He set the cup down, noting the surprise on her face.

CHAPTER TWENTY-THREE
Badur, November 1943

"Feeling better?" Pierre asked, struggling to slide the black brassard up the sleeve of his overcoat.

"Not really," Irene replied, taking another sip of water in an effort to lose the taste of bile.

"Do you want me to fetch Doctor Chamonix?"

"I'll be fine. Just need to rest. Think I'll give the funeral a miss though."

"Of course." Irene flinched as Pierre stroked her arm. To hide his disappointment, Pierre rearranged the plates of bread, cheese and apples. "Slim pickings for the wake," he mused, "Hope it's enough. You know what they're like round here when it comes to a wake. Never hear the end of it."

"Don't fret. You've worked wonders." She looked outside and saw Doctor Chamonix approaching. In the four days since he had told her she was pregnant, Chamonix hadn't mentioned anything to her, nor she guessed, to Pierre. It could only be a matter of time, even if she'd noticed quite the change in the Doctor's demeanour; more approachable if less confident, a hunched gait replacing his cocksure strut. And he'd started drinking coffee, or at least the muck that they made do with these days.

Stranger still, nobody in the village had mentioned the pregnancy, a minor miracle given that gossip was the lifeblood of Badur. Even so, she convinced herself neighbours looked at her differently, speculating behind her back who the father could be. Irritation replaced nervousness as she listened to endless, two-faced homilies about Henri's virtues.

She barely slept, or ate, and struggled to hide her grief from Pierre. Her only relief was, when alone upstairs, she danced the simple yet impossible steps that allowed Henri to return to her. For a few moments at least.

"Better get going," Pierre said. "How do I look?"

"Very smart. She straightened the armband before tidying his rucked collar. "Thanks, Pierre."

"For what?"

"For being so understanding."

Spurred on by her fleeting, all too rare kindness, he squeezed her hand and said, "The day I married you was the happiest day of my life." For once she didn't recoil as he kissed her. "Why the tears?" he asked.

"Why's life so cruel?"

"I've no idea. But at least we've got each other, eh?" He joined Chamonix outside the café and the pair of them strolled towards the church, warmly greeting other mourners as they did so.

Hoping the windbag tendencies of the parish priest, Father Lafont, would soon be in full flow, she climbed the steep, narrow staircase to the bedroom then drew out the suitcase from under the bed. Placing her hairbrush, make-up case and jewellery box on top of the clothes already packed inside, she closed the lid then placed the case at the foot of the bed. She straightened the bedclothes, fluffed the already plump pillows then took one last look around the bedroom, landing on the tarnished, silver gilt rimmed wedding photograph on the mantelpiece. Pierre beaming like the cat that got the cream whilst she managed a grin verging on a grimace, something her mother, never one to miss a flaw, had commented upon.

The clock on the mantel showed ten forty-four. The bus, if it came, and there was no guarantee of that these days, was due in six minutes. And even if it was late, Henri's grave in the village's, spartan, low walled cemetery, a good fifteen minute walk away in the woods, gave her more time.

It was inevitable Pierre would find out about the baby. The poor mite would be a lifelong reminder of her betrayal. She accepted life would be a struggle but she'd cope. All that mattered now was the child having a life filled with love. She thought about leaving a note but could see little point. Better to disappear altogether than leave Pierre an accidental tendril of hope laying in a shoddy sentence or misplaced word.

A mud spattered German truck pulled up outside. Weary, unshaven SS troops in filthy field green uniforms, dismounted and stamped their muddied boots to shake the stiffness from their limbs. Funeral latecomers hurried past, eager not to draw the Germans' attention. A soldier rapped on the café door and kicked the bottom panel. A thunderous hymn sprang from the church.

To Irene's relief, the bus was on time. She took her chance and went outside, locking the door behind her. The officer brushed the peak of his cap and spoke to her in German. For a split second she considered snatching his pistol from his holster and shooting the fucker. But the baby, her and Henri's child, checked her. So she smiled and shrugged, pretending not to understand. The officer pointed at the suitcase and asked in broken

French if she wanted help carrying it to the bus. Smiling but refusing, Irene continued the short but excruciating walk toward the bus expecting any second to hear a bellowing order to stop.

"Where to?" asked the bus driver.

"Nice."

"Return?"

"No. Single."

CHAPTER TWENTY-FOUR
Badur, August 1944

Shoulders aching, Guzco settled into his chair, removed his hat, found the bookmark and opened the weighty medical textbook at the letter "C" to read up on carbuncles, the subject of the morning's first consultation. Each night, he poured over books and studied patients' files hoping to understand their maladies and so prescribe appropriate treatments. Most times, he repeated Chamonix's prescriptions, hoping they would suffice. The patients never questioned his diagnoses; in fact many seemed happy just to be spending a few minutes with the slightly aloof, posh doctor from the north, before nattering with Lydia in the dispensary, from where she handed out tinctures, tablets, ointments but mostly gossip.

A young man walking past, tipped his cap then said, "Morning, Doctor." It took Guzco a moment to register he was being spoken to. Looking up from the image of an enflamed corn, he smiled then asked, "How's the little one?"

"Much better thank you." The baby had contracted jaundice. At one point Guzco had thought she wasn't going to make it. After all he was clueless about what to do but he hadn't bargained for the cantankerous local midwife, the Matriarch Lerond, to nurse the child back to health. Guzco quickly learned never to agree or disagree with the Matriarch, a woman quick to take offence but slow to admit to an error.

"Good. I'll call round tomorrow. Make sure your wife has plenty of rest."

"The Matriarch Lerond has already told me." The man set off but turned on his heels and said, "By the way, we've named her, Margot."

"A beautiful name."

The café's torn yellow canopy flapped in the stiffening breeze. Guzco glanced towards the aged church, basted by time and weather, its spire listing, towards the Vatican insisted the more devout locals. Angry, impish gargoyles, eroded over time, stared out. Several villagers queued outside the baker's. A one-armed man, another veteran from the first war, waited outside the butcher's with a parcel tucked under his good arm. The rusted tin sign hanging over the butcher's door signified it doubled as the village post office. Just as well, given the butcher rarely had meat to sell these days owing to the rationing. The cobbles glistened in the buttery sunshine.

The other shop, the greengrocer's come hardware store, offered a wide but thin collection of goods also made by the war's shortages. The grocer rearranged the jars most mornings to make it look more than it was. Everyone appreciated the deceit, while excitement gripped when humble swedes or turnips became available.

Gossips suggested the greengrocer had contacts with the Nice underworld, which enabled her to source black market goods. This rankled with many, Lydia for one, who viewed such unpleasant behaviour as tantamount to collaboration. But she was still willing to pay over the odds for under-the-counter soap, coffee and underwear.

Irene had worked three mornings a week in the shop, so naturally many villagers linked her disappearance to an underworld feud. Some thought she'd fled to Nice, others thought Paris. Matriarch Lerond chose New York as America was full of gangsters and women with loose morals.

As Guzco studied the bleached cigarette advert stencilled onto the greengrocer's flank end wall, Pierre, dishevelled with last night's wine lingering on his breath, stepped outside. The village had rallied around him after Irene's departure with men bitching about women, whilst women commiserated and shared confidences about their marital woes. Either way, Pierre didn't listen and sought comfort in the bottle.

"Morning, Doc. Coffee?" Guzco nodded, his eyes now resting on the war memorial and the wilting bouquet of flowers propped against the photograph of Henri Velous.

Guzco had always found Henri to be kind and open-hearted, the very opposite of his father. The young man's vitality and plans for the war's end had impressed him. Now Henri's death clung to the valley like humid air before a storm, invoking fear and resentment. Hushed, angry discussions took place between villagers over avenging his execution and finding the collaborator living among them. More fingers pointed towards Irene, her disappearance a sure sign of guilt.

But Guzco knew different. He'd read Irene's medical notes and discovered she was pregnant. A day later Henri was shot. A couple of days later, during Henri's funeral, Irene caught the bus to Nice and hadn't been seen since. The truth about her disappearance lay among these snippets.

Some nights he stood by the memorial, reliving Henri's final hectic thoughts about Irene but kept his suspicions from Pierre and also Henri's mother, Marianne Velous. She hadn't spoken since her son's murder, unlike her husband, who happily accepted Pierre's sympathies and free cognac whenever he set foot in the café.

Pierre set Guzco's coffee down. "Just been on the radio, Doc," he muttered under his breath, "Paris is surrounded by the Free French. Can't be long now."

"Let's hope so, Pierre," Guzco answered, desperate for the war to end so Badur could return to its rightful place as a forgotten backwater. Just how he liked it. Already talk had begun about the festival restarting after a near five year absence thanks to the Vichy banning order. The chance to be reunited, if only for a few seconds with Luisa and Bia through the festival dance's simple but impossible steps couldn't come soon enough.

A sharp pain coursed through his shoulders as the collected souls jockeyed for position, as they always did this time of year, to earn the coveted right to petition him. Not that it had ever helped any of them, but still they came. Guzco found their efforts beautifully futile. The last remnants of their humanity pushing toward him in the hope that he could end their stateless limbo. He never did. Why, he couldn't say, but he knew they'd return the same week next year, and every year thereafter.

The pain deepened, bordering on unbearable. He rolled his shoulders in an attempt to ease the agony, only managing to shift it from one spot to another. Then something caught his eye. A battered, two-tone Renault Monaquatre, with long canes and netting lashed to its roof, rattled into the square.

Jean and Marianne Velous climbed from the car. The flat-footed, crafty Velous loped towards the café. Marianne, carrying a spray of fresh wildflowers, headed to the memorial.

"Doctor," Velous said, nodding towards Guzco.

"Jean," Guzco answered, noting the calculating flicker in Velous' narrow, hawkish eyes. He sensed Velous felt no remorse for his part in his son's execution. A charlatan lurked beneath his scruffy, genial exterior.

Velous had brought Louis Foucault's body into the village, claiming he witnessed Louis' efforts to escape the Germans. Examining the corpse, Guzco had found numerous bullet wounds, convincing *him* that Velous had shot Louis in order to mask his collaboration. He also suspected Velous of stealing Louis' life savings, stashed in a biscuit tin beneath a loose flagstone

in his kitchen, a short walk from the Velous' farmhouse.

Guzco knew there would be a reckoning. He'd deny Velous' black soul a future. But there was no rush. After all, time is what he had in abundance. Besides, it wouldn't be right to break Marianne's heart so soon again.

"Heard the news, Jean?" Pierre whispered, setting a cognac down in front of him. "Paris is about to be liberated. Nice is expected to fall in a day or two's time. It's nearly over!"

Smacking his lips after downing the cognac, Velous shook his head, muttering, "What I'd give for my Henri to be alive to see it. German bastards."

CHAPTER TWENTY-FIVE
Paris, August 1944

Uncomfortable in the sticky summer heat, Irene set the dress down. She stood. The baby kicked. "You can't come soon enough," she said, holding her belly. "Life is hard enough without having to lug you around."

Once a storeroom, the haberdashery's basement heaved with boxes of old dress patterns and yellowing couture magazines. Dust-coated glass jars holding assorted off-cuts, buttons, hooks, brooches and lengths of thread rested on five sagging shelves lining the walls. On the table beneath, a Hurtu sewing machine sat beside a temperamental wireless, currently playing Maurice Chevalier. Irene's workbench was wedged beneath the barred, grimy window and her bed lay against the long unused fireplace, decorated with ornate tiles, some of them chipped.

Although little more than a hovel, the room had provided her sanctuary, a chance to start afresh, whilst the Proprietress' haughty, diffident company offered companionship. Of sorts. Only caring about Irene's skills as a seamstress, the Proprietress had never judged her for being pregnant or asked about the child's father.

Before dawn, each morning, Irene trudged with increasing difficulty upstairs to wash, swill out her smalls then prepare breakfast in the Proprietress' once grand apartment above the shop located behind the Place d'Italie. When she first arrived, there was a good chance of finding fresh eggs or bread to eat but now the food shortages were such that a stale crust was usually all she could rustle up, while the Proprietress still turned her nose up at the chicory coffee.

Each evening at seven o'clock sharp, she prepared dinner, lately a less than nourishing one or two vegetable soup, more often than not served cold due to the power cuts. She ate with the Proprietress. They rarely spoke, and only the sound of bone-handled cutlery scraping upon delicate, fine China plates broke the silence. When the Proprietress chose to speak, it was to connect with happier times; famous customers, her run-ins with Coco Chanel and the difficulties in sourcing good-quality cloth in these straitened times. "When all this nonsense is over, Irene," she liked to say, "We'll get the shop back to its former glories. It'll be a riot of colour and gaiety. You mark my words!"

Even if the city had calmed in the past weeks, German and Vichy snipers killed at random while the Resistance's makeshift barricades had turned the city into a maze of ripped up cobbles, felled trees and burnt out cars. Amidst all this chaos and hunger and fear, Irene remained surprised to see Parisian women risk their necks to bring their hats, gloves and dresses in for repair, thinking it strange they couldn't pick up a needle and thread themselves. "A favourite dress or coat offers normality, the familiar and comfort," the Proprietress explained, "And with us they are guaranteed exceptional service, which even the Boche cannot stop."

She listened to her employer on all matters couture, as she planned on opening a hosiery store when the war ended, thinking every woman would be desperate for fresh knickers after five years of making do. She'd even found the perfect shop around the corner in the Rue de Moulinet. A former milliners, light and spacious, plenty of floor space. Cheap rent too.

Returning to the table, she cursed to herself. The running stitch along the hem of the green chiffon dress was off a fraction. After unpicking and re-stitching the seam, she held the dress to the light and tugged to test the stitching's strength. Although the seam allowance was a tad generous and a loose thread needed unpicking with a stitch pick, she was satisfied. Being a seamstress required patience and a good eye but brought the satisfaction of a job well done whilst calming her nerves over the forthcoming birth. Better still, the hours spent engrossed with hems and cuffs and collars allowed her to forget Henri.

The light bulb flickered and then died, as did Maurice Chevalier on the wireless. Irene lit the kerosene lamp on the mantel and set about unpicking the loose thread, thinking herself a character from a Hans Christian Anderson fairy tale, locked in a basement doomed to stitch for the rest of her days. The baby kicked once more. "Like that story do you? I can't wait to tell you in person. What I wouldn't give for you my love. My life if needs be. Everything."

Some distance away, a shell exploded, shaking the basement's walls. The jars juddered and the light jerked in its socket. Small arms fire rang out. Any moment now, the Proprietress would shout down from the top step and ask Irene if she was well. Heart in mouth, she picked up the lamp, the dress and her sewing kit, and sat beneath the table and continued working.

Needing to pee, she struggled to her feet and ducked under the blouse and pair of threadbare knickers slung across from the washing line stretching between the window and the fireplace. She struggled to climb the stairs and was relieved to sit on the toilet. As she peed, church bells began to peal. Odd at this time of the night. The Proprietress tapped on the closet door.

"Won't be a minute," Irene answered, pulling up her drawers and then straightening her skirt.

"Hurry."

She opened the door expecting the Proprietress to dash by her. The landing was empty. Outside, the peals grew louder as more churches, including the great bells of Notre Dame, created a wave of joyous noise. People took to the streets, some singing *The Marseillaise*. The Proprietress stood by the open shop door, wearing an immaculate, fitted mauve velvet evening gown, studded with diamante and topped off with elegant satin evening gloves. Dazzled by the dress's bold colours, Irene rounded the mahogany counter, tidying a measuring tape and pincushion and joined the Proprietress, noting her make-up and the slight hint of scent. People ran past holding the *Tricolore* aloft, and shouting "Paris is free! We are free!"

The ground shook. Fearing the worst, Irene ducked inside but the crowds cheering grew wilder still. A handful of half-tracks rumbled along the street heading north, towards the Seine. Each vehicle bore Free French Army markings but had *Madrid, Ebro, Guadalajara* daubed on the front grills and the scruffy soldiers aboard shouted greetings in Spanish. The swarming crowds forced the vehicles to a halt. Parisians cheered, sang, danced and cried, sometimes all at once. The Proprietress gripped Irene's arm and whispered, "The Liberation has come."

As she broke down in tears, Irene's waters broke.

Still groggy from the gas, Irene awoke in a comfortable bed with fresh, crisp bedding. A tube attached to her right hand ran up to a plasma bottle hanging from a gibbet. Set beside the gibbet was a vase holding a large bunch of fresh flowers. She heard a child crying and looked for a crib but couldn't see one.

A young nurse smiled to reveal two rows of white, well-scrubbed teeth. "Mademoiselle Jonquet! How are you feeling?" She felt Irene's forehead with the back of her hand then took her pulse. She looked at the flowers and said, "They're from your employer. Aren't they beautiful!"

"What happened?"

"Don't you remember?"

"I remember tanks. And the soldiers, Spanish I think. People everywhere, cheering, singing, dancing." She checked herself, as she remembered her waters breaking. "Where is my baby?"

Looking uncomfortable, the nurse said, "There were complications, Mademoiselle. An emergency caesarean section had to be performed. But rest assured your daughter is well."

"A daughter!"

"Yes."

"Can I see her?"

The nurse hesitated. "Rest now, Mademoiselle. The doctor will be with you soon. He can answer all your questions."

"Why can't you?"

"It's best you speak to the doctor." She tidied the bedclothes and moved away, stopping to talk to a woman three beds down who was feeding her child. Irene ran her hand across her stomach and felt the dressing on her tender belly. "What have you done with my daughter?" she screamed.

Minutes later, another woman, certain in her virtue, entered the ward and approached Irene. The nurse, head bowed, walked a half pace behind. "Please, I just want my daughter," Irene said. The other mothers looked on in silence.

"I'm afraid that won't be possible," the woman replied in clipped, authoritative tones that matched her haughty features. The small silver crucifix resting on her high-collared blouse caught the sunlight filtering through the window.

"Why not?"

"Because your daughter has been put up for adoption."

As the other mothers coddled their newborns, or rested, Irene lay in bed and imagined holding her stolen daughter who she had named Isabelle. She told Isabelle about her dance to honour the Angel of Badur and to never be afraid because the Angel will always protect her. Perhaps she should tell them about Pierre, so they'd realise she was married and return her daughter to her. But what would Pierre do or say when they contacted him as they were bound to do? So, she kept quiet, thinking, plotting, planning and at night, whilst fighting the sedatives, she imagined dancing the simple yet impossible steps and drawing Henri out from the shadows. "See? She looks just like you, Henri." Henri smiled but always faded despite her pleading with him to stay.

Her despair drew her into a grief-addled silence that flummoxed the nurses, doctors and the condescending moral welfare officer who sought to explain the decision to strip Isabelle from her. The words washed over Irene like heavy breakers: "It's in the best interests of the child…you have no permanent home…you have no family…no husband…there are morality issues…" As the woman continued, Irene dug her fingernails into the palms of her hand and drew blood. She stored her rage, her silence liberating. All that mattered was finding Isabelle.

CHAPTER TWENTY-SIX
The Badur Valley, January 1946

With fog cloaking the narrow mountain road, Guzco, eager to get home, gunned the Citroen towards Badur. Seeing the festering boil on Chloe Jonquet's knee, his first thought were the Plague years. He'd made a hash of the procedure, twice having to retire to the latrine to gen up on boil treatments under a flickering lighter flame while Chloe's mother, Cecile stood outside asking if he needed anything for his bogus stomach complaint.

Struggling to make out the telephone poles lining the road, he wrestled the car around a hairpin, grounding the suspension and sending a plume of gravel skittering into the darkness. He liked driving: it offered freedom, speed, and a sense of control, especially with the Citroen's heavy steering and dull brakes. Rounding the next bend, a sharp right-hander, he accelerated, wiping condensation from the windscreen.

The car veered off the road, barrelling into a row of beech and larch trees. Guzco was catapulted through the windscreen, landing hard on the bonnet. For the first time in years, he lost consciousness.

When he came to, a man in a tailored blue three-piece suit and hand-stitched black Oxfords stepped toward him, each step accompanied by a high-pitched squeak. The sharp scent of expensive pomade clung to the air, catching in the back of Guzco's throat. He tried to flee to other dreams, but the soft, elegant whisper of metal on leather held him fast.

"A pleasant surprise, Master Domar," Massandar said, laying Caballero against Guzco's right cheek. "And all these souls craving your attention. You have been busy. To stay hidden for so long is testament to your powers of self-preservation."

"What do you want?"

"Your company of course!" He snorted then continued, "Hasn't Caballero worn well? Maybe you crave his hollow song once more."

"You left. To Genoa. With the horses. The Crusades."

"Genoa continues to serve me well. Greed and religious fervour are true alchemy. I made vast sums from those taking the Cross. For centuries since, Genovese merchants sought the services of the Banco di Dogali to fund cathedrals, churches, even the city's famous Lanterna. Although I love the irony of lighting a traveller's path, I shun acclamation; a hunter revels in stealth after all. Talking of the hunt, have you seen her?"

"Who?"

"Philomandra. The Angel sent to protect you."

"Never heard of her."

Caballero sliced. Guzco bled. "Are you sure? I've tracked her since the Plague years. What a glorious time that was, although I will admit, the speed of its advance surprised me. Flushed out many Angels though. Most I bagged but this hydra, Philomandra, still eludes me." He laughed, "What were you doing during those years, Angel? Cleaning your pots? Grubbing around these mountains as a goatherd or a farmer? Bearing children?"

"I tried to help."

"Of course, Badur. The village protected by an Angel skinned by the Devil. People flocking hoping to find respite from the Black Death. From evil. From me. Perhaps they should know the truth about you, the coward who cowered." He laughed, pleased with the pun. "The Plague made you famous, Angel. How noble of you to spend centuries in such a shithole."

Lifting Caballero, Massandar then smoothed his brilliantine-shined hair and straightened his black silk tie. Arshadne stepped forward, carrying the wooden box inlaid with ivory and ornate carvings of mythical creatures. She set the box down, unlocked it then raised the lid. Guzco's wings' translucent sheen remained undimmed. Shoulders burning, Guzco reached for them but Arshadne pulled the box away.

"Please," Guzco begged, allowing centuries of hopes to siphon.

"A game of dice to see if you can win them back?" mocked Massandar. His bland features narrowed. "Of course you would, but only Philomandra interests me."

"I told you, I've never heard of this, Philomandra."

"Then you are either a liar or blind. But no matter, there'll be another time, maybe even another war. Mussolini proved a valued ally. When he banned the Jews from public life in thirty-eight, the Banco di Dogali provided the expertise to sequester their land and money. I used the Nazi round-ups to flush Philomandra out, even in your backwater I recall. Came close once or twice. But *She* still evades me." He leaned closer, his sour breath causing Guzco to blanche. "But I'll find her. The hunt is more exciting when the prey puts up a fight."

"Is that all you want?"

"What else is there? You hide from your guilt and doubts in these mountains hoping birdsong or a soft breeze heralds Azekiel's arrival. Take it from me Domar, he isn't coming. And never will. Admit it, after killing the German, you felt nothing for him. Your morality is crumbling. Look at how you revel in your hatred toward Jean Velous, a true hero these days in these parts. No, the longer you wait for Azekiel, the more you sustain yourself on anger, hate, and jealousy, just as you did during your years as that derelict leper. Nothing wrong with that, I know those feelings well. But when you've had enough, I'll be waiting for you with open arms."

Guzco woke with a start, the light making him queasy. He lay in bed, in a white tiled, hospital ward. A statue of the Virgin being adored by children rested in an alcove above the door. His right leg was in plaster and the slightest movement was pain filled. A blurred figure sweeping from side to side approached, reminding him of his efforts with the scythe to clear the cemetery for Fachetti's victims. Scythes. Death. He raised his arms to shield himself, the pain unbearable.

The surly cleaner wrung out his mop releasing the smell of disinfectant. A dowdy no-nonsense nurse approached, her shoes squeaking on the still damp parquet flooring. "Doctor Chamonix," she said, straightening the blankets.

"Where am I?"

"In hospital, in Nice. You had a car accident three days ago. Fractured your skull, broke your right arm and five ribs. Monsieur Jean Velous found you. You owe him your life."

"I wish."

"The doctor will be doing his rounds soon. He wants to ask you about those scars on your back."

CHAPTER TWENTY-SEVEN
Aboard the Soviet ship Sikhali, The Mediterranean, August 1948

Glad to be rid of the unending monotony of the Russian Steppe, Luca stood on the bridge deck of the Sikhali, the antiquated grain carrier requisitioned to transport him and the eleven other Italian officers from Odessa to Palermo. He smoothed his cowlick and coughed. His chest rattled, a hangover from the typhus. With the water foaming against the hull, his fear of returning reared, a feeling for once not tempered by the joy of the warming sun. He had spent most of the voyage on this spot, staring out to sea, devouring every sight, the minarets of Istanbul, the glowering Dardanelles, and the islands that pitted the Aegean. Islands whose myths and heroes gilded his boyhood imagination. He whispered to persistent seabirds hovering overhead and his heart leapt at the sight of bottlenose dolphins skirting the ship's bow near Mykonos.

"Still can't believe that we're going home," muttered Pietro Orsi. He wore a saggy, double-breasted grey suit and sweat stained plain shirt and not the Red Army gymnasterka all the men had worn in captivity.

"Where did you get the suit?" Luca asked.

"The Captain. He has one for each of us. Makes him a class traitor in the cook's eyes, but we can trust the Soviets. Unlike that bastard Mussolini." He spat overboard. "Wish I'd witnessed him being strung up. Because of him, I doubt my children will recognise me."

"They will."

"I hope so. At least I survived. Thanks to Stalin, St Anthony and the Angels." By force of habit he made a sign of the cross.

"I thought Comrade Bronstein had converted you to communism," Luca said, recalling the infirmary's Political Officer's endless, gormless lectures regarding Stalin's genius.

"Of course. But it's always handy to keep the Angels on side. Just to be sure."

"Will you return to Sicily?"

"Yes to Canicetti. And Lavagna for you?" Luca nodded. "I knew a Lavagnan, on the retreat in forty-three. Perished when a German '88 shell hit the izba sheltering him. He talked of the rowing regatta."

"The Paglio de Tiguillio. I rowed for Lavagna. Rapallo beat us to the pennant that year." It surprised him that his efforts in thirty-eight still burned. Mussolini could fix that race but not a war.

"Bet it made you popular with the ladies though."

"Some."

"Anyone waiting for you?"

"Thought there was. Not so sure now." For six years he had cloaked himself in Greta's words at Principe Station. *"Come home to me Luca."*

But the war had purged her from his mind's eye. Were her eyes blue or brown? Her hair auburn or black? Was she left or right-handed? He took all of these things to be a sign that she was with someone else. But he still remembered her chuntering on about the Angel holed up in some French village and insisting that when he came home, they would wander the mountains in search of him. Back then he wanted, needed, to believe in such fairy tales to keep the fascists at bay and have something fantastical to believe in. But Christ alive, what he'd endured these past years. The smell of shit, blood and fear. The marches. The camps. The Kazak guards robbing the dying. Steal a man's soul if they could.

"Never heard from her. Most men, even the wife beaters, received letters."

"I got two," replied Orsi, sheepishly. "Perhaps she didn't know what to say."

"Greta always knew what to say. Daresay she's moved on and married."

"Sorry to hear that. But the fascists are gone now. We can build a new socialist future for Italy. We'll need good men like you."

"The war has made me wary of ideas. I lost too much to too many."

"What will you do?"

"Not sure to be honest. Maybe complete my medical studies."

"You'll make a good doctor; all those lives you saved in the camp."

"I could have done more."

"Nonsense. You did your best. That's all anyone can ask."

Keen to change the subject, Luca asked, "What about you?"

"The farm. Never going to leave." Orsi blessed himself and began to hum the opening bars of The Internationale.

But Luca thought different. When the typhus fever broke and he learned that most of the other captured officers had already been despatched to Italy he was pleased to have been left behind. Whether saving lives on the

Front or in the camps, survival became an end in itself. He relished the suffering that underpinned these visceral years and now found it impossible to comprehend returning to a life free of struggle. Without Greta, or his dead comrades, coming home seemed a pointless, hollow gesture. The stateless limbo in Odessa had suited him: skimming stones, the occasional rowing adventure, and earning rollockings from Russian and Italian players alike as he refereed football matches between the prisoners and hospital staff. Simple. No expectations. No disappointments.

Orsi grabbed his shoulders and hollered, "The Twelve Disciples are coming home comrade!"

The Sikhali's Captain, a heavyset, taciturn Ukrainian who wore his florid complexion with pride, appeared on deck. Despite his stern appearance, he was a reasonable man with a passion for submarines, peppering the mess walls with pictures of them, interspersed with the obligatory photographs of Stalin and Lenin.

Ignoring the pronouncements of the ship's NKVD officer, the Captain held little animosity towards his former enemies. Providing a suit of clothes for each man was his way of showing this. When he took the air after dinner, he liked to share a word with Luca who at first remained cautious to engage, a hangover from the hair-trigger violence of the Kazak guards. But despite the ever-present fear of denunciation, Luca appreciated the Captain's cautious warmth.

Below them one of the Italians promenaded, as he did from daybreak to sunset. "Why does he do that?" the Captain asked.

"Nobody knows. In the camps he spent the day walking around the perimeter fences. In Odessa he did nothing but walk around the hospital grounds. One time he hopped over the wall with the intention of walking home to Venice."

"A long walk."

"He returned two days later."

"I see. Yet you are happy to stare at the sea, Lieutenant."

"I am, Captain."

"A man can spend his life watching the water and feel he has not wasted his time. You were a sailor once?"

"I grew up on the coast. The sea fascinates me. It is never still, restless, in many ways like me. It was the thought of the sea that kept me sane on the Front and in the camps. Even in the most desperate times I could always find a way to reach it. And in Odessa we could wander down to the harbour."

"Do you have anyone waiting for you?"

"I thought I had. Not so sure now."

"I lost both my sons in the war. Oleg, my eldest, in a tank battle on the outskirts of Kharkov. Alexei drowned in the Pacific. They served the Motherland. Alexei would have been twenty-six this week. He was a good lad. They both were."

He handed Luca a photograph of a doughty, stern faced woman. She wore a loose fitting, plain dress set off by a string of pearls and sat in a high back chair. Either side of her stood two sombre young men, one in naval uniform, the other wearing the uniform of the Red Army. "My sons," he said with a hint of regret.

"And your wife?"

"Yes, my Natasha. She still mourns them. Makes life difficult at home. I spend my time at sea. She is the real love of my life. Never any need to explain anything to her." Handing Luca a wallet, he said, "It was Alexei's. He forgot to take it with him the last time he was home. Perhaps he knew death was waiting for him. Take it."

"I don't think I can, Captain."

"Please. I have no need of it, it holds too much sadness. You may need it in time. Remember a good Soviet citizen by it."

"No fraternisation with the fascist, Comrade Captain," barked the NKVD officer as he walked past. The Captain muttered under his breath and walked on.

Luca's thoughts drifted to his capture near the Don in forty-three and the gruelling forced march across the frozen Steppe. He and his three comrades became the focus of each other's world. If one fell or struggled to slog through the waist-high drifts, his comrades took turns to support him.

"Davai! Davai!" shouted the Russians. All the time they risked being shot should their struggles be spotted. Frostbite cost him two toes on his left foot, earning him the nickname of "Leper". Yet the men's devotion to each other remained unconditional, hewn from the barbarity of the world venting around them. They were assailed by starvation, beatings, frostbite, and the loss of hope, only sustaining themselves with rows over politics, football and women. They endured, even surviving, the fifteen-day, two thousand-kilometre train journey to Kazakhstan locked in a freight carriage with sixty other prisoners, many severely wounded. When the guards let them out at a watering stop, forty dead still stood among the living.

Yet within days of reaching the transit camp, his friends perished from typhus after it swept through the men's earthen hovels. Lice had hobbled Luca's medical skills. Powerless to stop the contagion spreading, he could only offer comforting words, boil tattered uniforms and plead with the vodka-soaked Russian medical officer for medicines, which never arrived.

Out of habit he looked at his bare left wrist and wondered how much the guard who had stolen his watch, a gift from Greta, had earned in cigarettes and vodka.

Gripped by an impotent rage, he began to sob. The ship's cook, labouring with two buckets of slops, appeared on deck. Heaving the swill overboard, he watched gulls dive into the water to feast before lighting a cigarette and shaking his meaty head in disbelief at Luca. He pointed to the horizon and whispered, "Sicily."

Drying his eyes, Luca searched in vain for Ustica, recalling his madcap plan for him and Greta to row from Lavagna in a goiter boat to rescue Papa. Everything was set fair until Greta demonstrated a lack of sea legs on her very short fourteenth birthday voyage aboard her uncle's trawler. He smiled at the memory but the dread of going home stirred. He daren't tell anyone, but fear of freedom now usurped fear of captivity.

CHAPTER TWENTY-EIGHT
Aboard the steam ship Cagliari, The Mediterranean, August 1948

Black smoke studded with cinders billowed from the SS Cagliari's funnel as Luca marvelled how nature could produce such bloodied sunsets. His ill-fitting suit that had brought normality on the Sikhali drew disdainful, pitiful looks, and his gaunt, jaundiced features further set him apart from the tanned, well fed passengers surrounding him. People he had fought a war for. The young, quick-witted, impetuous man who'd left Italy, returning as a ragged veteran, hounded by life.

A short, stocky woman in her sixties, her features carved by the sun and the cigarette, stood to his left. A wisp of hair escaped her floral patterned headscarf. Leaning against the metal balustrade, cigarette in hand, she smiled at Luca and asked, "Travelling far?"

"Home."

"Always nice to go home."

Luca raised a weak smile. Unused to everyday chatter, he didn't know how to answer. To his relief, the woman stepped away and sat on a bench. He stared into the water thinking back to that day when aged six or seven and on a ferry returning from Cagliari, he'd placed a scrap of paper inside a bottle, on which he written his name, address and a short note about being shipwrecked. He hurled the bottle overboard and promptly forgot about it. A month later, he received a letter from a girl roughly his age. She had found the bottle washed up on a Sardinian beach and wondered if they could become pen pals. He never wrote back.

He had always been impulsive; swearing in the Portico, shinning up trees, fighting the Balilla idiots. On the Front, he was little changed, charging into no man's land to retrieve the wounded, oblivious to raging fire fights. In the camp he once confronted the bestial commandant about the appalling living conditions. The dipso medical officer's intervention had spared him the firing squad.

He couldn't understand. He'd survived but his comrades, better men than he, had perished and now lay buried beneath the Russian Steppe. He baulked at the prospect of meeting their families, certain they'd wonder why he'd survived when their beloved sons and brothers had perished.

Greta long gone, Papa murdered, his comrades succumbing to typhus. Only Mama left. For years he had fought to survive yet now he had so little to live for. Death offered peace. Nobody would miss him. He glanced at the woman. He would like to know her name, a small event from her life, just to make things a touch more intimate. After all, he was about to share something precious with her.

Retrieving the Captain's wallet from his jacket, he breathed in the lingering coppery scent from the wallet's purse and then pulled out the Soviet bank notes and print of St Andrew, Ukraine's patron saint. He released his transit pass, issued in Palermo, into the breeze and stuffed the notes and picture between the slats of a whitewashed bench.

"Forgive me," he said to the woman. He clambered onto the railing and leapt, desperate to see his comrades again, the only people who truly understood him.

The water splintered upon entry, hissing its disapproval. "Greta!" he shouted. She has the deepest blue eyes, lustrous brown hair and a serious, yet beautiful face. Glasses too. She wears glasses. "Greta! Greta!"

The old woman, face frozen with shock, pointed towards him then shouted for help. His frail, typhus-addled body struggled to stay afloat. Exhausted, he sank, gagging on the water, the brine stinging his lips, eyes and throat.

The churning growl of the turning Cagliari's propellers receded allowing the sun-streaked water to calm him. Rapture replaced terror as Greta appeared before him.

"Work to be done, Master Meazza," said Lord Azekiel. "Work to be done."

CHAPTER TWENTY-NINE
Sainte Anne Asylum, Paris, August 1948

Irene yawned and stretched, grateful to have had a good night's sleep. Her first in weeks. In the bed beside her Justine, already propped up on her pillow, said, "Morning sleepy head."

"Morning. What time is it?"

"Six o'clock, just gone."

Rubbing the sleep from her eyes, Irene looked through the barred skylight above her. The rhythm of the drumming rain carried her back to the festival's dance. The day nurse, a sly, awkward customer, threw the ward doors open and chivvied the patients to get up. All did her bidding, except Justine.

"What's wrong with you today?" Irene asked.

"Don't like her," replied Justine, tugging at a strand of hair. "Says nasty things about me."

Irene wasn't surprised. Justine was convinced every doctor, nurse, orderly, and most patients in the asylum were plotting and scheming to lock her away for good. When her paranoia peaked, she howled abuse at everything and anyone until the doctor sedated her or had her bound and moved to an isolation cell. A day or two later, she returned and the delusional cycle began all over again.

Justine never offered a clue as to the cause of her condition, but then again Irene had finally invented for the doctors' benefit, a husband, Vincent, who had died in an Allied bombing raid on Cologne, whilst working as a forced labourer. For all the good it did in reuniting her with her daughter.

"Can I see your scar again?" Justine whispered. Although nearly thirty, a childish excitement gripped her.

Unable to fathom her neighbour's obsession, Irene drew down her blankets and raised her cotton nightdress to reveal the scar running across her belly. Agog, Justine whispered, "Did it hurt when they cut you open and took out the baby?"

"No. I was unconscious."

"Where's your daughter now?"

"Don't know. They took her from me."

"Why?"

"They didn't think I would be a fit mother."
"You seem fine to me."
"When I get out I will find her."
"How?"
"I need your help."

The doctor's office reeked of cigarettes and redemption. It contained a grand mahogany desk, leather backed swivel chair and two seats for visitors. A wooden filing cabinet and glass-fronted medicine cabinet stood against the wall and a locked, barred window looked over the asylum's fine gardens, alive with the summer. On the desk, sat his diary, notebook, an overflowing ashtray, a stack of files and a telephone, which he was talking into when Irene entered. He beckoned her to sit while concluding his conversation. Replacing the handset he said, "Forgive me, Irene, an urgent call."

As she'd learned to her advantage, Irene smiled. He was serious yet kind, devoted to his patients. *"One day you will be wise"*, Irene often thought during their sessions which could drag on for as long as one of Father Lafont's sermons. Since she'd been under his care, four long, largely pointless years, the doctor had acquired a wedding ring and a new cologne. Thankfully the rakish beard he had sported on their first meeting had long since gone, leading Irene to think his wife had the measure of him.

"And how are you feeling today?" he asked.

"Very well thank you, Doctor. How are you?"

"Very well. Thank you for asking." He read her file notes and without lifting his eyes said, "You've made excellent progress, Irene." Closing the thick file, he smiled in his bland, reassuring manner. He was about to speak when the flustered day nurse entered without knocking, "Sorry doctor, it's Justine Kopa. She's having another episode."

"Excuse me, Irene." He hurried outside, into the corridor, now resonating with Justine's screams. Taking her chance, Irene moved around the desk and scoured her file notes but found nothing of interest. Tucked in the back were several more pages. Still Justine screamed.

Irene rifled the pages without the slightest interest in these fuckers' opinion of her. Something at last. An application for adoption with "Approved" stamped, dated and signed. She recognised that bitch, the moral welfare officer's name and signature. There were two other signatures, a man and woman's. And an address.

Someone outside. The door opened. Irene stepped to the window, muttering the address over and over. The now flustered doctor lit a cigarette, took a deep draw then exhaled. He sported a graze over his right cheek. Justine had gone above and beyond.

Looking over the gardens, he said, "I've some good news, Irene. You can go home."

To where, she had no idea. Four years of her life lost. But she had an address.

CHAPTER THIRTY
The Badur Valley, April 1951

Dripping with sweat and hampered by his weakened leg and expanding girth, Guzco grabbed a tree branch to haul himself up the slope. He was running late, should be heading home by now. Even so it was a relief to be outside and look out over the flowering meadows with wave upon wave of birdsong filling the sky.

His injuries from the car crash had taken much longer to heal than expected. And once home, his convalescence saw him gain so much weight, Lydia had to let his trousers out. Twice. He blamed her cooking. Nothing to do with his gluttony for wolfing it down.

Some days during the long convalescence both in hospital and at home, he considered himself to be captive. First, with the hospital staff keen to get to the bottom of the scarring on his shoulders. Each answer he gave never satisfied them, and only led to more awkward questions until Guzco put a stop to things once and for all by talking of his near death at Verdun through gas and machine gun.

And when he was discharged, a good year after the accident, he found himself bedbound, listening to Lydia prattle on about life in the village, President de Gaulle, ungrateful colonies and the latest sightings of Irene. Mostly he ignored her tittle-tattle but his interest was pricked the morning Lydia told him Jean Velous had unexpectedly bought Louis Foucault's farm. "Thought them as poor as the rest of us, Doctor," she muttered judgmentally. "Just goes to show."

The news confirmed Guzco's suspicions that Velous had stolen Louis' life savings, although it would have been nowhere near enough to buy the farm outright.

The other item of gossip that most interested him, was the portrait of Irene left outside the café in February. Nobody had a clue who the mysterious artist could be; Lydia had her money on one of the uppity Lerond girls, while Matriarch Lerond, a regular visitor, thought it the hand of an outsider. Why, she hadn't the feintest notion but Guzco knew it was wise to agree with her. To everyone's surprise, Pierre hung the painting in the café. Lydia thought it odd as the picture would serve as a permanent, scolding reminder of what he had lost. "After what she did to him, I'd have thought he'd have burned the damn thing," she concluded.

But seeing the painting for the first time, Guzco understood why Pierre had kept it. The delicate, dreamlike brushwork perfectly captured Irene's serenity as she danced the simple but impossible steps. How, or why, Guzco couldn't figure, but the painting filled him with joy. Pierre treated the painting as an omen and now, every morning since, he waited on café's steps hoping to see Irene step off the morning bus from Nice. Guzco didn't have the heart to tell him she wasn't coming back, figuring it was better for Pierre to live in blind hope than heartbroken reality. Friendship can be cruel sometimes.

Soaking his aching feet in a shallow brook, he recalled the German soldier's final moments. Killing for survival had become a necessity long ago, but Massandar was right, he had taken pleasure in the German's suffering. In the years since, he'd fought to forget that dark, lingering delight. Time and again. Always without success.

Those same venal human traits continued to gain ground, pulling him further from the softer, kinder image he now liked to project through Chamonix's refined air and status. Massandar's jibes after the accident had been true all along.

How can I be the Angel depicted in legend?

To make matters worse, fate had decided to make the murderer and thief, Jean Velous, his saviour. Despite himself, Guzco gave the crafty, smug Velous credit for creating a myth around Chamonix's and Henri's deaths. Yet he remained desperate for Velous to get his comeuppance, preferably from the end of a rope. If not that, he could always deny Velous' soul peace.

Cheered by the prospect of revenge, he dried his feet, pulled on his socks and shoes, and stood. Before moving off, he paused to watch the chill, winter-flecked wind ruffle the sprouting grass and flowers. Smooth, billowing eddies fanned out in all directions, reminding him of the edgeless grace of a murmuration.

Revenge? What was I thinking of?

Perhaps it was time to head for a fresh start, a new life, free of the collections, doubt, Massandar, all of it.

Even if nobody else thinks so, I'm better than this. Know it in my heart. Just one step, that's all that's needed. Then one more and one more after that. I need to be bold, to trust myself, I've lasted this long. The blue lake. Can make a life for myself there. He moved

off, but it took only a few seconds for his mortal aches and pains to thin his determination. *I'll break free next year. Time'll be right next year.*

The sun had almost set as he crossed the flowering meadows, his mood lifted by the lingering scent and glorious riot of shimmering colour. He looked skywards, hoping to see a murmuration, but the starlings were still to arrive. He walked on, and within the hour, he stood beside Spinoza and Miriam's graves. Why he returned to these graves more than any other, he couldn't say but Spinoza's sacrifices and the leper's wisdom often proved a balm in these moments of resent filled doubt. Bravery and wisdom. Perhaps the two most important attributes in seeing off Massandar.

He fished in his satchel for the whale carving and, ignoring his aches and pains, he climbed up and into the towering beech tree standing guard over the graves. Halfway up, he found the perfect spot.

Lashing the carving to the branch, he whispered, "A new one to watch over you both."

CHAPTER THIRTY-ONE
The Port of Palermo Customs House, Sicily, April 1951

The beetle-browed customs official, a man in love with the small degree of authority his role afforded, still hadn't returned. Greta studied his musty office which depicted the efficient slovenliness of the Mussolini years to a tee. A desk and chair, two chairs for visitors, a bookcase with seven books and a tin wastebasket containing a fresh apple core and cigarette butts. On the desk sat an empty ashtray, a writing pad, a telephone and a gleaming Olivetti typewriter, with a tongue of carbon paper poking from the drum. A wobbly overhead fan gamely fought the humid, sticky air but with little success. The ghost outline of a picture frame stained the wall behind the desk. In all likelihood Mussolini.

She unfolded the Red Cross letter dated January nineteen-fifty. Again she hoped to read different words. They remained the same. Luca had boarded the Sikhali in Odessa and disembarked in Palermo in August forty-eight. Palermo Port Authority had a copy of Luca's transit papers for Genoa, signed and countersigned by the appropriate staff. Clipped to the Red Cross letter was a file letter signed by a naval doctor confirming that Luca, despite the lingering effects of typhus, had been passed fit to travel.

Pietro Orsi's letter, complete with hammer and sickle letterhead, apologised for not being able to help but noted Luca had the makings of a good socialist. The letter from the endlessly inquisitive, now retired, Carabinieri inspector, provided an exhaustive update on his trawl through hospital, sanatorium, even prison records for any sign of Luca. He'd found none.

She folded the letters then straightened her glasses as the official returned with a file. The misplaced confidence of a former fascist apparatchik still clung to him. No surprise, Italy remained littered with them. He sat then cleared his throat. "Sorry for keeping you, Signorina Perazzolo. My colleague informs me that there is no more information pertaining to Signor Meazza. The information provided to you by the Red Cross is correct. Signor Meazza arrived in Palermo on the day in question, received the appropriate documentation, underwent a medical assessment and to the best of our knowledge boarded the Cagliari for Genoa. The ship's manifest was accurate. I found a carbon copy of his boarding pass and a remuneration slip for returning prisoners of war. All I can suggest is that he landed in Genoa without presenting himself in accordance with the protocols. You must remember hundreds of prisoners were in transit during those sad times. Naturally, they did not appreciate the importance of record keeping and administrative order."

"But this was three years after the War had ended. You only had twelve men to deal with."

"Be that as it may, and may I say, I truly understand your disappointment, so many have suffered and lost due to the War but be it twelve or twelve thousand the same protocols would have been fully complied with."

"May I look at the paperwork?"

His cold, charmless eyes degraded the smile perched on his lips. "Unfortunately I'm not at liberty to share the information." He affected a look of disappointment, his thoughts already turning to his next task. He stood, scraping his seat over the parquet, and walked towards the door and opened it. "If you leave your details with my assistant, I will contact you if any new information comes to light." They shook hands. "Thank you for your time, Signorina."

Outside, Greta allowed her disappointment to fester. Coming to Palermo had proved a mistake. Official channels were closing down. There was little more she could do but accept that Luca had disappeared. Besides she had Massimo to consider.

His proposal was made in good faith. He was kind, generous of spirit, a long way from the arrogant fascist upstart idolised by Alesandro before the war. His work as an underwriter at the Banco di Dogali in Genoa was well paid and offered the chance of a comfortable, happy life. Most importantly, he adored her, and had encouraged her to go to Palermo, knowing they could never be truly happy with Luca standing between them.

Massimo had come to pay his respects to Greta's parents following Alesandro's death in Libya in forty-one. He looked uncomfortable when her father asked him who he worked for, quickly changing the subject to Alesandro's bravery and sacrifice for Italy. Greta recalled Alesandro's boasts about Massimo's connections to the secret police, OVRA, and his success in taking on the Reds and the Jews. Yet as much as she wanted to hate Massimo for his fascist links and the wrongs done to Luca's father, she detected a humility in him that set him apart. He'd been the only one of

Alesandro's friends who had come in person to offer condolences, marking him out as a decent man, perhaps with a conscience too. Better still he was handsome. She cringed recalling the incident outside the apartment when Luca, returning from college, had thought Massimo had come to arrest his mother.

Despite a broken nose and chipped tooth, Massimo never pressed charges and even wrote to her parents to apologise for his role in the fracas. That was the last Greta saw or heard from him until in the summer at war's end, they ran into each other in the Villeta Di Negro in Genoa. The fascist airs and graces and pin badge had gone. And he was still handsome.

The courtship took hold, ordered and contained. To outsiders they seemed the perfect couple, predestined for happiness. Yet Greta couldn't shake Luca from her thoughts, so much so that after Massimo had proposed, her first thought was of Luca and only then did she catch Massimo looking at her with a mixture of adoration and terror. She couldn't disappoint him. She was twenty-eight after all and bore the burden of her parents' expectation to cast off her infatuation with Luca and start a new life. She would accept his proposal.

As the *SS Messina* slipped from its moorings, passing a docked American battle flotilla, Greta held her glasses to the light, determined to remove the last vestiges of the smudge. She felt the thrum of the ship's engines as hectoring gulls hovered over a Palermo-bound fishing boat, sitting low in the water indicating a good catch. A crewmember wearing bright yellow oilskins, returned the waves of the two children standing near Greta.

Even with the Mediterranean drowsy and lifeless, she began to feel unwell, just as she had on her long dreamed of fourteenth birthday outing with her uncle. Luca had laughed like a drain when she told him they returned to harbour before reaching the open sea on account of her seasickness. She cried when Luca told her she'd have no part to play in rescuing his father from Ustica.

The hem of her linen dress rippled in the light breeze. The sun, rich and ripe, warmed her, but her stomach still churned. An elderly woman standing to her left coughed and then lit a cigarette. She was short, stocky and her hair danced in the squall. A bulging cotton bag sat beside her. "I watched a man jump to his death from this ship three years ago," she said. "A nice man too. But troubled. Broken hearted I'd say. So sad." She shook her purse and pulled out some bank notes. "He left these behind. Russian by the looks of things. Never had the heart to throw them away." After drawing on her cigarette, she muttered, "Sometimes life makes no sense at all."

She reached into her bag and pulled out a spray of roses and lavender. "Could you help me drop these flowers overboard, my dear. My rheumatics are playing up today."

"Of course," Greta replied.

"Be at peace," the woman muttered as the spray fall. Struggling to tame her hair, she limped to an empty bench and sat. Greta watched the flowers disintegrate in the *Messina's* wake and recalled Luca's words to her at Principe Station. "Trust me."

She had.

In the months after he was posted missing, her sobs would rouse her parents and Oona in the early hours. She dropped two dress sizes and grew more and more distant from her family, finding comfort in her grief and memories of her and Luca's real and imagined adventures.

But as the months passed to years, she found herself doubting her devotion. Being in love with Luca was the joy of her life, to lose him beyond comprehension, but she had the right to hope. No man should dictate her future. Oona's plainspokenness rescued her. "Do you want to end up like the Widow Rigazzi? You are beautiful, kind and smart, Greta. You can have any man you want. It's time to let go."

Now she had Massimo, the promise of happiness and wanting for nothing.

"Are you unwell my dear?" The old woman brushed Greta's arm. "Is it a man? It usually is. A beautiful girl should never be sad. Leave that to us old folk. Why don't we keep each other company for the remainder of the crossing. Sadness should always be shared. Do you smoke?"

"No, but please, I'd like to know more about this young man."

The woman lit another cigarette and collected her thoughts. "He seemed nervous, hunched, a bag of bones and wore a grubby grey suit far too big for him. We shared a word or two, nothing special, just tittle tattle really. Then to my surprise, he apologised, climbed onto the railing, ran his hand

through his cowlick and jumped. Perhaps if we'd spoken for longer, if I'd shared his troubles, he would still be here."

"Cowlick?" Greta's throat tightened. The woman nodded. "Never forgotten the way he ran his hand through it, while lost in thought." She looked out to sea and continued, "When he landed in the water, he shouted a name, Margareta or some such, I couldn't hear properly, but by the time I'd raised the alarm and the ship had turned, the sea had taken him."

She made a sign of the cross and continued talking but Greta wasn't listening. Instead, she pinched her forearm to stem the shock flaring through her.

"Trust me."

CHAPTER THIRTY-TWO
Paris, April 1951

Outside her apartment, Irene heard a child crying. Poking her head outside, she saw young Helene sitting on the apartment block's stairwell, her lips trembling, eyes damp with tears.

"What is it, Helene?" she asked.

"They were teasing me."

"Who were?"

"The other children."

"Why?"

"Because I don't have a mummy or a daddy."

"I'm sorry to hear that. Where are your mummy and daddy?"

"Dead. The War."

"I'm sorry. Many mummy and daddy's perished then. I'm sure they're still watching over you."

"Aunt says they are too."

"Then that is a comfort."

"She'll be angry with me though."

"Why?"

"Lost my door key."

"She'll understand."

"Doubt it." Nothing new in that Irene thought, the seven year old's wariness mirrored her aunt and uncle's diffidence. They were earnest, God-fearing folk who had passed on their cautious nature to the child, be it insisting she grasp the banister when climbing or descending the stairs, or that she never splash in puddles or play hopscotch in the courtyard during a winter smog. Such a cautious approach to life manifested itself in Helene's pinched, downtrodden features at odds with the wonder of childhood.

"I've an idea," she said. "You can wait for your aunt with me. I'll talk to her when she comes home."

Helene's face brightened. "Really?"

"Of course!" Irene leaned closer, "I'm baking madeleines. You can lick the bowl if you like."

"Why?" Helene looked at Irene as if she'd lost her marbles.

"Because it tastes nice."

"But won't the cakes taste nicer?"

"Probably."

"I'll wait for them then."

"Very well but come inside anyway. We'll leave the door open and you can leave your aunt a note in her letterbox."

The note astounded Irene, not only because of the neatness of seven-year-old Helene's handwriting but also her command of language which laid out in precise detail who the bullies were, the words they had teased her with, and her disappointment that this had carried on throughout the engrossing lesson about the French colonies.

After Helene stretched up on tiptoe to drop the note into her letterbox, Irene said, "Now Helene, how about a madeleine?"

"Yes please." A faint smile punctured the child's shyness.

Irene cursed as she dropped the scorching baking tray onto the two-ring stove. "They smell nice," Helene said, after the clattering came to a stop. "I love the smell of lemon."

"So do I," Irene replied, rinsing her scalded hand under the cold tap.

Flapping a tea towel over the cakes, she continued, "The village where I come from has been guarded by an Angel for many centuries. In times of trouble we turned to him."

"How do you know the Angel is a man?" The question stumped Irene. It had always been accepted that the Angel was a man. Nobody thought different. Until now. Helene waited for an answer. When one wasn't offered, she asked, "Have you ever seen the Angel?"

"No, but I know he's there. We have a saying, 'The Angel celebrates loss and the triumph of hope.' If you ask him, I'm sure he will keep you safe from your tormentors."

"Are bullies the reason you left your village?"

To Irene's relief, there was a tap on the half open door. Forgetting the cakes, Helene ran to her prim, austere aunt and sobbed. "Ssh my child," said her aunt, holding the scrunched up note in her gloved hand. "I have you now."

"The Angel has me too, Aunt."

"Which Angel would that be?"

"The Angel of Badur."

Helene's aunt look nonplussed. "Thank Mademoiselle Jonquet for her kindness, Helene."

"Thank you, Mademoiselle." Helene also threw a curtsey in for good measure. Irene kissed her on the cheek and left a smudge of lipstick. Wiping it off with her thumb, she whispered, "My door's always open, Helene."

Despite Aunt's misgivings, Helene began to visit Irene once or twice a week, to bake cakes and listen engrossed to Irene's tales about the mysterious Angel from her village in the middle of nowhere.

Away from her guardians, Helene shared Henri's boldness of thought and optimism. She asked sharp, intelligent questions that Irene often struggled to answer and sought to nullify by feeding her another slice of cake or tart. Helene didn't mind; she rarely, if ever, ate cake as Aunt frowned on sugar in all its forms.

At first, Aunt wasn't keen on her charge growing attached to the new concierge who she once described as, "too forward for her own good" and considered to be a woman not in keeping with her own hard-won social status. Irene offered to take Helene on day trips, but these were always firmly but politely rebuffed. That was until Helene's uncle pointed out the peace and quiet to be gained on Saturday afternoons if Helene wasn't in her room making that awful racket on her trumpet. Aunt relented, but on the basis that the trips were educational and character forming.

Each Saturday morning, after trumpet practice and tidying her bedroom, Helene, skittish with excitement, bolted downstairs (without holding the banister), and rapped on Irene's front door desperate to begin their next grand expedition. She hoped for another visit to the zoo after developing a fondness for giraffes, lizards and penguins. But not sloths as their spare, lazy movements and cloying fur scared her. Besides, an animal named after a deadly sin must be a bad thing. Sometimes she wondered what a Gluttony or Covetous would look like. But when she asked Aunt what a Lustful would look like, she was banished to her bedroom with a stinging rebuke following her down the hall. It was the same in school or church. No grown-up offered an opinion as to what a Lustful looked like and Irene had blushed when Helene asked a woman on the Metro one Saturday morning on the way to the zoo. The woman scolded Irene for raising such an ill-mannered child before changing carriages.

One trip took in the cavernous Natural History Museum in the Jardin des Plantes. Helene found the place fusty and off putting, full of shiny bits and bobs locked away in glass cabinets. Worse still were the sad looking stuffed animals in odd poses staring back at her. "We should set them free, Irene."

"Who?"

"The stuffed animals. Then find them a home in the zoo."

Irene hugged her and whispered so softly Helene couldn't hear properly. Not that it mattered. She loved Irene's hugs. Aunt didn't go in for that sort of thing but feeling another person's warmth allowed Helene to imagine her mother was holding her. That was what she liked best on her trips out with Irene. The sweets, cakes, hot chocolate and laughing a lot were lovely, but Irene's hugs made her feel special. Wanted.

"I think I was sent here to protect you," Irene once told her.

"Sometimes I wish you were my mother," Helene answered. Irene had squeezed her all the tighter.

When Helene announced that she wanted to learn to swim, Irene was happy to take her to Saint Germain baths. Helene, clad in a baggy swimsuit, and swimming cap, thrashed her spindly arms and legs in the water earning praise and tellings-off in equal measure from the whistle-happy instructor whose chlorine scented advances Irene rebuffed several times. Within a month, Helene had managed to swim a length of the children's pool without stopping and earned herself an extra-long hug from Irene. Tears too.

Irene's favourite part of the expeditions was arriving home with Helene still babbling away about lust or giraffes or the breaststroke. After cake and hot chocolate, she would lift the thin rug from the tiny living room floor to teach Helene the steps to her festival dance.

Helene proved a natural dancer, further releasing her from the staid strictures of life with her guardians. Once, red-faced and out of puff from her efforts but still able to scoff a macaroon, Helene asked, "Why did you leave your village, Irene? It sounds perfect."

"One day you will learn about the power of the heart to undo common

sense."

"Why not go back?"

"I hurt too many."

"Is that why you have no pictures on your walls?"

Irene tapped her temple and said, "I keep all my memories in here where nobody can touch them. New memories too."

"What are they?"

"Of our adventures together."

Helene wore her serious face to say, "One day we'll go to Badur to see the Angel. It will be our greatest ever expedition."

CHAPTER THIRTY-THREE
Badur, August 1951

Games of pat-a-cake and football broke out in the square among the children waiting for the bus to Nice. Guzco rolled his shoulders, the pain now sharper, more insistent. By tomorrow it would be intolerable. This year's festival couldn't come soon enough.

It was the right thing to do.

At first deciding to pause the collections left him uneasy, a touch guilty too for abandoning the souls to their fates, but thanks to both wars, hospitals, penicillin, the Matriarch Lerond's skills, even metalled roads, demand for his services had dwindled. He'd grown tired too of his self-imposed, centuries long, obligations, made worse by Jean Velous' ongoing heroic status.

There was something else. Something he didn't like to admit to. He *enjoyed* inhabiting Doctor Chamonix, not only for the social standing it conferred upon him throughout the valley but also the peace of mind he'd found. Not having the deaths of spinsters, widowers, quarrymen, drovers, farmers, weavers or teachers hanging over you, was a boon, especially as modern life, its rules, certificates, sign offs and testimonies that made the collections nigh on impossible to conduct.

Something to be said for the quiet life.

Much of his spare time was now spent with the minutiae of valley life where slights real or perceived were allowed to fester. The Festival Organising Committee sat at the apex of this world. He rued the moment Lydia had nagged him to join in forty-five, hoping he'd knock some sense into the other members.

Over the last six years their tiresome, drawn out meetings debated age-old thorny questions: the festival tent's siting in the square; seating arrangements; the order of the procession; eligibility criteria for performing the recitals; the age and size of the goats from Cresson. One argument, however, dominated all others. The rights and wrongs of changing the stew's recipe, a blessing in Guzco's eyes, heresy to the older Committee members.

Underpinning the Committee's combative nature lurked the rivalry between two men. The Committee Chairman, a devout Stalinist, and the Organising Secretary, a dyed-in-the-wool Gaullist. Both veterans of the first war, they staked positions in order to bait the other. Only Father Lafont's diplomacy prevented their verbal sparring spilling over into fisticuffs, just as well given their advanced years and similar respiratory complaints brought on by cigarettes.

And yet, despite the endless debates, motions and counter motions, nothing changed. Until this year, when Lafont had proposed at the Committee's February meeting, that the festival should honour the Angel *and* Henri Velous and Louis Foucault's sacrifices for the valley. For once the various factions united in agreement, while Guzco quietly seethed at the suggestion. In every subsequent meeting, he filibustered, raised obscure points of order and sought backroom deals to kill Lafont's idea. To no avail. Lafont became even more wedded to the idea, going as far to express his disappointment in Doctor Chamonix for objecting to such a sensible, sensitive proposal.

The June meeting voted to honour Henri and Louis in this year's festival. Guzco insisted the meeting minutes noted his objection. Worse still, Jean Velous revelled in the news. His part in the murders would be buried yet deeper.

Opening his now, well-thumbed medical textbook, Guzco baulked at the grotesque image of an engorged liver spot, the subject of his first consultation. Pierre set his coffee down and the sighed, his wine-soured breath grating on Guzco.

"The detective from Paris called last night, Doc. Just like Nice or Marseille, he found no trace of Irene. And this a man who boasts of always finding his quarry." Lighting a cigarette, he muttered, "She's never coming back is she."

Placing a consoling hand on Pierre's arm, Guzco replied, "Maybe it's for the best, Pierre."

"Doubt it."

"Don't be too hard on yourself. You're a good man, respected by everyone."

"Except the one person who really matters."

"Give it time."

"Can I ask you a question?"

"Of course."

"Were you ever married?"

"Once. Many years ago."

"Before the war?"

"Yes."

"What happened?"

"She died."

"I'm sorry. What was her name?"

"Luisa."

"And you never found anyone else?"

"No. She completed me, allowed me to dream."

"Is that why you came to Badur? To start again."

"In a manner of speaking."

To Guzco's relief, Jean and Marianne Velous pulled up in a gleaming, brand new Renault sedan. The front grill sported two silver chevron bands with bulbous chrome headlamps either side. Long canes and netting were strapped to the roof. Basking in the Committee's decision, Velous approached the café whilst Marianne laid freshly cut flowers beside Henri's shrine.

"New car?" Guzco asked.

"Beauty isn't she?" Velous replied. "Teak dashboard, plush leather sprung seats. Seven-litre engine. Garage owner said it's a better motor than de Gaulle's."

Marianne made a sign of the cross then walked towards the church, carefully placing a black veil on her head. Velous lit a cigarette, took a drag and then smiled, revealing a gleaming new pair of dentures. "Bought a new rifle as well, Doc. Beauty she is. Telescopic sights, the lot. Reckon this year's bird hunt will be the best in years. By the way, how's the leg?"

"Much better thanks."

"Lucky I found you. What if I hadn't been out hunting your precious birds that morning?" Guzco bit his tongue, wondering if the scoundrel would ever stop crowing about the rescue. Aware of Velous' Achilles heel, he asked, "How's Celeste?"

The smile left Velous. His cold blue eyes weighed up Guzco. "Fine. Still misses Henri of course. We all do. A finer son no one could wish for. This time of year is very difficult. The pain is still raw."

"Seven lives were saved that night."

"Seven Jews for my boy? No comparison, Doc. At least the Committee has decided to honour my boy. And poor Louis of course. Mustn't forget him. But who'd have thought it, eh? The Velous family highly regarded in Badur."

"It's most deserved," Guzco replied through gritted teeth. "Well, I mustn't keep my patients waiting, Jean." He stood, left some coins on the table for the coffee, then set off for his surgery.

"Always a pleasure, Doc. Drive carefully now!"

"Coffee, Jean?" Pierre asked.

"Please, Pierre. Any chance of a pick-me-up too?"

Pierre nodded and went inside. The coast clear, Velous pocketed two of the coins Guzco had left to pay for his coffee.

CHAPTER THIRTY-FOUR
Badur, The Holiday Cottage, August 1951

The proud, crowing cockerel woke Greta. Early morning sunshine breached the window's thin cotton curtains. Beside her, Massimo didn't stir. No surprise, it had been a long, tiring drive to Badur from Nice where they had spent the previous two days. The narrow, steep roads wound ever deeper into the mountains and more than once Greta was sure they would plunge down a scree lined gorge. Reaching the cottage, even in the dead of night, proved a blessing.

Amidst the sour odour of mothballs, she looked around the bedroom. Aside from the uncomfortable bed, overlooked by a copy of the Sacred Heart and a wooden crucifix, the only furniture in the room was two bedside cabinets, a wardrobe and a worn armchair. Oil lamps stood on each cabinet, their sooty deposits marking the damp-stained ceiling.

She put on her glasses, dressed, collected her handbag and went downstairs. The smell of damp greeted her. Light poured through the kitchen window, catching on the prancing dust particles. The only sound was that of a ticking clock. She stepped towards the sink and stubbed her big toe on a loose flagstone. Swearing under her breath, she turned on the single tap. Water spat into a saucepan which she then set to boil on the hob.

Whilst washing, she studied the photographs sat on the window sill. A young married couple on their wedding day. A man in naval uniform. Children astride a disinterested horse. One picture stood out. The young man was handsome with a mischievous glint and clearly proud of his fine shock of hair.

The creaking stairs heralded Massimo's arrival. Still half asleep, he drew Greta towards him, nuzzled her and said, "Want to go back to bed?"

"Later, darling. I need to go to the village and buy groceries."

"Very well," he replied, a touch disappointed. She kissed him, opened the kitchen door then stepped outside into the sunshine. A purring tabby cat curled around her legs as she breathed in the chilly air. Beneath the sun-flecked beauty, a derelict aura hung around the farmhouse. Weeds sprouted on paths, fences needed repairing, the door and window frames could do with a lick of paint and most worryingly, the front wall sported a series of large cracks. But despite all this and Massimo's disappointment to learn the cottage had no electricity, Badur's solitude matched her long held image of the place. Better still it was the perfect place for an Angel to hide.

The cockerel, a puffed up bruiser, long past his prime, walked alongside her before peeling away to strut around foraging hens. A young woman, in labourers clothes, left the Velous' farmhouse and walked towards a run-down barn. "Bonjour!" Greta shouted. The woman walked on without stopping or acknowledging her.

A large black car was parked outside the farmhouse, its grandeur out of keeping with the poverty of its surroundings. A ginger tomcat, lounging on the bonnet, paused from its ablutions to study Greta. Jean Velous wearing just his trousers, stood on his front step, scratching his groin, leering at her. Marianne stood on the bottom step tossing feed for the chickens from a battered bucket. Greta raised an awkward smile. Marianne scowled back.

Greta walked on, unnerved by her misfit hosts' reception. She reached the turning for the main road. A motorcycle's waspish engine note echoed and a red faced, out of puff cyclist struggled to thread a path through a flock of goats, his task made all the more difficult by the shepherd not lifting a finger to help. The cyclist hurled insults, roiling the shepherd who threatened to set his dog on the cyclist before both went their separate ways.

She hadn't told Massimo about her and Luca's pact to come to Badur. Thought it best not to, probably a step too far. When he'd asked her why she wanted to honeymoon in this backwater, she told him how much the legend of the Angel meant to her. He didn't seem convinced but went along with her wishes. To her surprise and shame, she had thought of Luca when Massimo accepted Father Biavati's invitation to kiss her after declaring they were now man and wife. His lips had tasted of almonds. She forced Luca from her mind as they walked down the aisle, garnering applause and congratulations until she shared a brief what-might-have-been smile with Luca's mother.

She stepped off the road and into the forest, already alive with birdsong. The air had a woody, earthy aroma. She stopped to drink from a small brook. The water was cold but redemptive. Shafts of sunlight threaded the canopy, creating a mysterious, illusory place. A place fit for Angels.

"Made it, Luca," she whispered before forcing herself to think of Massimo and his joy on their wedding day. He'd promised to love her to his dying day. "Thank you, Massimo," was her thin reply. Ever since, she had fretted this half-hearted reply had upset Massimo. If it had, he never said, nor did he seem angry or put out on their wedding night or during the short stay in Nice or during the drive to Badur.

Looking back to the thirty-eight regatta where their paths had first crossed, Massimo's fascism had bothered Greta. Now she no longer cared. Everyone had secrets from those days. Her's was Luca while Massimo's were bound to Mussolini. Best to keep a sympathetic conspiracy of silence and marry a decent, handsome man, besotted with her. Mama and Papa were happy. Oona too.

Feeling better, she reached a glade, guarded by towering beech trees and carpeted with a thick bed of leaves. Revelling in the isolation, the aged, mildewed carving of a whale nailed to a tree took her by surprise. She traced the outline of the carving with her hand. The breath left her. *"How can it be. Here? Of all places?"*

Opening her handbag, she retrieved the whale carving Luca had given to her years before when they climbed up the southern headland. She compared the carvings. They could have been a pair, matching each other in proportion and design, even down to the flourish of strokes on both flukes. She'd hoped to find somewhere fitting to leave her carving as a memorial to Luca, to say goodbye and no longer be a prisoner of her past. Fate, circumstance, decision upon decision, whatever it was, had brought her to this spot at this time. There was no point to think or doubt or try to kid herself anymore. Badur was telling her that he wasn't coming back. She wanted to cry but had no tears. No time for sentiment or self-pity. Live the hand dealt you.

She stretched up on tiptoe and hung Luca's carving from a low slung branch. Patting the bough for luck, she wiped her glasses on her sleeve then made for the village. Within fifteen minutes, she was crossing an ancient, two arch stone bridge. Badur sat on the far bank.

Each house was festooned with flags and gaily coloured ribbons drifting in the light breeze. Food, ironware, bedding and assorted junk sat on each doorstep.

The church bells struck seven as she reached the square to find a group of musty men, some dressed as labourers others in collar and tie, arguing over the raising of a large, ex-military field tent. Women and children unloaded chairs, benches and wooden boxes from a parked Studebaker truck still bearing US Army livery.

With the argument ringing in her ears, Greta entered the church and breathed in the lurid scent of incense, sin and polished wood. The cool, dark interior pressed on the optimism of the morning sunshine. The church was small, windowless with aged scorch marks scarring the walls. Carvings of a child's doll and a hawk, smoothed by decades of play, sat on the altar.

Forced to squint after stepping outside, she skirted the war memorial and approached the café where Pierre stood on the steps downing his early morning livener.

"She's going!" announced one of the tent party. A support pole gave way. Struts and guy ropes gave up the ghost. The tent collapsed.

"Why didn't you fix the stays!" someone shouted.

"That was your job," came the answer, as two men crawled out from the crumpled heap that had replaced the tent. The arguments started afresh, with fingers jabbed and insults hurled.

Smiling, Pierre straightened his grubby apron and drew out a chair for Greta. As she sat, she noticed the crescent-shaped dagger tattoo on his right forearm with *"Irene"* written beneath the blade's tip.

"Coffee, Madame?"

"Please."

"Would you like a croissant to go with your coffee? I have none but can run to the bakers if you wish."

"Just coffee, thank you."

Surprised to see a woman in his usual seat, Guzco sat at the next table, smiled and raised his hat towards Greta, who smiled back. Neither spoke and it was something of a relief for both when Pierre set Greta's coffee down in front of her then took Guzco's order. The arguments by the tent grew more heated. Two men, one in collar and tie, the other in dungarees and steel toe capped boots had to be pulled apart.

"Excuse me, Monsieur," Greta asked Guzco.

"Madame?"

"The men. What are they arguing about?"

A rueful smile crossed his lips. "In Badur it is the small things, the details that vex everyone." He wiped his mouth wondering what to say next. The truth. "The Germans abandoned the field tent when they left. Most villagers wanted to put it to use for our festival, but some, the communists

in the main, considered using a Nazi tent akin to collaboration. Where it is sited has become a proxy for this disagreement. Important to some, but not to most of us. I hope you will not judge us because of this."

"Of course not."

"Here for a holiday?"

"Honeymoon."

"Congratulations."

"And the festival."

Startled, Guzco asked, "You've heard of the Angel?"

"I'm from Lavagna."

"Where the Angel stepped ashore." He thought back to that day centuries ago. The boats, the headland, Isabella, Marta. Massandar.

"I grew up with stories about the Angel's bravery. Was it true Lavagna used to send fish to Badur to honour him?"

"That stopped before the First World War. The smell of fish after a week-long trek through the hills…not pleasant as you can imagine." For emphasis, he shuddered. "Once, it was the largest fare between Genoa and Marseille with claims of miracles, of the blind hearing and the deaf seeing. The festival celebrates loss but also the triumph of hope. Although its glory has dimmed, it remains dear to our hearts."

"It's good we honour tradition."

"The war taught us the importance of remembering."

"In Italy it's the same. We have come through dark times."

Nodding in agreement, a spasm of pain tore through Guzco's shoulders. He stifled a groan.

"Are you unwell, Monsieur?"

He raised an unsteady hand towards the pretty Italian woman. "Just a twinge, Madame. Rheumatics." The pain subsided sufficiently for him to relax.

After taking a sip of coffee, Greta said, "This is a beautiful valley, Monsieur. You are lucky to live here."

"I am. Can I ask what you do?"

"I teach biology in a secondary school in Genoa, although my lessons take place in a synagogue hall as the school was destroyed in the war and is still to be rebuilt. The Rabbi is happy for the hall to be used to honour those Genovese who helped his people escape the round ups."

"Italian Jews fled to Switzerland through the valley. Perhaps they once worshipped where you now teach. A pleasant coincidence, if true." He paused, unsure how much more to say. "In forty-four a German soldier hunting them down was killed in the valley. In retaliation, the Germans executed a young man." Pointing to Henri's picture at the base of the war memorial, he continued, "That's him, Henri Velous."

"There's a photograph of him in our cottage."

"So, you are staying at Louis Foucault's old place. I know it well. The dead boy's parents are your neighbours." Despite his discomfort, Guzco extended his hand. "Doctor Lionel Chamonix."

"Greta Ferrari."

"My pleasure, Madame Ferrari. If you are interested, an hour or so's walk into the hills from where you are staying are meadows full of the most stunning flora and insect life. At dusk you may catch a starling murmuration, a sight to gladden the heart. A biologist's dream I'd wager."

"It sounds it. Thank you." She finished her coffee, left payment and said, "A pleasure to meet you, Doctor."

"Likewise, Madame," replied Guzco, tipping his hat.

Bit of a coincidence. A Lavagnan woman in Badur at the time of the festival? His wounds throbbed.

The squabbling men ignored Greta as she joined the queue outside the bakery, where she soon became the object of furtive, nosey glances and weighings up.

Pierre set Guzco's coffee down. "What did you make of the Italian woman?" he asked.

"Very pleasant."

"For an Italian. Never trusted them. Fascists for one thing and they beat us in the thirty-eight World Cup. Bastards fixed the match. Everyone knows it. Mind you, the husband's a lucky man." He lit a cigarette then said, "The nuns have arrived."

A column of nuns from Sacre Coeur, led by Sister Francine, the Mother Superior, came to a halt beside the war memorial. Each nun, one or two flushed from their efforts, carried a chair with a cushioned seat, which they stacked beside the Studebaker. Why the nuns brought cushioned seats nobody, not even Guzco, could fathom. But all the same, he welcomed their silent if fleeting appearance, as it would prove a distraction from Greta and his aches and pains. For a brief, perfect moment, he felt a child's tiny fingers grip his left forefinger.

Pierre brought out a pitcher of water and glasses for the nuns. Each one thanked him as they took a glass. Their arrival calmed the tent party who now carried out each task without the childish rancour. Within minutes the tent was raised, leaving the field green canvas panels puckering in the breeze. Despite their success, the two factions refused to acknowledge each other's efforts.

A sharp clap from Sister Francine. The nuns lined up for the return journey to the convent. No words were spoken as Sister Francine considered conversation a distraction from devotion. But passing the café, she acknowledged Guzco with a curt nod. If he had a hero, it would be Sister Francine. After guiding the first group of Jews to the convent, over the next weeks and months, he found more Jews wandering the forest, lost, frightened and starving. Each time Sister Francine accepted them without question despite the Germans' repeated sweeps of the convent and its grounds. To this day where the nuns hid the Jews remained unknown. Sister Francine shunned acclamation, telling Guzco on one of the rare occasions she did speak, that it was, "the right thing to do, plain and simple." Just as centuries before when the nuns of Sacre Coeur had taken in the baby Isabelle.

"All will be well," Pierre mused, watching the nuns leave the square. "The Angel will aways be with us."

With the tent up, the seats were brought in and the stage set up. The Studebaker drove away, leaving a trail of diesel fumes. Guzco rolled his shoulders. The pain was much sharper this year, bordering unbearable.

How many centuries? How many lives?

He left the café still brooding over Greta and fearing tonight's petitioning.

This time sticking to the road, Greta found the return journey to the cottage harder, less peaceful. Even so, she had achieved something she had always

thought out of reach. Laying Luca's memory to rest had always seemed impossible, reckless even. But the carving and its mysterious twin, instead of prompting fear, provided an unexpected but welcome sense of relief. For that alone she was right to insist they visit the valley. The charming, if eccentric Doctor's phrase returned. "Celebration of loss, and the triumph of hope." The idea of celebrating loss appealed to her in a forbidden, pagan way. There was more to Badur than met the eye.

She set the shopping down to rub her aching hands. Despite her scientist's logic, all the oddities she'd witnessed this morning left her comfortable, at peace. Some things cannot be explained or understood. Just as it should be. Sometimes a little mystery is welcome.

Her delight was cut short by the blast of a car horn. Jean Velous waved as he drove past, while in the passenger seat, Marianne stared ahead with a dulled, lifeless expression. Greta waved back, grateful she didn't have to rerun the macabre gauntlet of stopping to talk to them.

A sheet of paper pinned to the cottage door flapped in the light breeze. Probably instructions or a telling-off from the landlady Greta thought. It was no note but a drawing of her walking through the forest. A man walked beside her. The artist had perfectly captured her likeness. Luca's too.

Unnerved, she folded the sketch and dropped it into her bag. Opening the door, Massimo greeted her with a kiss. "Want to go back to bed?" he asked.

CHAPTER THIRTY-FIVE
Badur, August 1951

It was pitch black inside the tent, the air stifling. Edgy and expectant, Guzco entered the moment the church bells struck one.

"Domar," whispered a man. He stood to the left of the stage, tall, willowy, in his late thirties, wearing ripped and muddied seventeenth century tunic and britches. Guzco baulked at the sight of the murderer, Pascale Penverne.

"Pascale, a surprise."

"Why say so, Angel? Am I not worthy of your time?" Penverne replied, rubbing the rope burns on his neck with his thick, calloused fingers. His broad, open features fooled many into thinking he was a good, kind man and betrayed his murderer's heart.

"Of course you are."

"Did you not tend to me at the gallows? Allow me to atone?"

"Yes. I only meant it has been a long time since I last saw you."

"So long that you forgot me?"

"I could never forget you."

"Funny isn't it. Your divine essence fails to adopt me, yet you were happy to take on nobler people." Penverne had come to taunt, not petition. Like the soldier, Sanchez, he'd borne a hard edge towards death.

"Makes me the proper sinner," he continued. "The slaying gave me pleasure, even if I paid with my life." He frowned. "Seem to remember you liking the dice, Angel. Just a pity you were such a poor player. Lost all your money and them tannery skins. Never seen a rage so fierce on a man. Thought you were going to knife him."

"You did."

"He swindled me so deserved the blade." Penverne's eyes narrowed. "There's us swinging, like dead leaves in the autumn breeze, the look on your face telling me you deserved this fate. Lucky your rope snapped though, that old skinflint, Douis, too mean to fetch up a fresh one for you, like he had for me."

Guzco recalled the noose tightening around his throat and the venal mob's hate-filled faces. The rope stretched then snapped, leaving him a gagging, retching wreck on the floor. "He's innocent," a woman cried out.

"The rope is shit," shouted another. As he was picked up, Guzco brushed against Penverne, gathering a fragment of the dying murderer's soul; not enough to take on his appearance but ample to experience Penverne's delight at plunging the knife into his victim's heart.

"You knew I was innocent yet you never spoke up for me," Guzco replied.

"Why should I? No one ever looked out for me. Now all I want to know is when I can be cut loose, from you, from everything. Done me time. Up or down suits me fine. Sick of all these whimpering fools around me. Even my shadow disgusts them. Just let me move on, Angel."

Penverne faded, leaving his toxic memory behind.

"Time is of the essence!" said the Watchmaker, running his forefinger along his shirt collar. "What are we without time! Nothing at all, just objects that bend and creak in the wind." Tidying his waistcoat, he stepped toward Guzco, removed his cap and bowed to reveal a thinning crown. Guzco had inhabited the Watchmaker between eighteen ninety-eight to nineteen hundred and two, after the Watchmaker had fled to Badur from Marseille a bankrupt, unable to settle his debts.

He held out a gold-plated watch then flipped open the case. Inside lay an emerald-studded face inlaid with silver Roman numeral hour markers. The centre of the face depicted sun and moon. "I forgot how skilled you were," Guzco muttered, struck by the craftsmanship.

"Once the finest watchmaker in the whole of France. This one I made in ninety-three. Barely lost a minute in all the years." He snapped the case shut then asked with a weary resignation, "How much longer?"

"Be assured when the time comes, you will know."

"If I can trap time in metal, it cannot be beyond you to tell me when I shall be set free."

"Patience my old friend. Think of the forbearance you showed to make that exquisite timepiece."

"Adieu, Angel. When the time comes, remember me." Returning the watch to his waistcoat pocket, the Watchmaker faded.

In need of fresh air, Guzco made for the entrance but a heavyset man, reeking of sulphur and other noxious substances, barred his path. "Angel?" The Apothecary said. "Been a while."

"Three centuries at least but still a pleasure," Guzco answered.

"Sixteen forty-eight if memory serves."

"There or thereabouts."

For seven long, puzzling years, Guzco had inhabited the Apothecary's eccentricities, tramping the valley in search of cures for ailments, some real, others spurious such as "pains in the mind" and "ongoing uncertainty". To nobody's surprise, least of all Guzco's, no cures for such maladies were discovered.

Bowing as low as his plump frame would allow, the Apothecary muttered, "Fate plays a strange hand sometimes. Like the day you found me on the mountain breathing my last after swallowing that Amanita mushroom and Alpine Knapweed concoction. What on earth was I thinking?"

"You always sought to stretch the boundaries of knowledge."

"I should have known better than to eat a mushroom as poisonous as Amanita. Although a dried version serves as a restorative for a variety of skin complaints."

"Useful to know," Guzco answered, thinking several of his patients may benefit from this knowledge.

"A chemist who succeeds in killing himself. Not great."

"A temporary setback. You were a visionary whose work has gone on to save countless lives."

"Really?" The Apothecary's mood lightened.

"Absolutely," Guzco lied. "Knotweed is used in many cures these days."

"So my death wasn't entirely in vain." He smiled. "But please Angel, do not forget me."

"Rest assured my old friend." The Apothecary faded, his ever inquisitive gaze flitting around the tent.

Exhausted and chastened by Penverne, Guzco stepped from the tent into pelting rain. Maybe Massandar was right; he had absorbed the worst traits of mankind; hate, anger and a taste for violence.

Or maybe not.

Penverne was strung up over three hundred years ago. Guzco should have swung with him. Perhaps he was lucky that day or maybe Philomandra had saved him by chafing the hangman's rope. Even so, his descent into hatred was not new. It had always lain within him. He couldn't sustain the virtues Azekiel demanded of collectors. That is why he had stopped collecting. But his human traits, for good or bad, had helped him to survive

his banishment. Maybe Massandar feared his imperfections as they were impossible to predict. Kindness one moment, hatred the next, hopeless infatuation blithely discarded. Only to be expected when inhabiting good, bad or indifferent lives. You aim to protect but inevitably you'll hurt as you try to balance perfection and imperfection. There's the rub, the sweet spot. Impossible to attain for the likes of him. No doubt the higher ups, this Philomandra for example, achieved such a state of grace. But not him. Not Guzco Domar.

He rested his left hand against the tent wall, raised his face to the rain and whispered, "Philomandra, take the souls in my care. End their and my suffering."

For one, fleeting moment, Philomandra stepped from the shadows. Why, she didn't know. Seeing sense, she slipped away. Guzco didn't spot her. But someone did.

CHAPTER THIRTY-SIX
Badur, August 1951

The following morning a frazzled, still sleepy Pierre greeted Guzco. "Early this morning, Doc."

Raising his hands to apologise, Guzco took up his usual spot then said, "Lydia and Matriarch Lerond are preparing the festival stew. The smell alone melts the teeth."

"My condolences. But tradition is,"

"As tradition expects."

While Pierre prepared his coffee, Guzco looked across the rain-shone cobbles towards the tent.

Did I really expect Philomandra to step from the shadows? She's never revealed herself to me. So why would she now? Pierre set his coffee down. *Of course. The Lavagnan woman. Carried secrets. Almost certainly. Maybe Philomandra is wise to her.*

A Berliet van pulled up. "Cresson's contribution has arrived," Pierre said after downing his morning livener. The van driver, a tall, rangy man with weathered, sleepy features half hidden beneath a fine beard, led two bleating Rove goats from the van. The blank-eyed buck stared at Guzco, who whispered, "Don't think about giving me the slip today."

"First sign of madness, talking to animals, Doc," Pierre said.

"I've a complicated relationship with goats, Pierre." Shaking hands with the van driver, Guzco then said, "Good to see you, Jean Baptiste. Thank you for bringing these beauties."

"My pleasure, Doctor. Cresson can look the Angel in the eye for another year."

"Certainly. Nervous?"

"A little. Rather wrestle a wolf truth be told."

"Lydia has every confidence in you. Remember, a dastardly look goes a long way."

"I've scared my poor daughters witless perfecting it."

Tying the goats to the van's rear bumper, Jean Baptiste then unloaded a lustrous two-metre replica wooden whale.

"It's magnificent," Guzco said, a touch jealous of Jean Baptiste's carpentry skills.

"Must admit she turned out better than expected. There's something else as well." He reached inside the whale's trunk and pulled a lever. The whale's jaw slackened. Another lever raised and lowered its fluke.

"Gangway, heavy load," a woman shouted. Lydia and the Matriarch Lerond's put-upon husbands pushed a wheelbarrow containing a milk churn across the square. After setting the barrow down beside an unlit fire to the right of the tent, they congratulated each other on a job well done. Pierre handed them a Pernod each, which they both downed in one mouthful, to the disgust of the Matriarch.

The sloshing churn was lifted from the barrow and its rancid contents poured into the aged cauldron hanging over the fire. Lydia sniffed the stew and half wretched. "Perfect," she groaned, her eyes streaming.

Unnoticed in all the excitement, a battered blue Citroen van pulled up beside the Berliet. Under Cecile Jonquet's watchful eye, the performers' costumes were unloaded.

Four year's older than Irene, Cecile was the very opposite to her sister. Calm, happy with her lot and preferring to go unnoticed. Her mother always thought she was the better dancer of the two but Irene, more pushy and confident had nabbed the festival dance ahead of Cecile when the chance arose. Not that Cecile minded. She settled for the role of festival costumer and with her diligence and eye for detail, nobody could recall a time when the performers' attire outmatched the acts themselves. And now her daughter, Chloe, was to perform the dance for the first time.

"Done for another year, Doctor," Cecile told Guzco, flexing her stiff, sore fingers.

"You've been busy, Cecile," Guzco answered, astonished by the intricate designs and delicate stitching for even the humblest garment.

"The haberdashers in Nice had some beautiful fabrics this year." Glancing at Pierre, handing Lydia his handkerchief, Cecile continued, "It's the least I could do. You know, after all that business with Irene."

"Of course. Thank you," Guzco replied, recalling Cecile's shame over Irene's disappearance and the damage it had done to her family's standing in the valley.

"My Cecile ran this up for me, Doc." Cecile's portly husband, slated to play the Devil in the pageant, wore a white cotton tunic depicting an embroidered boar hunt with hounds giving chase. "Beautiful isn't it. Almost as beautiful as my wife." Blushing, Cecile playfully whipped him with lengths of spare material she kept to hand for last minute alterations.

"How's Chloe?" Guzco asked.

Cecile's strained, shy features lightened. "I don't wish to sound boastful, Doctor," she whispered, wary of earwiggers, "But I truly believe Chloe is a better dancer than Irene. Watching her, time stops and my heart fills with joy. Yet to look at her who'd think something so extraordinary could pour from my plain, bashful daughter?"

Her words filled Guzco with anticipation. The tent was up, the nuns had supplied the cushioned seats, Cresson had brought goats, the awful stew prepared, and the terrible acts rehearsed. With luck, Chloe Jonquet could carry him to Luisa and Bia. The cloudless, blue sky matched his mood. For all its nonsense, the festival rooted him and the village in its history. Worthy of celebration.

Greta put on her glasses then buttoned her blouse. Massimo lay beside her, eyes half closed, enjoying the sun on his face. "Can't find it anywhere," she muttered.

"What?"

"My hairpin."

He rummaged under his blazer. "This it?"

Pinning her hair, Greta smiled, recalling the pin digging into her shoulder as they made love in the flowering meadows. Having sex in a place ablaze with life proved arousing, life affirming. And as Massimo's rhythm entwined with her own, pulses of desire and lust coursed through her as she clung to him, revelling in a giddying liberation. Perhaps she could love him after all. She just had to try harder.

But now half naked, hair messed up and searching for her left shoe, she felt self-conscious in front of him. He picked a blade of grass from her hair, kissed her cheek and said, "Enjoy that?"

"Of course. We are married."

"That's not what I meant."

"Forgive me, Massimo, that came out wrong. In the moment yes, it was wonderful, sensual, all the things I imagined and more."

Resting on his elbow, Massimo now ran the blade of grass along her cheek and said, "I'd never hurt you, Greta."

"I know."

"We can talk about anything."

But she knew it was wise to keep quiet about some things. He rested his head in her lap. The knee-high grass billowed around them in edgeless sweeps. "What I would give to remain in this moment." He sat up, his shirt slipping from his shoulder. "We should come back to this exact spot every year. On our anniversary."

"I'd like that," she lied, stroking his face. "I'm so grateful we found each other."

"Of course you are!"

Laughing, Greta stood and straightened her skirt. "Found something out today. Quite the coincidence."

"What?"

"Nothing. It can wait."

"Tell me."

"It's nothing really but that Doctor I mentioned, told me earlier that Genovese Jews hid from the Nazis in the valley. There must be a good chance they attended the synagogue where I now teach."

Now Massimo made a mess of buttoning his shirt. "Fucking Jews, will I ever be free of them?" he muttered impatiently. His tone was aloof, dismissive. Still fascist. A ridge of silence separated them, their rutting passion from a few minutes ago now forgotten.

CHAPTER THIRTY-SEVEN
Paris, August 1951

"Irene!" Helene shouted from the Saint Germain swimming pool's shallow end. Looking up from her sewing, Irene waved. Adjusting her swimming cap, Helene bellowed, "Watch me swim a length under water."

"Take a big breath!"

Wearing her serious face, Helene nodded. She took a deep breath, sank and pushed off from the pool wall, clawing the water in long, even strokes.

Irene returned to her stitching, pleased with the progress she was making on Helene's dress. The pool was quiet with a few diehards, now familiar faces, ploughing up and down. After all it was a boiling hot summer's day and people preferred to be outside enjoying the sunshine. A short *parp* on the whistle alerted Irene to the whistle-happy lifeguard's presence. To her relief, he was trying his luck with an attractive woman sitting further along. She glanced towards the deep end to see Helene burst through the water and grasp the pool wall, her chest heaving. Taking another deep breath, Helene set off on the return length.

Irene's thoughts turned to Badur. August 24th. Festival day. She wondered who'd be performing the dance today, probably one of those uppity Lerond girls or possibly the baker's frumpy daughter. No surprise there. Her parents were always angling to give her the role, even if the poor girl had two left feet.

She hoped Chloe would perform the simple but impossible steps one day. She had loved aping Irene during rehearsals and shared her timing, poise and grace, even at such a young age. Perhaps all Jonquet women were blessed with such elegance. Helene too.

She lifted the hem and ran her fingers across the stitching. Pleased with her progress, she glanced at the pool. She couldn't see Helene. She should have surfaced by now. A shrill whistle startled her. The lifeguard dived into the pool and swam down towards a shadowy, motionless figure lying on the bottom. Moments later, he breached the surface with Helene's limp body in his arms. He reached the pool wall and two other swimmers helped to lift Helene from the water. The lifeguard climbed out and gave Helene the kiss of life then pumped her chest, all the while pleading with her to wake up.

Helpless, terrified, Irene looked on, her thoughts landing on Henri.

"Live," she whispered. "Don't leave me."

"It's no good," said the lifeguard.

"Don't stop," pleaded Irene.

He rolled Helene onto her side and then thumped her back. Helene's lifeless body jolted under the impact. Her eyes opened and she coughed up a mouthful of water.

"Thank God," muttered the lifeguard, watching Helene's reddened, terrified eyes search for Irene.

"Swimming underwater?" Helene's aunt's features flushed with anxiety and rising anger. Her cold hazel eyes bore into Irene.

"She's done it before. Helene's a very accomplished swimmer," replied Irene, wilting under Aunt's gaze.

"She's barely seven years old! How can you expect her to swim two whole lengths underwater?" She turned to her grim-faced husband for support.

Irene hadn't expected this reaction, thinking they'd both be relieved to see Helene sitting up in her hospital bed, asking the nurse the best way to treat verrucas. Such a venomous dressing down had come as a surprise. "I knew it was a mistake to let you take Helene swimming, she's too frail for such exertions. Were you watching her?"

"I was, Madame, but turned away. Just for a moment."

"What's that in your bag?" She pointed at the canvas bag draped over Irene's shoulder.

"A dress I'm making for, Helene."

"Were you sewing while Helene swam?"

"Yes, but..."

"Yes, but nothing, Mademoiselle Jonquet. My niece was in your charge and through your neglect she very nearly drowned." Her gloved hand prodded Irene's shoulder. "I could have you arrested for child neglect."

Irene knew she should stay quiet. No good would come from the words forming on her tongue, she might lose Helene for good. But still in shock and desperate for the truth, forced her hand. "When have you ever paid Helene the slightest attention? When did you last hug her, laugh with her, listen to her stories? When was the last time you told her you loved her?"

"How dare you," came the answer. Aunt looked at her reticent husband who raised a manicured finger to his lips. To no avail. "When that child needed a home we took her in, and we have given her all the love she could ever wish to receive. Isn't that right, Bernard?" Her husband nodded, embarrassed by the queer looks they were receiving. "We've given that child a good, Christian, upbringing."

"But a happy one?"

Aunt bridled. "What gives you, a concierge and a poor one at that I might add, the right to argue with me."

"I have every right."

"Why?"

Irene checked her tongue but this stiff, arch snob standing in front of her had no idea of what she had endured to survive the war, life without Henri, and losing her home and family.

"Because, Helene, is my daughter."

CHAPTER THIRTY-EIGHT
Badur, August 1951

On the ancient stone bridge into Badur, Massimo cursed as he struggled to free his left shoe from the sticky bitumen. His foot came away but the shoe remained stuck. He shrugged his shoulders then said, "My favourite pair too. Not my day today."

The incident melted the awkwardness that had sat between them since leaving the meadows. "I'll buy you a new pair when we get home," Greta said, watching him pull the shoe free.

Villagers and valley folk, all wearing Sunday best, slowly gathered on or near to the bridge. Cigarettes were smoked, wayward children told off, old folk outbid each other's ailments, friends and foes waited to swap stories and renew rivalries while young men eyed young women who in turn cast glances at the lad they were sweet on.

The church bells chimed. Massimo checked his watch. "Quarter to six," he said. A corpulent priest wearing cassock and surplice with three terracotta pots, each one the size of a baby's fist, slung across his chest, approached. Behind him traipsed two altar boys one of them carrying an unlit thurible.

The priest stopped and introduced himself to Greta and Massimo. "I am sorry we have not had the chance to meet before. Father Alain Lafont, parish priest."

"A pleasure to meet you Father. Massimo Ferrari. May I introduce my wife, Greta."

"The couple from Genoa?" Massimo nodded. "*La Superba!* A wonderful city. Columbus himself hailed from there. And where would we be without Columbus?" Massimo looked nonplussed as Lafont then whispered, "I dare say Genoa's lowliest festival remains a much grander affair than our little event, but I hope you enjoy it, nonetheless. I understand the Velous' are your neighbours."

"Yes."

"They live in a fashion only they can explain, ever since their son, Henri, died. There is a daughter, Celeste, something of a recluse, but an extraordinary artist by all accounts. Modern stuff, all squiggles and circles. Not very Godly in my eyes but it is a calling. Of sorts." Lafont nodded his goodbyes and then hurried the altar boys along, leaving Greta to wonder if the mysterious Celeste lay behind the drawing of her and Luca. Guzco and Pierre ambled towards them. Guzco tipped his hat and asked, "Looking forward to the festival, Signora Ferrari?"

"Very much, Doctor. May I introduce my husband, Massimo?" Shaking Massimo's hand, Guzco asked, "Have you visited the meadows yet?" Massimo bristled. Greta forced a smile. "This morning. You were right, it is very beautiful."

"A treat for the eyes and the soul."

"When does it all begin?" she asked, keen to change the subject.

"The Procession begins at six sharp. Father Lafont considers tardiness a sin greater than lust or sloth but he has adopted a more relaxed approach than his predecessors who once insisted pilgrims cross the bridge on their knees. Ruined many a pair of trousers, although tarred roads have had other unintended consequences."

"I can understand," Massimo replied, studying his ruined shoe.

The church bells struck six. Cigarettes were ground out underfoot as pilgrims, seeking to banish guilty thoughts, took their place. The flirting youngsters stopped flirting, the old friends and old enemies promised to see each other next year and the wayward children were brought under control, with a slap around the legs if needs be. Before the final chime dissolved, a haphazard column snaked across the bridge. At its head, Lafont cleared his throat, again adjusted the pots and said, "Today we honour the Angel, who continues to protect, clothe, feed and shelter us. In turn we must now shelter him." Girding himself, he asked, "Who will shelter the Angel?"

"We shall," the adult pilgrims responded with varying degrees of enthusiasm. Eager to get on, Lafont set off towards the village and the procession shuffled forward, led by the Organising Committee, except the communist members who considered columns bourgeois and joined their families. The small troupe of costumed performers and musicians followed the Organising Committee, except Jean Baptiste due to the Gaullist committee members unhappiness at seeing a Cresson man playing Goliath.

The lay procession, as ever led by the Leronds, followed the performers. Tradition dictated those families who'd lived in the valley the longest stood towards the front leaving more recent settlers bringing up the rear. One over-excited young girl tripped and landed in another patch of tacky bitumen, earning a scolding from her mother, busy dabbing the tar stains on her daughter's hand with her spit-stained handkerchief.

Guzco nudged Pierre and said, "Over a hundred this year."

"Maybe," Pierre answered, eyes peeled for Irene. "Honouring Henri and Louis has swelled the numbers." His comment deflated Guzco.

En route to the square, Lafont stopped outside each house to collect the gifts left on doorsteps. He blessed each householder for their generosity then placed each gift in a rickety cart pushed by an old man wearing his threadbare Sunday best suit.

Within the hour, the procession reached the tent. Lafont stood beside the fire and beckoned Jean Baptiste, resplendent in his Philistine get-up, towards him. Jean Baptiste approached keeping the goats on a tight leash. Lafont placed his hand on the goats' heads and muttered a short, tentative blessing. The buck reared up, forcing Lafont to step back and John Baptiste to further tighten his grip on the leash. Wide-eyed and fearful, Lafont fished in his cassock pocket and pulled out the box of matches he used to light his morning and evening cigarettes. He struck a match and lit the thurible and then struck another to light the fire's kindling, saying, "Evil destroyed our church. The men who carried that evil remain unforgiven. Evil again struck with the murders of, Henri Velous and Louis Foucault, our very own valley Chevaliers." To murmurs of agreement, Lafont continued, "We ask the Angel to shelter those poor souls who perished here."

He swung the thurible over the cauldron. The heady aroma of incense mingled with the rank stew to create a thick stench. Within minutes, Matriarch Lerond announced the stew was ready to serve. She filled a bowl with the lukewarm slop then handed it to Lafont. He swallowed a mouthful and gagged. Through gritted teeth he said, "I bid everyone to share in the bounty of Badur."

Those brave enough waited in line to be served by the Matriarch and Lydia. Few could keep their first mouthful down, prompting children to promise their parents they'd behave themselves for the rest of the year if they were spared a portion. The leftovers were poured into two buckets for the goats, who both turned their noses up.

CHAPTER THIRTY-NINE
Badur, August 1951

A few pilgrims peeled away but most ambled towards the tent. Despite being aired for two days, it still retained its odour of sweat and sorrow, made all the more maudlin by the tired yellow light thrown out by the aged field lamps ringing the perimeter.

The cushioned seats, set out in the first two rows, were reserved for the Organising Committee and their spouses. Two were reserved for the nuns of Sacre Coeur. But as Sister Francine didn't hold with public displays, these seats remained empty. Two more were held in reserve for visiting dignitaries, although none had visited since eighteen fifty-three. That year the itinerant singer Florio Manastalgi, who had lied about his Badurian ancestry, was engaged to sing for a stipend of good wishes and a shoulder of pork.

But his tone-deaf, off-key aria come folk lament was so poor, the year's visiting dignitaries from Marseille fell into a state of near catatonia, mothers covered children's ears while the pious clutched rosary beads, besieging the Angel to put an end to his shrieking. Manastalgi received only half-hearted good wishes in payment, as villagers feared he had driven the Angel away. Ever since, singing and humming was frowned upon in the valley with whistling tolerated but not on religious holidays.

A newly fashioned dispute over seating entitlement for Organising Committee members' children had dogged this year's arrangements. Guzco had suggested allocating a cushioned seat to offspring under the age of eight as this was the age at which children could still be expected to require feeding, coddling or being scolded for excessive fidgeting. As no committee member had a child under eight, seating arrangements remained unchanged and all parties could claim victory.

The lower ranked families took up their usual spots. Waspish words targeted Massimo and Greta for sitting in the Lerond family seats, seven rows from the front.

"I think we should move," Massimo said to Greta, sensing the Matriarch Lerond's ire. As he and Greta stood, two of the uppity younger Leronds took their place, with, in Greta's opinion, undue haste. She and Massimo found two empty seats close to the entrance, where Guzco and Pierre stood beside a lugubrious gendarme, sent up from Nice to keep an eye on things.

"What happens now?" asked the gendarme.

"The pageant," replied Pierre.

"Is it any good?"

"Depends on what you mean by good."

"In that case, I'll go for a stroll. Keep an eye on things."

The blather of instrument tuning, coughs, creaking chairs and curious children came to an end as the Organising Secretary climbed onstage and stared out over the seventy or so strong audience. He cleared his throat and was about to speak when the communist committee members arrived to claim their cushioned seat.

Miffed by these baiting shenanigans, the Secretary cleared his throat once more and uttered, "Welcome. The tales you shall witness this evening are lost in the mists of time and shrouded in layers of history. We are proud to honour our Angel and pray that he continues to guard us. It has been agreed that tonight's performances are dedicated to the memory of, Henri Velous and Louis Foucault, our Chevaliers of the valley. As ever the Angel watches over them. Please enjoy the acts but don't worry if you do not. None of them last very long."

"Where was the Angel when we needed him?" The Secretary hadn't heard Marianne Velous' stern, clipped voice since Henri's death. No one had come to that.

Standing, she raised an accusatory finger towards Lafont. "The Germans murdered my son on the day we're supposed to celebrate the Angel's arrival. Yet, where was he that night?" Lafont looked flummoxed that the Angel of Badur's legend was being questioned. By a woman to boot. Her tone hostile yet certain, Marianne continued, "For centuries we were told to honour the Angel. Yet the truth is there is nothing worth honouring. Lies. That's all it is. All it ever was." Sweeping her hand across the entire Organising Committee, she continued, "Some of you made an accommodation with the Germans during the occupation. But today you sit among us, holier than thou, puffed up with self-importance, busy swearing fealty to our very own false idol."

Guzco was taken aback that Marianne's accusations had caused so much discomfort, even amongst dyed in the wool communists. Velous reached out for Marianne, but she waved him away. She faced Guzco and asked, "Doctor Chamonix, where were you when my Henri was murdered?"

"In the valley, Marianne. Been watching birds. Hawks, falcons and the like." Guzco realised his answer sounded thin, verging on pathetic. He caught Jean Velous' eye whose perennial self-satisfaction melted away as events spiralled beyond his control.

"Really, Doctor? The Nazis scour the valley for Jews, yet leave you free to watch your precious birds?"

"It's the truth."

"You were seen guiding the Germans through the forest that night." Gasps went up at the revelation. Velous squirmed as Marianne made his venomous lies to her public.

Heart racing, and broken, Guzco asked, "By who?"

"Irene Fontaine."

"Did she tell you that?"

"Who told me isn't important but it explains why Irene upped and left so soon afterwards."

"And why would that be?"

"To stop you betraying her to the Germans, just as you'd betrayed poor Louis Focault and my darling son."

Guzco caught the look of horror yet intrigue on Lydia's face. The Plague years had taught him that once people chose to believe something, however far-fetched, little can be done to change minds. Many pilgrims had morphed from bored, semi-detached attendees to the descendants of the flint-hearted, furtive men whose cold suspicion had once barred him from Badur.

Massandar's had a hand in this. The Nazi round-ups, Henri's murder, the Italian couple turning up, Velous poisonous words infecting Marianne. Massandar's setting traps. And if he can demolish the enduring, if fading, appeal of the Angel of Badur so much the better. He's close.

Only by telling the truth; about how he had slain, lied and lived as a coward in equal measure over the centuries could he cut Massandar adrift. He'd hidden in plain sight for long enough. His shoulders throbbed as the collected souls begged him to keep quiet. He couldn't. It was time to speak out. A hand rested on his shoulder. Closing his eyes, Guzco turned, not sure if he'd see Massandar's bland smile or Azekiel's scowl.

Instead, Pierre said, "You're wrong, Marianne. The night Henri was murdered, the Doctor guided seven Jews through the valley to Sacre Coeur. He's a hero, not a collaborator."

"Who told you this?" Marianne asked.

"Sister Francine when I visited the convent looking for Irene. She swore me to secrecy but now I can't allow a good man to be wrongly accused. Without truth where will this stop? Anyone can accuse anyone of anything and before we know it, all that's left is hatred. If the legend of the Angel tells us anything it's that we must look out for one another."

Her certainty and anger dented, Marianne glanced at Velous then said, "I know what I believe, Pierre. And what about Irene?"

"She was many things but not a liar." Pierre fought his heartache and shame to continue, "Please, Marianne, don't betray your grief with hatred. Stay and celebrate Henri's life with us."

"I'm sorry, Pierre." Marianne made her way out with her stumbling knave of a husband in pursuit. She didn't look back. The silence following her rang out.

CHAPTER FORTY
Badur, August 1951

With the audience still reeling from Marianne's outburst, two teenage girls, wearing pale blue dresses and whitewashed pumps, took to the stage. The shorter one nudged the taller one who cleared her throat and said, "People of Badur. An Angel came to us in our time of need and remained to protect us. The Angel is no hero but holds the true values of life dear. To allay fear, to never walk by, to give comfort to the sick and dying. We remain loyal to him and beseech him to remain loyal towards us."

Matriarch Lerond applauded her granddaughters and egged the other Leronds to join in as the clearly relieved girls departed.

The Organising Secretary returned holding a silver tipped staff, with which he tamped the boards, cleared his throat and set about reciting a soliloquy of inordinate length about the Crusades. Bored youngsters fidgeted as he droned on while many adults wore lost, faraway looks. Several even upped and left, shaking their heads as they walked past Guzco and Pierre.

To everyone's relief, the soliloquy ended, allowing the Secretary to milk the spare applause while two men, both members of the tent party, dragged a small wooden boat onstage. Both of them then shuffled two plywood waves, each topped with cotton wool, back and forth across the stage to create an illusory ocean. The Lerond girls now in green tunics, maroon leggings and black wigs returned to take up their places in the boat. The shorter one cast a small net overboard, theatrically wiped her brow, and landed the still empty net, saying, "Turn for home, brother. Mother sea has granted us another bountiful harvest." Both heaved on the oars, exaggerating the extent of their backbreaking labours. Offstage came a roar. The waves moved with greater vigour. "Whale! Whale!" The girls shouted. A bow-legged, stocky man wedged inside Jean Baptiste's model whale, staggered towards the boat. The whale's jaw slackened as it loomed over the girls who shouted in unison, "We are to die!"

Fluke raised, the whale tottered off stage. A moment later, a muffled yelp filled the tent. The sisters dragged the boat off stage in confused silence.

Lydia's husband strode manfully onstage. He wore hand knitted chainmail tunic, baggy and leggings with balsa wood wings, one a touch wonky, strapped to his back. A wobbly halo, made from a coat hanger, hovered over his head.

Cecile Jonquet's husband followed. Small, curved horns were glued to his forehead which along with his face, was slathered in red face paint. Instead of his usual devil's costume, this year he wore a hand stitched, navy blue, double vented, four button, three piece suit. The jacket draped perfectly from the shoulders while the trousers were also a perfect fit with their hems resting flush on his highly polished black Oxfords. Any tailor based in Paris's eighth Arrondissement would struggle to match such quality. Why Cecile had decided to dress her husband in this way for this year, she couldn't say. But she was glad she did.

"Who are you to bar my journey to Genoa?" roared the Devil.

"I'm an Angel, here to do the Lord's bidding. You will go no further."

"It is for Genoa I am bound, to carry the dead to the underworld."

"These souls are under my protection."

"A lowly Angel to stop me, Lucifer?" He drew out the short wooden sword tucked into his belt.

"The light shall always outshine the dark," replied the Angel, drawing his sword.

The Devil lunged, the Angel parried and then attacked. More near arthritic thrusts and counter thrusts ensued. No blows were landed yet both the Devil and the Angel were soon blowing hard, their supernatural powers hampered by their ample girths.

The combat captivated the children but those adults who had watched this doggerel for years looked on in quiet dismay, even if the Devil looked sharp in his suit. To everyone's relief, the Devil fell. Raising a hand towards the Angel, he rasped, "Make good time, Angel. I shall return. Evil stalks you and those you protect. Mark this: I shall find you and take my revenge."

He gave out a blood-curdling scream, startling the distracted and drowsy.

The breathless, phlegmy Angel looked out over the audience. "The Devil has been defeated. I leave Lavagna now for yonder mountains and the holy village of Badur to serve my Lord God. Honour the Angel, people of Badur."

A deep voice boomed, "The Philistines gathered their armies. King Saul and the men of Israel gathered to fight them. The Philistines stood on a mountain on the one side, and Israelites stood on a mountain on the other side: and there was a valley between them. And there went out a champion of the camp of the Philistines, named Goliath, whose height was six cubits and a span. He wore a helmet of brass and dressed in a coat of mail, carried a great spear and shield."

Children gasped as Jean Baptiste, wearing his Goliath costume, struck his much-practiced dastardly pose then bellowed, "Choose amongst you a man to fight me. If he be able to kill me, then we will be your slaves but if I prevail then you Israelites shall be our slaves!"

The narrator continued, "When King Saul and all Israel heard those words, they were dismayed, and greatly afraid."

The Secretary's insubstantial thirty-year old son, playing David, appeared onstage. Dismissed as a nancy-boy by some villagers, he wore a gold tinted satin tunic, gold sandals and cotton headband dyed gold by Cecile. In his right hand, he held a sling. Even on tip toe, he barely reached Jean Baptiste's chest. Undeterred, he shouted in a jarring tone, "Why should this uncircumcised Philistine, defy the armies of God?" Mention of circumcision drew giggles. Lafont shifted in his seat whilst the scandalized Matriarch Lerond looked daggers at the Secretary.

"It is I, David, who stands before Goliath. I was tending my flock when a lion and a bear took lambs. I slew them both. I will fight this uncircumcised Philistine."

Jean Baptiste pointed at the sling then guffawed with hammy delight, "You think you can fight me with that!"

David replied, "You approach me with a sword, spear, and shield: but I come in the name of the Lord whom you have defied. I will smite you." He raised the sling above his head then slung an imaginary stone. Jean Baptiste clutched his head and struck a final dastardly face. He fell heavily, causing the stage to shake and the lights to flicker. David, pleased with himself, stood over Goliath in triumph. His parents, still shamefaced over the filthy wordplay, gave their boy a half-hearted thumbs up in appreciation of his efforts.

"The Philistines fled when they saw their champion dead. David had slain him," concluded the narrator, leaving most of the audience to ponder why they wasted their time on such drivel, year after year.

And then they realized why when two more of the tent party, looking uncomfortable in their sixteenth-century era britches, tunics and clogs stood stage left. One struck up a simple melody on an ancient mandolin. The other lifted a small cylindrical drum onto his hip. The goatskin drumhead glistened. First he tapped the rim with his thumb, then began a slow, pulsing rhythm that reached far back into Badur's history.

Outside a soft twilight fell as inside the tent, anticipation grew.

Chloe Jonquet took to the stage. She was barefoot and wore a plain green loose fitting skirt and a white blouse bearing yellow and blue piped seams. Her long black hair hung loose.

She didn't move, preferring to allow the sparse melody to envelop the audience. The notes brushed lightly against people's hearts, stirring a sweet sadness or distant memory they couldn't quite recall. The rhythms built into a base, primal tune encouraging Chloe to move with a liquid, effortless elegance, allowing young and old alike to see a personal beauty and hear a song dear to *them* be it a symphony, a jig, a reel, a nursery rhyme, or ballad.

Allowed to glide inside their once half-forgotten memories, some recalled the smile of a lover, the sounds of their childhood, laughing with friends or forgot their disappointments. Others however, suffered pangs of regret over misdeeds, a lost love, the restless anger inside them or wondered why hope, in all its glory had abandoned them.

Even the gendarme experienced a twinge of happiness that had evaded him for years and distracted him from the two stick-thin, raggedy children mimicking Chloe's steps in the church doorway.

Greta reached for Massimo's hand but he shied away from her.

Guzco closed his eyes and stepped from the warm sea onto Lavagna's black sands where Luisa and Bia waited to greet him. Cradling their smiles, he held Luisa and said, "I've missed you, my love."

Wiping the tears from her eyes, she whispered, "I love you." Ignoring Massandar's taunts, he picked Bia up, kissed her cheek then said, "You've got big."

"I've made you something, Papa." Bia handed him a carving of a fish. It was plain, unadorned, not that Guzco cared. "It's beautiful," he said, "almost as beautiful as my daughter." She giggled and wrapped her arms around his neck, saying, "Stay with us."

Before Guzco could answer, Luisa whispered urgently, "Philomandra needs you, Guzco."

"I want to stay here, with you."

"Go to her. Then return to us. Life."

Spellbound, Greta's thoughts became enmeshed within the dance. The steps lacked precision but they conveyed the bliss of a moment's happiness. An inexplicable perfection, like breathing in a glistening, otherworldly air that spoke to something eternal within her. She glimpsed Luca, as the young boy berating Mussolini in the portico, as the defeated coxswain and as the young buck scrapping with the Balilla. She was eight again, beachcombing in Lavagna wearing her wellingtons and overcoat, the one with the shiny buttons. Soaking up these warm, near illicit memories, she failed to notice Massimo stepping outside.

The final notes faded. Chloe now still, her rapture undimmed. Silence shrouded the tent but welcome like a fine drizzle on a heat drenched summer's day. At first the applause was sparse, fitful even, but as the audience were drawn back to the present, a wave of adulation washed over the exhausted Chloe. The acclamation grew, encores demanded. But that was that. The dance was finished, dreams and fears extinguished. Chloe left to cheers, her proud parents' the longest and loudest.

The Secretary cleared his throat and began to speak but the clatter and crush of people making for the exit meant his closing comments, long agonised over, were ignored with only his wife and son staying on to listen. Beside them, Lafont nodded sympathetically to the Matriarch Lerond's lengthy, whispered tirade against the continuing enthusiastic references to circumcision.

In the square, fathers carried sleepy toddlers home. Some mothers and daughters, arm in arm, giggled about the wheezing Devil, Goliath's dastardly stare and wondered out loud why Chloe's dance had lifted their spirits. Other mothers and daughters kept quiet, wrapped up in life's disappointments.

Greta found Massimo looking over the river from the bridge. He seemed lost, haunted. "I saw them," he muttered.

"Who?"

"The Jews." He paused, struggling to make sense of his vision. "They surrounded the dancer. Each and every one of them." He shook his head. "It was Colonel Massandar's idea."

"What was?"

"To go after them. In forty-three. He was one for grand gestures, to show the Germans we could run Genoa without them sticking their beaks in. What could be easier than picking up a few Jews and packing them off to God knows where. I knew most of those arrested, some I counted as friends. If we arrived at a house and discovered they had fled, I'd want to leave it there, but not Massandar. He'd follow the SS into the mountains, as if it were a hunt or some such. Said he saw it as his patriotic duty."

"Why didn't you speak out?"

"Massandar wasn't a man to cross. Underneath his bluster and charm lay a black heart. Besides, nobody would have listened and I'd have got into trouble for speaking out. You remember how things were back then."

"But those poor people were Italian. Like you and me. You sent innocent men, women and children to their deaths."

He reached for her hand but it was her turn to pull away. "Why weren't you punished?"

"After the war, communism was deemed the greater threat. My time with

OVRA made me useful to the new government. The bank's governor was an old friend of my father's. He pulled a few strings. Believe me, Greta, I've been haunted by these memories, of seeing Jews being led away or hunted. I wouldn't wish my suffering on anyone."

"We all hurry to forget yet there's no excuse for what you did."

"I know. I thought I'd never be released from this torment. But the day we met in the Negri changed everything." He found the courage to look at her. "Meeting you gave me the chance to atone and begin to live an honourable, good life, free from Massandar's curse. I should have told you. Honestly, I meant to, but when you returned from Palermo and agreed to marry me, I took it as a sign that I had a chance of forgiveness. Please, Greta, find it in your heart to forgive me. Let's not think of the past but our future together."

Unsure whether to feel revulsion or pity for this stranger before her, Greta looked out over the river, her euphoria from watching Chloe dance now drained.

"Can you forgive me?" he asked.

"Let's head back," she answered, fearing their marriage had already run its course. She'd been a fool to allow her life to be shaped by another man's failings. First Luca and now Massimo. She would never accede to any man, ever again.

At the turning for the cottage and with the light fading Massimo took her hand and pointed skywards to a murmuration. Hours earlier, she would have been reduced to silence, probably tears, by such a tumultuous display of winnowing, shapeless splendour. But not now. Now the murmuration carried a hint of threat. For all its beauty, passion and intrigue, she was mistaken to insist on visiting Badur. Massimo's idea of a week in Ventimiglia would have been the wiser choice. His past would have remained hidden and she could have continued to live in acquiescent ignorance. That was impossible now.

Reaching the farmhouse, Massimo stopped to enquire about Marianne. Greta walked on. Another sketch was pinned to the cottage door, this one of Massimo in his Blackshirt uniform talking to a man Greta couldn't place. But beneath his matter-of-fact banality and forced smile, lay a pitiless cruelty.

She folded the sketch in half. Massimo didn't need to see it.

CHAPTER FORTY-ONE
Badur, August 1951

Guzco crossed the bridge, left the road and entered the woods. Consumed with thoughts about Luisa, he followed a familiar route until an hour, maybe two, later, he stood in the gathering gloom, beside Spinoza's grave, unsure what had brought him here.

"Help me, Guzco. Please," Philomandra pleaded.

Where are you?

She didn't answer.

"Best be quick, Domar." Massandar sounded confident.

Guzco started to run, with no notion of where to, or, for how long. Despite having tramped the valley for centuries, it now stretched before him as a foreign, petrified haze. Branches whipped his face. Roots, sets and burrows upended him. The odd owl, out on the hunt, harried him. The old carvings came thick and fast, some familiar, others long forgotten. At first they were a comfort, filling Guzco with confidence; this was *his* valley, *his* forest. The land *would* give up Philomandra.

Dawn broke blood red. Exhausted, he stopped to rest. The dawn chorus seemed to mock. His shoulders slumped, his thin courage struggled to stem doubt. He stood beside Spinoza's grave.

"Please, Guzco," Philomandra said. This time Massandar said nothing.

He set off once more, routes decided on whims and fanciful notions. Hours later he found himself back at Spinoza's grave. Again Philomandra pleaded and again Guzco set off, this time with a plan. *Run straight and true, don't deviate. Keep going. I'll find her Luisa. I promise.*

He passed through a glade of chestnut and beech trees and reached a shallow river. He stopped to drink. The water was cold, redemptive. Wiping his mouth he looked across the river towards a steep, wooded ridge, dappled by shadow. If memory served, the bothy was close.

Get to the top and get my bearings.

He stepped into the water. Birds erupted from the sentinel trees guarding the riverbank. Within two paces, the river swelled into a raging cascade and swept him away. Dragged under, he clawed his way to the surface, fighting for breath in the foaming deluge, hopes of rescuing Philomandra replaced by tumbling confusion. As he went under again, all hope lost, he grabbed at a large rock breaching the water. It slipped from his grasp, as did the next two but he managed to cling to the fourth boulder. He drew breath, safe, if half drowned. The riverbank was a hop and jump onto two more rocks away. Like a sodden Rove buck, he leapt and wobbled his way to dry land. Carvings of a whale, fish and falcon hung from three beech trees. Louis Foucault's place was two miles away as the crow flies. After all his efforts, he was less than an hour from Badur.

He heard a straining engine. The steep Cresson road must be near. He set off, shivering in the cold, murky air, scuffing up long dead leaves and needles, clinging to Chloe's steps, Luisa's smile and Bia's embrace.

"Not long now, Domar," Massandar insisted.

"Guzco, please," Philomandra whispered.

Reaching the road, Guzco looked in both directions. *Which way?* He'd no idea. Needing to rest and think, he sat on a dilapidated wall to gather himself and rest his raw, blistered feet.

From the east, another engine fractured the silence. A black Mercedes sedan's suspension bottomed on a pothole. The car's rear nearside passenger door flew open. A woman tumbled out and came to a halt in a misshapen heap. The Mercedes came to a shuddering stop. The woman struggled to her feet and cradling her left arm, staggered towards Guzco. Deep cuts and vivid, angry bruises marked her face. Her shredded blouse revealed filthy, bloody wounds to her torso. Even so, her quiet grace and splendour, beguiled Guzco.

Philomandra?

Help me Guzco. Please.

Massandar, dressed immaculately in a dark blue three piece suit, and black Oxfords, stepped from the idling, dust-covered Mercedes,. He popped an orange segment into his mouth and followed Philomandra, straightening his shirt cuffs, his shoes squeaking with each step. Arshadne and another man, cowed yet powerful, followed.

Philomandra threw off her blouse, unfurled her wings and swathed herself in them. They hung limp, forlorn, unable to extend to their full majestic height and breadth. Worse still, in her weakened state, she fell.

Arshadne and her companion sprang forward and pinned Philomandra face down. They took hold of a wing each, both beguiled by the beauty fanning out in their hands. The soft, elegant whisper of metal on leather

carried on the breeze. The centuries fell away. Arshadne's punches rained down. Massandar's wine-soured words. The mosquitos feeding frenzy. Caballero, sharp and deadly. The tearing flesh, the searing pain. Helpless.

Azekiel.

"No one is coming, Master Domar," Massandar answered, stuffing the sheath into Philomandra's mouth.

"Philomandra?" Azekiel muttered, stirring from his ledgers. "Why does Domar think of her?" Life and Death kept quiet.

"Hold her," Massandar ordered, placing his right foot between Philomandra's shoulder blades. Caballero rested in his thin fingers. Philomandra struggled to break free. The new slave struck her. In three swift incisions, skin, muscle and bone were cleaved and Massandar eased the left wing from its socket. "Blessed again," he whispered, admiring the shorn wing in his bloodied hand. Ecstasy creased his bland features. He handed the wing to Arshadne then placed his left foot between Philomandra's shoulders and butchered the right wing.

Revelling in the spasm of pleasure, he handed the wing to Arshadne, who carried them to the boot of the Mercedes.

"Enjoy the spectacle, Domar?" Massandar asked. "Wait. There's more." He nodded and his new slave raised Philomandra to her feet. Bereft, her splendour dimmed but still defiant, Philomandra raised her bloodied face to Massandar and whispered, "I shall not beg."

"Good," Massandar replied. He drove Caballero into her heart, twisting the blade for good measure. Philomandra's lost, tear-filled gaze settled on Guzco. Her legs gave way. The slave let her fall. Massandar squatted beside her and sighed. "Blood on my cuffs, see Domar?" Shaking his head, he rubbed at the stain with a crisp, white handkerchief.

"It's no good," he sighed, "It won't come out." Returning the handkerchief to his pocket, he looked at Guzco, smiled then said, "But thank you for drawing her out, Domar."

Breaking from his past, Guzco ran at Massandar but the slave picked him up and then dropped him onto the road. Massandar's cologne overwhelmed Guzco as he leaned over him. "As I told you, Angel, the hunt is all there is."

He returned to the Mercedes with his companion following. Moments later, Arshadne put the Mercedes in gear and it accelerated away, bucking over the pitted surface.

Guzco crawled to Philomandra. She was still alive but her breaths rasped and curdled.

Forgive me Philomandra.

Grew lazy. Indifferent to him.

He kissed her cheek but she had no soul to collect. Instead, another woman's features passed across her face.

Protect her when she comes.

Her hand brushed his cheek. Grasping it, Guzco fighting back the tears, said, "Don't leave me." Her eyes dulled.

Protect her when she comes.

She faded, leaving only the trace of her blood on the road.

Neither the scorching sun nor swerving, horn blaring cars could shake Guzco from his hours long stupor. Philomandra had sustained him. She offered hope.

Fucking immortality.

Kissing the ground where Philomandra had lain, he stood, stiff, sore. He looked in both directions, wondering what lay behind each horizon. He'd never know, wasn't interested to be honest. Home lay north.

Dawn, the next day, exhausted and starving, he crossed the bridge, waved to a passing driver and walked towards the square, ducking under sagging festival bunting, fluttering in the listless, heavy air.

"Been away, Doc?" Pierre asked, pouring his morning livener.

"Went up valley looking for Choughs. Lost track of time. Got into a bit of a scrape."

"Happens. Coffee?"

"Please."

"Missed a great party. The Matriarch Lerond had one too many and gave the Organising Secretary the mother of all bollockings for still allowing circumcision to be mentioned. And as for Lydia…" as Pierre continued with the gossip, Guzco sank into his usual seat, grateful to rest.

Villagers queued outside the baker's. Three boys and a girl playing football, argued over whose turn it was to go in goal. Father LaFont enjoyed his morning cigarette outside the church. A man with a parcel tucked under his arm knocked on the butcher's door hoping they'd open up early for him. Fat chance. The greengrocer polished each apple and then carefully, to some eyes over zealously, rearranged the artichokes.

It was good to be home. To the monotony of everyday life.

A dust-covered black Mercedes pulled up. The nearside rear window rolled down. Massandar leaned out. "You look tired, Domar, no surprise there I suppose. Forgot to thank you for your help. Couldn't have done it without you. And when Azekiel sends another for you, I'll be waiting." He wound the window up and sat back. Arshadne put the Mercedes into gear. The children jumped clear as the car turned then headed towards the bridge.

"Who was that?" Pierre asked, setting Guzco's coffee down in front of him.

"Tourists, after directions."

Finishing his coffee, he reached in his pockets for money to pay and drew out Bia's carving.

Perhaps there are some things worth living for.

"Why does this foolish fisherman causes me so much difficulty?" Azekiel asked. "Centuries ago, I ordered Domar's banishment. Who placed Philomandra near him?"

"I did," Life replied. The whip grazed her forehead.

Azekiel reeled in the sulphur-tipped thongs. "If the old ways were to hand I would not stop until your back is shorn of flesh."

"I acted in good conscience, Lord Azekiel. I thought it was wrong to abandon, Domar."

"Lord Azekiel," Death interrupted. "You are right to be enraged by the deceptions carried out, but any further punishment for Domar should be deferred until he returns. His banishment no longer serves a purpose. To prolong it further only reeks of spite."

"I am beholden to no one."

"But justice, or at the very least, the illusion of justice, remains one of your greatest powers. Retribution is important but hope of redemption equally so."

"What do you suggest? I despatch a phalanx to retrieve, Domar?"

"There is someone."

"Doesn't he remain impetuous?"

"That has been drained."

"His broken heart mended?"

"Sufficiently."

Azekiel gripped the whip's handle. Witnessing Massandar's barbarism had made him envious but the lickspittle was right. "Very well," he said. "We will send him to retrieve, Domar. But, at a time of my choosing."

CHAPTER FORTY-TWO
Lavagna, August 1952

Father Biavati scratched his nose, peered over his reading glasses then said, "And finally we wish the Lavagna crew success in today's Regatta." As the crew gathered in front of Santa Stefano's altar for the blessing, Greta's father whispered, "We'll need more than divine intervention this year. Rapallo have recruited an American national champion while Chiavari have Czech and Hungarian mercenaries. How's that fair?" Despite Mama shushing him, he carried on chuntering under his breath.

Greta watched the crew descend Santa Stefano's steps surrounded by ever hopeful supporters. The drummers began to play and Lavagna's finest set off for the harbour with the crowd's chants bouncing off the narrow streets in a cacophonous racket.

"We'll visit Alesandro," Mama insisted, while lifting her veil. Disappointed not to be part of the procession, Greta gripped Massimo's arm, held her breath and stared at the ground, as they followed her parents and Oona into the cemetery. Startled by an exploding firecracker, she glanced up at a sorrowful Angel. Without thinking, she looked for the ghosts of dead children.

"Everything alright?" Massimo whispered.

"Fine," she replied, annoyed for still being in thrall to Alesandro's childhood nonsense. Even so, she lowered her eyes and took another deep breath, desperate for the ordeal to end. As her parents recited a decade of the Rosary for Alesandro's soul, she grew lightheaded, excused herself and sought shelter in the Portico.

Minutes later Mama, her arm looped through Massimo's, found Greta sitting in the shade. "Are you unwell, Greta?" she asked wearing a knowing, expectant look which Greta had come to dread, especially when it became tinged with disappointment after she didn't announce she was expecting. If that wasn't bad enough, Massimo grew increasingly fretful over the delay in her conceiving. After all, they made love every night and he had brought home a welter of manuals and leaflets on how to increase the chance of conception by adding spinach, eggs and grape juice to their diet. She feigned interest while thinking how ridiculous these old wives' tales were. Besides, the Dutch caps ordered from the United States were proving effective.

The few days spent in Badur had changed her. Massimo's revelations left her feeling trapped inside a marriage with a festering hypocrisy at its heart. It wouldn't be fair to raise a child with a man whose past made him untrustworthy and impossible to know. To the outside world she remained a devoted wife, supportive of Massimo's ambition yet accepting his crimes gnawed at her self-worth, all the more so while teaching her less than interested pupils in the synagogue's hall.

Luca's mother bumped into them outside the apartment's entrance. Still dressed head to toe in black, she seemed uneasy, the once feisty, indomitable spirit that had sustained her and Luca, quenched. Raising a thin smile she embraced Greta. "How is married life suiting you, Greta?" she asked.

"I couldn't be happier, Signora Meazza," Greta replied, drawing in her rose water scent.

"I'm delighted to hear it."

Shaking Massimo's hand, she said, "A pleasure to meet you again, Signor Ferrari. How are things in Genoa?"

"Very good thank you, Signora."

"Here for the Regatta?"

"Yes," Greta replied, thinking back to Luca's efforts to claim the pennant for Lavagna in thirty-eight.

"Don't know why we bother," Papa mithered.

Trudging up the stairs, her mother said, "The poor woman must miss her husband and Luca, although she never mentions them."

"Maybe it's still too raw for her, Mama."

"Perhaps, but nonetheless it's heartbreaking to see her so reduced. They were dark days under Mussolini." Greta sensed Massimo tense. Not that it came as a shock. Despite expressing remorse for his role back then, his fascist connections had landed him the plum job with the Banco di Dogali and propelled him up the bank's hierarchy to head up property loans. A world of favours sought and favours repaid, one hand washing the other.

After a lunch of fish, salad and pasta, served on Sunday-best crockery, Greta looked out to sea from the dining room. The drummers still played. "At least the drummers sound confident this year, Papa."

"That's as good as it'll get," he replied, mopping up his sauce with bread.

"You never know. This year might be our year," Mama proclaimed with an air of optimism. "Think how happy you will be seeing our lads claim the pennant."

"They've about as much chance as Genoa winning the Scudetto."

"That bad, eh?" Massimo said. Papa failed to see the funny side.

Reaching the thronged harbour, Greta breathed in the salt-soaked air. Moored boats bobbed in oil-stained water. Her uncle greeted her with a bear hug. "You look well my dear," he said, the smell of cigarettes on his breath. Wiping his forehead with a grubby handkerchief, he turned to her father and muttered, "Seen the Hungarian fella yet? He'd give Hercules a run for his money."

Leaving Greta's father and uncle to bemoan Lavagna's chances, Massimo excused himself and wandered over to a group of men. Greta, Oona and their mother paid their respects to the Widow Rigazzi sitting under a parasol.

"Expecting yet Greta?" she asked.

"Not yet, Aunt."

"Get on with it, otherwise he'll start to wander. All men are the same when it comes to their urge to impregnate." Unfurling the parasol and jabbing it towards Oona, the Widow asked Mama, "You married this one off yet?"

"I'm engaged, Aunt," Oona interrupted.

"Pleased to hear it. Being the plain one, I always thought you'd struggle to land a husband." Before Oona could answer, she barked, "And why haven't I been introduced?"

"He works in Turin."

"That's no excuse my girl. I want to run my eye over him. Make sure he's worthy of you. I know a thing or two about men's carnality."

"Next time he visits, I'll make sure Oona brings him to meet you," replied Mama, embarrassed by her aunt's brazenness. Furling her parasol, the Widow sighed, "Better make it soon. My palpitations are getting worse. Now, help me into to the shade." Mama helped her towards a bench in a shaded area. An old man smiled a toothless smile and shuffled along to accommodate her.

"Always nice to see her," Oona said to Greta.

"She means no harm. At least she's honest."

"Although her honesty can be wearing." Waving the Widow goodbye, Greta and Oona stepped onto the beach. Cheers went up as the Regatta flotilla left the harbour walls and plied towards the starting buoy, a mile across the bay. The race announcer babbled ten to the dozen from the loudspeakers stretching along the shore. "He'll drive me mad," Oona announced. "Let's find somewhere quieter."

Greta spotted Massimo among some of Alesandro's old Balilla comrades. He looked uncomfortable, refusing the offer of wine and beer nor singing the raucous, bludgeoning songs. One of the men, worse for wear, placed an arm around Massimo's shoulder and sang:

Our law is the slavery of love,
Our motto is freedom and duty,
We, the Blackshirts will avenge,
The heroes that died to free you.

His comrades joined in with the fascist marching song, ignoring the unease spreading among the spectators. "Idiots," muttered Oona. "They're like that most weekends. Sitting on the harbour wall, drinking, cursing, shaming Alesandro's memory. Surprised Massimo wants to have anything to do with them."

"Loyalty is one of Massimo's best qualities. It's served him well," Greta replied.

The southern headland reared above them and Greta spotted the old tree she and Luca had climbed all those years ago, and where they had promised each other they would go in search of the Angel of Badur. At least she had kept her side of the bargain. To distract herself, she said, "Why didn't you tell me you and Frederico were engaged?"

"We're not. But he'll get the message. Eventually."

"Do you love him?"

"Yes. At least I think I do. He's no Victor Mature but he's a good man. Kind, sincere. And he knows what to do in the sack." She giggled as Greta affected a look of mock outrage. Removing windblown hairs from her face, Oona then said, "We don't keep secrets from each other. Don't think any marriage can last if there are secrets."

Greta blushed, her embarrassment saved by the soaring maroon fired

from the Race Umpire's boat. Cheers broke out the as the goiter boats set off through the choppy waters for the first marker. "Come on Lavagna!" Greta and Oona shouted in unison.

Within five strokes Lavagna were already trailing. A young girl, perched on her father's shoulders, watched the race through binoculars, recounting the growing distance between Lavagna and the other boats. "Perhaps it's Father Biavati's blessing," Oona whispered. "They should ask the Angel to come ashore again."

"Perhaps," Greta replied, shielding her eyes from the glaring water. "Papa will be fuming. We'll never hear the end of this."

"Especially as he had high hopes for Biavati to ascend to the Papacy."

The Rapallo boat was cut adrift by Zoagli and Chiavari who rounded the second buoy neck and neck. The homeward leg was nip and tuck, no quarter asked none given, the supporters' shouts drowning out the tannoy. The boats reached the shore with nothing between them. Both coxswains leapt onto the beach and sprinted towards the masthead topped with the fluttering, near sacred pennant.

"Chiavari by a whisker," shouted binocular girl as Chiavari's coxswain reached the masthead two paces ahead of his rival. He shinned up the pole, grasped the pennant, and then dropped to earth, his arms aloft in triumph. "Chiavari wins!" shouted binocular girl.

Ignoring the announcer's blather, Greta and Oona retraced their steps to the harbour where Chiavari supporters celebrated victory with songs and taunts for rival supporters.

The mood soured as Massimo's comrades charged the celebrating Chiavari fans. A bottle was launched and punches thrown. Two whistle-happy Carabinieri tried to break up the fight but as more supporters piled into the fracas, they retreated.

The Lavagna boat reached the shore to little fanfare. The shattered crew slumped over their oars. The coxswain tried to lift flagging spirits. His crewmates ignored him.

Greta spotted Massimo in the melee, his hands aloft as if surrendering. A fist caught him flush on the nose. "Massimo!" she shouted. Spotting her, Massimo, his nose bloodied, threaded a path through the scrum. But within two paces, a Lavagna supporter caught him flush on the mouth with a right hander. His attacker spat on him then shouted, "That's for packing Luca

Meazza off to Russia, you OVRA bastard."

Wiping the blood from his mouth, Massimo looked at Greta.

"Quickly, Greta," Oona said, grabbing Greta's hand and pushing a drunk aside. "We need to go."

"I can explain," Massimo shouted after them. But she didn't want him to. There was nothing left to say.

CHAPTER FORTY-THREE
Nice Bus Station, France, August 1952

Boarding the green and cream liveried Isobloc bus, Greta found an empty seat halfway down the aisle. She looked at her watch. Five minutes before departure. Shouts went up for buses to Marseille, Paris and Milan. Her heart jumped when an announcement was made for the Genoa bus. Again she studied the terminus building worried Massimo might appear. She hadn't left him a note, nor her parents, or Oona, as he was bound to ask them if they knew anything. When the dust settled after a few weeks she'd write to let them know she was safe and not to worry.

On the train home last night, Massimo had tried to explain but her revulsion towards him only deepened. The deportation of Genoa's Jews she'd learned to accommodate, as that was an abstract. But to arrange Luca's conscription after the fight on the apartment stairwell years before couldn't be ignored. Massimo had begged for forgiveness. She'd played along but had already made up her mind. Her husband had the man she loved, killed. Nothing would undo that fact. She would accede no more, it was time to start again. Alone.

The bus driver, heavyset and unshaven, sat in his seat, tilted his cap and rattled through the towns and villages where the bus would be stopping. Ever cautious, Greta only relaxed when she heard, "Badur."

In the mountains, the bus struggled up single-track roads, receiving the driver's encouragement and applause broke out from the handful of passengers when it crested a summit. A middle-aged woman, who had also boarded at Nice, sat beside Greta and recounted tales of illness, family death, de Gaulle's failings, the shortage of cheese and her allergy to dogs. After hours of listening to these woes, Greta was relieved to hear the bus driver holler, "Badur next stop!"

Pierre watched the bus pull in. Again no sign of Irene. Disappointing, but no surprise. The sight of Greta lugging two suitcases towards him was a shock though. Walking out to meet her, he smiled and said, "This is a pleasant surprise. Coffee, Madame?"

"Please, Monsieur."

As he prepared the coffee, for once Pierre didn't look at Irene's portrait but pondered why the attractive Italian woman had returned. And for how long. From the weight of the suitcases it could be for some time. And where was her husband?

News of Greta's arrival spread. Unused to see people returning to Badur, villagers extended daily errands to watch her. Questions about her previous stay were raised and incorrect answers given.

"She's hiding a dark secret," the Matriarch Lerond told the baker's wife as they studied Greta's reflection in the bakery's front window whilst pretending to examine breadsticks. At the Matriarch's insistence, the baker's wife delivered a dozen free baguettes to the café but Pierre remained tight-lipped. Even Father Lafont, out for an early afternoon stroll, couldn't shed any light on the conundrum.

Guzco, on his way to examine a patient's wart outbreak, shared everyone's surprise to see Greta. Philomandra's death reared. Fearing Massandar's return, he tipped his hat, cast an artful eye over Greta then said to her, "A pleasure to see you again, Madame."

"Likewise, Doctor. Would you care to join me?"

"I have a patient to visit. Perhaps tomorrow. How is your husband?"

"He died, late last year."

"My condolences, he struck me as a thoughtful, decent man."

"He was," she lied again.

"How long are you staying?"

"Just a few days."

"Until tomorrow then."

For the rest of the day, Greta nursed her coffee, nodding to passers-by and enjoying the stillness of village life but changing seats twice to avoid the sun. With darkness falling, Pierre asked, "Madame. Is everything alright?"

Startled, she fished in her purse for a few coins. "Sorry Monsieur. I lost track of time."

"Don't we all sometimes."

Handing Pierre payment, she asked, "Monsieur, do you know of somewhere in the village where I could possibly stay for a few nights?"

He had a spare room. But that seemed indelicate. Velous was doing up Louis Foucault's old place, hooking it up to the grid and was even having a swimming pool, of all things, dug out. He had an idea. "The baker has an apartment above his shop. Been empty since his mother died. I can make enquiries if you wish."

"I do not want you to go to any trouble."

"It's no trouble at all. Are you hungry? A plain old cassoulet but nourishing and filling nonetheless."

"That would be wonderful."

CHAPTER FORTY-FOUR
Paris, September 1952

Irene stubbed out her cigarette and took her time applying fresh foundation, blusher and lipstick. She blotted the excess lipstick and tossed the tissue in the bin. After brushing then pinning her hair, she admired herself in the dressing table mirror. "You'll do," she muttered.

From the wardrobe she retrieved the green pencil dress she'd run up the week before. The seams were flat and the double stitched hems would have had the Proprietress purring. Sliding the dress over her slip, she studied herself from various angles, pleased how the tight fit flattered her figure while offering a touch of sophistication. Just as she wanted.

Propped against her perfume bottle was an envelope addressed to her in a child's neat handwriting. She retrieved the letter from its envelope and read it for the hundredth time.

"Hello Irene,

I hope this letter finds you well. I'm not supposed to write to you, Aunt has forbidden me. But I am going to anyway.

The train journey to Caen was long and boring, only made exciting after I locked myself in the toilet. Aunt couldn't find our tickets so the guard threatened to put us off at Lisieux. Aunt thought him common and a poor ambassador for Breton people, but thankfully she found the tickets and we were allowed to stay on board.

I like Caen. But not nearly as much as Paris. I miss the zoo most (but not the sloths). There isn't as much to do and Aunt won't let me go swimming, a shame since the local baths are three hundred and sixty-seven paces from our front door. I did ask Uncle to take me, but he is too busy with work and I also think he is afraid of getting a telling-off from Aunt. But at least my verrucas have cleared up.

I have settled in at my new school, the lessons are both rigorous and enjoyable for the most part, although the girl sitting next to me smells and struggles with her times table. But she has invited me to her birthday party. Aunt has promised me a new dress, although I want to wear the one you made for me.

I visited my parents' graves yesterday. It was sad, Aunt cried. I tried to but couldn't. All the same it seemed strange looking at a patch of grass with my real Maman and Papa buried beneath it. They aren't lonely though. An Angel guards them and I was reminded of all the stories you told me about Badur. I still hope we will go there one day to meet the Angel. I miss our days out together. Most of all though I miss your hugs.

I must go now. I will write soon to let you know how the birthday party went. Hopefully there will be cake. And lemonade. But not chocolate cake as I don't like that.

All my love

Helene.

PS *I still dance the steps you taught me (although quietly because my bedroom floorboards squeak).*

Irene rested the letter against the perfume bottle and lit another cigarette. She'd been a fool, convincing herself that the partial address she'd memorised from the doctor's file would lead her to her daughter. In fact, the sole link was the austere front door on the Rue de Tivoli that sported a brass plate bearing the adoption agency's name. Blinded by her despair and oblivious to its meaning, she had traipsed the area asking wary shopkeepers and café waiters if they knew of any seven-year-old girls living in the neighbourhood. None did. But one Tuesday afternoon, a young girl roughly seven years old, left an apartment building, four doors up, with a stern, prim woman scolding her for slouching. In that moment, Irene convinced herself that she'd found her daughter. Better still, a handwritten sign pinned to the apartment's main door asked for persons interested in the position of concierge to enquire within.

When her veil of yearning lifted, she realised Helene didn't look like her or Henri, while the child's bright, inquisitive mind was a reaction to her repressed upbringing. Even so, she loved Helene; a substitute love but love all the same. To see Helene whisked away broke her heart, made all the worse by the police inspector's threats to send her back to Sainte Anne if she ever went looking for Helene.

Shutting the bedroom door, she wedged the purple bath towel, a Christmas gift from Helene, beneath it. Satisfied there was no draught, she wedged rolled up newspapers into the bedroom's rickety window frame. With the time on the mantelpiece clock reading ten forty-four, she plumped a pillow taken from her bed and set it down in front of the gas fire. She sat in front of the fire, opened the gas tap then lay her head on the pillow. Her thoughts turned to Henri and the daughter who she would never know. In the hissing, bittersweet air she railed at the life denied her yet fought the tears, desperate not to smudge her make-up.

Above her, the smarmy new tenant sang along to a song on the wireless, Maurice Chevalier by the sound of things. When their paths crossed, on the stairs or if he knocked to collect a parcel, Irene often felt uneasy around him. Her throat caught on his cologne while his rich, foreign voice flattered with empty platitudes. The wireless fell silent.

Heady and a little drowsy, her bitterness waned. Henri's passion had liberated her. Better an hour with him than a lifetime of making do with Pierre. And in Paris, she had shown the world her skill with needle and thread. Now she has the gumption to decide she wants nothing more to do with it. The clock showed ten forty-four. Six minutes. She closed her eyes and danced those simple but impossible shapes that spoke of life's carnal beauty.

"Henri," she muttered, impatient to be reunited with him.

PART THREE

PART THREE

CHAPTER FORTY-FIVE
Badur, August 1969

Pleased with progress on the whale carving, Guzco stood to shake the stiffness from his right leg. Standing too quickly, he felt giddy and leant against the mantelpiece to steady himself. As the dizziness cleared, he studied his ageing features in the mirror and swept his thinning grey hair over the growing bald patch.

Some immortal you turned out to be.

Life in Badur ground on. The starlings' arrival, once an annual harbinger of hope, was now another jarring reminder that another dull, listless year had slipped by. Hemmed in by the humdrum, he longed for a touch of war, pestilence, even famine. Suffering offered excitement and adventure. Perhaps it was time to start collecting souls again.

This torpor extended to the surgery. Years of thumbing medical textbooks had made him an expert on skin conditions, just as well given Badurians' susceptibility for lesions, rashes, boils and carbuncles of varying size and irritation. Many an hour was spent lancing pustules, scraping dead skin and prescribing ointments and tinctures. Why more meaty conditions so rarely presented themselves remained a mystery. Lydia was at a loss to explain this plague of skin complaints. But she remained the source of valley gossip. Another family leaving to find work, the latest slight to the Matriarch Lerond and the ongoing intrigue of the greengrocer's links to the Nice underworld. Guzco ignored most of her blether but did note that Lydia's interest in Irene's whereabouts had waned and replaced with titbits surrounding Greta and Pierre.

He'd lost count of the times he'd been forced to listen to Pierre pining over Greta. Why she was still in Badur after all these years was a conundrum, especially given her intelligence and kind, gentle nature. Surely life beyond the valley offered a more rewarding life.

Watching the pair navigate their clumsy, drawn out courtship, Guzco realised while he was bound to death, love flourished all around him. Lydia had her husband and family as did Cecile Jonquet. Marianne and Jean Velous shared a love of sorts and Henri and Irene's love had produced a child. John Baptiste even found love in sixty-two whilst playing Goliath. Christ, even the Matriarch and Patriarch Lerond rubbed along, largely on the Matriarch's say-so.

His sole connection to love was the festival's dance and those sacred, stolen moments with Luisa and Bia. But Chloe Jonquet's dancing days were nearing their end and with nobody to replace her, he feared losing his wife and daughter for good. And where would that leave him? Probably the same lonely, unforgiving existence he had endured as the leper. To clear his mind, he decided to brave the lashing rain and go for a stroll.

The deserted square's rain-shone cobbles glinted in the recently installed lamplight. Apart from the light in Pierre's bedroom, every building was wreathed in darkness. A dog barked as he ran his hand over the war memorial.

I hope you're well Irene. And your child.

Turning up his collar, he walked on as far as the bridge and watched the fast flowing river slap against the piers. Wishing he had worn his hat, he ran a hand through his sodden hair, again disappointed to feel the bald spot. A pair of car headlights blinded him. The car pulled alongside. The passenger window wound down. *Massandar?* Heart racing, he turned for home.

"Excuse me, Monsieur, can you help?" asked a woman. Her voice was unfamiliar. Guzco stepped towards the window and breathed in the stale air of cigarettes. A sleeping toddler lay on the back seat.

"Where are you headed?" he asked.

"The Velous' farm. But we are a little lost."

The driver grunted his displeasure.

"It's not far."

As he gave directions, the driver lit a cigarette and, for a flaring second, lit up the woman's attentive, attractive face. Thanking Guzco, she wound up the window and the car reversed back across the bridge, turned and set off for the Velous' farm.

Guzco headed home. With luck he'd finish the carving before daybreak.

"Told you it wasn't far," said Helene, now wondering if it was a mistake to come to Badur. Sometimes long held promises are best forgotten. Maurice drew on his cigarette and kept quiet, as he had for much of the long drive south. Keen to lessen the tension, she said, "Another ten minutes or so."

"No thanks to you," he snapped. "Lucky you weren't piloting the Apollo or Armstrong wouldn't have found the moon, let alone set foot on it." Helene bit her tongue. Their daughter, Audrey, gripping her ragdoll, stirred and asked, "Are we there yet, Maman?"

"In a few minutes darling."

A month ago, Helene had returned to Paris for the first time since leaving for Caen. The plan was simple. Persuade Irene to come to Badur with her, Maurice and Audrey, a long shot given that Irene had never replied to any of her letters. At first Irene's silence had upset her, but as she settled in Caen and made new friends, memories of Paris faded into a soup of jolting Metro trips, a lingering fear of sloths and Irene's hugs.

She wanted Badur to be a fresh start for her and Maurice. Life together had grown staid and suffocating, tinged with the threat of violence. Irene's tales about the Angel answered a need she couldn't explain. Maybe she was clutching at straws but just this once, she wanted to take a risk. And if she was going to go to Badur, Irene must come too.

Of course, Aunt thought such a long journey irrational. After all, there's plenty of nice places to stay in Normandy and Brittany an hour or two away. It was madness to travel so far, making it perfect for Helene.

Arriving in the old apartment block's bleach scented lobby, a fleshy, breathless char leaned on her mop had asked, "Who have you come to see, Madame?"

"Irene Jonquet," replied Helene, savouring the rush of old memories. The char frowned. "I'm afraid Irene is dead." She made a sign of the cross then whispered, "Suicide. Gassed herself."

Stunned, Helene grabbed the handrail and sat on the bottom step. She fumbled in her handbag for her cigarettes. "Heard she had a broken heart," the char continued. "Long-lost lover from America by all accounts. Never got over him. Those American GIs broke many a girl's heart back then, my sister's for one."

The new concierge, a spindly, jovial woman, invited Helene into Irene's old apartment. Despite new wallpaper and furnishings, faint traces of the many happy hours Helene spent here with Irene still lingered.

The concierge produced a bundle of letters and old photographs of Helene. At the zoo cowering in front of the sloth enclosure, beaming in her cap and swimming costume at the Saint Germain baths, playing hopscotch

in the damp courtyard and puffing out her cheeks whilst playing her trumpet.

Struggling to hold back the tears, Helene read each crinkled letter and discovered the treasure trove of embarrassing, prim comments she'd written aged seven to fourteen all the while cloistered in her aunt and uncle's sealed off, socially awkward world.

Leaving Gare St Lazaire for home later that day, she was more determined than ever to honour Irene's memory by going to Badur. Woe betide Maurice if he objected.

CHAPTER FORTY-SIX
The Holiday Cottage, Badur, August 1969

The crowing cockerel woke Helene. Maurice lay asleep beside her. Daylight breached the bedroom's thin, lemon coloured curtains. Amidst the claggy odour of fresh paint, she sat up and stretched. Aside from the spongey bed, the only furniture in the bedroom was two bedside cabinets and a wardrobe. Long redundant oil lamps stood on each cabinet, their soot stains still visible on the cracked and bowed ceiling from which hung a garish pink lampshade. Above the bed, a wooden crucifix and a large copy of the Sacred Heart hung from the recently whitewashed wall.

Struggling to button her blouse, she tiptoed across the landing to look in on Audrey, still asleep, her ragdoll tucked under her arm. Wary of the creaking steps, Helene descended the stairs. The kitchen's air was sticky and musty. Dust danced in the rays piercing the venetian blinds, which the mealy-mouthed landlady had insisted should be kept closed at all times. Searching the loose-hinged cupboards, she found mouse droppings, crockery, bone-handled cutlery, old saucepans, a jar of coffee but none of the promised food. She flicked the switch and a reluctant lightbulb slowly came to life.

She opened the back door and breathed in the creosote scented breeze. She stooped to coddle a purring tabby cat rubbing against her calf. The cat then followed her along the narrow, paint spattered path towards the swimming pool, its pale blue water glistening in the weak sunshine. Reaching the pool, she sat and lowered her legs into the water and watched the ripples fan out. Fear tinged excitement gripped her. She hadn't been this close to a swimming pool since the episode in the Saint Germain baths all those years ago.

Aunt and Uncle had blamed Irene for the accident. But slipping beneath the water that day had been her doing. She'd found a place where the bullies couldn't tease her with chants of, "Helene Jassaron, your Maman's gone."

The more they taunted, the more she craved anonymity, something the pool's deep end had offered. Lying on those cold tiles watching the flabby swimmers pass overhead, she thought herself a real-life mermaid, until everything went fuzzy and that hairy brute of a lifeguard, the one had taken a shine to Irene, thumped her on the back and forced her to cough up a lungful of water.

The idea of losing Audrey to such whimsy froze her blood but imagining Aunt's disbelief, Helene stripped to her underwear and dived in. The shock of the cold forced the breath from her. She swam both the out and return length underwater. Brushing the wall, she treaded water, basking in the peace. A flock of starlings so dense they blackened the sky, passed overhead. A solitary bird of prey, exuding blissful menace, followed. She sank, and revelled in the muffled, sloshing silence, a mermaid once more. She breached the surface, gasping for breath. But full of life.

Back at the cottage, while waiting for the burbling cafetiere to brew the coffee, she sang along to a jaunty France Gall song on the transistor and was intrigued by the aged black and white photograph set on the mantelpiece of a handsome, mischievous-looking young man. Cursing after stubbing her toe on the loose flagstone the landlady had warned her about, she took Maurice's coffee up to him.

He pulled her towards him and tugged at Helene's damp bra strap, forcing her to spill the scalding coffee over him. "Shit," he cried as she wriggled from his grasp. Straightening the twisted bra strap, she said, "I'm popping into the village to buy groceries. Keep an eye on Audrey."

Maurice grunted and inspected the vivid scald marks on his chest and right arm. Watching Helene put on fresh underwear and a new blue skirt and matching blouse, he muttered, "You wearing that?"

"It's the latest fashion."

"Makes you look fat."

Stung by the barb, Helene hesitated. Maybe he was right. Perhaps she should change into her jeans and an old blouse. But no, she was twenty-five, a mother, more than able to make her own decisions. The skirt and blouse suited her complexion and figure. And besides, she was on holiday. Sod him. She smoothed the skirt, straightened the blouse and put on her canvas pumps. Tying her still damp hair into a ponytail, she decided not to wear any make-up.

The insults had begun not long after their wedding, itself hastily arranged after Helene discovered she was expecting Audrey. Maurice's sniping further sapped her self-worth which had never recovered from the bullies' taunts and Aunt and Uncle's ham-fisted efforts to protect her from life's cruelties. Despite now being a wife and mother, Helene still sensed Aunt's disappointment when she visited their grand house in Caen's poshest suburb, filled with gaudy antiques and much to Helene's horror, stuffed animals. The visits were tense, largely silent, awkward affairs, a weekly ritual Helene continued out of duty and Audrey's fixation with Uncle's fine moustache.

Checking on Audrey, she went downstairs and stepped outside, leaving the stiff back door ajar. Passing the Velous' house, she spotted Jean standing at the kitchen window, lighting a cigarette. Marianne offered her a crabby-eyed nod from the front gate. Inside the rusted hulk of Velous' old Renault, a chicken pecked at the worn driver's seat, watched by a ginger tomcat lounging on the bonnet.

A car pulled up. Helene recognised the driver. The old man who had given her directions last night. Guzco smiled as he climbed out and said, "So you found the cottage, Madame."

"Think we'd still be looking without your help, Monsieur."

"Not the easiest place to find."

The returning flock of starlings split into chevrons to confuse the harrying hawk. "Good hunting my friend," Guzco muttered.

As Helene walked on, he approached Marianne, shocked by her frail, washed out appearance. Velous' illness was taking a toll on Marianne as well. After her outburst at the fifty-one festival, she seldom left the farm, despatching Jean to lay flowers at the war memorial and light a candle in the church for the repose of Henri's soul. Now Jean's chronic emphysema left him bedridden and unable to undertake these tasks, Pierre had taken it upon himself to lay fresh flowers beside Henri's picture and light a candle in the church for the repose of Henri's soul.

"Wasn't expecting you today, Doctor," she said.

"I was just passing, Marianne, so thought I would pop by and check up on Jean."

"There's little change I'm afraid."

Affecting concern but pleased that the valley's last bird hunter could no longer ply his trade, Guzco followed Marianne inside, bracing himself for the reek of human waste, sweat and cigarettes. Velous, dressed in faded pyjama bottoms and a stained vest, still stared out from the kitchen window. He sported a week's worth of stubble and his thick, curly grey hair sat in an unruly clump on his head. Stubbing his cigarette out in the overflowing ashtray set on the draining board next to him, he whispered breathlessly,

"New car, Doc?"

"Picked her up a couple of days ago."

"Citroen eh? Always been a Renault man, me."

"Each to their own, Jean. How are you feeling?"

"No puff."

"If you stopped smoking you'd still have some," Marianne snapped.

"Here we go again," Velous answered, with a shake of the head. "Nag, nag, nag. What do you think, Doc?"

Thinking it wise to keep quiet, Guzco washed his hands under the hot tap. After drying his scalded hands on a grubby tea towel depicting Nice's promenade, he asked Velous to undertake a lung function test. A simple enough procedure according to the textbook.

"Well, Doc?" asked the wheezing Velous, his bloodshot eyes for once fearful. The same look he wore in fifty-one after Marianne's outburst at the festival.

"No change, Jean, but Marianne is right about the cigarettes."

"A man must have some pleasures. And as I can't hunt anymore, Monsieur Gitanes offers me some solace. Dare say you're pleased to hear that."

"The birds yes, the cigarettes not so much," Guzco replied, this time washing his hands under the cold tap. After drying them on the grubby towel, he shook Velous' skeletal hand then said, "See you soon, Jean. No cigarettes."

"Yes, Doc. Drive carefully now."

Marianne handed Guzco a carton of eggs and walked him to the front gate, her eyes searching Guzco's face for signs of optimism. Standing at the window, Velous drew on a fresh cigarette then doubled up from a coughing fit.

Guzco sighed, "There is little more we can do, Marianne, except keep him comfortable and make sure he takes his medication. The smoking doesn't help."

"Even Matriarch Lerond cannot get him to give up," she replied, dabbing the towel on her eyes. Surprised by tough as teak Marianne's display of emotion, Guzco sat beside her on a weathered bench outside the gate. Her calloused right hand, the fingernails thick with dirt, reach for his hand. A nosey chicken approached.

"Forgive me, Doctor," Marianne muttered, "I can't imagine life without

him. She paused, lost in thought, possibly recrimination. She wrung her hands, wiped her mouth and shot Guzco a furtive, downtrodden look. "I know he helped the Nazis, doctor, but so many people did, even if it was just by acquiescing. But what was I to do? I had two children to raise with a husband who seemed ashamed of them." Again she paused. "But since Henri's death, Jean has been my rock. Then there's Celeste." Making a sign of the cross she paused, caught up in thought. "I very nearly died bringing that girl into the world. Something broke inside me that night. Ever since I've done my best to protect her. Perhaps coddled her too much to keep her out of harm's way. Now I wonder how she'll cope when I'm gone."

"Daresay you have a few more years in you, Marianne."

"I'd like to think so. Never smoked or drank. Said my prayers at night, observed the commandments."

"You do know you're held in the highest regard."

Unused to praise, Marianne's dowdy features brightened, "Me?"

"Yes."

She brought her left hand to her mouth, revealing the thin gold ring binding her to her scoundrel of a husband. "Very kind of you to say, Doctor. Try my best. I'm about to take Celeste her morning coffee. Would you like to come?"

"Why not," he replied, struggling to remember the last time he had enjoyed Marianne's company, let alone offered the chance to meet the reclusive Celeste.

CHAPTER FORTY-SEVEN
The Velous' Farm, August 1969

"This way, Doctor," Marianne said, pointing her orange thermos towards the ramshackle barn.

Taking his chance, Guzco asked, "Will you be attending this year's celebration, Marianne?"

Marianne's unusual warmth cooled. Shaking her head, she replied, "No. Someone knows what happened to Henri that night. "Even now they keep quiet." Guzco bit his tongue. Surely Marianne now connected her husband's collaboration to her son's execution. But she didn't. Or couldn't bring herself to face this terrible truth. "I'm just glad my mother isn't alive. Stern woman she was, stopped smiling when she turned sixty but she never missed the festival. Drummed its importance into me. Break her heart if she knew I no longer attended."

To change the subject, Guzco said, "I gave the family staying in Foucault's old place directions late last night."

Testy Marianne returned. "Bretons can you believe. She's a haughty, ill-disposed creature. But the husband and daughter are charming. The swimming pool drew them here."

"What do you mean?"

"It was Jean's doing. He heard swimming pools are now must haves among the rich and famous. Bardot, Delon, Sinatra, they've all got one. 'Why shouldn't we?' Jean thought. At first I thought him mad, but the pool has proved a selling point."

The barn drew near. Its bowed timber walls were near rotten and the rusted corrugated tin roof sported several patch repairs. The reek of fresh paint and epoxy resin added to Guzco's alarm about going inside.

A large hand-painted sign hung over the entrance proclaiming, *Museum of the History of the Baddur Valley*. Noting the incorrect spelling, Guzco's eyes were drawn to the aged, scabbed scythes, shovels and pitchforks propped against the open doors. Setting the flask down, Marianne rummaged through an old beer crate sat on top of a metal filing cabinet and handed him a bicycle lamp.

"You'll need this," she said, steering him inside. The barn's cool, chemical-tinged air sat at odds with the gathering morning heat.

"These belonged to Jean's father," she said, pointing to a nineteenth century horse-drawn plough, reaper and thresher. "He was the first farmer in the valley to embrace modern methods. Yet his forward thinking was met with suspicion. Little changes. Even today the Velous family are treated as outsiders. Explains my Jean's view of the folk round here."

Thinking of Velous' collaboration, Guzco replied, "Sometimes it's best to let go."

"Easier said than done, Doctor, old slights cast long shadows."

A child's bicycle, its chain and tyres perished, lay against the thresher. "Henri's bicycle." Marianne's voice wavered. "Never had the heart to throw it out." Guzco rang the bicycle's bell. It had seized and its strangled tone reminded him of a leper's bell.

Ahead of them reared a giant steam tractor, all wheels, pulleys and gauges. "Wonderful isn't she," Marianne said. "Cost us a pretty penny but I think it adds majesty to the collection."

She moved on, her torchlight flitting between cobweb strewn rafters and the discarded engine parts, jerry cans, even a petrol pump, littering the floor. The acrid chemical scent grew stronger.

She patted the flank of a majestic, seventeen-hand black stallion standing on a wooden plinth. "My uncle bequeathed it to me. He was once the finest taxidermist in France. Indoors, I have a photograph of him preparing an African elephant for the Natural History Museum in Paris. He could stuff anything."

"An unusual talent."

"But rewarding. He had accrued quite the fortune by the time he died. In his honour, I took up taxidermy. At first I found it baffling but now I relish bringing such magnificent beasts as these back to life." Her torch settled on two stuffed red squirrels sat on a table. A third squirrel lay on its side, glowering at Guzco through its glass eye. "Those German children couldn't keep their hands off anything," Marianne muttered, righting the prone squirrel. "Then the parents had the cheek to ask for a refund. Can you believe that, Doctor?"

"Scarcely, Marianne."

The stuffed animals offered a sense of the macabre and grotesque as Guzco grew a touch light headed. Torchlight landed on an adult male Rove goat. The armature for mounting the skin, a latticework of chicken wire

and balsa wood, lay exposed around the goat's shoulders. "Jean bagged that fella a year or two back," Marianne told him. The goat's saturnine eyes bore into Guzco.

Everywhere I go, there you are.

Beyond the goat, lay a low-ceilinged room, its grimy window set in the far wall the only source of natural light. Guzco stood at the doorway and shone his torch inside. Drawings, hundreds of them, lined the walls. Intrigued, he stepped into the room. Several piles of sketches lay stacked on a paint spattered table. Beside them sat an ashtray holding a cigarette, its smoke curling into the toxic air. "Sorry, Doctor," Marianne said, "Celeste doesn't like people coming in here."

Ignoring her, Guzco flicked through the drawings. The fourth one astonished him.

Here in this space? How can it be?

A near perfect likeness of Marta dancing.

"Look like you've seen a ghost, Doctor," Marianne said, moving towards him.

"In a way I have," he replied. Pointing at the drawing, he asked, "Do you know the girl in the picture?"

"Not a clue." Marianne's light flitted over the sketches fastened to the walls. "Jean goes mad at the clutter, once threatened to set light to it all. He's never understood Celeste."

One drawing fluttered in the draught, catching Guzco's attention. He levelled his torch on it. The sketch was of an elderly, curly-haired man striking an actorly pose and reciting an oration. *Giacomo?* Beside Giacomo a sketch of Spinoza was pinned to the wall and beside Spinoza rested the kind, wise leper.

Bewildered, Guzco ran his eyes over more sketches. He knew every character in them. Some he had loved, others feared, despised or misunderstood. The bill-hooked priest who had regaled the mourners at the plague pit, Fachetti astride his charger, the fishermen hauling their vessel through the Lavagnan mist, Poseidon and the goat dozing beneath their favourite tree.

"This one's my favourite." Marianne's torch landed on a sketch of a fisherman struggling to haul his vessel ashore. A peasant woman and her daughter looked on.

Luisa and Bia?

A wave of confused yearning reared through him.

"Extraordinary isn't it," Marianne whispered, as if in church. "When I look at these pictures I see all of life's complications and sadness. But also its beauty. Most of the people round here see Celeste as a loner, an imbecile. But her drawings tell me she's the only sane one among us."

Guzco lingered over another sketch beneath the window. "There's better ones to see, Doctor," Marianne said. He stayed put and studied the drawing of Henri slumped against the war memorial. A grief-struck Irene stood over him.

"Celeste knew about the affair." Marianne paused to clear her throat. "And their plans to elope." She touched the sketch as if trying to divine Henri's spirit. "I wouldn't have minded. He'd still be alive. Safe too. Even with that strumpet. Some days, when I'm undone by sadness, I come here to be with him."

The fumes added to Guzco's confusion. A toxic chemical flare tore through his bloodstream. *Muffled German shouts – Giacomo's hammy recitations – Marta dancing beside the boulder – A woman climbing into the stallion's belly - Velous tearing away the lichen gauze to reveal Philomandra to out of puff Germans.*

Without thinking, he whispered, "Forgive me, Philomandra, I should have saved you. I should never have been chosen. Luisa, Bia, I'll be home soon. I promise."

He stumbles from the boulder – the hectoring souls demanding freedom – Massandar eggs them on.

He came too outside the barn with Marianne standing over him, flapping a rag. She smiled a gap-toothed smile and poured him a cup of coffee from the thermos. "You gave me a proper fright, Doctor. The fumes can do that. But after a while they help dull things." Drinking the coffee, Guzco reeled from the sight of blood on his hand.

"Don't fret, it's only paint. You knocked over a tin when you fainted. I've turpentine in the house. It'll come off in no time. But rest a little longer, until you get your bearings."

"Can I meet Celeste?"

"One day, maybe." She took a sip of coffee then asked, "Were they old patients of yours?"

"Who?"

"Bia, Luisa and Philomandra. Unusual names."

"They are, Marianne. And yes, you're right. All former patients."

"From before the war?"

"Yes."

"Another place then."

"Very much so."

Tipping away her coffee dregs, Marianne helped Guzco to stand. Brushing the dirt from his jacket, she said, "Forgive me for saying, Doctor, but in the barn I sensed a malaise in you. Take it from one who knows, don't grow disillusioned. That way bitterness lies ahead. Find someone to share your life with."

"Easier said than done, Marianne."

"Only if you dare not to look."

Even in this toxic fug, Guzco bristled at the thought that *Marianne Velous* pitied him.

"I forgot the turpentine, your eggs too," she said. "Wait there, I'll fetch them."

She scuttled away, leaving Guzco to wonder and fear, how Celeste knew so much about him.

CHAPTER FORTY-EIGHT
Badur, August 1969

Crossing the ancient stone bridge, Helene was surprised by Badur's careworn and fragile appearance. Not at all how she had imagined. One or two houses stood empty, their doors and windows boarded up, with weeds sprouting through cracked render. Ducking beneath faded bunting strung across the street, she cast a mystified, wary eye over the pots, plates and moth-eaten blankets left out on doorsteps. On one step, a girl of an age to Audrey, twiddled the knobs on a television set.

She calmed upon reaching the square. The ancient church, bullet-riddled war memorial and higgledy-piggledy shops and houses were exactly as Irene had described, right down to the weathered cigarette advertisement on the greengrocer's flank wall, the rusted post office sign above the butcher's and the café's torn, yellow striped awning.

She stepped inside the church and breathed in the cool, damp air tinged with the lingering scent of incense and candle wax. Several candles of remembrance burned. On the plain stone altar sat a wooden doll and hawk, their features smoothed and discoloured from years of absent minded fondling. Tracing her hand along an aged scorch mark, she heard the faint echo of footsteps and children's laughter. Spooked by the eerie, other worldly atmosphere, she stepped outside and studied the scarred war memorial. The young man's weather-stained photograph at the base of the memorial matched the photograph in the cottage. "What is your story?" she muttered, tidying the bunch of aged, brittle flowers lying in front of the picture.

She heard laughter. Three middle aged men, one in suit and tie, the other two in workmen's clothes stood in shade outside the bakery looking at her. Another man, a little older than the others, joined them. He wore shabby dungarees, a filthy shirt and frayed cap. He muttered something. The others laughed without taking their leering eyes off Helene.

Glad Maurice wasn't here to say she should have worn something plainer, she walked towards the café where Pierre stood, nursing his morning livener. On the table in front of him sat a cardboard box containing the bunting. Seeing Helene, he pushed the box across the table, tidied his waistcoat and said, "Good morning, Madame."

"Could you tell me what time the butcher's opens, Monsieur?"

"In a few minutes. A coffee while you wait?"

"Thank you." Taking a seat, Helene, still uneasy under the men's glare, reminded herself to buy salad vegetables for lunch as the greengrocer set about displaying fruit, vegetables, buckets, mops and an ironing board outside her premises.

The thought struck her that whenever Irene talked about Badur, she never mentioned family, friends or work, or if she had, Helene, so wrapped up in legends and fables hadn't listened. She wondered if the waiter knew Irene but then recalled Irene telling her she'd left Badur for the hurt she had caused. Probably wise to leave it for a day or two.

Setting her coffee down, Pierre asked, "Here for a holiday?"

"Yes."

"I hope you enjoy your stay."

"Thank you."

An elderly man in suit, collar and tie, walked towards the men standing in the shade but stopped several paces short and refused to acknowledge them. The man in dungarees made a hand gesture which the others found funny. Aware he was the butt of the joke, the elderly man struck a haughty, almost imperious pose and nodded to the young priest, standing outside the church, enjoying a quiet smoke.

A fraught air of violence hung heavy among the group, as to why, Helene had no idea.

Pierre reached into the box and pulled out the tangle of bunting. He sighed with frustration.

"Can I help?" Helene asked.

"Thank you but no, my waitress will be here soon enough. She can lend a hand. After all this was her idea."

As she did most mornings, Greta stood at her window, breathed in the bakery's rich, sugary scents and watched the village stir while sipping coffee and nibbling on a croissant. The emergence of this agreeable ritual in part explained why her original plan of staying in Badur for a day or two now stretched to seventeen years.

Yet her stomach still tightened each time a strange car pulled up, the knot only loosening when Massimo didn't step out, in search of forgiveness. Now when he crossed her mind, she felt pity rather than anger. She had done the right thing in making Badur her home, no longer in thrall to any man and free of expectation.

The sparse apartment served her needs, containing a bed, armchair, drop leaf table and two chairs, a wireless and now a television set. On the table, next to a jar of loose change she used for the gas metre and bus fares, rested a framed picture of her with her parents, Oona and Alesandro taken on Lavagna's beach. The kitchenette boasted a two-ringed hob and butler sink while the small, damp privy and its temperamental cistern sat across the landing.

If she had one wish it would be to see the sea, as apart from Oona, it was what she missed most about Italy. In the early days, Oona visited every year with Frederico, now her husband, and their three daughters. But last year, only the youngest girl had accompanied Oona and she soon tired of the silence sheathing Badur especially after falling out with the latest batch of uppity Lerond youngsters.

Every couple of months or so, she caught the bus to Nice, to shop, visit the hairdresser's, watch a film and withdraw books from the Central Library. Thrillers mostly, but also the odd work of non-fiction. Treating herself to lunch in a cheapish bistro, she studied the latest fashions and hairstyles, embarrassed that her couture and coiffure remained in hoc to dowdy, post-war Genoa. She stayed in an inexpensive but well-appointed pensione a short walk from the Promenade, whose owner was always welcoming and circumspect.

And in the summer, she roamed the woods, plotting the plethora of carvings and usually found herself in the flowering meadows, lying in the tall grass, listening to the thrum of insects and birdsong. She had found her heaven.

She enjoyed Doctor Chamonix's authoritative company, grateful too that he never sought a romantic attachment. Then there was the unwitting companionship of the baker and his wife; talking, laughing and snoring in their apartment, below her. Their bouts of heaving, bedspring-damaging sex, a nightly occurrence when she first moved in, were now sporadic and short-lived. Their daughter, the jewel in her father's lazy eye, left croissants outside Greta's front door each morning, her quiet generosity reaffirming Greta's love for the village's odd but kindly inhabitants.

Several men had tried to woo her. One even named his prize buck in her honour. Yet she rebuffed each advance. Even so, Pierre still took exception to each would-be suitor's efforts, banning them from the café on trumped-up charges of drunkenness or uncouth language. And there was the rub.

She knew Pierre was besotted with her. Underneath his handsome if gruff exterior, lay a kind, lost soul. But first Luca and then Massimo had made her wary of defining herself by men. And there was Irene. Pierre remained in thrall to her. On this basis alone she thought it wise to reject him if he ever summed up the courage to ask her out.

Besides, where could they go? Badur's sole nightspot, if you could call it that, was the café. Pierre wasn't one for tramping the woods or mountains and he often professed at length his revulsion for Nice and towns in general, seeing them a hotbed of rogues and hucksters. The courtship, were it ever to happen, would bear a striking resemblance to their daily routine, the sole difference being a snifter or two at closing time.

After finishing breakfast, she washed up then retrieved one of the suitcases from under the bed. She loosened the straps and threw open the lid. On top lay the new cotton blouse and plain black skirt she'd bought in Nice the week before.

Enjoying the sensation of wearing fresh, still creased new clothes, she pinned her hair and bemoaned the appearance of a few grey strands. Applying a little rouge and lipstick she was certain she could still pass for thirty-five. At a push, given her fiftieth birthday was around the corner. She tightened the buckle on her scuffed sandals. On the next trip into Nice, she'd buy a new pair.

She picked up the notebook resting on her smalls and studied the two sketches left outside the cottage during her honeymoon. She compared the drawings to the photograph of her and Luca taken on Lavagna's harbour wall in thirty-eight with Luca holding his copy of *The Odyssey*, her birthday gift to him that year. The likenesses were identical in every respect. As always, a chill ran through her.

She had badgered Doctor Chamonix about arranging a meeting with the mysterious Celeste but each time he muttered his apologies. Once or twice, she had staked out the Velous' farm hoping to pin Celeste down about the drawings. But she remained elusive, as if she knew someone was watching her.

Next, Greta re-read the retired Carabinieri inspector's letter. The words she knew off by heart but they still stung. He never traced the mysterious Colonel Massandar within the Banco di Dogali or OVRA, Mussolini's secret police. Why Massimo claimed he was following this ghost's order remained a mystery, as was his denial in packing Luca off to the Russian Front. Like so much from the fascist years, truth and lies were inseparable.

She knew she should face the truth about Massimo and his far-fetched tales surrounding Massandar. Asking Doctor Chamonix for his view on the matter seemed a start. She trusted him but even after all these years, still not enough. Maybe next month. Best to keep her past secret in order to enjoy a quiet present and a hopeful future.

Returning the sketches and letter to the notebook, she set off for work, arriving at the café the precise moment the church bells struck eight. She greeted Helene, and in true Badurian fashion, sized her up.

The rust-pocked Studebaker, its US Army livery now faded, pulled up. The moon-faced driver dropped from the cab, hitched his trousers over his belly and walked to the rear of the lorry.

The old man in collar and tie and old man in dungarees avoided each other's glare.

The Organising Secretary and Chairman's annual joust was moments away.

A dust cloud flew up as the festival tent was unloaded from the lorry and dropped onto the cobbles. Staves, poles, ropes and the wooden stage sections followed. After a break for a coffee and a Pernod, delivered by Pierre, the gang set to work.

"To the left," the Chairman said. The men shuffled to the left.

"To the right," the Secretary replied. The men shifted right.

"Left!"

"Right!"

"Left!"

"Right!"

The lorry driver released his grip. "When you two have finished arguing, let us know where you want us to put the damn thing." The others followed suit. The tent fell to the floor, kicking up more dust.

"Too far left and its light is blocked by the church!" the Secretary asserted.

"Too far right and the baker will be upset," the Chairman retorted.

"He is always upset!"

"Probably because he is a Gaullist."

"Only a communist could think that. I've never known a happy communist."

"Happiness is a capitalist construct. To be happy is to be bourgeois."

"You don't even know what bourgeois means!"

"I do. It means you're a fucking class traitor!"

"Your subtlety does you justice."

"Capitalist!"

"Communist!"

"Capitalist!"

"Communist!"

"Turd!"

"Gentlemen please!" shouted Guzco upon arriving. "Why not raise the tent in its usual spot?" His annual bout of common sense allowed the Chairman and Secretary to break off from their insults, each certain they had secured a victory, of sorts, for the year.

Minutes later, the nuns from Sacre Coeur arrived with the cushioned seats. As their number dwindled, so the cushioned seats became even more sought after, leading to the Organising Committee holding lengthy negotiations over chair entitlement. In true Badur fashion, nothing was agreed but the Committee's members, bar Guzco, luxuriated in endless proposal and counter proposal.

The nuns stacked the seats beside the tent then accepted a glass of water from Pierre. Sister Francine, now frail and a touch stooped, clapped her hands. The nine nuns lined up. Sister Francine clapped again, and the column moved off.

With the tent pitched, the stage and seats were installed. Electric lights were strung up around the interior and wired to the nearest lamp post (the electricity company didn't need to know). A piano was manoeuvred inside the tent, its growling strings reminding Greta of distant thunder. There was nobody to play the piano, but the Organising Committee agreed having such a fine instrument on hand gave proceedings a sense of grandeur.

"Looking forward to this year's festivities?" Guzco asked Greta as she set his coffee down.

"It brings back memories, Doctor. Are you?" She started to untangle the bunting as Guzco rolled his shoulders in an effort to ease his discomfort.

"Yes and no," he replied, thinking of the centuries squandered waiting for Azekiel's return.

"Do you think there is any truth to the story of the Angel?"

"A story of sacrifice is always worth telling, Greta. It may be fantasy, but I think we all live in partial fantasy, needing our lives to be fulfilling, yet unable to achieve this through our own labours. To dream a little is no hardship."

"You surprise me. You're a man of learning, of wisdom."

"In moderation."

"Yet you mither over the festival's decline."

"Someone must, otherwise the Secretary and Chairman would throttle each other, albeit very slowly, and it would fall to me to resuscitate them." After sipping his coffee, he continued, "Like last year's uprisings in Paris, I have sought change. Not on that scale of course, but discreetly with the minimum of fuss. Jean Baptiste as Goliath, the mechanical whale, and pushing for new acts all challenged the status quo. It was a shame that the mime artist liked a drink, the tightrope walker suffered with an inner ear infection and the plate spinner owned no plates."

"Pierre was right not to lend him any."

"He was, but it didn't make for a great spectacle." To ease the pain, he shifted once more then said, "To answer you, Greta, I don't believe in the story of the Angel, but Badur is dying. The quarries have closed, our young must move away to find work. Soon the village will be abandoned, reclaimed once more by the forest, leaving nothing but our ghosts behind. For most valley folk, the festival has become a chore but I like to think that for those few hours the Angel's myth binds the village to its past."

"A history worth recounting."

"Agreed." After taking a sip of coffee, he said, "Forgive me for asking, but why did you stay?"

Setting the bunting down, she thought for a moment then said, "I almost

went back in sixty-four but couldn't for one moment imagine life in Genoa. Although Italy is booming, the fascists' legacy is still poisonous. That poison does not exist here."

"Perhaps our Angel found an imperfect peace in the valley. A plain splendour."

"The irony is I have feared Angels since childhood."

"An obscure phobia."

"When I was little, my brother convinced me the Angel statues in Lavagna's cemetery cursed children for breathing in their presence or even just looking at them. I took this to heart. Remember fainting once so engrained was my fear, on my wedding day I held my breath and avoided their gaze. Now here I am in a village that celebrates an Angel's sacrifice."

"Fate, Greta. But all the same, I'm glad you stayed." He laughed.

"What is so funny, Doctor?"

"I've just remembered. Another of Badur's odd rules that allowed you to live with us for so long."

"What rule is that?"

"Statues of Angels or anything else for that matter are not permitted in the village's cemetery for fear of upsetting our very own Angel."

"Can't say I ever noticed," Greta replied, embarrassed to admit that whenever she attended a burial, her childhood phobia still weighed heavily enough for her to hold her breath and keep her eyes fixed firmly on the ground.

Helene stepped off the road and set the shopping bags down to rest her aching hands. Badur hadn't matched up to Irene's vivid descriptions. A sense of decay lay in the village, its people relishing their petty squabbles. But she'd hide her disappointment from Maurice.

At first, he hadn't wanted to come to Badur. No surprise. He never wanted to go anywhere these days. Even taking Audrey to the swings or to the zoo to see her beloved chimpanzees had become a chore. Easier to sit on the sofa, buried in a newspaper, complaining about the corrupt politicians, foreigners and communists destroying France. But when Helene showed him the pictures of the cottage and its swimming pool, the long drive, expense and hassle were all forgotten. She didn't dare ask him why he'd changed his mind, just in case he did. Maybe the holiday *would* bring a spark back to the marriage.

He was sat at the kitchen table when she arrived.

"Did you get eggs?" he asked.

"Oops," she replied setting the bags down.

Sighing, he returned to his day-old *Le Monde*.

CHAPTER FORTY-NINE
The Holiday Cottage, Badur, August 1969

The following morning after her swim, and again fending off Maurice's heavy handed advances, Helene set off for the village to buy bread, eggs and milk. The decrepit Velous peered out from the kitchen window while Marianne stood at the front gate striking a bucket with a ladle, calling to her chickens.

Deciding to take a short cut through the woods, Helene stepped off the road and followed a narrow, leaf strewn path. Birdsong and the rustling foliage filled the spaces around her. She swayed along to the breeze borne melody. "Look Irene!" she shouted. "I'm dancing. In Badur!"

"Help me, Guzco, please," a woman whispered.

"Who's there?" Helene replied, her rapture short lived.

"Help me, Guzco, please."

To her left, someone or something, crashed through the undergrowth. Roosting starlings took to the wing, their panicked cries and fleeting shadows disorientating Helene. Hanging from the tree opposite were carvings of a fish and a boat. Odd. So far from the ocean. Moments earlier, the forest had granted her the freedom to dance, but now the same steepling trees caged her. With little clue what direction to take, she seized upon the shafts of sunlight studding the ground and ran, ducking under branches and skipping over exposed roots until exhausted, she leant against a tree to draw breath. She peered into the murk for sight or sound of her stalker. Nothing.

She heard a lorry shift gear and its engine strain as it tackled an incline. She threaded a path through the trees towards the welcome sound of modern life, only stopping to drink from a shallow stream's cold, redemptive waters.

Refreshed, eyes peeled for anything out of the ordinary, she stepped onto the Badur road and waved to a passing cyclist. He ignored her. She was in two minds. Return to the cottage for Maurice to complain all the more about not having eggs for breakfast or carry on towards the village. Seeking the quiet life, she decided to carry on towards for Badur.

The tent walls billowed in the soft breeze, rousing Helene's curiosity.

Peering inside, the odour of sweat and sorrow greeted her. On a small stage, a slight, barefoot woman wearing a leotard and leggings, skimmed across the floor, the only sound her feet scraping the wooden boards. Helene recognised the dancer's bold, fantastical steps. She'd spent hours in her bedroom perfecting them, hoping to earn Irene's praise and with luck, a hug. Her thoughts drifted inside these sacred, perfect moves.

She's sitting in the back of a large car, possibly a Mercedes, travelling along a dusty, pitted road. Aunt and Uncle sit either side of her. Every movement jars, the pain excruciating. She asks the driver to stop but Maurice, reeking of cologne, turns from the front passenger seat and tells her to be quiet then orders the driver to accelerate.

"Where's Audrey?" she asks.

"Far away from you that's for sure," Aunt brays.

"Help me, Guzco," she whispers.

The car bottoms out over a pothole. It slows. Just enough. Seizing her chance, she opens the car door and tumbles out. She gets to her feet and staggers towards the trees calling to Guzco. The car shudders to a halt. Maurice, Aunt and Uncle step out.

The dancer spins, each rotation faster than the last until she is a shifting, near shapeless shroud of movement. She comes out of the spin and stretches into a series of beautiful arcs, cleaving time and motion and forcing Helene further into her vision.

Too weak to run, she must stand and fight just as the ancients taught her to do. Her malign family step closer. She unfurls her wings to protect herself but falls. Aunt and Uncle are on her.

"Pick her up," Maurice orders, unsheathing a knife.

"Help me Guzco. Please."

The searing pain announces the cleaving of her wings. Aunt and Uncle's grip slackens.

"Put them with the others," Maurice again orders.

"She's yours if you want her, Domar," Maurice hollers. The kindly Doctor steps forward as Maurice plunges the dagger into her heart, and twists for good measure.

As the cold seeps through her fevered bones, she smells the sea and hears a gentle lullaby. "I am with you," the Doctor says. But she's not afraid. There's no need to be. Not anymore. "Here is Life," she whispers.

Head bowed, her face obscured by a mane of tumbling, jet black, sweat-soaked hair, the dancer is still. The spell broken, Helene cannot understand why a vision which should appal has left her as blissful as the moments following Audrey's birth. Audrey. *Her* Life. The dance points to a life lived with passion. This isn't a place of far-fetched fables and customs, but a place of liberation. Irene's greatest kindness was Badur itself.

Chloe Jonquet, now returned to her reticent, waif like self, gathered up her belongings and left Helene wallowing in the unruly peace of mind swaddling her.

Outside the café, Guzco greeted her with a tip of his hat. "So, you've had the privilege of watching Chloe Jonquet dance."

"She's remarkable," Helene replied, unsure why the kindly doctor had featured in the vision. "Is there a story behind the dance?"

"Legend has it that a girl danced for the Angel of Badur upon his arrival in the village. The dance cast a spell, condemning him to love her for all time even though he can only see her in dreams."

"A beautiful tale."

"Not if you are the Angel."

Helene spotted Pierre and Greta behind the bar, their movements perfectly choreographed by years of proximity.

"Are you enjoying your stay?" Guzco asked her.

"It's all I imagined and more."

"I'm pleased to hear it." He offered his hand, "Apologies, I should have introduced myself yesterday. Doctor Lionel Chamonix."

"Helene Delfour." Sensing she could trust him, Helene asked, "Do you know the woman in the painting hanging over the bar, Doctor?"

"Irene," Guzco whispered, glancing over his shoulder towards Pierre. "Pierre's wife. Or rather, she was. Towards the end of the War she ran off, to where nobody knows. Best not mention it if Pierre is within earshot. Irene broke his heart. Why do you ask?"

"She told me so many stories about this place."

"You know her?"

"When I lived in Paris. We were close."

"How is she?"

"She died, several years ago."

Stunned, Guzco studied Helene before saying, "I'd always hoped she would come back."

"She said she had hurt too many."

"Maybe." He leaned forward then whispered. "Could I ask a favour, Madame? Please say nothing about this to Pierre. He still harbours hopes that she will come home one day."

"The portrait tells me that some things are best left unsaid."

"Thank you." Guzco relaxed. He could trust Helene. Although an outsider, she instinctively understood the attachment valley folk have to avoiding hard truths. His thoughts turned to tonight's petitioning.

Returning to the cottage, Helene found Maurice and Audrey by the pool. The tinny transistor played a maudlin Francoise Hardy love song. Maurice, re-reading his *Le Monde*, didn't acknowledge Helene as she sat on a lounger.

"What kept you?" he asked.

"I was watching a girl dance."

"Did you remember the eggs?"

"Yes. Bought you a paper too."

"Thanks. Tell me, what's with these morning swims?"

"When I was younger, I liked to swim."

"Never mentioned it."

"Never felt the need."

His sunburned chest and belly repelled her. How easily she had fallen for his cheeky grin, blue eyes and flashy Triumph motorcycle, thinking him a French Steve McQueen.

She had had crushes on boys in school or at the factory but always simpered from afar until one day, much to her surprise, the cute junior accounts clerk asked her if she'd like to go to the cinema to watch a Catherine Deneuve film. Such were her eighteen year-old's nerves, it took her over three hours to decide what to wear. She wanted to look nice for him after all. But the moment the cinema fell dark, her beau lunged for her, causing her to scream, much to the annoyance of those around her, not least her would-be suitor.

That was the sum of her experience with men until the brassy Bernice, from Accounts, explained that Maurice's frequent visits to the typing pool were to see her.

Within three months of their first date, a trip to the funfair, she fell pregnant. Maurice ever the gentleman, asked for her hand on bended knee. Aunt was set against the marriage, as despite Maurice's attempts at flattery, she took against him, thinking he lacked the gumption to make a good husband, let alone father. But the chance to become a wife and mother, offered Helene a new start, free from her claustrophobic home life. Despite Maurice's tendency to sulk, she was certain he'd prove Aunt wrong. Marriage and fatherhood would be the making of him. Within weeks, she realised Aunt was right.

Maurice was an arsehole, only interested in sex, a full belly and controlling her. But she'd made her bed and for the sake of the child growing inside her, she had to accept her life, thinking those screeching feminists calling for greater rights for women promoted an illusion as far-fetched as Irene's Angel.

Her face a picture of concentration, Audrey carried a tray with the pink plastic tea set towards Helene. She handed Helene and then Maurice imaginary cups of coffee.

Maurice examined the empty cup before setting it down on the edge of the pool. "Watch this, Audrey," he said. He jumped into the pool and sank. For a brief, shaming moment Helene hoped he might stay under but he breached the surface, gathered Audrey up, ignored her screams and dropped her into the water. After recovering from her coughing fit and now revelling in the noise and anarchy of the moment, Audrey shouted, "Look, Maman, I'm swimming!"

"Well done, Audrey!" Helene replied, recalling her near drowning in Saint Germain baths.

"She'll be swimming the Channel by Christmas," Maurice said, as Audrey squealed with delight. Hoping to make use of his rare, good mood, Helene said, "The girl I saw dance is performing in the village tomorrow."

"Sounds like a waste of money."
"It's free."
"Suppose we ought to see something of the place."

CHAPTER FIFTY
Badur, August 1969

The tent's beams and spars creaked and groaned. The church bell chimed once. Guzco spotted a movement in the shadows. Baby Isabelle's mother, still bare foot, hair shorn, her face bruised, grew anxious and turned away causing her threadbare dress to swirl.

"Please, there's no need to be afraid," Guzco whispered.

Eager for news, she asked, "My daughter. Did you take her to the nuns at Sacre Coeur?"

"Yes. They took Isabelle in."

"Isabelle? Is that the name you gave her?"

"Yes. Broke my heart to give her away. But the nuns raised her well, even if they found her wilful."

"Like her mother then."

"I visited each year; left alms, the odd carving too, but never spoke to her, thinking that too cruel. I'm only sorry you never saw her dance."

"A dancer?"

"Best I ever saw."

She swelled with pride. "My daughter, the dancer." Calmer now, she continued, "After Papa sold me, I only ever saw myself as a chattel. And when the cow he traded me for ran dry, he claimed I'd placed a curse on the poor beast. That's when the tales of me being a witch began, spread by the priest after I refused his advances, even though I had just been widowed and still mourned my husband." She clenched her fists, her eyes now glistening with rage. "Maybe if I had done, I'd have been left alone and not taken up that accursed mountain." She softened. "Thank you for saving Isabelle and giving her a life. I'm glad she found happiness."

"She had a family of her own. Her descendants live in the valley to this day. You live on."

"Really?"

"The Jonquets are good people." Thinking of Irene, he said, "Although some possess your wilfulness."

"Never thought such things happened to the likes of me."

"Is there anything else you would like to know?"

The question wrongfooted her. "What else is worth knowing? I don't ask you to promise me something you've no way of keeping. You saved Isabelle. That is enough. Thank you."

She took up the simple but impossible steps, her joy in movement life affirming. Guzco was captivated by her grace, rendering his pain worthwhile. She began to fade. He held out his right hand to her. She brushed it with her left hand. Guzco's doubts abandoned him and he revelled in a state of bliss. And then she was gone and the doubts returned.

Henri Velous wiped his glasses, the once confident, optimistic young man now soured by pessimism. He studied Guzco with a critical eye, then said, "Am I supposed to say something?"

"Most do."

"I'm not most people."

"Then say nothing."

"But that seems a waste."

"Only if you think so."

Smart arse.

"In that case, how are Irene and the baby?"

"Irene left Badur."

Panic replaced Henri's confidence. "Where did she go?"

"Nobody knows," said Guzco, to spare his feelings.

"Not even Pierre?" Guzco nodded. "And my father? Did he have anything to do with it?"

"He's dying."

"Why should I care."

"What do you mean?"

Henri shook his head and sighed, the brash confidence now tainted by bitterness. "We knew Papa was a collaborator, probably Milice too. Earned a fortune from it. When the Germans arrested me, Papa was with them. I thought he'd try to butter the Germans up, to get them to release me. Even as the firing squad assembled, I still hoped he'd do something. But he looked, on smoking and joking with the other soldiers. His was the last face I saw. Even then he gave nothing away." Sadness tinged by confusion gripped him. "Why did he betray me?"

"Only he can explain."

"He only ever spoke with his belt or fist."

"Your mother still leaves flowers by the memorial and lights a candle in the church for you."

"For all the good it does. All I see is *him* looking on as the German officer gives the order to fire. My only comfort was to think that Irene and our child were safe, yet that is denied me." He stepped towards Guzco. "Bring them home, Angel, even if I have to stay in this limbo forever." Before Guzco could answer, Henri faded.

In the dank half-light, time peeled away and opened up a path to Guzco's earliest days in Badur. Spinoza's slight, supple form stood before him, his wounds at the hands of Marlinka still visible.

"Are we alone?" Spinoza asked. He seemed nervous, unsure why he was here.

"Yes."

"Good. Didn't want to come at first. Feared Fachetti and Marlinka might still be here. I'll never understand. All that suffering, pain and terror they inflicted."

"Give any man the order and nine times out of ten they will obey. Instruction absolves."

"Then all hearts are black."

"Most, not all. Yours for one."

"Kind of you, Angel, although I wish I could sing a happy tune once in a while. I despair of the laments but whenever I open my mouth it's their words that pour forth." He tensed and looked towards the exit.

"What is it?" Guzco asked.

"Fachetti is close."

"Relax, it's only you and me here."

"If I can come to you, who's to say Fachetti cannot?" Spinoza stepped away, slowly dissolving into the enveloping darkness. "Let me sing of happiness once more, Angel. That's all I ask."

Guzco left the tent aware that each of this year's petitioners represented a pivot in his time in Badur. Spinoza had saved him from Marlinka and Massandar's cruelties. Missing Henri's death by a matter of minutes enabled him to remain as Chamonix. Isabelle's mother had freed him from the bondage of leprosy. The revelations surrounding Celeste's painting pointed to something more profound.

Massandar is rolling the dice once more.

CHAPTER FIFTY-ONE
Badur, August 1969

The following morning, with the bunting finally strung up around the café, Pierre watched Greta sweep the floor. This was his favourite part of day, alone with Greta, enjoying a coffee and a smoke, listening to her talk. Odd, given he used to frown upon Irene gossiping, thinking it trivial and intrusive. Time spent with Greta, even on trifling matters, was time never wasted.

But like so many things to do with Greta, he considered gossiping life-affirming, alongside her many other enthusiasms; the insect life in the meadows, a diving hawk's menace, the baker's lemon tarts or the plot twist in the latest *Sherlock Holmes* adventure she was reading. Her vitality softened the pain that still scarred him over Irene. So much so that when she spent a night in Nice, he counted down the minutes waiting for the bus to arrive, desperate to see her step off.

Yet each time he tried summoning the courage to reveal his feelings, Irene's departure befuddled his tongue. Bursting into silence is how he thought of it and long hours were spent trying to concoct a way of Greta finding out he loved her without having to go to the trouble of saying so.

Chamonix had once shushed him to say, "Pierre, I knew men who maimed and killed without a moment's thought. But those same men, when involved with a woman, will dissolve to the meekest, mildest, most nervous of creatures. Love is a terrible, beautiful thing that can cause the heart to melt or glow. Nobody else can say the words. Tell her. And save me from your constant prattling."

"Spotless," Greta said, as she stirred her coffee. After taking a sip she asked, "Did Doctor Chamonix ever marry?"

"Before the war."

"What was his wife's name?"

"Luisa."

"Why does he never speak of her?"

"He told me once she completed him. I never asked about her again, some things are better left unsaid."

"Is that why you never speak of your wife?"

Uncomfortable, wondering what she was driving at, he shrugged. "What is there to say? Irene left. For years I hoped she would return, but now I'm not so sure."

"Why?"

To buy time, he lit a cigarette. "It's complicated and I'm a simple man."

"You're too hard on yourself, Pierre."

He leaned forward, elbows on the table. Its legs creaked. "Irene was passionate and wilful. Despite being born and raised here, valley life never suited her. She was always on at me to leave. Nice, Lyon even Paris. But I could never leave Badur, happy to run my pokey little café, seeing the same faces, having the same conversations day in day out. When people told me they'd seen her with other men I thought them bitter gossips picking apart our lives because they had nothing else to talk about. Denial is a powerful, destructive emotion. So when she upped and left, my heart broke. But looking back, what surprises me most is that she didn't leave sooner."

"But you keep her painting."

"Some customers like raising a glass to her on New Year's. We are nothing if not custodians of tradition. Anyway, why do you ask?"

"Something the Doctor said the other day about Badur offering an imperfect peace. I thought of you when he said it."

"Really? Should I be worried?"

For once not weighing up the consequences, Greta placed her hand on his. "Of course not." She looked at him beyond friendship. Pierre's floundering heart skipped a beat until the heartache of Irene's departure muzzled him. "Better get on," he said, pulling his hand away, "Festival day is upon us."

"As you wish," she replied, wondering what had prompted her to be so forward. To lessen the tension, she outlined the next set of chores. Pierre heard the odd word, "*goat, stew, seat, bread,*" all the while furious with himself for lacking the balls to tell Greta he loved her.

The nine o'clock bells pealed. Guzco, still perplexed from last night's petition, took up his usual spot. His ashen appearance took Greta by surprise. "A little under the weather, Doctor?" she asked.

"The stew is being cooked."

"Of course." Her concern melted.

"You weren't asked this year?"

"No," she snapped.

Last year, the Matriarch had invited her to help prepare the stew. A great

honour according to Pierre, and a sign that she was now a fully-fledged Badurian. But Greta's excitement soon soured when her suggestion of replacing the bones and gristle with pork, chicken and wild herbs was dismissed out of hand with the Matriarch asserting Greta didn't understand the stew's significance in Badur's history. Moving an iota from the original recipe was tantamount to blasphemy and in all likelihood would bring disaster to the valley. More importantly, the ingredients were guarded with a righteous fervour by The Organising Committee. Hours later, she gagged on the putrid liquid fermenting on Doctor Chamonix's hob, while Lydia and the Matriarch congratulated themselves on a job well done. She wasn't surprised her help hadn't been sought this year.

"I'm sorry to hear that," said Guzco, "But tradition is,"

"As tradition expects."

Over the next hours, festival preparations took shape. Jean Baptiste and his gangly six-year old son arrived from Cresson. The doe and buck Rove goats reared up on Guzco. Jean Baptiste practised his dastardly Goliath face on terror-struck children and a crowd gathered around the wooden whale to watch him oil and polish his leviathan from snout to fluke.

Greta made herself scarce when Lydia and the Matriarch Lerond's put-upon husbands, assailed by Lydia's screeched instructions, wheeled the barrow carrying the stew towards the unlit fire. The pair then ignored the Matriarch's outrage while downing their Pernod snifters, courtesy of Pierre.

Everyone stood well back as the thoroughly refreshed pair then tipped the stew into the cauldron hanging over the unlit fire. Lydia stepped forward, sniffed the contents and wretched. "Perfect," she said, placing a lid over the noxious slop. Her eyes streamed.

Under Cecile's watchful eye, the performer's costumes were brought into the tent. Cecile told Guzco about the struggles she'd had to find good-quality yarn this year. But the costumes still displayed exquisite design and intricate embroidery, even earning praise from the Matriarch Lerond, a sign that the Jonquets' rehabilitation into the valley's polite society was now all but complete.

With each tradition, come chore ticked off, Guzco's excitement built at the prospect of seeing Luisa and Bia. To kill time, he returned home and put the finishing touches to the new boat carving, its sleek lines and yellow and red paint scheme bringing him particular pleasure. At five-thirty, he returned to the cafe, relieved to see a reasonable turnout. The mandolin player and drummer tuned their instruments as Jean Baptiste, clad in his Goliath get up snarled at terror struck tots. People, wearing Sunday best, milled around. Teenagers flirted. Children petted the stupefied goats and the elderly complained to each other about their conditions.

Quarter to six rang out. Pilgrims gathered on the bridge. As Guzco collected Pierre, it began to rain. "Good turnout this year," Guzco said, nodding to new arrivals.

Pierre muttered under his breath.

"What was that?" Guzco asked.

"Sorry. Rehearsing my speech for Greta. Today's the day I'm going to tell her." Guzco said nothing, certain that when the time came, Pierre would again grow tongue-tied.

To calm Pierre, he said. "Perhaps the rumours around Father Jerome have encouraged a few more people to attend."

"Manastalgi," Pierre replied, unfurling his umbrella.

"Could be," Guzco said, thinking it was brave or foolhardy for the new parish priest to ignore the Organising Committee's objections and insist upon singing. He unfurled his umbrella.

On the bridge, Father Jerome, already drenched, adjusted the three rattling terracotta pots slung across his chest and then tuned his guitar. Not yet thirty with a pleasant, plump face sporting a hint of shaving rash, Jerome greeted pilgrims with a broad smile and hearty handshake. Behind him, two altar boys, tried to impress a group of girls, sheltering beneath umbrellas, with their thurible skills.

Jerome's arrival had caused a stir. He was young for starters and insisted on conducting mass in French and not Latin. But his optimism marked him out from that old stick-in-the-mud Lafont, now retired to a seminary near Arles. Much to her disgust, the Matriarch Lerond's husband had wagered Lydia's husband a leg of lamb that the new priest would one day become Bishop of Nice.

Jerome greeted Guzco with a rain spattered smile.

"Still planning to sing?" Guzco asked.

"Very much so, Doctor," Jerome replied enthusiastically. "I know about the festival's traditions, but to honour its medieval roots, I'm convinced my madrigal will add a new, exciting flavour." His smile invoked the spirit of the naive ingénue.

"Manastalgi," Pierre repeated.

The Secretary, jockeying for prime position in the procession, glowered. The siting of the tent and entitlement to a cushioned seat were but minor affectations compared to singing.

The six o'clock bell struck. Cigarettes were ground out, wayward children gathered in, and the elderly helped up. The flirting teenagers rejoined their families while stealing glances at the girl or boy who had caught their eye. Taking his usual spot with Pierre, Guzco greeted several familiar faces. A column of mostly black umbrellas stretch the length of the bridge beneath which stood the damp but stoical pilgrims.

Helene, Maurice and Audrey, buried beneath her anorak, weaved among the crowd, unsure where to stand. Spotting Guzco, Helene pushed into the line behind him, apologising to the nose-out-of- joint couple whose place she had taken. "You decided to come, Madame," Guzco said.

"Yes, Doctor," Helene replied. "May I introduce you to my husband, Maurice, and my daughter, Audrey?"

Maurice raised a half-hearted, flinty-eyed smile as he shook Pierre and Guzco's hands then asked, "She said there's food laid on."

"Depends on what you mean by food," Pierre replied.

Audrey dropped her doll onto the rain-soaked pavement. Picking it up, she tugged the hem of Helene's overcoat and whispered, "I need the toilet, Maman."

"There's a toilet inside the café," Pierre said. "Two minutes away, across the bridge."

"I'll take her," Maurice said. "Better than standing around here getting soaked."

Handing Helene the umbrella, he took Audrey's hand and led her to the front of the procession, earning a queer looks first from the Matriarch Lerond, and then the Secretary and finally the lanky, largely disinterested Gendarme who'd drawn the short straw to keep an eye on this year's proceedings

As Maurice and Audrey hurried by Jerome, the priest cleared his throat,

adjusted the guitar then said, "Today we honour the Angel who continues to protect, clothe, feed and shelter us. In turn we must now shelter him." Girding himself, he asked, "Who will shelter the Angel?"

"We shall," the pilgrims responded with scant enthusiasm. Ignoring the now sheeting rain, Jerome strummed his guitar and sang in a clear, pleasant tone, *'From whence did good...'*

Hollering, "Manastalgi!", the Secretary with a vigour at odds with his age, tore the guitar from Jerome and hurled it over the bridge parapet and into the river. It landed with a light *splosh*.

"Didn't see that coming," Pierre muttered to Guzco.

"Me neither."

Father Jerome dashed to the riverbank and then waded into the river after his beloved six string, now drifting downstream. Realising his faux pas, the Secretary hurried after Jerome but stopped at the water's edge to remove his shoes and socks then roll his trousers above his knees. He waded out into the water and sank, leaving his toupee bobbing on the surface. Thanks to the speedy intervention of the policeman, he was spared drowning, much to the disappointment of the communist committee members.

"Let's get you home, Vincent," his wife said as, all fingers and thumbs, she returned the sodden wig to its rightful place.

"But what about the acts, the speeches. *My Speech?*" He wore the pained look of a gelded colt.

"There's always next year. Isn't that right, Doctor?" Guzco, kneeling beside the Secretary, nodded. "Things wouldn't be the same without them. But now go home, find some dry clothes and then pour a glass or two of cognac into you."

"Perhaps water acts are the way to go, Doc," Pierre said as he and Guzco trailed the policeman and small group of pilgrims walking downstream and every now and then encouraging Jerome not to drown. The rain beat a steady rhythm on their umbrellas.

"Help!" pleaded Jerome, clinging to his guitar.

"At least he's caught his guitar," Pierre said.

"I was beginning to worry," answered Guzco. "Do you think the pageant will go ahead? Chloe's dance at least."

"Doubt it. Not with the parish priest floating towards the Mediterranean. Someone should have warned him about Manastalgi."

"I did. But he wouldn't listen."

"He'll know for next year."

Rounding a bend, the river's current slowed enough to allow Jerome to grasp at a low-hanging branch at a cost of releasing his guitar to the current.

A thin, pallid stranger dropped his rucksack took off his ill-fitting, double breasted, grey jacket, found a toe hold and climbed up and into the tree. Reaching a collar, he straddled the branch and inched towards Jerome. Taking hold of the stricken priest's shoulders, he waited for the rescue party, led by the bold policeman to wade out to Jerome.

Looking on from the riverbank, Pierre said, "Fancy a livener Doc?"

"Better see to Father Jerome first," Guzco replied, watching the rescue party lead Jerome to safety.

"As you wish," Pierre replied, the butterflies in his stomach swirling at the prospect of speaking to Greta. He set off for the café.

Guzco attended to the priest, whose only concern was for his guitar, a prized family heirloom, bequeathed to him by an uncle who had once played it on a lesser known Tino Rossi recording. Thanking Guzco for his kindness, Jerome was escorted home by his rescuers.

The gallant stranger brushed the bark stains from his trousers before offering Guzco his hand.

"An honour to meet you Guzco. Luca Meazza."

CHAPTER FIFTY-TWO
Badur, August 1969

"Guzco? I am Doctor Lionel Chamonix and I'm pleased to say I have been all my life."

"Guzco Domar, the Soul Collector who gambled his wings to Massandar. Before Chamonix you were Louis Foucault, a farmer, and before him Therese Adalansis a bookkeeper and before her Bruno Dax a policeman and before him Serge Reynaud, a quarry labourer."

"I'm sorry, Monsieur, you're mistaken. These names mean nothing to me," Guzco replied with disdain but fretting over how this stranger knew so much about his past lives.

"Hold me."

"I'm not in the habit of hugging."

"It will help you understand." Guzco ran his hands along Luca's back. His wings shifted.

"An Angel?" Guzco muttered with disbelief.

"Charged with bringing you back." The shrunken, slightly lame old man in front of him didn't match the Guzco spoken about in hushed, revered tones by other Collectors.

Dumbfounded, Guzco muttered, "I'd all but given up hope of ever returning. Tell me, is Azekiel angry with me?"

"Of course. But then he's always angry with everyone. After Philomandra, he wouldn't risk sending another Collector for you. Life and Death changed his mind."

"He's right to be wary of Massandar."

"I can match him."

"Master Meazza," Guzco sighed, "You may be adept at shinning up trees and inching along branches but you've faced nothing like Massandar."

"I stared down death in the War."

"That's as maybe, but understand, Massandar is as much an idea as a presence, able to inhabit your thoughts, set traps and lure you on. All without you knowing. Chances are he already knows you're here. Keep your wits about you."

"I shall." Luca tilted his face towards the rain and recalled saying his goodbyes to Greta at Principe Station and their promise to come to Badur.

At least he'd kept his part of the bargain. "Travelling through the mountains was a joy. To experience taste, touch, smell, pain, fear, even hunger again. I followed your route to learn of your struggles. But best of all, I was free to remember."

"Thought remembering was frowned upon."

"It is. But up here, whose to know?"

Despite the rain, a small crowd had gathered in the café with everyone keen to discuss Father Jerome's near drowning and subsequent rescue by the scruffy stranger. Among them were Monsieur Jonquet's, Devil, Monsieur Lerond's, Angel and Jean Baptiste's, Goliath all three masking their disappointment by guzzling the free gin and whiskey served up by Pierre. Not the good stuff but knock-off bottles gathering dust beneath the counter. Already the tale had entered the festival's pantheon of fables, with one or two wondering if it was the last Badur would see of the happy-clappy priest.

Greta busied herself taking orders while listening to eyewitnesses outbid their companions' accounts. Outside, a handful of people stood around Maurice's table. "Never seen the like," the Matriarch Lerond, whispered to Lydia who nodded in agreement.

Stepping into the tent, Helene again drew in the scent of sweat and sorrow as she sat on a cushioned seat. Chloe Jonquet stood on stage. She was barefoot and wearing a plain green loose fitting skirt and a white blouse bearing yellow and blue piped seams. Her long black hair hung loose.

"I'm afraid the pageant has been cancelled, Madame," she told Helene.

Seizing the moment, something she wouldn't have dared, even yesterday, Helene said, "Would you still dance for me, Mademoiselle? A strange request I know. But watching you yesterday, something stirred in me." Chloe seemed unsure. "Please," Helene insisted, "It would mean a great deal to me. And an old friend."

Laughter spilled from the café, its notes chiming with the pelting rain

drumming the tent's roof. Chloe swayed in time to this odd percussive ensemble. Within three steps she was lost to the simple but impossible steps, her movement tearing through the silence like a wound, splintering time into something sharp and wild. Controlled rage, both beautiful and feral.

Marvelling at the raw, balletic beauty before her, Helene fought back the tears. "Thank you, Irene," she whispered, no longer a cuckold or punchbag but capable, proud and not beholden to anyone. Except to Audrey. No longer would she accede to a life half lived, doing Maurice's bidding. Irene and The Angel of Badur had loosened the doubts shackling her since childhood.

Grateful he'd taken the chance to come to the tent on the off chance, Guzco looked on, astounded by the beauty unfolding before him. Marta's fluid movement was pure yet destructive. She punctured the air like a blade, carving shapes too fierce for words. Rising. Falling. Stopping.

He stepped onto Lavagna's black sands. Luisa and Bia greeted him. Brushing Luisa's cheek, he kissed her, lost for words, unable to take his eyes from her.

"Don't fret, my love," Luisa whispered. Wiping the tears from his eyes, she said, "I love you."

"My love, my love."

Bia giggled as he picked her up. "Did you bring my present?"

"Of course!" He handed her the boat carving.

"Keep it, Papa. Use it to sail home to us."

Out of breath and sweat-shined, Chloe came to a halt, her long black hair masking her. The rain still drummed but the laughter had deserted them. Even so, Helene knew she had witnessed perfection.

Luisa! Bia! Come back. Please!

"Your wife is very beautiful," Luca whispered. "Your daughter too."

"You saw them?"

"Of course. I see everything you do, Guzco." Nodding towards Helene, he continued, "Even her hopes and fears."

Guzco stowed the carving in his jacket pocket and smiled at Helene, who returned the favour.

I wonder what she saw.

"Wait here, Luca."

Outside the smoke-choked café, Guzco spotted a three sheets Jean Baptiste among those gathered around Maurice's table. Wondering what was going on, he squeezed past the onlookers to see Maurice wolfing down a bowl of the stew. Audrey sat beside him holding a glass of water to her dolly's lips. Maurice wiped the empty bowl with a slice of bread then said, "Any chance of seconds?"

"Seconds?" a slack-jawed Monsieur Lerond muttered.

"First time in living memory," Monsieur Jonquet replied.

"Five francs he heaves."

"You're on."

"Hospitalisation can't be out of the question. Strange folk, Bretons."

Pierre, holding a tea towel, depicting an Alpine scene, over his mouth and nose, ladled a second helping of stew into Maurice's bowl. Keeping the bowl at arm's length he hurried back and, admiring Maurice's pluck or stupidity, he set the bowl in front of him. Audrey scrunched up her face in disgust. "Smells like poo, Daddy," she said.

With everyone focussed on Maurice, Pierre, growing edgy, spotted Greta emptying ashtrays inside the café. Smoothing his tie and shirt, he approached her. She looked up at him and smiled.

"I need to speak to you, Greta. Can we go outside?"

"It's still pouring."

"We can talk in the tent. Please, it won't take long."

"Very well," she replied, bridling at his bossy tone. Apologising to the communists, still waiting for their free tipple, she followed Pierre, past

Maurice's table and towards the tent.

"Greta?" The voice sounded familiar, drawn from a previous life. Thinking it an aberration, she stopped in her tracks. Luca stood at the tent's entrance. She relived their steam shrouded promise to each other at Principe Station. Thirty years later, here he was. Overcome, speechless she stumbled into Pierre's arms.

Guzco pushed Luca back inside the tent and then helped Pierre lead Greta back to the café. First, he took her pulse and then rested the back of his hand against her forehead, something she found a tonic. Better still, a lullaby and the smell of the sea steadied her frenetic thoughts.

"I thought he was dead," she whispered.

"Who?" Guzco asked.

"Luca."

"What did she say, Doc?" Pierre asked, at the end of his wits.

"Nothing to worry about," Guzco answered a touch too quickly. "She hasn't eaten all day. Felt a little feint."

Greta looked past Guzco, hoping to see Luca but only saw familiar faces studying her, some concerned, others intrigued. She waved Guzco away then hurried outside towards the tent. There was no sign of him. Her legs gave way once more. This time the baker caught her. "Let's get you home," he said.

Pierre stepped forward but Guzco rested a hand on his shoulder and said, "Let her be, Pierre. Tomorrow is soon enough."

The midnight bell chimed. With brittle memories calcifying, Greta stood at the window watching the breeze crease the tent's walls. On her wireless, a jaunty Sylvie Vartan sang about love. A few cackling, slurring stragglers hung around the café toasting each other with glasses of whatever came to hand. Pierre, among them, but apart, looked up to her apartment. She stepped back, still mortified by her earlier public display of emotion.

She studied the photograph of the two of them taken on the harbour wall in thirty-eight. The young man clutching *The Odyssey*, could be the twin of the young man she saw outside the tent. How could that be? For starters, Luca would be near fifty now, whilst the man she glimpsed was in his twenties. Lots of men sport cowlicks but the clincher was the callow, broken look behind his eyes. Whatever Mussolini had thrown at him, Luca's blue eyes always shone with wit and warmth. No, the young man couldn't have been Luca. She was a fool for even grasping at such a misplaced hope. *But why does it stay inside me, like a dormant infection?*

Doctor Chamonix's first ever words to her, now gnawed. "The lost can be found."

The past was gaining ground on her once more. She'd promised herself never to be owned by it, ever again. There was only one thing to do.

CHAPTER FIFTY-THREE
Badur, August 1969

The clock in Guzco's living room chimed three, as Luca, soaking both his feet in tepid salt water, wolfed down a third slice of pear tart.

"So the kilns are still working then," Guzco said. "That's where I started. Akin to hell in many eyes. I can still taste the sulphur to this day."

"Azekiel retains his enthusiasm for them. Apprentices are still graded there," Luca straightened and feigned a deep onerous voice to announce, "Kiln work is dismissed by all those trumpet blasters, one string harp pluckers and flesh worshippers, but kiln work is the making of us all!"

"Impressive mimicry."

"Too much time on my hands." He licked his fingers, then said, "I hope you don't mind but I must ask. Is there anything you miss?"

"Sleep. Dreams. To shutter thinking for a few hours would be a comfort. I found solace in the valley though, must have examined every tree, blade of grass, stream and river. To see a murmuration is a majestic moment. But since Philomandra's death I haven't wandered as often or as far. In truth, I've not wanted to do much of anything. I was trained in perfection, to guide, cradle, help, collect yet remain apart. Difficult to sustain when you've been abandoned."

Carvings of birds, fish, whales and boats littered the room, some finished, most discarded. "Impressive carvings though," Luca said, pointing at a hawk.

"Trinkets that help pass the time."

Rain lashed the windows while a gust of wind snuck beneath the floorboards, lifting the carpet. Luca ran his finger around his plate and again licked the crumbs.

"Why is Greta here?" he asked, unable to skirt the issue any longer.

"She came to Badur for her honeymoon. After her husband died, she came back. Ever since, the valley has shielded her. And now you show up."

The cuckolded prisoner of war replaced the confident young man. "To my shame, a coward's way out. Rational thought was a luxury in the camps, time spent there rendered immaterial. Our past, present and future was in the gift of the guards. Watching my comrades perish, survival became a luxury. I convinced myself that Greta no longer wanted me and that there was no life for me in Italy. Mussolini killed Papa. Guilt ravaged me for surviving. So I decided to take my chances with death."

"You failed to trust yourself, Luca, that the world had no space for you when you came home. Yet there was ample."

"When I saw Greta, all I wanted to do was to tell her I love her and to explain."

"Explain what? That you are an Angel? Here to take Doctor Chamonix, another Angel, away?"

"She deserves to know."

"To know that you had such little faith in her and chose death? She married, lost that man, and years later you appear! You no longer have or deserve a place in her life except to be a sad, bitter memory."

"I love her."

"But not enough to trust her." He studied Luca's troubled features, unsure if the young man had understood. He tried a different tack. "For years life in the valley rested upon the weather and the harvest. Death was all purveying, land and children routes to survival. I witnessed people share unforgiving, rigid lives driven by circumstance and Church law. The great advances in science and medicine allowed love to flourish. It's good to be able to love who you wish. Now choice is abundant. Yet still people cling to the old nostrums of life and death. You chose death when you jumped."

"Hopelessness dulled me."

"Perhaps your eagerness for death explains why you were chosen. Death tempers people's daily thoughts. I've witnessed enough of it to value life to its very last drop."

"Why do you think you were chosen?"

"They wanted my brother, Jose, not me. He was much more capable than me in every respect. I killed him and in that act, I interrupted our fates. There will be such an event that stalled your fate."

"Mussolini? The War? Cheating death in the camps?"

"Any of those."

"I've never thought of things in that way before."

"You've not had centuries of banishment to contend with."

"But look at what you've achieved in Badur."

"In hoc to dreams, hoping for this moment."

"Amongst apprentices your stoicism and service are legendary."

"If I could recall such an emotion, I'm pretty sure I'd feel proud."

"You should."

"But before we maul ourselves with adulation, I have to attend to a dying man."

"My instructions are to bring you back without delay."

"Luca, I have been *waiting centuries*. I've survived war, plagues, famine, the cold, the heat. I skirted childbirth by a whisker, but had the misfortune of several drunken, rutting husbands. I've witnessed murders, fought and killed. Endured centuries of loneliness, mocking goats. I've *menstruated* for fuck's sake! And let me tell you, that's no fun at all. No, three days is a small delay. But a stray word or look from you and everything will unravel. There's an old bothy in the woods. You can stay there whilst I attend to Velous. If we leave now we'll reach it by daybreak."

"Very well, Guzco. Three days. And then we leave."

CHAPTER FIFTY-FOUR
The Holiday Cottage, Badur, August 1969

Waking with a start, heart racing, Helene looked up at the damp patch on the ceiling, its whorling pattern beautiful yet disturbing. The bed springs creaked under duress from Maurice's fart. She slipped out of bed, gathered up her clothes and tiptoed outside. After checking on Audrey, she crept downstairs and stepped into her one-piece black swimsuit, the one Maurice told her was tarty.

Shivering in the dawn air, she dived into the water. Again the cold took her breath away as she swam a length underwater. Breaching the surface, she took a breath then sank until her feet rested on the pool's concrete floor. Above and around her, the water moved in a dense, slinking motion. Safe, out of sight, the young girl who'd almost drowned in the Saint Germain baths promised to return to Badur one day to again witness the dance and its promise of a life not stifled by her overbearing guardians or violent, belittling, ignorant husband.

She caught sight of a hazy figure standing poolside. She surfaced and climbed out. She was alone but on a lounger weighed down by a stone, lay a sheet of paper, its edges curling in the breeze. It was a delicate pencil sketch of her gliding through the water.

Confused, she looked along the path towards the cottage, the landlords' farmhouse, and the woods beyond. Nothing, save for the odd chicken and the tabby cat sunning itself on the patio.

Reaching the cottage, for once she locked the door behind her. Just in case. Leaving the sketch on the kitchen table, she filled the cafetiere and set it on the hob. Waiting for the coffee to brew, she peered through the venetian blinds but saw no one but swore after stubbing her toe on the loose flagstone. The pain was short, sharp, frustrating.

Not wanting to wake Maurice, she crept into the bedroom and set the coffee down beside him. His hand snaked out and grabbed her arm. She broke free then said, "Going to the village. Need eggs," Her fear of him trumped the mystery artist.

"When you get back then. No more playing hard to get."

Without replying, she dressed quickly and drew her damp hair into a ponytail. Audrey, standing on the landing said, "Dolly wants to go for a swim, Maman."

"Daddy will take you after breakfast."

Hurrying downstairs, she heard Audrey say, "Dolly wants to go for a swim, Papa."

Relieved to have escaped Maurice clutches, Helene unlocked the back door and stepped outside. She left the door ajar in order not to disturb him and earn a telling off when she returned.

Nothing stirred, even the Velous' house lay silent. Usually the old girl was out by now feeding the chickens with her pervy husband looking out the grubby window. The old girl must have left the sketch on the lounger. Her way of being friendly. Odd way to go about things but there you are. Country folk and all that.

This time she kept to the road. Just to be sure.

Arriving in the square, she walked past the bleary-eyed gang who had erected the tent yesterday. Uneasy in their glare, she hurried to the café, where Pierre was downing his morning livener. He straightened his waistcoat then said, "Good morning, Madame. A shame you didn't get the chance to see the festival in all its glory yesterday. Coffee?"

"Please." She took her seat, her unease shifting to annoyance with the leering men.

Pierre scratched his stubble. "Usually the priest recites a prayer or two, blesses a broken toaster or bike tyre, gags on the stew and then takes himself off. A close shave with his maker is not expected."

"How far did he drift?"

"Two hundred metres, there or thereabouts."

"I'm glad he's safe."

"So am I. A dead priest is not a good look. By the way, how is your husband today?"

"Fine thank you. Why do you ask?"

"Nobody can remember the last time anybody ate two platefuls of the stew. One, come to that."

"Maurice has a very healthy appetite."

"And a cast-iron constitution. He was the talk of the village last night."

"He'll like that. He likes being the centre of attention." She glanced inside the café, her eyes drawn to Irene's portrait.

"My wife," Pierre said, a touch ruefully.

"She's very beautiful."

"Irene was the prettiest girl I ever met. Between you and me, Madame, I found it hard to believe we courted, let alone married. She broke my heart but now I hope she's happy."

"That is very gracious of you."

"I've learned that it isn't healthy to let memory cloud life."

The Studebaker arrived to a round of sarcastic applause from the tent party. The driver jumped down from the cab, hitched up his trousers and waved away the jeers. Over the next hour or so, the festival was packed away for another year. The Secretary was a noticeable absentee but it was clear to all concerned that things ran much more smoothly than usual without his small-minded interferences.

From her window, Greta watched Pierre carry the coffee and Pernod snifters out to the tent party and water for the nuns arriving from Sacre Coeur. He looked towards her. Embarrassed, she stepped back and opened one of her suitcases sitting on the bed, wondering why regret existed in the human condition. It's nothing more than a waste of time and emotion. Fighting the temptation to look at Luca's picture, she set about writing two notes. One for the baker, the other for Pierre.

The baker's note took next to no time. Pierre's however proved much more difficult as the growing pieces of crumpled paper scattered around the table attested to. She was ending something with the one man who had never asked her for anything. Yet what would she have done if he had revealed his feelings? Falling in love with the valley and Pierre was irresponsible. Irrational. Love is for the young and foolish. As you get older life is to be tolerated, endured. The festival's faded glory and bizarre rituals showed her this. She should have stayed in Badur for those few days and then moved on to teach biology to bored pupils far, far away, leaving Lavagna, Genoa, Luca and Massimo behind.

Finally happy with the letter, Greta placed it in an envelope and rested it beside the baker's note, against her money jar. She wiped her glasses, brushed her hair, applied a little lipstick, put on a new light cream jacket and opened the apartment door. Seeing Guzco on the landing, took her by surprise. He was holding the croissants left by the baker's daughter.

"How are you feeling?" he asked.

"Much better thank you, Doctor. A good night's sleep has done the trick."

"Then you won't mind if I check a couple of things." He sensed her despair. If he still had his wings, he'd take her under them. She sighed and checked her watch. Ten forty-four. The bus was due. She sat on the bed. Guzco took her pulse and felt her forehead with the back of his hand. Again she heard the lullaby and smelled the sea.

"Everything is as it should be. Pierre has given you the day off. Rest up. Eat and drink plenty of water."

"Yes, Doctor. Sorry for yesterday."

"Nothing to apologise for, Greta. Such moments makes life interesting. Who did you mistake my nephew for?"

"Your nephew?"

"Yes. From Toulouse. He's here for a walking holiday."

"He reminded me of someone I was close to, a long time ago." She stood, first straightening her jacket and then tidying its collar.

"He set off at dawn for a trek in the mountains," Guzco said with a mischievous tone, "Although judging by his hangover, it may not be a pleasurable experience. I'd hoped to introduce him to you in the café this evening." Noticing the cases, he asked, "Going somewhere?"

"Lavagna. I haven't been back since my mother's death. Oona has been nagging me to visit. My parents' apartment is still empty. I'll move there and then decide what to do next."

"Does Pierre know?"

"No. He'll only try to change my mind." Picking both letters up, she hid her heartache by adopting a matter-of-fact manner. "Could you give him this? It explains everything." Handing Guzco the second note, she said, "Could you give this to the baker? The rent is paid up to the end of the month and I'm happy to leave my furnishings. Also, there's a library book by the sink that needs to be returned. Could you arrange that?"

"Of course but are you sure about this, Greta? Sometimes it's best to

think on things."

"Spent too many years thinking, Doctor. Half the problem."

"I respect you too much to try and change your mind. But let me drive you to Nice, if only to spare Pierre."

"I'll take the bus. I don't want to look as if I am slipping away." She knew she owed Pierre his dignity but she owed herself more, even if it meant being cruel. "I must begin to live again."

Struggling with the cases, Guzco staggered through the doorway and down the stone steps. Greta stole a final look around the apartment, realising for the first time how small it was.

For once the bus was early, and its driver, sharp featured with insincere eyes, took the chance to enjoy a quiet smoke. Red-faced from his efforts, Guzco set down the cases, rubbed his hands and waved to the Studebaker driver as he drove off.

"I'll miss you, Greta," he said.

"I'll miss you too, Doctor. Thank you for your many kindnesses."

"Come back. One day."

"Perhaps."

They hugged, Guzco drawing in her crisp, sultry scent, Greta again smelling the sea. Her hands brushed the aged scar tissue running down his shoulder blades. "War wounds," he said.

"Not the scars from having your wings amputated?"

If only you knew.

The bus driver stubbed out his cigarette. "Where to?" he asked her.

"Nice, please."

"Return?"

"No. Single."

After loading her suitcases, the driver took his seat and started the engine. Pierre hurried from the café. "Where are you going?" he asked Greta, while glancing at Guzco for reassurance.

"Lavagna," she replied, unable to look at him.

"Why?"

"Madame," interrupted the driver, a man lacking a sense of the romantic.

"One minute, Monsieur, please," Pierre pleaded.

"I've a timetable to keep to."

"This bus hardly ever runs to time, so why talk of timetables now!" Greta

touched his arm, covering Irene's tattoo. He looked wounded, desperate. "As much as I love it here, Pierre, I must go. I gave the Doctor a letter. It explains everything."

"What can you say in a note that you cannot say to my face, Greta?"

"Please, Madame," the driver insisted.

Fighting back the tears, Greta kissed Pierre on the cheek then whispered, "Thank you for saving me." She boarded and took her seat. He meant so much to her but she needed to trust herself.

Pierre stood on the bus's bottom step. Something, fear or shyness, he couldn't figure, held him back. Instead in a despairing rage, he tore off the bus's left windscreen wiper and began to flail the windscreen with it. "You bastarding bastard! You can't take her from me!" he yelled.

"That wiper belongs to the bus company!" the driver shouted.

Red faced, veins throbbing, Pierre levelled the wiper at him and hollered, "Bastard bus. First you took Irene from me and now, Greta. Do you know the hours of wasted hope I spent on you? And did you ever help me?"

"I'll have the police onto you for this."

"Just leave, Monsieur, please," Guzco urged.

The bus pulled away. Greta pushed her glasses up her nose then swept a stray lock of hair behind her ear. She gripped the seat in front not daring to look back. Pierre, out of breath from his efforts, hurled the wiper after the bus and muttered, "Don't go, Greta."

Sister Francine clapped her hands. The nine nuns lined up. She clapped again and the column headed for Sacre Coeur with the cushioned chairs. Passing Pierre, the wizened old nun whispered, "I'm sorry."

Pierre read the note sitting at the table where he and Greta always took their morning coffee. Finishing the note, he laid his glasses on the table and rubbed his stubble. "She loved it here, Doc. She once told me Badur had allowed her to lay her past to rest. So why leave?"

"It is not that simple, Pierre," Guzco replied, thinking of Luca.

"Simple?" Pierre threw his hands in the air, "My life ground to a halt the day Irene left. Each time the bus pulled in, I hoped she was aboard. Day after day, month after month, year after year I held these hopes. What a waste. She was never coming back. She always wanted more; more than I could give her. Excitement, passion, risk. None of those things were in my gift. But Greta…" Fighting the tears he continued, "She dared me to hope that I'd find love again."

He put his glasses back on and read, *"I came here to find peace, a fanciful misguided notion when I realise that all along I have been hiding from despair. From the moment I stepped off the bus, you were there to support me. You have always been so gentle and loving, the kindest friend and confidante. Sometimes I wished we could have a life together but the sadness inside me would at some point lead me to betray you. You do not deserve that."*

Folding the letter, he then said, "I never told her I loved her, Doc. And that is the worst feeling a man can take to his grave. What should I do?"

"I'd have thought that obvious."

CHAPTER FIFTY-FIVE
The Holiday Cottage, Badur, August 1969

Climbing from the pool, Helene found another sketch weighed down on the lounger. This one showed Audrey thrashing in the water, her face one of panic. Alarmed, she decided to ask the landlord or landlady if they knew who the artist was and put an end to this threatening nonsense.

Skirting the loose flagstone, she brought Maurice's coffee up to him. To her relief, Audrey was sat on the bed beside him with her dolly. "Can I take Dolly for a swim, Papa?" she asked.

"No," Maurice snapped, stifling a yawn.

"Will you take me and Dolly swimming, Maman?"

"I have to go out Audrey but ask Papa, nicely this time, and I'm sure he'll change his mind."

"Please, Papa," Audrey pleaded.

Maurice sighed. "Very well but let me drink my coffee first."

Screeching with delight, Audrey bounced up and down on the bed and shouted, "Look, Maman. Dolly and me are dancing."

Helene smiled. Audrey's dance reminded her of her first clumsy steps in front of Irene, while Maurice, wary of the hot coffee slopping around his cup, told Audrey to sit still or he wouldn't take her swimming.

"Eggs and a newspaper," he shouted, as she went downstairs.

Leaving the back door ajar, Helene set off but seeing the Doctor's car parked outside the farmhouse, she decided to ask the landlords about the mystery drawings when she returned from the village.

Maurice drifted off to sleep. Audrey nudged him. He didn't stir. Even Dolly couldn't wake him. Growing impatient, and telling Dolly to be quiet, she crept downstairs. The back door was open, the gap big enough for her to squeeze through. Again telling Dolly to keep quiet, she ran along the gravel path towards the pool with the nosey tabby cat a few paces behind.

Seeking the comfort of the familiar, Jean Velous' cloudy eyes scoured the bedroom. They landed on the striking portrait of Henri hung between the Sacred Heart and large crucifix hanging from the opposite wall. He looked to his right and saw Doctor Chamonix, standing in front of the mahogany wardrobe where he stashed much of his illicit wealth. Past the chest of drawers, laden with his medicines, he saw Marianne, sitting beside him. The room was silent except for her creaking chair and the oxygen feeding his fetid lungs through a mask. The window was half open to chase out a stifling cigarette and piss-addled scent.

The still drawn, plain green curtains flapped in the light breeze, allowing enough light into the room for Guzco to notice the thick layer of dust coating every surface. He unbuttoned Velous' pyjamas then laid the stethoscope on his chest.

"Jean told me he smells the sea when you examine him, Doctor," Marianne whispered.

"Pleased to hear it," Guzco replied, buttoning the pyjamas. "But I think you should fetch Father Jerome." Stunned, Marianne hurried into the hall and called for Celeste.

Velous lifted the mask and rasped, "That you, Angel?"

"Yes."

"Thank God." He grabbed Guzco's lapel. "I should've saved Henri. I deserve to die with such a lie on my lips. But please, spare Marianne the truth. Allow her a few happy memories of our time together."

"Why?"

"In my own way I loved her. Besides, you were sent to watch over the valley, even the likes of me."

"How did you know?"

Velous smiled but said nothing. Even now, at the end of his life, he wanted to get one over, but Guzco had waited years for this moment. "Why should you be shown mercy when you wronged so many?" he whispered, "You helped the Nazis hunt down those poor Jews. You even shared a joke with them as they murdered your son. Ever since, you've basked in lies and deceits, happy to see innocent people defamed."

"And for all that and more, I ask for forgiveness."

"Too late for that. What's more," Guzco paused, revelling in this moment,

years in the waiting. "Henri fathered a child. Yet because of your greed, and your hate, you never knew them."

"A grandchild?" Violent hope lit up Velous' deathly features. "I'd give my soul just to see them."

"It's not in my gift, Jean." *And even if it was I'd deny you.*

"Please, Angel, I beg you." Guzco remained unmoved.

Massandar was right all along. Strip away the sheen of Chamonix's respectability, and rage and jealousy still cling to me, fuelled by every slight, real or imagined. I should be better than this. I can be. I know I can. But why do I still want, no, need Velous to writhe with pain and anguish in his final moments? And then deny his soul? What have I become? Massandar's acolyte?

"Doctor." Guzco turned to see Marianne standing in the doorway. She seemed distracted, in shock. "It's the young Breton girl She needs you."

Torn between saving Audrey or denying Velous peace, Guzco hesitated. "The child, Doctor!" Marianne shouted, loosening Massandar's grip. Guzco hurried into the hall. A short, heavyset woman, no more than forty, knelt over the limp, unconscious, Audrey. Both of them were ringing wet with the scent of chlorine clinging to them.

Velous squirmed. His eyes landed on Henri's portrait but he died staring up at the nicotine-stained ceiling, the mask torn away, his lips curled around one last word. Marianne kissed her dead husband's forehead, closed his eyes and wondered what he'd tried to tell her.

Shouting, "I am with you, I am with you," Guzco pumped Audrey's chest then pinched her nostrils to give her the kiss of life. He leaned back and placed two fingers on Audrey's neck, checking for a pulse. There wasn't one.

"Please, Doctor," the woman urged. Guzco redoubled his efforts. Still nothing. Isabella and Marta reared in his panicked mind's eye from that fog-bound night centuries before.

Please Azekiel, let this child live.

Nearing the main road, Helene doubled back thinking if the landlady didn't know who the artist was then perhaps the Doctor could help. Having both of them in the house would save time.

As she climbed the steps towards the farmhouse, she noticed the old man wasn't in his usual spot by the window. She heard a commotion coming from inside. Perhaps she could help. She'd done a bit of first aid training in the factory. She knocked. No answer. She opened the door. To her horror, she saw the kindly Doctor frantically pumping Audrey's chest.

Speechless, she looked on, the pain of Audrey's birth nothing compared to the pain now racking her. The panicked midwife working feverishly to unblock Audrey's airways. Audrey's first smile, her first tooth, her first step, her first word. She wanted, needed, to lash out at her parents, Aunt and Uncle, Maurice, even Irene for leading her to this cursed place.

"I'm with you, I'm with you," Guzco shouted, as again he searched for a pulse. Still nothing. He leaned away and allowed his head to drop, unsure if there was any point carrying on.

"Please, Doctor," insisted the woman. "Protect her when she comes."

"Please, Doctor," pleaded Helene.

He rolled Audrey onto her side and then struck her on the back. Once. Twice. Audrey's torso jolted and lurched under the assault but her fingers flickered for a spare, petty moment. To the outside world the flicker meant nothing. But on this grubby hall floor, in a run-down farmhouse in the middle of nowhere, it meant life. Audrey's eyes half opened. She gagged, coughed up a mouthful water and then fought for breath. The fingers on her tiny right hand wrapped themselves around Guzco's left forefinger.

Helene, now sobbing, brushed away the wet hair clinging to her daughter's face. "Papa fell asleep so I took Dolly swimming on my own, Maman. But I forgot she couldn't swim."

"We'll have to teach her then," Helene answered, smiling through her tears.

Guzco's hands shook as he removed his glasses to wipe the sweat from his eyes. It was better to save life than take it. A hand rested on his shoulder.

"Thank you, Doctor," the woman said.

Putting his glasses back on, Guzco, looked at the woman, now cleaning her thick, horn rimmed glasses. He'd seen her before but couldn't remember where or when. He froze. It was the same unremarkable face that years before, had passed across Philomandra's dying features.

"He's gone, Celeste." Marianne and her daughter held each other and sobbed.

CHAPTER FIFTY-SIX
The Velous' Farmhouse, Badur, August 1969

Jean Velous' open larch wood coffin lay in the farmhouse's rarely used but well aired front parlour. Velous was dressed in his best suit of clothes and shoes. Rosary beads were wrapped around his clasped hands. Marianne, tired, drawn and wearing a plain black dress and matching shoes, sat beside the coffin, accepting murmured condolences with a weary smile and odd word. An empty chair sat beside her.

Guzco stood behind Lydia and her husband in the shuffling queue waiting to pay their respects. "Any news from the hospital, Doctor?" Lydia asked.

"The little girl is expected to make a full recovery."

"Thank God." She made a sign of the Cross. "And her parents? Can't imagine what they have been through."

"A little shocked but apart from that they are fine."

"That's a relief. You're a hero, Doctor."

Indifferent to the praise, Guzco moved forward, leaned into the coffin and kissed Velous' cold, waxy forehead. *Even in death you look untrustworthy.* He counted to ten before approaching Marianne.

"Thank you for coming, Doctor." Marianne's voice was strained and a touch hoarse. With his eye drawn to her wedding band, Guzco said, "If there's anything you need, Marianne, just ask."

"Saving that poor little girl was enough. Is she well?"

"On the mend."

"And her parents?"

"Shocked but they'll live."

"Never wanted that pool to be dug out, but Jean said it would be a money-spinner."

"No harm done. Where is, Celeste?"

"She's not comfortable in crowds." Marianne's expression made it clear their conversation was over. Lydia nudged Guzco aside to embrace Marianne. "I'm so sorry for your loss, Marianne, no finer man ever trod the valley's soil."

If only you knew.

Guzco glanced for one final time at Velous and could have sworn his old foe was smirking. He slipped into the kitchen, acknowledging other mourners sipping cheap wine and nibbling on bread and cheese. He stood at the dirt-streaked window. An ashtray piled with cigarette ends and a half-smoked packet of Gitanes sat on the draining board. For years he'd plotted his revenge, yet now it felt bittersweet, hardly worth the wait. But if he hadn't been in the farmhouse, Audrey would have perished.

Leaving the farmhouse, he skirted a few loitering mourners and headed for the barn. The heady aroma of resin and paint once more assailed him as he rummaged in the filing cabinet for a lamp. He found one which worked only after a good shake. Its thin shaft of light created other worldly shadows among the jumble of machinery and stuffed animals. He weaved his way through the collected junk. The sight of the indifferent goat still startled him.

A cigarette tip glowed in Celeste's studio. "Thought I'd see you today," she said, half blinding Guzco with her torchlight.

Shielding his eyes, he replied. "Wanted to thank you for saving, Audrey."

"Anyone would have done the same. By the way, I found this floating in the pool." She held up Dolly. "Had one similar when I was little. Mine was made from wood though. Henri carved it from a single piece of larch. Maman fashioned a dress for her from an old scarf. Loved, Beatrice. She went everywhere with me."

"Do you still have it?"

"I'm far too old for dollies now, Doctor!"

Guzco lit up the far wall. "Can I ask you about the drawings."

"You weren't supposed to see them. Maman shouldn't have let you."

"It wasn't her fault, honestly. But they fascinate me."

"No surprise. They're about *you* after all."

"How did you know?"

"Philomandra."

"You knew her?"

Setting her lamp down, Celeste took a final drag on her cigarette then stubbed it out in the teeming ashtray. "Found her hiding in here a few days before Henri's murder, battered, bruised, desperate to find you, Doctor. At first, I thought she was a Jew escaping to Switzerland until she told me this fantastical tale about her being an Angel sent to protect you from the Devil himself and how she'd managed to give him the slip but he was still after her. Didn't believe her at first. An Angel here? In this hovel? I'd have been carted off to the asylum if I told anyone. But there was something about her, difficult to spot at first on account of her wounds. But when she stepped from the shadows," She paused to straighten a pile of sketches. Time bought, she continued, "She was perfection, Doctor. In every way. Never seen the like."

She was.

"I sheltered her. Brought her food. Clothes too, Maman's favourite silk blouse and her best jacket and skirt too. Two days later, the day of Henri's funeral, a big car, bigger than Papa's old Renault, pulls up and this smooth-talking fella, full of smiles and smarm, asks me if I've seen her. I spin him a yarn but he orders the man and mute woman with him to search the barn."

"And they found her?"

"As if. I hid her inside the horse just like the Greeks did in Troy all those years ago. You know Odysseus, and all that stuff." Despite her childlike manner, there was a poise about Celeste, a sense of control, defiance almost.

"Fancy some fresh air, Doctor? Don't want you fainting again." She opened the grimy window. "Dressed for, Papa," she said, noting Guzco's surprise to see her dressed head to toe in black. "Not that he deserves anybody's pity. Nasty man. Beat me and Henri all the time, Maman too when the mood took him. I used to think the beatings were my fault, that if I prayed even harder, they'd stop. But no matter how much I prayed, nothing changed. With or without the drink, he was a bad man, plain and simple. Burned my Beatrice on the fire." She looked outside and asked, "Did you take his soul?"

"Sorry?"

"Philomandra told me that's why you're here, to collect souls. Only you weren't very good at it, so she was sent here to keep you out of harm's way. Did you take Papa's?"

"No. I didn't think him worthy."

"Good. He gave Philomandra up to that man." Her words stunned Guzco. "You remember, the year Maman accused you of being a collaborator. Papa stormed in here. Never seen him so angry. He took the belt to me, demanding I tell him what I knew about Henri's death. I told him I didn't know anything. But it didn't matter. He kept hitting me, saying over and over it was my fault Henri had died and if I'd been normal, none

of this would have happened. I'm sure he'd have killed me if it wasn't for Philomandra. Where she came from I'll never know, but all the same, I'm glad she did. Scared Papa witless. I told her to leave, that he wasn't a man to cross. She fled. I followed her into the forest but lost track of her. That Massandar fella and his cronies must have found her. Daresay Papa helped them hunt her down. Must explain how he could afford the swimming pool and the finery on display around here."

Guzco's stomach tightened. Even dead, Velous had managed to get the better of him.

"I knew the exact moment when she died." Celeste took her glasses off and cleaned them on her sleeve. "I was wandering the woods, calling out to her but all I heard was the blunt echo of my voice. I crossed a river, a stream really, crossed it hundreds of times before. Then this stabbing pain in my chest strikes me down, and I'm washed away in a torrent. That's the moment Philomandra died. Sure of it. The next thing I know, I'm clawing at the water, the breath leaving me. And as I'm drowning, all these lives sped through me, all sorts; some cruel, some kind, some sad, some happy. Then, I'm on the surface gasping for breath. Alive. Ever since, I've drawn. Turned me into a hermit, shackled to your memories, Angel. Maman thought I'd a gift, a revelation, especially after I drew Henri by the war memorial with Irene looking over him. When he saw the drawing, Papa said nothing. But he never raised his hand to Maman or me again. Philomandra protected us from him." She paused, chastened by her brutal, solitary past..

There's something else too." She turned her back to Guzco, unhooked her dress then raised her slip over her shoulders. Holding his torch up Guzco winced as he inspected the aged welts and scars around her neck and upper shoulders. As he levelled the torch on her back, two tightly bound wings shifted beneath the calico binding.

Protect her when she comes.

"Not every day you end up an Angel. Must have been Philomandra's gift for saving her. Long for the day when I can use them."

"Who knows?"

Pulling her slip back down, Celeste shook her head then said, "Only you."

"But you stayed hidden from me."

"Had to. Massandar knows everything about you, so I stayed hidden.

Only it's clear now he doesn't know about me. Not yet anyway. Best if it stays that way. To protect Maman, like I used to protect her from Papa. Besides, I'm not cut out to roam the earth looking to do good or bad. Happy to stay home and chronicle your stories."

"So why help me now?"

"Drew this last night." She held up a sketch of Luca and Massandar. Massandar was brandishing Caballero.

It was dusk by the time Guzco reached the bothy, now little more than a pile of stone buried beneath a thicket of brambles. He crawled inside. Faded obscenities and betrothals covered the walls. There was no sign of Luca.

Hunched against the cold, lungs burning, limbs aching, Luca trudged through the starlit night, listening to his illusory Russian pursuers, barking orders and obscenities at each other. He scrabbled after his old comrades, the risk of coming across Massandar outweighed by the chance of redemption.

"Keep up, Luca!" they shouted as one.

"Please, I want to explain," he shouted after them. They ran on.

CHAPTER FIFTY-SEVEN
Pierre's Café, Badur, November 1969

When news of the letter reached the Matriarch Lerond, she fetched Lydia, who in turn fetched Guzco, who hurried to the café. Pierre's tired, red eyes spoke of drunken sleeplessness. He sported a week-old beard. Worse still, he stank to high heaven.

"Heard you received a letter from Italy," Guzco said, his eye drawn to the glinting bus windscreen wiper nailed above Irene's portrait.

"It's got a Genovese postmark," Pierre replied, holding the envelope up to the light. "Not sure if I should open it. After all, the last letter an Italian wrote to me didn't carry the best news."

"Open it, Pierre."

Pierre tore open the envelope. He turned the letter over. Hope drained from his face. "It's from, Oona." He read on in silence. When he'd finished, he set the letter on the table then rubbed his beard.

"Well?" Guzco asked.

"She's not coming back." Pierre downed his morning livener. "Oona thinks I should visit Lavagna."

"Sounds promising."

Pierre downed another livener then replaced the stopper in the Pernod bottle. "Not going all that way just to make a fool of myself."

"What are you afraid of?"

"What good will it do, Doc? I finally pluck up the courage to tell her, and she ups and leaves."

"You took years! What are you going to do? Rot in the village, drinking yourself to death, shuffling from day to day wondering what might have been. Don't live in the past, look to the future. Would Greta have left, if you had told her how you felt about her?"

"But if she says no? What then?"

"Then for those few seconds you'll have lived with passion, hope, excitement even. And earned my respect."

"But she can have her pick of men."

"Remember what her note said about her feelings for you?"

"Only of not wanting to hurt me."

"And of sharing her life with you?"

"Don't remember that." He waved Guzco away. "Besides, I'm too old to go charging off to Italy."

"Tell her, Pierre. If not for your sake then for mine. To spare me your constant whining."

Outside, Jean Baptiste stepped from his nearly new Berliet van. He nodded to Pierre then shook Guzco's hand. "Got here as soon as I could, Doctor. Your message sounded urgent."

"I need a favour, Jean Baptiste," Guzco replied. Unsure when or if Luca would return, he needed to remain in Badur. Jean Baptiste was the one he trusted to give the plan he and Oona had cooked up any chance of success.

An hour later, Jean Baptiste and Pierre, now washed, shaved and dressed, squabbled over having the radio on for the long drive to Italy. Pierre invoking the curse of Manastalgi, preferred to travel in silence whilst Jean Baptiste wanted to listen to his favourite jazz station.

Watching the van pull away, with the sound of Duke Ellington in its wake, Guzco drew his coat tight and walked home. A storm gathered in the snow-coated high valley, the strengthening wind flexing the trees. He hoped helping Pierre find happiness so long frittered, would reduce the lingering guilt he still felt for denying Velous' soul. Massandar had beaten him again. The dice always rolled in his favour.

The bitter north-easterly rattled the windowpanes as he opened his front door. The sweet, unctuous smell of Lydia's lemon tart greeted him. "Dinner in ten minutes," she shouted from the kitchen. "Pork stew."

He sat by the fire, opened his knife and set to whittling the tail fin of the whale carving he had started earlier in the week. The keening wind funnelled down the chimney. Guzco swore he heard Massandar laughing.

"Dinner ready yet?" he shouted.

"Five minutes."

The blade caught on a stubborn knot. Guzco's frustration grew. His knifework became rushed and clumsy. The wood split along the grain, leaving it fit only for kindling. He tossed it on the fire and again asked if dinner was ready.

On the mountainside, grief wrapped guilt still hoodwinked Luca into thinking he was tramping the Russian Steppe.

In the bitter, ceaseless cold, the prisoners' ice-bound balaclavas give them the appearance of withered aliens, ever fearful of another random beating from the Kazak guards. They're lashed to each other to prevent one dropping to the ground through exhaustion and dying at the hands of the cold or a bullet.

Stiffened corpses mark the way, their frostbitten faces imprinted with suffering, bodies contorted, magnifying the survivors' awareness that death stalks them. Only survival and friendship matter.

He trudged on, instinct and hope his guides while trying to shake off his imagined Russian pursuers by hiding amongst the rocks, wading into freezing streams or climbing ice-scarred trees. He'd hide for days, his pursuers shouting and bawling surrounding him. A world that did not run to the governance of Angels. When he moved on, he shunned the hamlets and isolated izbas, certain the Soviet peasantry would betray him in order to collect the bounty on his head.

Lost in yet another valley, sheltering from yet another storm and yet again cursing immortality, Luca's stooped, wind-lashed comrades passed within one hundred paces of him.

"Stop! Wait!" he shouted. They walked on.

He stepped from his bolt-hole to follow but within seconds, his comrades were devoured by the driving snow and howling wind. Madness to follow. Better to stay safe and strike out when the bludgeoning storm abated. They couldn't get very far. In his stricken state, a slither of hope settled in him. His long, weary but bold march was about to bear fruit. He crawled back into his hideaway and curled into a ball in an effort to fend of the cold. The only thing that mattered to him now was their forgiveness. After that, the Devil take the hindmost.

Dawn broke. The storm had abated. Stiff and frozen, Luca crawled from the shelter. Three sets of fresh footprints trailed towards the next valley.

Hopes raised, he followed, weaving through the drunken supporters from Lavagna's rival villages, all shouting their boats on. Near the southern headland Greta, wearing her wellingtons and red coat, the one with the shiny buttons, rubs a pebble for luck and flings it across the flat water. "Sixer," she says. "Bet you can't beat that."

"'Course I can," he answers, hurling a fragment of scree down the mountain's shoulder but disappointed to see it peter out as a threer.

CHAPTER FIFTY-EIGHT
Lavagna, November 1969

In the grey, washed-out morning, Greta stood at her living room window, watching the large merchantman plough through the choppy sea towards Genoa. Distracted by squawking gulls wheeling overhead, she looked towards the southern headland and imagined a young girl and the oddball boy she'd met at an old maid's funeral, shinning up an aged beech tree in order to shout into the gale.

The sea view confirmed that coming home had been the right thing to do. Better still, her parents' apartment offered a degree of comfort she'd long forsaken in Badur. All she had to do now was summon the courage to visit their graves and put an end to Oona's nagging. She put on her coat, one of her mother's hand me downs, and left the apartment to take her regular morning stroll along the harbour.

The level crossing barriers were down to allow a Pisa bound train to roll through. With the barriers raised, she walked to the near deserted quayside, alive to the tune of creaking ropes straining to keep yachts tethered to bollards. A blue and yellow goiter boat lay upturned outside the Yacht Club enclosure. She wished Papa and Uncle had lived to see Lavagna's victory in this year's Regatta, even with two Yugoslavs in the crew.

Luca made good progress, for once able to appreciate the stern, barren beauty surrounding him as he tracked iced footprints along a ridge that plummeted on its eastern face towards a small lake with the bluest water imaginable. He reached a fork in the path. One route led towards the lake, the other towards the giant boulder he'd passed months earlier. The footprints snaked towards it. Luca followed them. Within the hour he patted the boulder for luck and then drank from the nearby stream, recalling the moment he'd almost surrendered to its current whilst bathing.

Refreshed, he looked for fresh tracks, while rehearsing what he'd say to his comrades about football, politics and lovers, real or imagined. There were no tracks, only unblemished drifts. Confused, he scoured the terrain, expecting to see his comrades trekking towards the lake or perhaps doubling back. The only other sign of life was the falcon circling overhead in languid, broad sweeps.

He had been tricked. Months wasted, thanks to his petulance laced guilt. He should have listened to Guzco and stayed in that run down bothy. Out here, exhausted and starving, he was easy pickings for Massandar. The bitter wind whipped up the fresh snowfall, blinding him. Panic set in. Shadowy outlines pricked the white out. There was only one thing to do.

He tore off his jacket and shirt easily enough but his stiff, frozen fingers struggled to unwind the calico binding wrapped around his torso. Growing frustrated with his cack-handed efforts, he swore under his breath, wary of Azekiel's anger until, no longer bound, a beguiling sense of purpose flared through him. The wings slowly furled, catching the buffeting wind and lifting him an inch, maybe two off the ground. Safety was three wing beats away.

"Seize him!"

A pair of muscular arms and hands erupted through the snow and grabbed Luca's ankles, stymieing his ascent. Stunned, Luca thrashed his wings to break free. He rose five, six feet into the air, his efforts drawing out a man from beneath the boulder who clung on to Luca.

I don't understand.

"You will Master Meazza." Massandar stepped through the squall to face Luca. Arshadne, clad in an anorak, thin britches and worn boots, stood beside him. Massandar reached inside his sable overcoat and retrieved a sheathed knife.

Leaving the harbour, Greta walked the short distance to Lavagna train station and stood on the Genoa bound platform that sat tight against the shoreline. Her favourite spot. A porter, busy sweeping the platform, nodded to her. Out at sea, three fishing boats, weighed down with the nights catch, returned to port with hectoring gulls in attendance. Sea legs or no sea legs, she'd ask her cousin to take her out in the boat he had inherited from Uncle. Oona could come too, and afterwards they'd visit the cemetery and finally pay their respects to Mama, Papa and Alesandro.

To keep the boats in sight, she ambled to the end of the platform. A sharp, searing pain tore through her right shoulder forcing her to cling to a lamp post for support. Struggling for breath, she watched Luca sink beneath the waves, goaded by the cemetery's Angels, their brutish, alabaster faces twisted with rage. Both vision and pain passed but seconds later, another agonising spasm gripped her.

Luca beat his wings furiously, desperation clawing at his burning chest. He cleared the boulder but the man clung to him. Exhausted, Luca made one last attempt to shake him off. He failed.

Massandar's frenzied shout split the frozen air, "Hold him, or he's lost!"

They crashed together in a tangled heap on the eastern ridge, fists flying, their hoar-white breaths clouding the frigid sky.

The snow beneath them shifted a fraction.

The pain lifted. Greta rested on a weathered bench etched with sweethearts' initials. The boats fell from sight, just as she had for all those years in Badur. Running away was a mistake. She should have rid herself of Massimo, accepted the barbs of all and sundry but lived on her terms. Oona was right about her. She *really* was little better than the late Widow Rigazzi, alone, feared yet pitied, no doubt a couple of years away from interrogating nephews and nieces on their marital prospects before droning on about her ailments.

The horn's blast signalled the arrival of a non-stop Genoa-bound train. The porter checked his watch. Greta, for once seized by reckless desire, buttoned her overcoat and walked to the platform edge, wishing she'd worn her scarf to keep out the cold. "One step forward, or one back?" she wondered. Closing her eyes and with the Angels' manic laughter drowning out the onrushing train, she stepped forward.

A rumbling, cacophonous roar punctured the morning stillness. A sheet of

snow and ice detached itself from the mountain and slipped towards the valley floor, slowly at first but accelerating as it grew in mass. Tumbling fists of rock and ice assaulted Luca. The air forced from his lungs, his screams muffled by the racket, he was tossed down the mountainside, powerless in this rapid, shredding descent. A shooting pain ripped through his right shoulder. On he rolled, yawing and pitching until he came to a halt, soon buried beneath the onrushing avalanche.

In the pitch black, winded, unsure of his bearings, he tore at the compacting snow, the claustrophobia overpowering.

I won't die here...I won't let it happen...not like this.

"You Fool! With me!" Azekiel ordered.

The train sped on towards Genoa, leaving a buffeting column of disturbed air in its wake. "Are you alright, Signora Ferrari?" asked the startled porter.

Greta nodded but began to shake, "I am. Thank you." She pushed her glasses up her nose then offered an embarrassed, wanting-to-be-gone smile. "Must have been daydreaming. Forgive me, I didn't mean to alarm you."

"No need to explain, Signora, we all experience such moments." He escorted her to the bench.

"I'll be fine," she said wiping her glasses and wanting to be alone. The porter brushed the peak of his cap and returned to his sweeping duties but kept an eye on her. A few minutes later, feeling stronger, she stood.

"Feeling better, Signora?" asked the still wary porter.

"Much better, thank you. I'll head home now."

"Allow me to escort you to the underpass." He took her by the elbow and led her to the underpass steps. She thanked him. He nodded, wished her well and watched her descend the stairs.

Outside the Town Hall, the shock of the past few minutes forced her to stop. How quicky the impulse to die had consumed her. One more step was all it needed. She had almost taken it too, only stopping because she imagined herself sitting beside Pierre in the café, enjoying a smoke and a coffee, blethering about everything and nothing. Too late to go back though. Too embarrassing.

The ripe odour of goat filled her nostrils.

A nearly new Berliet van, with French number plates pulled up outside the Town Hall. Jazz music wafted from its radio. The passenger climbed out and buttoned his overcoat. He walked towards her, his flat-footed, clumsy gait as always reminding Greta of doubt.

"So this is Lavagna," Pierre said.

"It is," Greta replied.

"Pretty enough. The sea too. Handy."

"Very."

He wiped his mouth, fighting doubt. "Oona wrote to me. The way you left. So suddenly."

"I had to leave, Pierre. Something happened that brought the past too close."

"We can't live in the past. Everything I need begins and ends with you." He paused, expecting Irene's loss to silence him again. There was no sign of her, leaving him free to say, "I love you, Greta."

CHAPTER FIFTY-NINE
The Badur Valley, January 1970

As the juddering bus wound its way up the narrow mountain road, Audrey, wearing a pink balaclava and matching scarf to keep out the cold, asked, "How much longer, Maman?"

"Not far now," Helene answered without having the slightest notion.

"Will we find Dolly?"

"Hope so." Helene waved her hand to clear the cigarette smoke, wishing she had ignored the woman puffing away behind her and left the window cracked. Feeling sick, she stared into the mist-tainted woods and whispered, "Guzco Domar," the name now a palliative whenever the world crowded her. Such as the moment Maurice recounted Audrey's accident to a mortified Aunt and Uncle and further proving their misgivings as to Helene's fitness to be a mother.

"Had you forgotten the incident in the Saint Germain baths?" Aunt complained in the kitchen that evening as Helene peeled vegetables for dinner. "Just as well Maurice was there. He has his faults, what man doesn't, but he's the kind of man you need, Helene. Strong, loving, protective." Helene said nothing, appalled by her aunt's change of tune.

Maurice took to arriving home from work smelling of cheap wine and cheaper perfume, berating Helene for her failures, as a wife, and a mother, growing angrier still when she fended off his drunken, violent advances. Her hopes for the holiday in Badur bringing them closer now seemed fanciful, juvenile. Maurice had returned poisoned, the last vestiges of kindness leeched from him. There seemed no way out for her but she kept quiet, accepting of her lot, if only for Audrey's sake.

Until last night, New Year's Eve. Maurice stumbled through the front door with lipstick smeared on his collar, his neck covered in love bites. As President Pompidou, stiff and pompous as ever, addressed the nation, Maurice flaunted his infidelity, complained about communists, foreigners and his dinner not being on the table. "Worst mistake of my life, letting you trick me into marrying you," he slurred. "Doubt the kid's mine too."

"Wish she wasn't," Helene answered, for once not holding back. "Audrey needs a proper father, not a drunk, philandering brute."

She ducked under Maurice's plate as it flew towards her. She straightened.

He was on her, pinning her against the wall. Raising his hand, he said, "You've had this coming for a while, you bitch."

"Go ahead. I'm not scared. Not anymore."

And as the Marseillaise faded, and France Gall began to sing about her broken heart, uncertainty gripped Maurice's soused features.

"Do you hear me? I'm not scared!"

"Maman," a sobbing Audrey called out from her bedroom.

She never expected her and Audrey to leave home first thing on New Year's Day, while Maurice slept off the booze. She couldn't stay with Aunt and Uncle. That would be the first place he'd come looking for them. Besides, they'd try to persuade her to go home to spare their blushes. Only one place sprang to mind, even if she hadn't the faintest idea what to do when she arrived.

"Badur!" the bus driver shouted, keeping an eye out for Pierre.

"We're here, Audrey!" Helene said, mustering as much enthusiasm as her weary bones would allow.

"I need the toilet."

Stepping from the bus, Helene saw Pierre outside the café, enjoying a quiet smoke. Greta hurried passed him and said, "Why didn't you wake me?"

"I wanted to let you sleep, my love."

She waved the library book at him. "Thought I told you the bus driver agreed to return the book to the library for me? It's been overdue for months. Doesn't do to upset librarians. Trust me." She ran towards the bus, waving the book. The driver opened the door and said, "Nick of time, Madame."

"Thank you for your help, Monsieur, here's ten francs. It should cover the fine. If not, let me know and I will cover any shortfall."

"Book any good?" he asked, looking at its cover.

"Very."

"*The Odyssey*. Not really a book man but think I'll give this one a go."

As the bus pulled away, Pierre crossed the square towards Helene and Audrey. "A pleasant surprise, Madame," he said, picking up both suitcases.

Audrey tugged the hem of her mother's coat and whispered, "Bursting, Maman."

After Audrey had spent a penny, Helene led her to a table where Greta had set down her coffee and for Audrey, an apple juice and a toffee. With the toffee gumming up Audrey's mouth, Helene basked in the sunny but freezing winter air, aware of the two old women watching her from the bakery. Even though exhausted, she knew in her bones she had done the right thing. Maybe Badur wouldn't suffice but she could always move on. Life would be a struggle but she didn't want Audrey to grow up in the hateful, spiteful world Maurice had prepared for them. Perhaps those screeching feminists were onto something after all.

Her certainty was short-lived when she caught sight of her crabby former landlady setting a posy of flowers beside the war memorial. Drawing her overcoat tight, Marianne approached the café. "Didn't think we'd see you again," she said.

"Couldn't stay away, Madame."

Marianne nodded. "I'm pleased your daughter looks so well."

"Thank you," Helene replied, the terror of those moments returning.

"Do you have someplace to stay?"

"No."

Marianne pushed the cottage's front door open, and said, "It'll soon warm up once the fire is lit."

"It'll be fine, I'm sure," Helene replied. Audrey slept in her arms.

"The poor mite is exhausted," Marianne said, with a hint of concern. "Let her sleep for an hour or two and then come up to the farmhouse to eat with us."

"I don't want to put you out, Madame."

"It's no trouble. You look like you could do with some rest as well." She opened the venetian blinds. Dull winter light flooded the kitchen. Handing Helene the keys, she said, "The boiler is playing up so there's no hot water. The plumber is due tomorrow. But he's not the most reliable of men."

"I'm sure we'll be fine. Thank you again."

"It's no trouble. No trouble at all." Unsure of what to say next, Marianne looked at the photograph of Henri and said, "You're very brave. I wish I had your courage."

"The truth is I had no choice. My daughter deserves a happy life."

"I know but all the same…" Marianne had no words. "See you in an hour or two. Forgot to tell you. The swimming pool has been drained. Oh, and remember the loose flagstone." She pointed to the floor and then left.

"Is this our new home, Maman?" Audrey mumbled, rubbing her eyes.

"For now, yes," Helene answered.

"Is Papa coming?"

"In a few days maybe. He has to work."

"Will he be nasty to you again?"

"No"

"Good. I don't like it when he's nasty to you."

There was a light tap on the door. Celeste stepped into the kitchen with sheets and towels. She set them on the table and left without speaking.

Too tired to make the bed, Helene pulled the heavy woollen blanket and quilted bedspread over Audrey. The room hadn't changed but the smell of fresh paint no longer lingered. Lying beside Audrey, she listened to her daughter's breaths slow and grew sleepy herself.

It was pitch black. Audrey was still fast asleep. Stiff necked, Helene yawned, rubbed the tip of her freezing nose then threw her overcoat on and came downstairs. The kitchen's warmth took her by surprise as did the roaring fire in the hearth. Coffee, cheese and a loaf of bread sat on the table. Two sketches rested against the loaf. In one Audrey, bored and listless, stared from the bus window. The other showed a young woman dancing with, to Helene's untrained eye, Chloe Jonquet's limitless grace. Her heart skipped a beat. The dancer was Audrey in ten or so years.

From her coat pocket, she fished out the sketch of Audrey swimming. She'd kept it to hand to remind herself how close she'd come to losing her daughter. She tore the sketch into small pieces then threw them onto the fire. As they curled in the flames, she whispered, "Guzco Domar."

As the cafetiere bubbled on the stove, The Beatles' *Ob-La-Di, Ob-La-Da* played on the transistor. There was a knock on the door. Celeste entered.

"Excuse me, Madame but we'll be eating soon. Nothing fancy just a cassoulet."

"Thank you," Helene replied.

"There's something else." Celeste held Dolly up. "Hung on to her in case you ever came back."

CHAPTER SIXTY
Badur, January 1970

Soaking in the bath, Guzco gripped the pumice stone and set about the corn on his left big toe. He considered the callus worthy of an article in a learned Parisian or Roman medical journal. Rubbing complete, he returned the pumice to its usual resting place between the taps and picked up a bar of peach scented soap. Lathering his right foot, he spotted a chilblain and wondered if that ancient bottle of calamine lotion still lurked in the bathroom cabinet.

He sat back and smiled, thinking how happy Pierre and Greta now looked, despite the quietest courtship in the history of Badur and probably beyond. The pair of them radiated a happiness that could power every home in the valley. Nobody, not even the Matriarch Lerond, seemed bothered that, technically speaking, they were living in sin as Greta had yet to divorce Massimo. Still, all in good time.

Stepping from the bath, he wrapped a towel around his bulging midriff and then searched the cabinet for the calamine lotion, finding it hidden behind a never opened bottle of after shave. He rested his foot on the side of the bath and slathered the lotion over the chilblain.

After dressing, he went downstairs to eat the roast chicken and salad, Lydia had left out. A familiar figure, dressed in a grubby grey suit, stared into the living room fire.

"Wasn't expecting to see you again. Where did you get to?" Guzco asked.

"Long story. You wouldn't be impressed," Luca replied.

"Probably not."

"Should have heeded your warnings about, Massandar. Cost me a wing."

"Another wingless Angel in Badur. I stay hidden for centuries yet within an hour of arriving, you very nearly unmask us both."

"I'm sorry. How is, Greta?"

"Happy."

A short, thin to the point of emaciated, man, clutching a leg of roast chicken in one hand and a clipboard in the other, stepped from the kitchen. Maggots trailed behind him. He wore a top hat lined with sheets of yellowing paper and a morning suit; its elbows patched, cuffs shiny, the buttons replaced with silver coins. The trousers' arse was worn through, and his boots' over polished black uppers had come away from their soles. The stench of putrefaction overpowered Guzco. The stranger bit into the chicken leg then set it down on the dining table. "Always partial to a bit of chicken. Even nicer with a sprinkling of salt," he said, after wiping his mouth on his sleeve.

"Pardon me, Monsieur. Who are you?" Guzco asked.

"I could ask you the same question," he replied, piqued by the question. "I am Death. Or if you prefer, the Grim Reaper, Thanos, Azrael. Many names, many lives. Most expect a tall, hooded, skeletal figure with a scythe. Sorry to disappoint."

"You've come for me?"

"Just the names on this list." Death tapped the clipboard with his right index finger.

"What's taken you so long?"

"That is not my affair." Handing Guzco the clipboard, he said, "Read out the names. Once they are uttered, I become responsible for their passage."

"I don't understand."

"Domar, I'm here to collect nine hundred and forty-six souls. Nothing more, nothing less. I'm not in the habit of debating such matters."

Guzco ran his eye over the list. "Nine hundred and forty-six. Did I help that many?"

"Can we get on?"

"Before we start, can I ask if you know what happened to an Irene Jonquet. I think she died in Paris."

The stench of decomposition ripened. "Why do you presume one woman's death weighs more heavily on me than any other? Do you know how many die each and every day? Do you expect me to have intimate knowledge of each and every one? You must have been taught that I'm blind to age, worthiness or time."

"I ask in good faith."

"Faith indeed, when will they learn." He turned to Luca, ran his left hand over the dozen or so wristwatches running the length of his right arm, and said, "Unless we begin this instant, I'm leaving."

"Please, Guzco," Luca said.

"Will they be safe?"

"You question me, Domar?" Death asked.

"Not at all. I just want to know where you are taking them. I deserve to know."

"They'll be safe, Guzco," Luca again interrupted, "Azekiel will see to that."

Scattering maggots while nodding in agreement, Death said, "My brother always honours his word."

"In that case, I'm happy to proceed."

"Finally," Death muttered. "Now read."

Guzco put on his reading glasses, cleared his throat and read, "Henri Velous (part), Lionel Chamonix, Louis Foucault, Therese Adalansis, Mattieu Dax, Armand Batralanza, Genevieve Cordesa, Idaline Fontaine, Vincent LaFont, Penelope Gironche."

As each soul left him, their final thoughts bled through his mind. Hopes, fears, regrets and uncertainty formed streams of excited chatter. Their faces flitted across Death's face. Male, female, old or young, each soul gazed upon Guzco for a final time before being consumed by Death.

"Pascalle Penverne, Etienne Malapense, Alain Serpontier, Gautier Baldarachim, Jean Focquet, Sadie Mas, Amelie Rallotelli, Mercian Lautage, Guido Borchetti."

He reached further back until only three names remained. "Sylvie Jonquettille, Rebecca Shibovitz, Yalakan Spinoza."

Guzco returned the clipboard to Death, who ran his eyes over the pages. "All done," he said matter-of-factly. Biting into the chicken leg, he faded.

"What happens now?" Guzco asked, catching his reflection in the mirror. To his delight, a ruddy but doubt-ridden fisherman studied him.

"Nothing will be left to chance this time," Luca replied with a hint of threat.

CHAPTER SIXTY-ONE
The Badur Valley, January 1970

Freed from Chamonix's seventy-year-old body, Guzco matched Luca stride for stride as they crossed Badur's bridge, stepped off the road and entered the woods.

Under a snow-filled sky, Guzco stopped in a clearing to gaze upon Badur for one last time. He had all but given up this day ever arriving. But now it had, his struggles, joys, mercies and cruelties meshed into a teeming, unsteady mass of life in all its flawed glory. His skin pricked at the finality of the moment. The urge to stay gripped, to secure the fate of the slain villagers he'd sworn to protect. Leaving broke that oath. He trusted Celeste to look out for them. Bacuali's children too. At least Doctor Chamonix's disappearance would be a welcome source of gossip for years to come.

Luca beckoned Guzco on.

"Sorry. Difficult, saying goodbye," Guzco answered. Carvings of boats, fishes and whales surrounded them. Some were new, most were old, near rotten, mostly forgotten. But they each held his triumphs, failures and merely getting by.

"Need to go," Luca insisted, growing impatient with his aged companion's sentimental attachments.

"Greta never stopped loving you, Luca."

Luca hid his disappointment over the bittersweet, what-might-have-been words. After all he was an Angel. Angels aren't supposed to possess such feelings. Work to be done and all that. But even so, love triumphed within him. "And I'll always love her," he answered.

"Nothing wrong with love. Even for the likes of us."

They hurried on through the moon shone forest, Luca out in front, setting a course beneath low hanging branches, swerving exposed roots and snow covered burrows. They reached a stream. "Can we rest?" Guzco asked, still keen to wallow in memory.

"We press on."

"What are you worried about?"

"Thought that obvious."

"Massandar isn't coming. Too smart for that. At least let me drink."

"Be quick then."

Guzco scooped up a handful of water. It was cold, redemptive. *I'll miss all this.*

Within the hour, they were wading through the snow-cloaked meadows. "Keep going," Luca said, aware Guzco was beginning to lag, while he struggled to abate his own fears.

By dawn, they had reached the boulder, its windward face buried beneath drifts. Just to be sure, Luca probed the base of the boulder with the tip of his boot while Guzco greeted the Ostler and Weaver. Both hunkered beneath the overhang, stamping their feet and blowing into their hands to fend off the biting cold. "Took your time," complained the Weaver.

"Keeping well?" Guzco asked, surprised and embarrassed in equal measure to see them. Their grim faces were answer enough. An awkward hour passed. Luca, eyes peeled for Massandar, the Weaver and Ostler chuntering to each other about the injustice of their situation, Guzco looking out over the neighbouring valleys for once free from fear or hope.

"That hawk's coming straight for us," said the Weaver, pointing skywards to a falcon arrowing towards them. The hawk slowed, extended its wings and gently landed on the boulder's surface. The tang of sulphur sullied the mountain air.

"Out. Now," a man commanded.

Azekiel stood on the boulder, unfurling his whip. Certain deference was called for, Guzco said, "Lord Azekiel, forgive me, I made a mistake and…"

"Spare me your prose, Master Domar."

Pointing towards the Weaver and Ostler, he continued, "Chance led us to these two. But the other one, Isabella Scalini, is still missing. You will find her. And before you say anything, Mistress Celeste Velous' is now responsible for your valley and all folk therein. Past, present and future, leaving you free to find the Scalini woman. By all accounts you're her best, possibly only hope."

"Does that count as praise?"

"No."

"Where do I begin?"

"I would have thought that obvious."

"To you maybe."

Azekiel flicked the whip toward the stream. Its tail unfurled and the sharp crack shattered the silence. "You gave her up here. It is only right your search begins here."

"Find her Guzco," said Luca. "She is all of us."

Guzco waded into the stream. Shocked by the cold, old doubts crept in. *I'm a fisherman, not cut out for this.*

Yes you are.

Does that count as praise, Lord Azekiel.

Yes. Now get on!

Guzco lay in the water but to stay the moment, he gripped the riverbed. A child cried. A mother shushed her. The child's tiny, perfect fingers gripped his left forefinger. It was time. He gently prised the child's fingers apart and gave himself up to the current's siren pull.

Entwined with the water, he slewed downstream and just as a river gains strength from its tributaries so Guzco grew in confidence and purpose.

Why not me?

On he flowed, tumbling over ledges, spiralling through eddies, accepting the cruel privilege handed to him.

Celeste examined the drawing, scarcely able to believe her eyes. Her wings flexed beneath the calico binding. She thought of burning the sketch, hoping fire might extinguish her fear. The drawing had come to her in a frenzy, the sweeps of the pencil, broad, bold but meticulous. She had little idea what was taking shape until she held the sketch up to the grubby light seeping through the barn's window.

Odd to draw your own death.

She scrunched up the drawing and tossed it onto the table. Outside, a storm brewed, the barn's timbers creaked, agitated crows stomped around the roof, squawking their tuneless chorus. She threaded her way around and between her parents' miserable collection. The torch gave out and she stumbled into Henri's old bike, the one she'd coveted as a child, especially as she had to make do with the doll.

A car, Mercedes by the look of things, pulled up outside the farmhouse.

Relieved Maman had taken Helene and Audrey into Badur for groceries and to lay fresh flowers beside the war memorial, she picked up one of the rusty, blunt scythes, propped against the door.

Arshadne opened the Mercedes' rear passenger door. Massandar stepped out, straightening his cuffs. As ever he was immaculately dressed in a tailored, green check three piece suit and tan brogues. Not a single slicked hair was out of place. He reached inside his jacket pocket and pulled out a worn leather sheath. The soft, elegant whisper of leather on metal announced Caballero's unsheathing.

Guzco.

"Haven't you heard? Guzco's gone," Massandar said.

Papa's wine addled features edged across Massandar's smile. She'd seen that look many times, usually before a beating or a whipping. She'd always accepted them, had no choice but to, even when she'd done nothing wrong. She gripped the scythe all the tighter. *Fight or accept?*

Massandar beckoned Arshadne with a flick of Caballero. She set the ornate wooden box on the ground her eyes blazing with long dimmed passion. Catching Massandar unawares, she turned to face him and in a scratchy, weak voice, unused for centuries, she muttered, "Enough."

"Always knew it would come to this," Massandar said. In one swift, deft movement he plunged Caballero into Arshadne's heart then twisted for good measure. She fell.

Any pretence of flattery abandoned, he stepped over the stricken Arshadne and moved towards Celeste, desperate for the arousal cleaving wings would bring.

Celeste stood her ground. Out of fear or bravery, she couldn't say. She looked into Massandar's smooth, unblemished features, his cologne catching on the back of her throat.

The movement was swift, brutal, taking them both by surprise. Celeste raised the scythe for a second time and brought it down on Massandar's right arm. Caballero fell from his grasp. Deep rust tinted, gashes to his right cheek and jacket sleeve announced the extent of the scythe's carving. Alive with rage for *all* the times Papa had struck her, Celeste raised the scythe for a third time. *Finish the job.* Massandar backed away, arms raised in blood-soaked supplication, his sheen of perverted superiority replaced by bewilderment that this lowly creature, a woman of all things, had bettered him.

"At my time of choosing," he spat, climbing into the Mercedes' driver's seat.

"I'll be waiting. Fucker." Celeste slashed the Mercedes' bonnet with such force, the scythe's blade buckled.

The accelerating Mercedes sprayed her in slush and mud. After wiping her eyes, she noticed a wooden chest inlaid with ivory and ornate carvings of mythical beasts sitting skew whiff in the Mercedes tyre tracks.

She knelt beside Arshadne. Struggling to breathe, the long-fallen Angel rasped, "You're safe?"

"Yes, thank you."

"He promised me my wings back if I served him. The evil I've witnessed in the hope of paradise. Took shelter in silence." She coughed up a mouthful of blood and tightened with the pain. "I am ready Angel."

Celeste kissed Arshadne's cheek. The fallen Angel's final thoughts overwhelmed hers. "

Free at last – from him – from my guilt – a fool – a perfect fool – all that suffering – prizing my wings over the lives of children – one day without rancour is all I crave now.

Arshadne exhaled and faded, her blood staining the earth.

Marta danced her simple but impossible steps, skittering over the water in unsullied perfection. Wanting, needing to revel in the beauty of this moment, Guzco gripped the water but couldn't prevent it slipping through his hands.

Marta was joined by Isabelle, Irene, Chloe, and all the other women whose steps had allowed people to drift through their own hopes and fears, both light and dark. Together, this elegant, otherworldly Corps slowed the river's impatient current, as if time itself paused to watch. A sight to gladden the heart, a sight to tell Guzco that beauty and compassion is in abundance.

"Come home to us," Luisa whispered as he slipped under Badur's ancient stone bridge.

Soon, I promise my love.

The river grew broader and deeper, its current stronger, until a day, month or maybe a year later, his river borne odyssey neared its end. The teeming sea growled, happy to have him back in her clutches.

Drawn out towards the deeper waters, the swell gripped and pummelled Guzco. A thunderous roar rose up from the depths, overpowering him. Until. Silence. Until. Stillness. Until. A whale's mournful lament serenaded the man floating towards the surface. Guilt and fear in equal measure coursed through Guzco. And then relief and joy.

"Jose?"

"Told you one day we'd have great adventures," Jose answered.

"To find the lost?"

"Aye, if needs be."

Guzco allowed the caress of foam-tinged waves to lift him and Jose to their futures.

At last, Guzco Domar had his wings back.

ALSO BY JIM O'SULLIVAN
FROM RYMOUR BOOKS

For Tom Casey, there isn't a right or a wrong side, just the side he lands on